GOOD ENOUGH

OTHER BOOKS
BY KELLY ELLIOTT

Coming Soon
Take Me Away (December 22, 2020)
Fool for You (April 2021)
Boggy Creek Valley series (Spring 2021)

Stand Alones
The Journey Home
*Who We Were**
*The Playbook**
*Made for You**
*Available on audiobook

Meet Me in Montana Series
*Never Enough**
*Always Enough**
Good Enough
Strong Enough (February 9, 2021)

Southern Bride Series
Love at First Sight
Delicate Promises
Divided Interests
Lucky in Love
Feels Like Home
Take Me Away (December 22, 2020)
Fool for You (April 2021)

Cowboys and Angels Series
Lost Love
Love Profound
Tempting Love
Love Again
Blind Love
This Love
Reckless Love
*Series available on audiobook

Boston Love Series
Searching for Harmony
Fighting for Love
*Series available on audiobook

Austin Singles Series
Seduce Me
Entice Me
Adore Me
*Series available on audiobook

Wanted Series
*Wanted**
*Saved**
*Faithful**
Believe
*Cherished**
*A Forever Love**
The Wanted Short Stories

All They Wanted
*Available on audiobook

Love Wanted in Texas Series
Spin-off series to the WANTED Series
Without You
Saving You
Holding You
Finding You
Chasing You
Loving You
Entire series available on audiobook
*Please note Loving You combines the last book of the Broken and Love Wanted in Texas series.

Broken Series
*Broken**
*Broken Dreams**
*Broken Promises**
Broken Love
*Available on audiobook

The Journey of Love Series
Unconditional Love
Undeniable Love
Unforgettable Love
*Entire series available on audiobook

With Me Series
Stay With Me
Only With Me
*Series on audiobook

Speed Series
Ignite
Adrenaline

COLLABORATIONS
Predestined Hearts (co-written with Kristin Mayer)
Play Me (co-written with Kristin Mayer)*
Dangerous Temptations (co-written with Kristin Mayer)
*Available on audiobook

GOOD ENOUGH

KELLY ELLIOTT

Prologue

"Ninety-eight bottles of milk on the wall, ninety-eight bottles of milk! Take one down and pass it around, ninety-seven bottles of milk on the wall!"

Mommy laughed as Daddy and I sang as loud as we could. "Goodness, how much longer until we get to the beach house?" she asked as she looked back at me.

"We just started the trip! We've got hours to go before we get there," Daddy said, then turned and winked at me. "It's our song, right, sweetheart?" He smiled, the sun shining on his hair, and I smiled back.

Suddenly, Mommy started to scream, and Daddy turned back to the road. Loud sounds from outside caused me to look out the window. Cars were driving all wrong. One was coming right toward us. "Oh my God! Oh my God! Frank!"

I closed my eyes and didn't open them, even when I felt everything flying in the car and hitting me. Mommy screamed again, then everything stopped, and I couldn't hear her anymore. At least until I heard another lady screaming and loud voices all around me.

"Call 911! Someone, call 911!"

"You need to get your little girl out of the car!"

Someone grabbed me, and I cried out. "Mommy!"

"Do not open your eyes, Timberlynn," Daddy whispered as he took me from my seat. "Do you hear me? Keep them closed."

I nodded and buried my face in his chest. "I won't. I pwomise." With my eyes closed tight, I slapped my hands over my ears, hoping all the loud noises would stop.

Daddy wrapped his arms tightly around me. "Don't do this. Please don't take her from us! God, please. I need someone to take my daughter! Please, I need to help my wife!"

Daddy moved me, and I was placed in someone else's arms. I instantly cried out. "Daddy, no! Please don't leave me! No!"

He stopped and looked back at me. "Timberlynn, I need to go get your mommy out of the car."

My eyes drifted past Daddy and I looked at our car all bent and out of shape. "Daddy?" I yelled as a woman's voice called, "Go! I've got her. Get her out of the car!"

"Daddy!" I shouted again as I watched him run to the car.

"It's okay, sweetheart. Shh...your mommy and daddy are fine. Just close your eyes."

I didn't listen to the stranger. I watched as Daddy ran to our car. It was the wrong way up. The wheels...I could see the wheels. Another man, a policeman, helped Daddy get Mommy out of the car. Then Daddy screamed so loudly, making both me, and the stranger holding me, jump.

"Oh, no," the stranger whispered and quickly turned me away from Daddy. She looked at me and smiled. "Your name is Timberlynn?"

I started to cry harder, but I nodded.

She smiled and wiped the tears from my face. "It's going to be okay, Timberlynn. It will all be okay."

I looked past her and saw Daddy on the ground, Mommy sitting in his lap. She was bleeding, and he was crying as he rocked her. Why wasn't she getting up to come get me? I tried to run to him, but the strange lady held onto me tightly.

"It's okay, Timberlynn. It's okay."

She buried my face into her chest, and even at my young age, somehow I knew she was not telling me the truth. That nothing would be okay. It would never be okay again.

Chapter One

TANNER

I sat on Trigger and stared out over the open pasture as I got ready to rope with Chance. You could almost feel the winter storm about to come in and blanket the distant Colorado mountains with snow. Right now they had patches of snow that only hinted that it was winter. My body ached to be home, though. To see the Montana mountains I had grown up in and loved so much. I sighed and looked down.

My ankle ached ever so slightly, and I rotated it completely out of habit. I'd broken it months back when I jumped off Trigger and landed wrong after winning the final round in Tulsa. I had taken some time off of roping after that to let it heal and stayed at my folks' ranch back in Montana. It wasn't anything that kept me from roping, though, and I could have easily pushed through the pain, but I needed that break. It was more of a mental break than a physical one, even if I didn't want to admit it to myself back then. And now I yearned for the Montana skyline to be replaced by this Colorado one.

With a deep inhale, I took in the crisp winter air. The sun would be sinking behind the mountains soon, ending another night out on the road. A strange feeling of yearning hit me once again, and I couldn't shake it. What was it that was making me feel this way lately? This longing to be home wasn't anything new, that's for sure. I loved being home on the ranch, but roping had always been my passion. At least, it had been up until my brothers all started to settle down and work with my father on the ranch. I missed them so damn much lately, and tonight it seemed that there was something else I was missing as well. I couldn't put my finger on it, even though I tried. That pissed me off and made me feel less in control. Control was what kept me on that horse and kept me winning on the circuit. Not being in control meant my life and my career were both at the mercy of fate...and I didn't like that one damn bit.

The sound of the crowd from the arena usually got me fired up, sparking that side of me that yearned for the chase, begged for the adrenaline rush, but not today. I'd been feeling off for the last month, and I knew Chance, my roping partner and best friend, could sense it. Truth be told, neither one of us had been ourselves for a while, and neither of us would admit that our hearts had been somewhere else other than roping.

"Tanner?" Chance asked.

"Yeah, sorry, I was taking a minute," I said as he rode up next to me and stopped. He stared out at the same scene I had been captivated by only moments ago.

"Is your head in this ride, dude?" Chance's voice sounded strained.

"My head's in it. Yours?" I asked, motioning for Trigger to turn and face Chance. Trigger was my five-year-old gelding I'd bought when he was three from a friend of my father's for five-hundred dollars. Never dreamed he'd turn out to be such an amazing horse when I first broke him. He was cowy, meaning he could watch a cow come out of the shoot and stay on it like no one's business. We were a perfect fit, and he was one hell of a horse. With Trigger, I had four Wrangler NFR Qualifications and one World Championship as a header. This coming year I had a feeling we would be on top again if Chance and I stayed healthy, didn't break our damn necks, and got our shit together. Three months ago, it had been pretty much all I had thought about. Winning another championship. Then everything seemed to shift when I had gone home for my brother Ty's wedding. That was the day I had met her.

Timberlynn.

I glanced back to Chance and waited for his response. He paused, and it spoke volumes.

Chance rubbed the back of his neck. "Honestly? No, I ain't in it. Not at all. I think it's the end-of-the-year shit. Or maybe she's still in my head. I don't really know."

I nodded because I had no clue what to say to him. It had been a long year for both of us. Chance and I had been best friends for as long as I could remember. It hadn't been a surprise to anyone when we started roping together. The two of us were the male version of Forrest Gump and Jenny's peas and carrots. We just worked together so well. Me the header, Chance the heeler. And we were good. Damn good. When we had our shit together, that is. This year, hell, this year had been a challenge for both of us, though, and we had been tested a lot.

Chance had found himself in love, and I had found myself without my best friend for the first time in years. Not that I wasn't happy for him, mind you, because I was. He had met a girl, fell for her, asked her to marry him, and without another word, she left him. Just like that. Left him for some city slicker guy who promised her the moon and stars under the bright lights of New York City. I think a part of Chance knew she would never have been happy with him on the road as much as we were now. It takes a strong-ass woman to handle a man being on the road for months at a time, knowing the temptations that we are faced with on a daily basis. The damn buckle bunnies were in abundance, no matter the venue or the city. That was the name given to women who prowled around rodeos looking to hook-up with the cowboys, especially those who won buckles. Some of them had even been known to steal the buckles as some sort of trophy.

"You're better off without her, you know," I finally said after we both sat there in silence for a good minute or two.

He sighed. "Yeah, I know. Still fucking hurts, though."

"You sayin' you want a longer break than just Christmas?" I asked, already knowing his answer. Hell, I was hoping for the same answer I wanted to hear.

"It was a rough year last year. Your ankle injury and all. My whole...I'm in love...debacle. I know we haven't missed a New Year's Eve Buck & Ball before, but I feel like I need some time off, Tanner. I'd like to just be home with my folks, spend some time with the family. Help my dad out on the farm. Just...take a few weeks' break, maybe even a month."

I let a small chuckle slip through. Chance gave me a slight smile because I'm positive he knew I was feeling the same way.

"Maybe we both need a break," I said as I looked back at the arena. "You thinking what, Alexandria, then we head back out on the circuit? That gives us a good month at home."

A look of relief crossed his face, and I couldn't help but wonder if there was something more to this break than what Chance was telling me. He looked at me as if he was thinking the same damn thing about me. "I'm good with that. It gives the horses a break as well. I'm sure Banker wouldn't mind being turned out for a bit."

He leaned over and gave his horse a pat. Banker bobbed his head as if agreeing with Chance. Hell, this life we were living was hard on everyone involved, including the horses.

Just then, the crowd grew louder and cheers could be heard. A small spark of excitement filled me, though not for the normal reasons. This time, I'd be going back home soon, and that was enough to get me excited about the ride.

Chance looked back toward the arena before he focused on me once more. "I think we need to give them all something to talk about when we're finished tonight. You in?"

I nodded. "I agree. Let's leave with a big fuckin' bang and win this round."

Chance and I made our way to the arena. Trigger always got antsy when we were in the box waiting for them to turn the steer out. I could practically feel his body vibrate from the excitement of going after the cow, and I knew exactly how he felt.

My heart thundered in my chest as we waited for the steer to be loaded up. Once I got Trigger where I wanted him, I gave the nod and the steer was off. He was hardly out of the shoot, and Trigger had just broke the line before I roped his horns and I saw Chance's rope sail down toward the back feet. Next thing I knew, we were facing each other and Chance was pumping his fist like a mad man, causing Banker to buck slightly from his rider's crazy antics. Chance then tossed his hat in the air. I watched in shock, wondering why in the hell he was spooking his horse like he was. Banker was a gentle gelding; he didn't like a lot of show and Chance knew that. Even the crowds cheering could hit him wrong sometimes. If we had a good ride, Chance knew to hold it in until he dismounted. It had been a good run, but he was acting like a damn fool. But then, my eyes moved to our time. Three-point-five seconds. Holy shit.

Three. Point. Five.

We had just tied the arena record. The world record time was three point four. Only three other teams had achieved that score, and this had been the closest we'd ever come. Three point six had been our team best previously.

The crowd in the arena went wild. The next thing I knew, the cameras were in our faces, buckles were in our hands, and we were giving interviews left and right. Neither one of us mentioned to the media the break we had intended on taking, though. There was no need to, not when we were riding the high of winning. Not to mention, it was a nice payday for both of us, so that kept the high even higher for a while.

By the time we got the horses settled and headed to the hotel, I was exhausted. But I still had enough in the tank to take a shower and pack up my bags. I knew Chance would want to leave first thing in the morning, and I was more than ready to head on out of Colorado and make our way back to Montana. The weather looked to be good for traveling, and I didn't want to press our luck with it being mid-December and trying to drive back pulling a horse trailer. Storms could easily kick up as we drove through the Rockies, and we needed to avoid that at all costs.

A knock on my hotel room caused me to pause for a moment. I knew it wasn't Chance, so that meant it was someone looking for a good time, which I wasn't in the mood for.

"Shit," I mumbled as I made my way to the door. With a towel still wrapped around my waist, I opened the door to find a brunette standing there. I'd recognized her as one of the buckle bunnies who showed up to some of the bigger events.

Her gaze moved greedily over my body. I knew what she was here for, after all. Her look should have sparked something inside me, but it did nothing. Not a damn thing.

"Figured you might want to celebrate, cowboy." The brunette stepped forward and gave me a sexy-as-sin smile. Her fingers moved softly up my chest as she purred, "I'm all yours tonight, Tanner, and trust me when I say that I know how to ride and will definitely last for longer than eight seconds. Hell, I really like ropin' too." Her hand slipped around my neck before she spliced her fingers through my wet hair and gave it a gentle tug.

I had no doubt she knew how to ride. Hell, she'd probably ridden against more cowboys than I had in my time on the circuit. And a few months ago I might have ushered her into my room and let her do just that to me. But not tonight.

"I was told by your partner that you liked brunettes."

All I could do was stare at her. It was true. I liked brunettes, I liked blondes, redheads, hell, I wasn't prejudiced when it came to women. I loved all women, all shapes and all sizes. I also respected the hell out of them because I knew my mother would personally hunt me down and cut off my balls if she ever found out I wasn't treating a woman right. It was part of the reason I kept the sleeping around to a minimum, even though my reputation said otherwise. I didn't contradict it; I did like an occasional hook-up. Contrary to what everyone said, though, I wasn't a manwhore like some of the other guys out here. Don't get me wrong, I liked sex. A lot. But I never slept with the buckle bunnies.

Chance, on the other hand, hell, he had gone on a fucking binge after Jessica had left him. I swore he would sleep with any woman who looked at him. And as much as I really wanted to let this woman into my room, especially since I hadn't had sex in a few months, the girl currently running her tongue over my jaw wasn't the girl I wanted to be with. I lifted my arms and pulled her hands back as I gently pushed her away from me.

With a smile, I shook my head. "As much as I appreciate the offer, sweetheart, not tonight."

The woman stood there with a stunned expression on her face. It wasn't often cowboys turned down a beautiful woman, and the one standing in front of me was indeed beautiful. She looked past me into the room, probably to see if I had someone else already waiting for me. She frowned and then looked back at me. "You're saying no?"

I nodded. "That's right, I'm saying no."

This had become the latest in a string of the word no I seemed to be giving women. None of them caught my attention, hadn't since I'd been back home, truth be told, and I was beginning to wonder if something was majorly wrong with my cock since nothing got the bastard hard. Not. One. Thing. Well, that was a complete lie. My nightly dreams of Timberlynn got me plenty hard simply thinking of her. And it didn't mind when I thought about her in the shower either.

The brunette took another step closer to me. I took a step back. "You're actually turning me down?" she asked again, this time with a bit of laughter in her voice.

"It's not you, you're beautiful. And you have a smoking hot body. I'm just not interested." I sighed and rubbed the back of my neck, wishing she would just move along to the next guy.

"Tanner, you have no idea what you're turning down, and I most certainly won't offer it to you again." She snarled her lip up at me as if I had offended her.

"I'm pretty sure I do, and I'm not interested in what you have to offer, but I'm sure you'll find a cowboy who roped tonight and is looking for a meaningless fuck. You'll probably find countless ones in this hotel alone if you look harder, although maybe you're only interested in the buckle winners."

It was a dick thing to say because she flinched and took a step back. We both knew every word was true though.

"Screw you, asshole." She turned and stomped away.

Without another glance in her direction, I closed the door to my hotel room and locked it. The sooner this night was over, the faster I could head back home. Fuck. I was so exhausted I didn't even bother putting on a pair of boxers. Just dropped my towel and fell onto the bed, knowing what I would dream about the moment my head hit the pillow. Well, not what...but who.

◆ ◆ ◆

The drive back to Montana from Colorado felt like it was taking forever. Chance slept damn near the whole time. I was positive it was from his previous night's adventure. This morning the brunette from last night had passed me by in the lobby and told me she found another buckle winner and thoroughly enjoyed being with Chance last night—yeah, whatever, that hadn't caught me off guard in the least bit. But I also saw Chance saying goodbye to another woman—a hot blonde—when I had gotten back from my morning run.

I'd woken up with a smile, still thinking about the dreams I'd had of Timberlynn and knowing that we were headed home today. I needed to burn off some energy while I waited for Chance to get his shit together. So, even with my ankle giving me hell, it felt good to run, especially in the cool, crisp Colorado air.

By the time we had gotten the horses and all of our saddles and other equipment loaded up, it was damn near almost nine in the morning. Chance looked like he hadn't slept a wink, and when he told me he'd ended up with two women in his room, I knew I would be the one doing most of the driving back to Montana. That asshole. I wasn't looking forward to the fourteen-hour drive.

I reached for the radio and turned it on, barely turning up the volume.

"I'm awake, dude, just trying to rest my body," Chance said.

With a quick glance his way, I asked, "Rest your body from what, sex? Is it becoming that hard for you? Can't handle having sex more than one time a night?"

He laughed. "Yeah, rest my poor aching body. I never in my life met two girls who could move like they did. It was their first threesome, and they evidently wanted to make the most of it."

"Is that right?" I asked with a slight chuckle. "And did they?"

"I think my cock is broken, if that tells you anything. I never had anyone ride me like that. I'm actually afraid to have sex again. Pretty sure I sprained my dick."

This time I laughed. A full-on laugh. "That's what you get. You used condoms, right? God knows how many other men they've slept with. The brunette stopped by my room last night, and I shooed her away."

Chance chuckled. "She told us in the bar. She's no longer one of your fans."

"I'm sure I'll survive. Worked out for you obviously."

He sighed as he sat up and stretched. "I'm serious, man. This meaningless sex just to get my rocks off...I honestly can't stand myself in the morning."

I chuckled. "Never thought I'd hear you say something like that."

"Yeah, well, my mother would be pissed if she knew what I was doing."

I nodded because she would. "You know, I've seen that blonde you were with a number of times, mostly with Bill Clapper."

Chance stopped moving. "Bill Clapper? You've seen her with him? A lot?"

I shrugged. "Yeah, I guess so. Enough that I actually thought they were dating, but I guess not. Why do you sound so freaked out?"

"Bill Clapper is married, Tanner."

I laughed. "Does that surprise you, Chance? Lots of guys cheat on the road, you know that. It's nothing new."

He shook his head and then ran his hands down his face. "Holy crap. Holy freaking shit."

"What is wrong with you, dude?" I asked.

"Bill Clapper doesn't cheat. He's got a hot wife. A really hot blonde wife, or at least that's what I've heard. I've actually never seen her since she's known to stay back at the hotels. She doesn't like to watch him ride, for some reason. I do know they got in a serious fight yesterday at the bar, or at least that was what Kenny told me last night. Bill's wife apparently stormed away after a pretty heated argument. Fuck. My. Life. I was with a married woman, and not just any married woman. Bill Clapper's wife. Shit. Shit. Shit."

"Dude, you're not even sure it was his wife. It might not have been."

Chance quickly pulled out his phone and typed something into it. If I thought he had been freaking out a few minutes ago, that was nothing compared to how he was now acting. "Oh my God. I'm dead."

"What is it?" I asked as I looked over at him.

"It's definitely his wife. I spent the entire night with Bill Clapper's wife...in a goddamn threesome!"

I looked at him and nearly lost it laughing when I saw his stunned expression. I focused on the road and tried to contain the laughter, but I lost the battle. Bill Clapper was one of the bull riders on the circuit. He also roped, but bull riding was his thing. He thought he was good. I knew good, and Bill was okay. Both of my brothers, Brock and Ty, were PBR World Champions. Bill Clapper wasn't up to that level for a reason. He was cocky, mean as hell, and he didn't like anyone making him look or feel bad.

"Tanner, this is not funny. This is...this is bad. If he finds out, he'll kill me."

I lifted my hand up and tried to control my laughter. "I'm sorry. Listen, I'm almost positive you're not the first guy she's slept with. I've seen her coming out of a few hotel rooms, so I'm going to guess she's not that faithful. Maybe he knows his wife sleeps around. I mean, if she didn't go back to their hotel room last night, where else would he think she was at?"

He paused for a moment and thought about it. "That's true. God, the things that woman knew how to do with her tongue. Almost makes it worth sleeping with a married woman."

I frowned and shook my head. "You really are a whoring bastard, do you know that?"

He cringed slightly then sighed. "I've been trying to get over a broken heart here, Tanner."

"And now, apparently, you've got a broken dick, dumbass. Whatever, all I'm saying is if you sleep around like you have been, it's going to catch up to you. One way or another. Take these next few weeks to get whatever it is out of your system. And when we get back out on the road, you have to stop thinking with your dick, before some crazy bastard decides to cut it off."

I could feel his eyes on me. "Speaking of that. What's going on with you?" he asked. "When was the last time you even hooked up with anyone? The brunette, I can't even remember what her name was. Anyway, she said she went to your hotel room and you turned her away...said you were a dick to her."

"She was right, on both counts."

He snorted. "You've got something you want to tell me? Like a girl you're seeing whom I don't know about? Are you secretly gay? Which I'm completely okay with and all, just so you know."

My head snapped to look at him as he raised his hands up and said, "Hey, I'm not one to judge if you've found yourself batting for the other team."

"I'm not gay, asshole. I'm just tired of the meaningless sex. Tired of bedding women I'm not ever going to see again."

Chance remained silent for a few minutes before he cleared his throat. "Dude, did you hit your head or something? You're talking more like a forty-year-old than a guy who is twenty-five."

"No, smartass."

"Are you...wait...are you saying you want to settle down? Who is she?"

"No, I'm not saying that. I'm just tired of it all. I mean, tired of everything."

He laughed. "Tired of what? Sex with women who don't want anything in return but a simple night with you? Dude, you've always had the women falling at your feet, that's your problem. You've never had to work for their attention a day in your damn life."

I rolled my eyes. "I want something different, but I don't know what it is. Ever since Ty's wedding, things have felt...different. I don't know how to explain it."

Chance diverted his attention out of the passenger side window before he said, "Dude, I get that. Both your brothers are settling down, getting married. You want that too. There's nothing wrong with that. Hell, I wanted it with Jessica. I was ready to give up roping if she had asked me to."

I nearly slammed on the brakes. "What!"

"I'm not saying I was going to give it up, I'm just saying I would have if she'd asked."

"How is that any different, Chance? Were you actually going to tell me you were ready to give up roping? Like isn't there some guy code...bros before hos or some shit like that? We've been friends and partners for a long ass time, man."

"I'm just saying things change. People change and there isn't anything wrong with that. I know someday I'm going to settle down. I thought Jessica was the one; she wasn't. But she was the first woman who made me want something more. It's okay to want something more. That's all I'm saying."

I turned and quickly shot him a look. "Are we talking about me or you? You're the one who just said you would have given this all up for a woman, and you weren't even going to bother to fucking tell me!"

"It's a moot point now, T. No point in even talking about it."

"But you were ready to walk away. Don't you think that was something you should have shared with me? And what's to stop you from walking away when the next Jessica comes around?"

Chance sighed. "All I'm saying is that someday I'm going to meet someone and I *will be willing* to give this up. You can't fucking fault me for thinking she might have been the one."

"I guess not, but when were you planning on telling me?"

He sighed. "For fuck's sake, I wasn't going to leave. I'm just saying, if I met someone who asked me to walk away from this, someone I loved and wanted to start a family with, I'd walk away. Don't tell me that you wouldn't..."

I gripped the steering wheel and felt my jaw tighten.

"You would and you know it, asshole."

Chance drifted back to sleep for a few hours, and when he woke we remained silent for a bit. The radio played and we were both lost in our own thoughts until I broke the silence between us.

"Are you tired of doing this? Is this little holiday break, or whatever you want to call it, your way of telling me you're done, Chance?"

"No. I don't know, Tanner. Maybe?" He said with a sigh. "Is it too much for me to ask for a break? I'm tired. Exhausted. We don't need to do all these smaller rodeos. Let's just take a break until the beginning of the year. I'm not asking you to find a new partner. I'm simply saying things change. Right now I need a break."

Chance rubbed the back of his neck, then dropped his hand in his lap. "I need to be home with my family. Get my head back on straight. You're not the only one tired of all the meaningless women and being away from home."

We both remained silent as I drove north. The emptiness that had been present since Ty's wedding was beginning to grow more and more, to take root and form a solid foundation, and it was throwing me. I wanted to talk to Chance about it, but I knew he was going through his own crap. Plus, I had just given him hell for even mentioning the idea of giving up roping. The next few weeks would be good for us. We both needed the break— from roping and probably from one another. And I needed to also take this time to figure out why I kept dreaming about one woman and one woman only.

I had no idea where the road back to Montana would take us. And honestly, I was too damn tired to care right then.

Chapter Two

TIMBERLYNN

I stared out the window of my small two-bedroom apartment in Atlanta as the rain came down in sheets. I had moved into this place two years ago with a fellow nursing student. It had been my first place on my own, and I had instantly fallen in love with it. Something that was earned completely by me, and that had meant a lot.

I grew up without needing a single thing. My father, who was a doctor, gave me everything I ever asked for, and then some. But this apartment was the first thing I paid for each month with the money I made working on my own. It had been one of the most freeing moments of my life when I walked in with my own key—it meant something, something huge. I didn't need to use the money that my father had deposited into my bank account for monthly expenses all through college. I didn't need to ask him for anything. I often couldn't help but wonder if that was my father's way of showing me he loved me. By dumping money into an account and telling me to buy whatever I wanted.

I closed my eyes and sighed. I had hardly talked to my father the last three months. Did he even realize how little we talked? Not that our conversations were anything great, even on a good day. It was mostly me calling to check in. He would ask how I was doing. How I liked the new job, and if I needed anything. I asked how he was doing, if he was working long hours, and when we might be able to get together for lunch or dinner. I always got the same reply on that last question.

"Soon, princess. When things calm down."

Opening my eyes once more, I stared out the window. Daddy's latest girlfriend, Sherry, was his main priority, second only to his job. Not his daughter.

The drops of rain that ran down the window blurred the view of outside, and a part of me was thankful for that. I closed my eyes once more and imagined the beautiful, snow-capped mountains of Montana and Utah. I had fallen in love with Utah after a college ski trip there a few years back. Park City had become my dream. The place where I would lay down my roots and start my life. Start the job I truly dreamed of doing. That was until my cousin Kaylee sent me pictures of Hamilton, Montana. When I went there for her wedding, I fell head over heels in love with it. The memory of me and Kaylee sitting on the swing while she told me about her life for the last few years made my chest ache slightly. God, how I had missed her. She had always been there for me. In both the good and bad times.

Kaylee was older than me by four years. Her father was my father's brother, and it wasn't often we got to see each other. But when we did, it had always been a blast. Once I got to college and lived closer to Kaylee, we grew closer. She was like a sister to me. I had told her all my fears and worries, and she listened to them and offered such amazing insight. She was my rock when I needed something strong and sturdy in my life. When she decided to move to Montana, I was heartbroken, but I had to hide it. The last thing I wanted to do was crush her dreams. Plus, I knew it would be good for her to leave behind her own demons. Her fiancé had killed himself a few years ago, and I hated seeing how sad and lost she had been through that. I knew the move to Montana was what she needed. So I hugged her goodbye and watched her follow her heart, knowing the only thing that would ever separate us was the miles. Watching her choose love spurred something in me, and I realized I needed to follow my own dreams.

But after visiting Kaylee, I knew Montana was a strong contender for my move. I never thought anywhere could be more beautiful than Park City. Boy, had I been wrong. Of course, I wasn't sure I'd admit that a certain cowboy who had occupied my thoughts...and dreams... had something to do with me leaning more toward starting my new career in Montana instead of Utah.

I couldn't help but smile at the memory of Tanner Shaw. He was handsome, with those pale blue eyes and dimples when he smiled.

"Timber?" Candace, my roommate and best friend, called out my name as she walked into the apartment.

"I'm in the living room," I answered.

"Hey, sorry I'm late. How was your day at the hospital?"

I sighed and turned back to face her. "Awful."

She frowned. "That bad, huh?"

With a nod, I walked over and dropped onto the sofa. "I simply wasn't made to be a nurse."

Candace smiled. "It's okay if you don't like it. But you are a damn good nurse."

I shrugged. "I had to be."

She gave me a confused look. "Why?"

With a roll of my eyes, I chuckled, not wanting to get into the details. "No reason."

"You could always go back to school. Learn something new and then you'd have two degrees!"

I scrunched up my nose. Candace was always the optimistic one of our little group of two. I, on the other hand, always waited for the floor to fall out. In my almost twenty-four years of living, nothing had ever seemed to go right for me. I didn't even get to pick what I wanted to do for a career. That decision was left up to my mother. My mother had put a letter in her will, telling me what career to choose in case she died before I started college. My father kept it until my senior year of high school and then gave it to me. He sat there while I read it, that same neutral look on his face he had perfected not long after my mother passed. It was the kind that showed zero emotion, so I never truly knew how he felt. About anything, including me. Before my mother died, my father made me feel like I was his everything. After she died, he slowly drifted away, leaving me to constantly wonder what had happened to his love. Did he resent the fact that I lived and she died? I knew my father loved me, but he had never showed it since that fateful day.

When I opened that letter and read it, I wasn't even shocked. My mother asked for me to follow a career in nursing like she did, and like her mother before her. I knew I had to do it, not only for her, but for my father. I wanted to please him. Maybe this could be the one thing I got right, and he'd finally be proud of me. Maybe even make him want to spend more time with me. It had been years since my father had really paid me any sort of attention, other than the occasional moments he told me he was proud of me. The first few weeks after my mother died, he had clung to me as if he were afraid I would slip away from him like she did. We did everything together. He was the one who first introduced me to horseback riding at the suggestion of the therapists I talked to each week. After that day, I spent a few months hardly speaking at all. There was safety in my silence. I knew my father was worried. Once I sat on my first horse, though, it all came back to me. I remembered all the times my mother had talked about the horse she had when she was little. She was there with me. From that point on, horses were my life. Once I resumed talking and acting like a six-year-old, I noticed my father spending less time with me and more time at work. He also spent more time in our home office where he drank a lot. One night when I walked into his office he was crying. I quickly ran to him, and he held onto me so tightly, I thought I wouldn't be able to breathe. He kept whispering that he was sorry. What had he been sorry for? That memory flooded my mind at random moments.

It wasn't long after that that he met his first of many girlfriends. Women who were more interested in his money than him...or his young daughter. Daddy hired Rachel, my nanny, and from that point on she did everything with me and for me until I was able to do things on my own. I hadn't realized until I was older how unavailable my father had been during those years. Every event I had with my horses, he promised he would show up, only to tell me he had an emergency surgery or an event that he couldn't get out of. It wasn't until I got to high school that I stopped asking altogether.

"Timber, did you hear me?"

I shook my head and let the memories go. "What was that?"

Candace slumped back on the couch, her light brown hair piled on top of her head in her signature messy bun. Her hazel eyes looked at me with a questioning gaze. "Why didn't you change majors if you didn't like nursing?"

With a humorless laugh, I shook my head. "You know why. I couldn't."

She stared at me with sadness in her eyes. "Timber, I know you did it because it was what your mother wanted you to do, but you could have changed it. Maybe if you had talked to your dad, he would have understood."

I shrugged. I didn't have the heart to tell her it was a last-ditch attempt to win my father's love. And like all the other attempts, I had failed. I simply wasn't good enough in his eyes.

I remembered that day like it was yesterday.

"I'll make you and Mama proud of me."

He stood from behind his desk, walked around it and stared into my eyes. My heart had picked up, and for the first time in years, I thought I saw a spark of happiness. And it was there because I was doing something he and my mother wanted.

"I'll be the best nurse, Dad. I swear it."

He smiled, placed his hands on my shoulders and kissed me on the forehead. "Oh, Timber, I know you will, sweetheart. I know you will."

It had been the first show of affection from him in years. In that moment I saw his acceptance and love. We had gone out to dinner that night to celebrate, and it was when my father kept mentioning how great of a nurse I would make that I realized I had sealed my own fate. I signed up for a future I knew I wasn't going to be happy with, all to make my father happy. If I had told him I wanted to work with horses, maybe even own a horse rescue, he would have looked at me like I was insane. So, I pushed my dreams to the side. How foolish I had been. It had only pulled me further away from my father.

With a sigh, I looked at my best friend. "I did it hoping to make my father happy."

She rolled her eyes. "He certainly doesn't act happy about it."

A rush of sadness swept over me. "It's complicated, Candace, and I really don't want to talk about it."

With a forced smile, she nodded, and I decided it was time to change the subject. "Kaylee invited me back to Montana for Christmas. She said she has some news she wants to share, and she'd love to have family there."

Candace smiled. "I wonder what it is? She can't already be pregnant, could she?"

My own face broke out in a wide grin. "I think she is!"

Candace grabbed my hands and we both jumped around and screamed, acting like middle school girls. Candace had met Kaylee only a handful of times, but it was hard not to fall in love with my cousin. She had a way of making everyone her best friend. I sure hoped Kaylee was pregnant. Plus, it would be another reason for me to pick moving to Montana over Utah. That and the blue-eyed man I couldn't stop thinking about. But I refused to acknowledge that reason.

"How can her parents not want to be in the picture?" Candace asked, dropping my hands and taking a step back. "I just don't understand it."

I shrugged, a sadness coming over me. I had told Candace about how cruel Kaylee's parents were. How they basically didn't want anything to do with her unless they needed her for something, like a party where they could show her off or brag about her. Once I got into college and Kaylee told me more about it, it was strange to me how her father and my father were nothing alike, yet similar in so many ways. I sometimes saw the love in my father's eyes when he would look at me; I simply couldn't figure out why he couldn't show it. That was so unlike Kaylee's parents, who probably only had a child to give off the appearance of a well-rounded and happy family.

"If I ever have kids, I'm using your father and Kaylee's parents as examples of how not to parent."

I forced a laugh, but clearly missed what Candace said.

Candace regarded me closely. "Are you okay?"

I nodded. "Sorry, what did you say?"

She pulled her scrub top off, revealing a white tank top underneath, as she made her way toward the kitchen and reached into the refrigerator for a beer. "I said, were you able to get off work to go visit her?"

I glanced at my blurry reflection in the window. My blonde hair was pulled back into a ponytail band, the hazel eyes looking back at me seemed so empty. It was a reflection I had seen for as long as I could remember.

I sighed and pushed away the sad thoughts and feelings. Tomorrow was my twenty-fourth birthday. The day my trust fund was finally mine. The day I could finally follow my own dreams.

"No," I said to Candace, "they told me I couldn't get Christmas off. I haven't paid my time, apparently."

She sank into the couch. "That sucks. Can no one pick up your shifts?"

"It doesn't matter. None of it does, because I quit today." I kept my gaze on the window as I answered, but I could feel Candace's eyes on me. I knew if I turned around, she would be giving me one of her open-mouthed, shocked looks. Then she would launch into a sermon about how irresponsible I was being. I held my breath and waited for it. Her wrath would be nothing compared to what I could expect from my father when he finally found out. Of course, I would be a coward and not tell him until I actually left.

"You did what?"

"I quit," I repeated.

"Um, Timber, you do realize that you have bills to pay? I can't afford to cover your half of everything until you find something new."

"Of course, I know that," I said as I faced her. "I wrote you a check for the next six months' rent and utilities."

She stared at me in disbelief. Candace knew I came from money. She simply didn't know how much money. I got a job as soon as I started college and worked as much as I could without it affecting my grades. Since my father paid for my tuition and living expenses, I tried to never touch the extra money he put into my account—I simply let it grow. I had hired Cory, a financial advisor, the moment I turned eighteen at the advice of my father. He was happy to see I was looking out for my own future, and even more impressed that I wasn't going to "piss away your mother's money," as he put it.

"What! You just wrote me a check for the rent for six months?" Candace asked, her voice higher than normal.

"Yes, because I didn't want to leave you in a lurch. I'm not only going to Montana for Christmas, I'm going to stay. At least, I think I am."

Candace smiled, but I saw the instant sadness in her eyes. "Your horse rescue and training stables, right?"

I nodded, but her smile faded and worry etched across her face. "I thought that was always just one of those...*what if* dreams. I didn't realize you were serious. I'm going to miss you so much, Timber."

My chest squeezed. "I'm going to miss you too, but I know this is the right thing to do."

She sighed. "Can you make money off of that kind of venture?"

I gave her a cocky grin. "Don't worry. It's all going to work out." Candace didn't need to know I had enough money with my investments and the money in my trust fund to last me the rest of my life if I simply wanted to live off of that alone. But I needed a purpose, I needed to follow my passion.

She shook her head as if trying to shake off some confusion. "What a pair we are. Isn't it always me saying things will work out and you're the one saying nothing will go right?"

We both laughed.

Candace stopped laughing and looked at me seriously. "How are you able to write me a check to cover the next six months? I mean, I know your dad is wealthy and all, but six months' worth of rent money, Timber?"

I let out a breath. "Tomorrow I have access to the trust fund my mother left me. Well, actually, it was her trust fund, and when she died it went to me. I didn't have access to it until I turned twenty-four. Honestly," I said with a halfhearted laugh, "I think my father has forgotten about it. Anyway, I want to use that money to find myself a nice-size piece of land. Something with at least one stable on it and a house. It doesn't have to be anything big, but I want the space to be able to grow my business. And with what I saved up during college from working and not touching the allowance my father gave me, I have a nice nest egg. Covering the rent for six months isn't going to be an issue."

My father had liked to remind me that it was my mother's money and that I should be grateful that she left it to me. She came from a wealthy family herself. Her father had invented some medical equipment to help monitor oxygen or something like that. That was how my mother and father had met. Through their parents. My father, along with his father, who was also a doctor, came up with one of the top allergy medicines prescribed to date.

"I know you wouldn't leave me stuck. I'm just surprised you would up and quit. That isn't like you at all, Timber."

I let a wide grin move across my face. "I know! It's not like me and I love it! Since I was a little girl, I knew my soul was connected to horses. They have helped me through so many times in my life when I felt alone or frustrated with my father's lack of interest."

"Don't even get my started on your father!" Candace said.

I grinned. "This is my way of paying it back to the horses. I know I can do this. I *know* I can be successful at this and do something I love as well."

Candace flashed me her brilliant, confident smile. "I believe in you, Timber. You're going to do great things; I feel it too."

"And just think, you'll have the apartment all to yourself. You can have crazy sex and not even worry about me hearing it."

Her cheeks turned red. "It was one time!"

I couldn't help but laugh. Candace had let herself have one crazy night of mindless sex with a hot guy she met at a club about a year ago. They'd kept me up nearly all night with the moans, groans, and pleading for it to be harder, faster, take me into your mouth, deeper. Ugh. It was the longest night of my life. No amount of burying my head under my pillow made it stop.

My face scrunched up at the memory, and I quickly pushed it away. "I can give Henry the rent check if you want and tell him it's to cover my half for the next six months," I said. "That way you don't stress, and I won't stress."

"Are you not planning on coming back to Atlanta at all?"

I swallowed hard and shook my head.

Her eyes widened. "What about all your stuff?"

With a quick glance around the apartment, I faced her. "Sell it, keep the money, I don't want any of it."

"What?"

"I'm starting fresh!"

She shook her head in disbelief and then looked around as if taking the apartment in before she focused back on me. "I don't think you have to pay for six months, Timberlynn. Our lease is up in four months. This is the perfect excuse for me to find a smaller place closer to work."

"Well, I'll write you a check for at least four months, then."

She simply smiled and nodded. Her eyes looked troubled, and I hated that she was worried about me. Oh, how I would miss her and her mothering nature.

"Besides, maybe I'll meet a handsome cowboy and have some of my own mindless hot sex where I'm begging the guy to give it to me harder."

Candace laughed as her face went red again. Then she tilted her head and narrowed her eyes at me. "What about

Ty's brother...what was his name again? The one you said was so good looking. You couldn't stop talking about him when you got back home."

My chest did that weird flutter at the mention of Tanner.

"Tanner, that's it!" Candace said. "I can't believe I forgot his name with as much as you first talked about him. You said he was hot and had a smoking body."

I deliberately kept my voice light. "Oh, he did, but I'm not even sure he'll be there. He ropes for a living and might be out on the road."

"Ropes?" Candace asked.

"Yeah, I told you what he did for a living."

She stared at me with a blank expression.

"He ropes the steer's head, and his partner ropes the back feet."

"That's right. Cowboys aren't really my turn on. I must have forgotten it the moment you told me."

I laughed.

She gave me a grin. "I do remember you saying something about how you'd like to see what he can do with his rope."

I spun around on my heels and made my way toward the hall that led to my bedroom, praying she would drop the conversation about Tanner. "I wish I'd never told you that!" I called out over my shoulder. "I was drunk when I said it, remember? Drunk speak should be sacred."

Candace followed me into my room, a teasing, mocking tone in her voice. "Was that really just the booze talking, Timber? You've never mentioned being attracted to any guy, drunk or sober. Well, I mean, since dickhead. That was a pretty big confession for you."

"I never said I was crushing on him. I said he was cute."

She leaned against the windowsill and smirked. "No, you said, wait, let me think of the exact words..." She tapped her finger on her chin as if deep in thought. "Oh, that's right! You said he was one of the hottest cowboys you'd ever saw, and you could totally see yourself sitting on his face. Maybe even being a reverse cowgirl to his cowboy."

My mouth fell open, and I smacked her on the shoulder. "I *never* said that!"

She laughed and sat down on my bed. "Fine, but we both know you thought it. And come on, Timber, even with the few dates you've been on, you've never once mentioned them afterwards."

I sighed. Candace was right. I had gone out a few times with some guys, but none of them ever made me feel like Tanner did simply from his smile. Or that husky voice of his. I thought of the way he held me in his arms that night when we danced.

Is it getting hot in here?

"Tanner is very cute, but he is also never home with the job that he has. I also heard rumors that he's a player. I'm not interested in that. I'm not interested in a relationship, period."

"Don't let your daddy issues ruin all men for you."

I laughed.

"So, you don't want to fuck him, then?"

This time I was positive my jaw hit the ground. "Excuse me? You are blunt today, aren't you?"

She shrugged. "I believe in getting to the facts. Now, answer the question. Do you want to fu..."

I put my hand up and shot her a pleading look. "Please, stop. No, I do not want to sleep with him."

Ugh. I wasn't only lying to myself, but to my best friend as well.

"The last thing I want or need is a meaningless hook-up." I prayed she didn't hear the slight waver in my voice. From the moment I met Tanner Shaw, I had done nothing but dream about him. Lord, that smile. Those eyes that left my heart beating like hummingbird wings. But I knew a guy like Tanner was not the type of guy I needed in my life. I, unlike my best friend, was a realist. Not a romantic fool who believed the words of good-looking men who promised you the moon and stars. Been there, done that. All it had left me with was a broken heart and fifteen extra pounds when I laid in bed for a few weeks and cried my tears into ice cream and potato chips night after night.

"Well, I can't fault you there. Are you thinking you're ready to settle down, start a family, maybe?"

My body froze for a moment before I faced her. "Settle down?" I laughed a humorless laugh. "From my experience with men, all they do is try and win your heart, then once they get it, toss it to the ground and stomp on it."

"Timberlynn, I know you've had issues with your daddy, and the guys you have dated haven't been exactly what you were hoping for. But not all men are jerks. Maybe you need to give love a second chance. Or, at the very least, enjoy someone's company." She wiggled her brows as she said, "Someone like Tanner, perhaps?"

It felt like tiny needles were pressed against the back of my eyes. It wasn't like I didn't want to fall in love again. I was simply too afraid of it. My own father had broken my heart over and over until I thought it had turned to stone. My throat worked hard for a few moments before I found the words to speak. "I can't."

"You can't, or you won't?"

"Both." I smiled in an attempt to lighten the mood. "I'm afraid this girl's heart is boarded up and closed for business."

Candace sighed as I reached into my closet and took out my suitcase and set it on the bed. "Well, from the pictures I saw of this Tanner, I'd totally let him do very wicked things to me."

With a wink in her direction, I replied, "It's a good thing I'm not you, then, isn't it?"

Chapter Three

TANNER

Chance lived about forty miles north of my family's ranch. I dropped him and his horses off, along with my back-up horse, Banker, then helped to get the horses settled before heading to my folks' place. I had thought about giving them a heads up, but decided surprising my mother would be more fun. With Lincoln, my older brother Brock's wife, pregnant with their second baby, my mother was occupied with what was happening in his life. My oldest brother Ty had gotten married a few months earlier to Kaylee, Lincoln's best friend, and was settling into his new life as well.

Kaylee and Lincoln had moved to Hamilton a few years back from Atlanta, Georgia, and had turned my family's world upside down. For the good, of course. Both Brock and Ty, once sworn bachelors like myself, had fallen hard and fast for their wives. I really couldn't blame them—both women were amazing in their own ways.

Brock never stood a chance with Lincoln. She was smart, independent, sweet, and simply adored Blayze, my nephew and Brock's son from his first marriage.

Ty and Kaylee...hell, everyone knew they were meant for each other long before the two of them knew it. Ty put up a good fight in resisting the fact that he had fallen in love with Kaylee, but eventually he gave in to the love bug, and was now living on the dark side with Brock. I couldn't help but smile when I thought of my brothers. It was clear they were both happy, and I was happy for them. A part of me was envious of their lives, but I wasn't even remotely ready to settle down. At least, I didn't think I was. Every time I thought about it, though, I couldn't help the emptiness I felt in the pit of my chest. I had no idea what in the hell I was longing for, and the more I tried to figure it out, the more pissed off and frustrated I became.

After driving down the long driveway that led to the ranch barn, I pulled up and parked. The moment I got out of the truck and shut the door, Trigger made it known she knew exactly where we were.

Home. Even she was happy to be here.

I smiled and walked back to the trailer where I opened the gate and quickly walked in. I ran my hand over Trigger's solid body and smiled. "You know we're home, don't you, girl?"

She bobbed her head, causing me to laugh. "Okay, let's get you to the barn so you can say hi to all your buddies and eat. Then it's out in the pasture you go." I led her out of the truck and into the barn.

"What in the hell is this?"

The sound of my brother Ty's voice caused me to stop and turn to face him. "What? You're not happy to see your little brother?" I asked with a grin.

Ty shook his head and made his way over to me. He gave me a quick hug and slap on the back before his eyes swept over me, most likely looking for the obvious injury that had me coming home early. My folks thought I'd be home for Christmas Eve, but that was still a week away. "Is everything okay? Dad told us about Colorado. That's awesome, Tanner."

I nodded. "Thanks, and yeah, everything is okay."

"You're so close to that world-record time, I figured you would be heading to the next event to ride the high."

With a forced smile, I shrugged and resumed walking Trigger to her stall. "We decided to end the year on a high note."

When he didn't say anything, I turned to face him. His eyes narrowed in on me. "I thought you weren't coming home until closer to Christmas, bro, what happened?"

It was best, to be honest, especially with Ty. He always seemed to know when something was off, and if I tried to hide it from him, he'd see it all that much more. "Chance needed a break, and to be honest, I needed one too. My head hasn't been in it the last month or so. I think we're both just tired from going at it so hard. And Trigger here, she needs a break herself."

"You only have her?" Ty asked, glancing back at the trailer.

Chance and I both brought two horses out on the road with us. Just in case anything happened to our go-to horses, we always had a backup. "Yeah, I left Hank with

Banker and Miller. Chance is going to turn them all out together. It will be good for them to stay with each other. Trigger could care less about those three, and simply wants to be spoiled here and given apples every day by Mom. Banker and Miller, I swear, are best buds."

Ty ran his hand over my horse's back. "She wins you a shit ton of money, she needs to be treated like a queen and she knows it."

I smiled and started to lead her into the stall. After getting Trigger settled with fresh water and some food, I closed her stall and released a deep breath. I'd turn her out in a bit, but for now she needed to chill in the barn, especially after that long ride from Colorado. "Damn, it's good to be home," I said.

"Mom's going to be over the moon. She missed having you here."

With a scoff, I shook my head. "She got used to me being home with my ankle."

"Hell, she ain't the only one. I miss your hands helping out on the ranch."

"You've got Brock," I stated as we made our way out of the barn. When I stepped outside, I paused for a moment and took in the view. The Sapphire Mountains to the east were covered in snow. As my eyes moved down the range, I saw the open pastureland that was part of my family's ranch. Crystal Lake stood at the base of it all, reflecting the mountains in her crystal-clear blue water. My three older brothers and I learned to fish and swim in that lake. Simply seeing it brought a peaceful feeling over my entire body. I couldn't see the log cabin that sat to the side of the lake, but I felt that familiar pull to it. Someday when I retired from roping, I was going to talk to my folks about buying it. There was nothing more beautiful than this ranch.

"Damn, that sight never gets old," I said as I looked up at the clear blue sky, then back out over the ranch. The pastures were clear of snow, and the cows grazed lazily along with the horses.

Ty followed my gaze. "No, it sure doesn't. Come on, let's get you up to the house so Mom can smother her baby with attention. It will give Lincoln a reprieve for a bit. Mom's been all over her with this pregnancy. She swears it's a girl because Lincoln has been so sick these first four months."

"A girl again?" I asked. "What does Brock want?"

Ty smiled. "A healthy wife and child."

I nodded. "I don't blame him for that." I glanced over at my truck.

"Don't worry about the trailer. I'll have one of the guys take care of it," Ty said.

"Nah, that's okay. I'll do it so I can drive my truck up to the house."

Ty stared at me for a moment. "You staying in the main house or the lake house? Or you could bunk with Greg and Jimmy again."

My hand went to the back of my neck as I rubbed it and chuckled. "Probably the main house. With it being Christmas and all, I'm sure Mom will like having me at the house. Besides, bunking with Greg and Jimmy isn't all that fun. And the lake house would be too lonely being by myself."

Ty laughed, but I was positive he felt the same rush of sadness sweep over his body that I had. Christmas had always been hard for our mother, ever since our brother Beck had died in the Marines five years ago. It was a topic she didn't like to talk about, and at times I knew I wasn't the only one who just wanted to remember our brother. Talk about him. Miss him openly. Mom was getting better at talking about him, though, since Lincoln and Kaylee had come into our lives. In a way, it was almost like Beck sent these two women to us to help us ease the pain.

Ty cleared his throat and gave me another slap on the back. "I'll meet you at the house. Let me call Brock and let him know you're home. You might be the only reason he'll drag himself away from Lincoln."

"They still acting like a newly married couple?"

Ty rolled his eyes. "I swear the two of them are sickening with the way they love on each other." He acted as if he was going to gag.

"Please, like you don't act the same way when Kaylee comes around."

My brother smiled, and I couldn't help but notice how his eyes seemed to dance with happiness. The same happiness I saw in Brock's eyes. Hell, even in my own parents' eyes. A sharp pain hit me in the middle of my chest, and I rubbed my hand over it, willing it to go away.

"Let me get this trailer off and put up and I'll meet everyone up at the house," I said as I tried to shake the feeling.

Before he turned to walk to his own truck, Ty placed his hand on my shoulder. "Is everything really okay, Tanner?"

I let out a deep breath. "I think so. I'm feeling a bit... lost right now. I think being home is going to help me sort a lot of things out."

"It's that time of year. I used to feel the same way when I was on the road. The holidays are hard on each of us. I miss him too."

I nodded. "That's just it, I wish it was just Beck...but it's something more."

His brows drew closer together as he regarded me with a concerned look. "What's going on, Tanner?"

With a scoff, I shook my head. "I don't know for sure, but I think Chance might want to walk away from roping."

His brows shot up. "No shit?"

"Yeah, no shit."

"We need to have a beer and catch up."

"Or six."

Ty nodded. "After Christmas, me, you, and Brock, let's head up to the lake house if the weather is good. Just to hang out."

I smiled. "I like the sound of that. It's been awhile."

"Since Beck."

We both looked out toward the mountains and stared at it in silence. The two of us searched for something, or someone.

I dropped my gaze. "I feel like my world is about to turn upside down and I have no fucking control over anything, Ty."

When I looked up and turned to face my oldest brother, he smiled. "Sometimes the only way to get your control back is to let it go."

I frowned. "That makes no sense at all. You start on the eggnog a bit early, man?"

With a deep laugh, he hit me on the side of the arm and started toward his truck. "I'll meet ya up at the house, Tanner."

I shook my head and made my way over to the trailer. Suddenly, I was more than ready to get up to the house and see my folks.

Chapter Four

TANNER

The moment I stepped through the back door, my mama wrapped her arms around me and hugged me like she hadn't seen me in years. "Tanner, sweetheart! You came home early!"

I looked past her at Ty, who grinned. My father stood next to him, with an equally big smile on his face.

Mama pushed me out at arm's length and gave me a once-over. "Nothing is broken this time, right?"

I laughed. "No, just in need of some R and R."

She beamed with happiness. "Then you came to the right place."

My father stepped up and gave me a quick hug with a hard back slap. "It's good to see you, son. Ty and Brock can use the extra hands to help out around the ranch."

With a hard glare, my mother pointed at my dad. "Ty Senior, did you not hear the boy say he needed some rest and relaxation?"

Dad laughed and shook his head. "If the boy wanted to relax, then he ought to have known better than to come home."

Mama rolled her eyes and let out a long sigh before she faced me. She cupped my face and smiled up at me once more. I could see the happiness dance in her eyes, and it made my heart swell. "I'm so happy to have you back home. How long are you staying, sweetheart?"

"A month or so."

She nearly shouted as she pulled me in for another hug.

I caught sight of Brock as he walked into the kitchen. Blayze, his six-year-old son, was right on his heels. "Well, look what the cat dragged in."

"Uncle Tanner!" Blayze cried out.

I bent down and caught him as he ran and jumped into my arms. "Holy cow, boy, you need to stop growing!" I said while I gave him a quick look over.

"Tell me about it," Lincoln said as she entered the room.

I smiled as I looked at Lincoln. She was carrying a sleeping Morgan and had a glow about her that screamed she was expecting another baby. Of course, the small baby bump was another clue.

"Lincoln, how are you?" I asked as she made her way over to me. I leaned down and kissed her on the cheek. "You look beautiful, as always."

Brock quickly took Morgan from his wife's arms like a man who handled a baby all the time.

"I'm doing wonderful. I'm so glad you made it home early!" she replied as we hugged.

"So am I." I looked down at her stomach. "When are you due again?"

She laughed. "Tanner, please, mark it in your phone! You keep asking. May fifteenth!"

I pulled out my phone and did exactly what she asked me to do. After a quick glance around the room, I looked back at Ty. "Where's Kaylee?"

"She should be here..."

"Hello!"

The sound of Kaylee's voice came from the front of the house. When she walked into the kitchen, she stopped and looked at me, then broke out into a brilliant smile. "Well, holy shi..."

"Kaylee!" Lincoln warned.

Kaylee rolled her eyes and made her way over to me. "Fiddlesticks. The youngest Shaw brother is back in town. Ladies, hold onto your panties!"

I laughed and hugged her. She turned her face and whispered into my ear, "I've got a Christmas surprise for you."

When I pulled back, I replied in a hushed tone, "Oh, yeah? Am I going to like this surprise?"

She chewed on her lip for a moment and then answered, "I think so, if what I saw at the wedding was any indication."

I frowned, confused by what she meant. "The wedding? Your wedding?"

Ty and Kaylee had gotten married last September and were still in the honeymoon phase of their marriage judging by the way my brother was currently staring at his wife.

I turned my gaze away from Ty and Kaylee, only to have it locked onto *her*. Those hazel eyes that from my memory reminded me of the colors of fall.

Timberlynn Holden.

Her face brightened from across the room as she took in the sight before her. Everyone followed my gaze and my mother gasped. "Timberlynn! Oh, my goodness, another surprise!"

I looked over at Ty, who simply stood there with a stupid-ass grin on his face. It would have been nice if he had given me a heads up that Kaylee's cousin was going to be here. The last time I saw her was at the wedding, when Dirk, my brother Brock's best friend, and I had both made it our mission to get to know her better. She was beautiful. No, that wasn't even the right word for her.

Stunning.

Breathtaking.

Those words didn't even begin to describe Timberlynn. She was all of them plus. Her blonde hair was down and fell in soft ringlets around her face, making her look younger than she was. Her eyes seemed to dance with excitement as my mother and Lincoln both showered her with attention. Blayze, of course, jumped in on it and asked to squeeze in and hug Timberlynn as well. Lucky little bastard.

Timberlynn took it all in and kept a sweet smile on her face as she said hello to everyone. When she got to me, her expression didn't change at all. Like she wasn't the least bit affected by my presence. Unlike me. My heart immediately began to race the moment I saw her. Looking at her now, my body temperature heated up, and for a few moments I swore I couldn't think straight. I might even have forgotten how to speak.

"Hi, Tanner, how's the roping going?" Timberlynn asked in a nonchalant tone.

"Good." The word came out sounding strained. I cleared my throat and tried again. "It's good. Everything is great."

She smiled a bit bigger, and then turned to look at Morgan. Brock's eyes met mine, and he looked as if he was trying not to smile, but I saw the corner of his mouth twitch ever so slightly. That ass. I looked away and searched for Ty. He was talking to Kaylee in a hushed whisper.

"Timberlynn, I'm so glad you could make it for the holidays. How long are you staying?" my mother asked while I made my way through the kitchen. Blayze grabbed my hand and pulled me toward the living room, saying something about a new saddle and how he had asked Santa for that and a new horse. I wanted to hear Timberlynn's reply to my mother—no, needed to hear what she said—but I missed it.

As I approached Ty, he looked over at me. I shot him a dirty glance and the bastard acted as if he had no idea why. Even going so far as to raise his arms up and mouth, "What?" to me. Jerk.

"Ty, you free to talk for a second?" I asked as Blayze dragged me past him.

"I think so." He followed us out of the kitchen and into the living room.

"Uncle Tanner, I asked Santa spafacially for a saddle like yours. I want to learn to rope like you, and Daddy said I needed to be in your saddle."

"Spafacially?" I asked as I turned to Ty.

"Specifically," he said with a slight smile. "But, buddy, I think what your dad meant was you needed to ride with Tanner, in his saddle, while he roped a calf."

Blayze stared at the two of us as he let what Ty said sink in. Then he shook his head. "Nah, I think I need Uncle Tanner's saddle. And a new horse."

I couldn't help but laugh. I turned and asked in a hushed voice. "What happened to bull riding?"

Ty looked at Blayze, who had been searching through the few presents that were already under the tree.

"He's given that up. He saw your interview a few weeks back in Kansas and declared he was going to be a roper, like you. Brock and I think it had something to do with the two pretty trophy girls standing on either side of you, though."

I lifted my brows in surprise. "No shit? He does know there are trophy girls in the PBR as well."

"Oh, he knows. Apparently, he likes the blonde one. The kid has a thing for blondes."

There was no way I could stop the smirk from moving across my face. The kid was a Shaw for sure.

"I don't even have to tell you how relieved Lincoln is at this new direction Blayze has gone in."

"I would imagine. He done with the mutton busting?" I asked as I headed over to my nephew. I couldn't lie to myself and ignore that I liked having Blayze look up to me like that.

"Yes, another thing Lincoln is relieved about."

I chuckled. "Blayze, Santa hasn't brought any gifts

yet, buddy. And I don't think a saddle will fit under the tree."

"Oh, I know it won't be here, it'll be at my house on Christmas morning. I heard Grams telling Daddy she wrapped some presents for me and put them under the tree."

I bent down and picked up a present. It did indeed have Blayze's name on it. "If she catches you snoopin', she'll take a present away," I warned.

Blayze stopped picking up the wrapped gifts and stared at me with a shocked expression. "We best tell her it was you snoopin' then."

Ty laughed from behind me, and I did my best not to laugh as well. "Then we'd be lying. Your daddy raised you not to lie," I stated.

Blayze looked guilty as he pushed his hands into his pockets and took a few steps away from the tree. "Aw, man, I bet Santa doesn't bring me the saddle now."

Ty walked over to Blayze and ruffled his hair. "Nah, I think you're allowed one peek, but that's it."

Our nephew's face lit up and he smiled at Ty. "It's a good thing Santa don't believe in washin' your mouth out with soap like Grams does when you lie." He took off toward the kitchen. I watched him until he left the room and then turned to glare at Ty.

"Why didn't you tell me Timberlynn would be here?" I asked in a whispered tone.

"Does it matter if she's here or not?" he asked while he folded his arms over his chest.

"No," I answered too quickly.

"Then why do you look like you're flustered, Tanner?" That asshole was obviously enjoying this.

"I'm not flustered. Why the hell would I be flustered?"

He shrugged. "I don't know, you tell me, bro."

I laughed when I saw him looking at me like he knew exactly why. "You think I like her?"

"I don't know if you *like* her, but I think you find her attractive."

"So did Dirk."

"Yes, but you danced with her a number of times at the wedding, and the next day you couldn't seem to keep your eyes off her at breakfast. And your face lit up like the Fourth of July when you saw her walk into the kitchen just now. Trust me, I'm not the only one who noticed."

I scoffed. "Please. Have you seen her? She's gorgeous. Of course I'm going to notice her. I was just taken by surprise, that's all. A warning would have been nice, asshole."

"Then why are you pissed off I didn't tell you she was going to be here?"

"I'm not pissed off, Ty. I was just surprised to see her, like I said."

He nodded and started back to the kitchen. "Good, then you won't be mad to find out she's going to be staying here in the main house. With you."

My mouth dropped open. "What? Why isn't she staying with y'all?"

The bastard only winked at me and headed toward the kitchen. And I still didn't know for how long she was staying. Goddamnit, my blood pressure had to be through the roof right now.

"Ty? Ty!"

He didn't answer. I cursed under my breath and followed him back into the kitchen. The air seemed to change the moment I stepped into the room. I had a hard time hearing my own thoughts as my heart started to beat in my damn head and race faster in my chest. Jesus, I needed to be worried about stroking out with the way my blood was racing.

I walked over to Brock, then reached for Morgan who was now awake and taking in the scene in the kitchen. The moment she saw me she smiled, and my heart did a little happy dance. "You missed your favorite uncle, didn't you, sweetheart?" I asked as I scooped her into my arms and promptly bounced her around. She giggled and then shoved her finger damn near up my nose.

"Tanner, would you mind showing Timberlynn up to the guest bedroom?" my mother asked as she walked up and took my niece right out of my arms.

"Hey, I was holding her."

"You've got plenty of time to hold her. Timberlynn's been flying on a plane all day, and I'm sure she would like to get settled."

"I've been driving all day and night, ya know," I countered. That earned a dirty look from my mother, and a chuckle from Brock.

My mother ignored both of us and kept talking. "She's going to be staying here with us since Ty and Kaylee are redoing the second bath. It'll be easier for her."

I looked over at Timberlynn. She hadn't been paying any attention to our conversation since she was deep into one of her own with Lincoln and Kaylee.

As if she could sense my eyes on her, she looked over at me. Fuck. My. Life. I couldn't help but notice the way my breath caught in my throat and my chest seemed to squeeze with that familiar ache I'd been experiencing lately. Never mind I couldn't pull my eyes away from her, even if I wanted to. She tilted her head and regarded me for a moment before she turned her attention back to my two sisters-in-law. A part of me willed her to look back at me.

Okay, this is a new feeling. Well, not new. I felt it the last time I saw Timberlynn too.

Brock slapped me on the back, breaking the weird spell I was under. "You better watch out there, Tanner."

"For what?" I asked as I faced him and frowned.

He winked. "You're dangerously close to letting our mother see you're attracted to Timberlynn."

I pushed him away from me and rolled my eyes. "I am not attracted to Timberlynn. She's not my type."

"It's a good thing then, since it sounds like we'll both be staying here. I won't have to worry about you attempting to sneak into my room and have your wicked way with me."

My heart jumped into my throat as I turned to see Timberlynn standing there. "I, um...I didn't mean what I just said...what I meant was...ah. I...you are my type, totally my type, but I...no, what I mean is..."

I could feel Brock staring as he tried not to laugh while Timberlynn looked at me like I was the last man on Earth she'd ever want sneaking into her room. It had been purely a joke to call me out on my comment about her not being my type—by confirming it, I was coming off like a real ass. Hell, why had I even said that?

"Right," I said as I cleared my throat. "Let me show you up to the guest room." I looked down at the floor and asked, "Luggage?"

"Right here!" Ty said, pushing the suitcase into my chest. "She's a light packer."

Timberlynn chuckled. "Not really, there's another one by the front door. I packed to stay at least a month or two."

"A month or two?" I nearly shouted.

Timberlynn pulled her brows in and asked, "Is that a problem?"

"A problem?" I repeated.

She nodded.

With a half shrug, I replied, "No, why would it be a problem?"

Timberlynn gave me a smile that didn't reach her eyes, then made her way to the living room. A few moments later she reappeared with another suitcase. I reached for it as well, and she simply shook her head and gave me a polite smile. "I've got it, but thank you."

I motioned for her to go first, down the hall to the steps. As she walked up them, I looked everywhere except in front of me. The last thing I wanted to see was her ass on display right at eye level. I had no idea why this woman had such an effect on me, but she certainly did. "You're going to turn to the left when you get to the top of the steps," I called out.

"Left at the top, got it!" She did as I said and started down the hall. My betraying eyes landed on her ass, and I internally groaned. Why did everything about her have to be so damn perfect?

"It's the last door on the left. It's above the garage and all the way on the other side of the house, so you don't have to worry about being quiet or anything."

Timberlynn glanced back at me quickly and laughed. That one action nearly had me tripping over my own feet.

Okay, settle down, Tanner. It's not like she's the first pretty...no, beautiful woman, who has ever smiled at you.

"I'm not going to be throwing any parties," she said. "But good to know." She stopped in front of the closed door and opened it slowly, as if expecting something to jump out and scare her. When the door fully opened, she gasped and walked into the room.

"There's a reason I'm sure Kaylee wanted you to stay here. There's a lot more room and privacy," I said as I sat her suitcase down near the king-size bed.

Timberlynn spun around and giggled. "This room is huge! Oh my gosh, look at this reading nook." She made her way over to the bench that sat under a large window.

"Open the curtains if you really want to see something," I said, making my way over to stand next to her.

As she pushed them back, I watched her face. Her smile faded and a look of utter wonderment moved across her face. "Oh, my goodness. Wow. That is...I've never... wow."

"Those are the Bitterroot Mountains. Wait until you see the sun set over them. It's left me speechless on more than one occasion."

Timberlynn turned and looked at me, a curious expression etched on her face.

"What?" I asked.

"A sunset left you speechless?"

With a half shrug, I replied, "I'm not afraid to admit to something that moves me. This…" I said as I motioned to the view, "always leaves me in awe."

She smiled slightly, and without looking back at the view said, "I can see why it would. It's breathtakingly beautiful."

For a moment I didn't know if she was talking about the view, or something entirely different.

"I'm not sure how much you got to see of the ranch when you were here for the wedding, but if you didn't see Crystal Lake and the Sapphire Mountains from the second floor of the main barn, you'll have to check it out. I mean, you've got a good view of it from the ground, but the view from the loft balcony is pretty amazing."

Her eyes searched my face before she quickly looked back out the window. "I didn't get to stay for long last time I was here. Just long enough to visit with Kaylee. I had a new job waiting back in Atlanta."

"Nursing, right?" I asked as I slipped my hands into the front pocket of my jeans.

"Yes, you remembered!" she said, her voice practically giddy. She faced me, and for a moment something flashed in those beautiful eyes of hers. Today they looked almost gray. With specs of gold and green sprinkled in them.

"Your eyes?"

Her teeth dug into her lip. "What about them?"

I shook away the trance. "I thought they were more green."

She smiled and looked down at the floor. "They change colors. Sometimes they look more green, especially if I'm wearing certain colors. Other times they look almost..."

"Gray," I whispered.

Timberlynn nodded. "They're weird."

"They're beautiful."

Her eyes widened in shock, and she shyly looked away before she focused back on me. "No one has ever really noticed they change colors."

"No one?" I asked in disbelief. "Not even a boyfriend?"

Her smile faltered for the quickest moment before it was back. "No, not even a boyfriend." Her eyes moved up to where my cowboy hat should be. "Your hat. Where is it?"

I chuckled. "My mother hates it when we wear them in the house."

Her gaze seemed to be burning the image into her mind. "I don't think I've ever seen you without it on."

I lifted my hand and ran my fingers through my short brown hair. "It's not often I don't have it on. I think the only time you'll see my father, Brock, or Ty without our hats on is here in the house. Mom's rule."

Her gaze jerked back down to mine and we stood there in silence for a few moments before she looked away from me. "Well, thank you so much for showing me the room, Tanner."

With a step back and away from her, I nodded. "Sure. I'll, um, let you get settled, I'm sure you want to visit with Kaylee."

Timberlynn nodded and followed me toward the door. "Are you home for long, or will you be heading back out on the circuit?"

I walked out into the hall and faced her once more. Fucking hell, the woman was beautiful. Her eyes looked directly into mine, and I had a hell of a time focusing on speaking when she gave me her full attention. "H-home?" I stammered.

She nodded. "Are you only home for Christmas?"

I shook my head to clear my thoughts. "No. My roping partner, Chance, wanted to take some time off, and truth be told, I did as well. I'll be home for a month, maybe longer."

The corner of her mouth twitched with a hidden smile. "Oh, that's nice. I'm sure your folks will be glad to have you here for the holidays."

"My father is—he's ready to put me to work on the ranch."

She laughed lightly. I was instantly hyper-aware of my entire body and how it reacted to this woman. *What in the living hell is happening to me*? I found myself absently rubbing my chest to make the crazy sensation go away.

Timberlynn looked away for a moment, her cheeks slightly pink. "Do you, um...stay here at the main house while you're home?" she asked, turning her attention back on me.

For the briefest moment I almost said no. Maybe the safest place I needed to be was as far as possible from this woman. She was a temptation I wasn't sure I could ignore, and I really didn't want to ignore her. "Yeah, my bedroom is on the other side of the house here upstairs."

She gifted me with another one of her amazing smiles. "Then I guess we'll probably be seeing each other often. Maybe. I guess. I'm not sure." She laughed and pushed a piece of her blonde hair behind her ear.

"I hope so," I heard myself saying.

Her eyes lifted to mine and she pressed her lips in a tight line before replying, "Me too."

I took another step back as a sudden urge to kiss her hit me from out of the blue. "I didn't mean what I said about you not being my type. My brother was giving me a hard time, and it seemed like an easy way to make him stop."

Her brows lifted in surprise. "So, I am your type?"

"Hell yes...I mean...you're different."

"Different?" she asked, one brow arched in confusion.

"Different good. Definitely good."

She attempted to hide her chuckle. "Different good. Okay, then, good to know."

I rubbed the back of my neck and tried to ignore the heat in my cheeks. "I'm gonna stop talking before I dig myself in deeper."

"Smart move."

"See you around then," I said as I tipped my head and then quickly turned and walked down the hallway.

I barely heard her reply.

"See you around, Tanner."

Chapter Five

Timberlynn

I told myself not to watch him walk away, but I could not pull my gaze from his retreating body. My heart raced in my chest, and the moment he reached the steps, I quickly stepped into the room and quietly shut the bedroom door.

My forehead dropped against the cool wood, and I took in a long, deep breath, then exhaled. "Oh dear," I mumbled. "What in the world was that, Timberlynn Holden?"

I walked over to my phone and pulled it out. Candace was the last person I had texted, so I pulled up her message.

Candace: I miss you already. Let me know when you get there!

Maybe Candace was right. I needed to let my guard down some. But a guy like Tanner...handsome, an unbelievable body, someone who wasn't looking to settle down...I couldn't open myself up for that let down.

I quickly sent Candace a reply.

Me: Made it safely. It's cold here, but just as beautiful as I remembered it.

Candace: And Tanner? Is he home?

I sighed as I replied.

Me: Yes. For at least a month.

Candace: Gurl...you better get on that!

Laughing, I almost called her but sent a text instead.

Me: Shut up! I'll call later tonight or tomorrow.

A light knock at the door had me freezing in place as I placed my phone down. "Come in."

Kaylee poked her head in and gave me a huge smile. I instantly felt a rush of happiness wash over me. "Is the room okay?" she asked as she stepped in and shut the door behind her.

"Is it okay? Look at that view!" I pointed out the window as Kaylee walked up to me.

She looked out the window and sighed. "Do you see why I left Georgia?"

I laughed. "I thought you left because Lincoln moved here."

She wrapped her arm around mine. "That was one of the reasons, well, the biggest reason. By the way, I sort of let it slip your birthday was the other day. Stella wants to make you a cake to celebrate. Hope that's okay."

Smiling, I looked at her. "That is so sweet of her. And so kind of them to let me stay here."

Kaylee waved her hand off like it was nothing. "Trust me, you'll be more comfortable here, and I'm positive Stella loves having another woman in the house."

"Plus, the newlyweds want their privacy still, I'm sure," I added with a wink.

My cousin Kaylee never blushed, at least I had never seen her blush, but a light shade of pink splashed over her cheeks and she looked adorable. "I'm not going there. Back to you. Are you still considering Montana as a potential new home?"

With a shrug, I dropped her arm, turned, and picked up one of my suitcases. I tossed it onto the bed. "I am. It's here or Utah."

"Utah?" she asked with a shocked voice. "Why would you want to be there when you could be here with me? Has Utah gotten a second visit from you?"

I flashed her a snarky smile. "No, I've only been the one time. You do make a good argument, cuz."

Kaylee let a smile play across her face that screamed she was hiding a secret. Maybe even two. I was dying to ask her if she was pregnant but decided to let her tell me when she was ready. One look at her, though, and I knew she was. She just had a look about her. And her eyes seemed different. Yes, she was madly in love, but there was something else in there. "I have something to show you tomorrow that I think will sway you to pick Hamilton."

I laughed. "Is that right?"

"Yep. I know you have a job and all."

I bit into my lip. "Well, actually, I don't have a job. I sort of quit when they wouldn't let me off for Christmas to come here."

"What?!" Kaylee gasped as she sat on the bed and looked at me with a stunned expression. "Timberlynn, that is not like you to do something like that. You've always been such a planner. Are you able to simply quit like that?"

I hated when people told me I was a planner. Everyone assumed I had laid out my life when, in fact, everyone else had done it for me. And out of guilt, I had gone along with everything that had been asked of me. I was so tired of always living by a set of rules I never implemented for myself. "More like my life was planned for me."

Kaylee frowned and looked down at her hands.

"I'm sorry, Kaylee. It's just that for the first time in my life I'm totally free. No one is hanging anything over my head, and I feel like I've finally stepped out of the shadow of my mom."

"You don't have to tell me you're sorry. If anyone deserves to do what in the hell they want, it's you, Timberlynn. Have you, um, have you heard from your dad lately?"

I scoffed. "No. I'm pretty sure he's forgotten that when I turned twenty-four I got my trust. Or he simply forgot my birthday."

"I had forgotten you got your trust fund!"

I nodded. "Cory did an amazing job growing it, Kaylee. I can buy some land with a house on it. I'd even be happy with a fixer-upper."

Her eyes widened as something struck her. "Wait, your dad didn't call you on your birthday?

I shook my head and tried not to let the hurt feelings come rushing back. When I crawled into bed on the night of my birthday, I cried myself to sleep. It was the first time my father had totally forgotten my birthday. Sure, he'd missed countless parties, or showed up to them late. But he never forgot my birthday. Ever. "No, if he'd remembered, I'm sure he would have just lectured me on what he thought I should do with the money instead of actually saying happy birthday to me."

"I'm sorry, Timberlynn."

With a humorless laugh, I went on. "It's okay. But, the good news is I can pay cash for a place and still have some money to start a breeding and rescue business. I've already looked into the area here and asked about the potential need for another trainer. There's a demand for someone to train horses. Jumpers, dressage. Oh, and to breed more Dutch Warmbloods, Oldenburgs, breeds that are amazing for dressage competition."

"You want to get into breeding as well?"

I shrugged. "I wouldn't mind. My main focus will be the training and horse rescue, though."

Kaylee smiled. "Is that not needed in Utah?"

"It is, but there are more trainers there than here. So, another point for Hamilton. To be honest, I wasn't sure how many people competed in dressage, but there's a large number in the area."

Her smiled widened. "So, total freedom?"

I nodded. "Total freedom to finally do what I want."

"And a chance to put the past behind you."

"That too!" I said, trying to make my voice sound light, refusing to let the past creep into the now. It didn't always work, though. I often had nightmares about my mother and the car accident. My father holding her in his lap. So much blood. The way he screamed her name. It was an image I knew I'd never forget.

"Hey, are you okay?" Kaylee asked.

I nodded as I pushed the memory away. "Yeah, I'm fine."

She looked at me like she knew I was far from it.

I waved my hands to ward off the conversation. "Honestly, I want to put it all behind me and move on."

She nodded and let out a sigh. Then she wiped a tear away.

"Are you crying, Kaylee?"

It was her turn to wave me off. "God, I'm so emotional. I just hate that that bastard hurt you like he did. I hate that your daddy is a jackass, and I hate that you're still thinking of moving to Utah!"

I laughed. "It's in a distant second place as of right now."

She gave me a wobbly grin.

"Kaylee, I'm not running from anything. I just want to do what I want to do with my life right now."

She looked away and shook her head. "I don't know why our parents have to be so...I don't even know the word I'm looking for, to be honest with you."

I reached for her hand. "I know, Kaylee. I know."

"I'm so sorry your daddy is the way he is. I hate it for you."

With a forced grin, I squeezed her hands. "It is what it is."

Kaylee sighed, then changed the subject. "Does Candace know you're leaving Atlanta?"

I scrunched up my face and nodded. "Yes, she knows, and it broke my heart telling her. I'm hoping she'll be able to come visit me wherever I end up settling."

Kaylee winked. "It'll be Montana."

A chuckle slipped free. "It is beautiful here."

"I'm going to spend the next few weeks convincing you that *this* is home. *This* is where you belong, here with me, I just know it."

With a half shrug, I replied, "Maybe. We'll see."

"Grrr, you're so stubborn." She stood and wiggled her brows. "And then there's Tanner. He'd make a great guy to move on with."

My head jerked up and my gaze caught hers. "Tanner? You've got to be kidding. I'm not the least bit interested in him."

Lies. Lies. Lies.

She laughed. "Please. Everyone in that room saw the way he looked at you when you walked into the kitchen. And you tried to play it off, but I saw it in your eyes. They lit up when you realized he was already home."

I stood. "Don't be ridiculous. Nothing lit up."

"Uh-huh. You can tell yourself that, but I saw the spark between y'all."

"You're mistaken and clearly riding on the high of your own romance. There was no spark. The short amount of time I was here for the wedding, I got an earful about Tanner Shaw. Have you forgotten?"

Kaylee walked over to me and kissed me on the forehead. "Oh, sweet cousin of mine. If there's one thing I've learned about the Shaw brothers, it's that you cannot believe everything you hear. Really, you can't believe anything you hear. Just enjoy yourself, Timberlynn. Tanner really is a sweet guy and fun to be around. I promise you."

I forced my body to relax. "I'm sure he is, but I'm not interested in starting any sort of relationship with a guy who travels damn near a hundred percent of the time for his job. And look at the man! I'm sure women fall at his feet."

"I can't argue with you on any of that. But I can tell you that it's okay to have a little bit of fun while you're here." She gave me a sinful smile.

My mouth dropped open. "Are you seriously telling me to sleep with him?"

She winked and headed toward the door. "I never said that, you just assumed it's what I meant. Your brain went straight to the gutter obviously."

"Ha ha, very funny. But that's good because it isn't going to happen." Even though a part of me wanted it to happen. It had been so long since I'd been with a guy. I didn't have much experience with men. A couple meaningless hook-ups with guys who were friends, but that was the extent of my experience. I had a feeling Tanner Shaw was wise beyond his years when it came to sex. The thought of Tanner simply kissing me, though...Lord, I knew if that ever happened, there would be some serious emotions that went along with a kiss. And emotions are not what I was looking for. Not now, anyway.

Something moved across Kaylee's face, but she simply nodded. "I'll be downstairs. Freshen up and I'll see you in a few. Stella has dinner nearly ready."

Relieved that she let the subject of Tanner go, I relaxed the sudden tension in my shoulders. "Thank you, Kaylee. I'll be right down."

Once the door clicked shut, I stood and made my way over to the window. The sun had started to sink in the blue sky, and a brilliant orange and pink color cascaded down over snow-covered mountains. I took in a deep breath and slowly let it out. I couldn't argue with the fact that I'd fallen in love with Montana, even before I ever visited. The pictures Kaylee sent had captured my heart instantly. I could honestly see myself living here. There was only one problem...and his name was Tanner Shaw. I made a vow to myself right then and there that he wouldn't be an issue. He simply couldn't be. This move was about me and my future, and Tanner Shaw was not part of that.

Chapter Six

TIMBERLYNN

When I walked into the kitchen of the Shaw family home, I paused and took in the sight before me. They were all talking at once. Some laughed, some argued with one another. An adorable little laugh came from Morgan somewhere in the room, Blayze was informing Stella he didn't need help getting something out of the oven, and Ty Senior was standing in the middle of it all, wearing an apron that said, *Give me a kiss and you'll get a cookie.*

It was everything I had ever dreamed a family would be like. I couldn't help but smile as I took in the room. A strange feeling of want hit me right in the middle of the chest. Or maybe it was self-pity that I had never had this sort of experience with my own family. Whatever it was, I wasn't sure if it made me sad or happy. When Ty Senior moved to the side, I saw why baby Morgan was laughing, and my insides melted on the spot.

Oh, good Lord. This is going to be harder than I thought.

Tanner held Morgan and lifted her up, then dropped her quickly to kiss her on the cheek. She laughed each time, and when she laughed, it made Tanner laugh. The sound of his laughter made me sigh internally. A feeling I really hadn't felt in a very long time moved over me. It was more of a longing than anything. For a quick moment I wanted to make Tanner laugh like that. I wanted Tanner's attention.

I was actually jealous of a baby. I shook my head to make the thought go away.

"There's something very sexy about a man with a baby, isn't there?"

I jumped at the sound of Lincoln's voice. A nervous laugh slipped free as I realized I'd been caught staring. "Yes, there is."

Lincoln gave her a knowing look. "I'm so glad you decided to come and spend Christmas with us, Timberlynn. Kaylee was over the moon when you told her you were coming."

I was relieved Lincoln had moved on from my obvious gawking of her brother-in-law to another subject. Lincoln adored my cousin Kaylee, and the feeling was mutual. They were the best of friends and reminded me a lot of myself and Candace. "Well, when she invited me, I knew I had to come. I miss seeing her, and getting a chance to visit the area longer will be a good thing."

Lincoln grinned and looked around the kitchen.

"How are you feeling?" I asked, glancing down to her stomach and then back up.

"Wonderful! This time around I don't have the morning sickness like I did before."

I raised my brows. "You know what that means, don't you?"

She laughed. "You sound like Stella. She's insisting it's a boy."

"Smart woman. I've heard girls make you sick more, so maybe she's right."

Lincoln's gaze searched the room until they found her husband. Brock was just as handsome as the other two Shaw brothers, with brown hair and blue eyes that seemed to look deep into your soul. He had been a professional bull rider and had retired recently. Kaylee's husband, Ty, had also been a professional bull rider, but a car accident ended his career a few years back when he was at the top of his profession. Both of them worked the family ranch now and seemed to be perfectly content with their lives.

"Does Brock have a preference?" I asked.

"No, not at all. He simply wants me and the baby to be happy and healthy."

Kaylee had told me a little bit about Brock's first wife. She had died only moments after giving birth to their son, Blayze, so it was not surprising that he'd be worried about Lincoln.

"Is Blayze excited to be a big brother again?" I asked.

Lincoln's face beamed with happiness. "He is very excited and has no problem telling everyone he needs a baby brother. He loves Morgan, but I think he wants a brother like Brock has with Tanner and Ty."

"I can see that. Are they all very close? Brock, Ty, and Tanner?" I asked, looking back out over the family.

"Yes, the three of them are thick as thieves."

With a chuckle, my attention was once again brought

back to Tanner and Morgan. She was standing in his lap, her fingers in her mouth as he spoke softly to her. She was nine months old and seemed to be able to hold the complete attention of the man holding her. Lucky little girl.

"Timberlynn, I hope you like chicken fried steak!" Stella's voice caused me to drag my attention away from Tanner and Morgan.

"It's one of my favorites!" I replied with a smile. "Is there anything I can do to help?"

"You are a doll. Yes, if you wouldn't mind grabbing the salad out of the refrigerator and taking it to the table in the dining room. There should be some homemade ranch dressing in there as well."

"I'm on it!" I said as I made my way through the kitchen. One thing I had noticed back in September when I visited for a few days was how Stella and Ty Senior had a way of making a person feel right at home. Like you were part of the family. I never had that growing up. A surge of anger and jealousy raced through me. If my mother hadn't died in that car wreck, is this how life would have been for me? A happy mother and father who loved their children so much you could see it practically beaming from their bodies? I wasn't going to go there again. I pushed away the negative thoughts and headed to the dining room.

Blayze soon appeared at my side and walked next to me as he carried in the rolls. "You sure are pretty," he said as he set the rolls on the table and faced me.

I couldn't help but laugh. He was a little Shaw in the making. "Why, thank you, kind sir."

Blayze jutted out his chest some. I could instantly picture a younger version of his father doing the same thing. Hell, any of the Shaw men. "I did have dibs on Kaylee, but Uncle Ty won her heart. You know, Uncle Tanner and Uncle Dirk both said they had dibs on you at the wedding."

That caused me to raise a brow. I ignored the way my stomach jumped a little at this bit of news. "Did they now?"

He nodded. "Yep. I heard them call it on ya. I'd like to go ahead and call dibs too."

I was positive my mouth was slacked open and my eyes were as wide as saucers.

Stella appeared out of nowhere, shaking her head. "Good Lord, boy. There's no calling dibs on a girl at any point in time."

"But, Uncle Tanner and..."

"Blayze..." Stella sternly warned. "A gentleman doesn't call dibs on a young lady. The boys were kidding, isn't that right, Timberlynn?"

My head jerked between the two. I wasn't sure if I should laugh, be angry, or maybe get a little excited. Both Tanner and Dirk were beyond good looking. I had to admit, it was a confidence boost for sure.

"Um..."

Stella tilted her head as she watched me.

I swallowed hard and said, "That...that is right. It most certainly will not win the heart of any woman...er ... girl, um...to, ah...to have dibs called on her."

Blayze looked as if he was thinking that through. "Then I take my dibs back. So, does that mean I've got a better chance of winning your heart since they called dibs and I didn't?"

I shot a glance at Stella who was attempting to keep from laughing by covering her mouth with her hand.

"Well..." I said, trying to hide my own smile now as I tapped my fingers on my lips. "I think I might be a bit old for you, Blayze."

"I don't mind waiting."

Oh dear.

"You're too late, buddy," Tanner said as he walked up. I quickly looked over at him and felt my stomach drop. Those dimples...they made my knees feel weak. He stopped next to me, and I forced myself not to feel the heat from his body. "I do believe Miss Timberlynn is going to go horseback riding with me tomorrow morning so I can show her the ranch." He leaned down and whispered loud enough for me and Stella to hear. "I'm hoping she'll think it's a date."

Blayze furrowed his brows and asked, "When I got my horse and saddle from Santa, I was gonna ask her out, but you asked her out before me?"

Tanner looked over at me, waiting for me to answer.

Stella now had her hand over her mouth, her eyes darting back and forth between her son, grandson, and me. She found this humorous. What in the heck was I supposed to say? I looked at Stella once more for guidance. She simply jerked her chin toward Tanner. What was that supposed to mean?

"H-he did, Blayze, and I said..." Another look at Stella and she nodded ever so slightly. "Um, I said yes."

With a dramatic roll of his eyes, Blayze tossed his hands in the air and let them fall to his sides. "This is why I should have tossed my hat in earlier. I knew it."

"What in the world?" Stella said as I finally lost the battle and laughed. Tanner did as well, rustling Blayze's hair.

"Sorry, buddy. Maybe next time," Tanner said as he smiled at Blayze, then looked over at me and winked.

My stomach fluttered, and I pressed my hand against it. I swore my breath seemed to be caught in my chest.

"Oh, poor Brock and Lincoln," Stella said as she placed her hands on Blayze's shoulders and guided him back to the kitchen.

Tanner watched them leave and then faced me. "Sorry, it was either that or you'd be forced to go on a date with my six-year-old nephew."

Blayze would have been the safer option, I thought to myself. "He is...something else," I said as I followed Tanner back to the kitchen.

"You have no idea."

"We're not really going riding, are we?" I asked, peeking over at him.

He looked at me with a sexy smirk. And there went my stomach once again. "Of course we are. You already agreed to go with me. No take-backs at this house."

I tried not to smile. "It was under false pretense."

"If we don't go, Blayze will know. Then he'll think he can officially call dibs on you again."

We had stopped right outside of the kitchen. I couldn't help but let my gaze move over Tanner's frame. My God, the man was utterly gorgeous. A body that screamed he had serious muscles under his jeans and button-down shirt. Blue eyes the color of the sky right after a fresh spring rain, and hair that clearly looked like he ran his fingers through it when he was thinking about something or maybe when he was frustrated. My fingers itched to do the same. I balled my hands into fists to fight the urge to touch him.

For some unknown reason, I found myself wanting to spend some time with Tanner, even though I had sworn off him only minutes ago. There was something about being with him that made me feel so different. What kind of different I wasn't sure of yet, but I liked the way I felt around him. If I were being honest, I liked the way he made me feel when he gave me that brilliant smile of his.

My cheeks ached from smiling. "Well, we can't have that now, can we?"

A brilliant smile erupted on Tanner's face. "No, we can't." He motioned for me to walk into the kitchen ahead of him. I couldn't wipe the smile off my face if I tried.

So much for my vow to stay away from the man. And all because of a six-year-old.

Chapter Seven

Tanner

"You're up early."

I turned from brushing my horse to see Ty standing on the other side of Trigger's stall. "Going for a ride."

"A ride?"

"Yeah, I'm taking Timberlynn out and showing her some of the ranch."

He stared at me for a moment and then nodded. "You taking Trigger?"

"Nah. I asked Timberlynn last night over dinner how experienced of a rider she is, and she said she grew up riding. I asked the guys to saddle up a few horses for me. I just wanted to get some time in with Trigger before I turned her out."

Ty nodded and then gave me a pondering look. "You like her."

"Of course, I like her. She's my horse, dumbass."

Ty sighed. "Not the horse, you idiot. You like Timberlynn."

"What?" I practically shouted, which caused Trigger to jump. "What do you mean?"

The way the corner of his mouth rose into a slight smirk pissed me off. "I mean, you like her. Dude, like I said yesterday, we all saw the way you looked at her when she came in with Kaylee. And last night at dinner you couldn't keep your eyes off her."

"You're insane," I replied as I walked Trigger out of her stall and toward the corral. I opened the gate and let her in. I was planning on turning her out to pasture this afternoon. She was so damn happy to be back home.

"Am I?" Ty asked. He tried to look as if he was considering the question.

"Yes, you are. She's an attractive woman, of course I'm going to take notice when she walks into a room."

"And the eye-fucking from last night? Was that me going crazy?"

I shot Ty a dirty look. "Just because you're in love doesn't mean the rest of us are lining up to give up our freedom."

"Then it won't bug you to know Dirk's in town and will most likely be seeing her too."

That caused me to frown, and unfortunately, Ty caught it.

"Was that a frown on your face, little brother? I didn't peg you as being afraid of a little competition."

"I'm not worried about Dirk," I stated.

He laughed. "So you do like her!"

I glared at him. "What if I do?"

That caused him to take a step back, his eyes wide. "Wait, are you admitting you like her? 'Cause if you are, can you say that again so I can record it and send it to Brock?"

"Why would you need to send it to Brock?" I asked, confused by where the conversation was going.

"We have a bet going on when you finally get hit by Cupid's arrow, and I just won it."

I stared at him, open-mouthed. "You just won it? Because I said I liked Timberlynn? I've liked plenty of women before. I like Lindsey."

Ty dropped his phone to the side and jerked his gaze up to meet mine. "Dude, no. You can't compare the two. Christ, you have a lot to learn, little brother."

I laughed. "How so?"

He sighed. "Lindsey is your fuck buddy. The girl you hook-up with when you come back into town and there isn't anyone around. Timberlynn isn't a fuck buddy, and if you even think for one second I'm going to let you..."

I held up my hands in defense. "Whoa, Ty. Jesus, calm the hell down. I didn't say I wanted to fuck her. I mean, I wouldn't mind that, but I think she's nice and I'd like to get to know her a bit. Then maybe have sex with her." I wiggled my eyebrows.

He closed his eyes tightly, shook his head, and then looked at me again. He moved like he was ready to punch me.

I quickly took a step back, ready to flee. "I'm kidding! I really do want to get to know her better. And yes, I'll admit it. I like her, and I wasn't planning on telling you or Brock because I knew you'd make it a big deal. Exactly like you're doing right now."

"Did you hit your head or something?" Ty asked.

"No?" I said with a laugh. "Why?"

"You actually like a girl and want to get to know her. Like you want to know her beyond just sleeping with her?"

I let out a heavy sigh. "Why is that so hard to believe?"

"You've never shown interest in being with one woman. Ever."

With a half shrug, I headed toward Pogo's stall. "You act like I'm gonna ask her to marry me."

I stepped into Pogo's stall and slipped on his bridle. When I glanced back at Ty, he was on the phone.

"Brock, you need to get to the main barn. Now."

I rolled my eyes and led Pogo out of the stall and to the tie-up area to get him saddled up since the guys hadn't gotten to him yet.

"Something is very wrong with our brother. He wants to get to know Timberlynn," Ty said into the phone. "Yeah. No. Not like that. Yes. No, I'm serious. He admitted he liked her. I'm dead serious. You owe me a hundred bucks."

He walked up to me and pressed the back of his hand to my forehead. I slapped it away. "Get the fuck away from me."

"No fever," Ty said, then swept his gaze over me. "He looks normal too."

"For fuck's sake, you two are assholes," I mumbled as I put the pad on Pogo and then went to get his saddle. Jimmy came walking around the corner with Rosie saddled up.

"Got her ready to go for you, Tanner. You'll just have to adjust the stirrups for Miss Holden."

Jimmy was one of the ranch hands who had worked for my father for as long as I could remember. I swore the man never slept. He was up before anyone and last to call it a night, every single day. When I was home with a broken ankle, I bunked with him and Greg, and they taught me a thing or two about drinking, card playing, and how to be the best cowboy you could be. They were rough around the edges, but damn good guys. I saw why my father trusted Jimmy like he did.

"Thank you, Jimmy, I appreciate you getting her ready."

He tipped his cowboy hat at me and replied, "It's good having you back home, son. You got Pogo?"

I nodded. "Yeah, I'll get him ready. Thanks."

"Enjoy the ride. It looks to be a nice morning."

I glanced past him out into the field and smiled. Although it was brisk out, the sun was shining full force, making it the perfect day to ride. "It does, indeed."

When I didn't hear Ty talking anymore, I turned to see he was nowhere to be found. Thank you, baby Jesus, he was gone. I finished getting Pogo ready and pulled out my phone. I told Timberlynn to meet me at the barn at eight. It was almost that time, and I suddenly felt nervous.

"Okay, you two. We're taking a pretty girl out to show her the ranch. Pogo, no flirting."

The seven-year-old gray thoroughbred snorted and bounced his head, almost as if he was offended. He was a retired racehorse my mother had rescued a few years back. He loved riding the trails but get him to an open pasture and he practically shook to be let loose. He was my second favorite horse on the ranch.

"Yeah, you act like you won't, but I know you will."

I walked up and ran my hand over Rosie. She was an eight-year-old standard breed mare with an attitude, but she was one hell of a horse. She had a beautiful canter, and she loved a good run when she was set free. "What about you, girl? You ready to show off some?"

Rosie looked me straight in the eyes, and I knew her answer.

"I thought so. Let's take care of her, okay?"

Rosie nickered and I laughed.

"So, are you some sort of horse whisperer?"

The sound of Timberlynn's voice made my chest squeeze slightly. I attempted to ignore it, but when I turned and saw her, the tightness grew, and my voice got lost for a moment. I barely managed to walk over to her without falling on my face.

She looked beautiful, dressed in riding pants, a black vest, and a pink hat with a yarn ball on top of it. She gave me a smile, and I was pretty sure something inside me cracked. Right then I knew nothing was ever going to be the same again. She was fucking adorable, and I wanted to know everything about her.

"You look cute," I heard myself saying before I could think better of it.

She tilted her head as she let her eyes roam over me. "You look handsome, as usual."

I lifted my brows and then laughed as I tipped my cowboy hat at her. "Sorry, I didn't mean to say cute."

"No? I don't look cute?" she teased as she spun around and motioned with her hands down her body.

"No, I mean, you do look cute. I mean, yeah, you look adorable in that. Um, I mean, you're pretty...looking. You look pretty adorable looking. No, wait."

Timberlynn laughed and walked up to me. She placed her hand over my mouth and softly said, "Thank you, Tanner."

A shot of heat raced through my body, starting from her hand on my mouth. I wanted to grab it and slowly kiss up her arm, hoping that it led to other places on her body I could kiss. Too bad she was covered up with clothes.

When she saw the way I looked at her, she backed away and dropped her hand. Her face flushed, and she cleared her throat. She had let her guard down, and that was something she must not do often. I was going to make it my mission to get her to let it down completely.

"Kaylee let me borrow a pair of her riding pants."

"Will they keep you warm enough?" I asked.

She glanced down and then looked back up at me. "I think so. How long will we be out riding?"

"Not long. The temperature is unseasonably warm, but still not warm enough to make it a longer ride."

Her eyes widened in both shock and amusement. "Unseasonably warm? It's thirty-eight degrees outside, Tanner. I can barely feel my toes!"

"It's gonna get up to forty, though."

Timberlynn laughed, and it sounded better than anything I'd ever heard. I mentally made a note to do whatever I could to hear it more often. It surprised me how much I wanted to be around her. Hear her laugh, see her smile. It should have made me want to run for the hills, but it didn't. I honestly didn't want to think too much about the reasons why. At least not right now. Or later. I'd think about it after our date was over.

She may not want to admit it, but this was a date as far as I was concerned.

"Okay, then, forty is warm," she said. "I'll need to remember that in my decision-making process."

She walked up to Rosie and started to run her hands all along the horse's body. She picked up one foot and examined the shoe and hoof.

"Decision-making process?" I asked, watching her look over the horse. It was sexy as hell to watch her. She was clearly in her element, and fuck if it wasn't a turn on. I had to look back over to where Jimmy was so my dick would stop thinking of all the things it wanted to do to Timberlynn.

"Yeah, I'm trying to decide if I want to move to Montana or Utah."

I shot my gaze back to her and tried like hell not to let this bit of information show on my face. Timberlynn in Montana for good? Jesus, that did things to my chest and stomach. Trying to blow off what seemed to be excitement at her announcement, I scoffed. "Please, tell me you're kidding."

She stopped what she was doing and looked at me.

"Utah or Montana?" I went on. "There isn't anything to think about. Montana all the way."

The corner of her mouth rose slightly. "You're biased."

"Hell yes, I am. I'm also not blind. Have you been to Utah?"

She folded her arms across her chest and gave me a hard stare. "Yes, I have. When I was in college, a few friends and I went to Park City. I fell in love with it up there."

I couldn't argue with her on that one.

"Fine, Park City is nice, but Montana is beautiful. There are so many gorgeous things to see here."

Her eyes turned dark for the briefest of moments as she let her gaze quickly roam over my entire body before she looked back to the horse and said, "Yes. I've discovered that."

I couldn't help the smirk that I knew was on my face. So, she was attracted to me as well. I could most definitely work with that.

When she finally finished giving Rosie a once-over, I untied Pogo and motioned for her to lead Rosie away from the paddock. "Shall we see the ranch?"

"I'm ready."

As we walked toward the path that would lead us west, I saw Ty and Brock heading our way. I groaned, especially when I saw the shit-eating grins on both their faces.

"Where are you two off to this morning?" Brock asked, his eyes bouncing between Timberlynn and myself.

"Tanner invited me on a ride."

"Did he?" Brock asked as he looked directly at me and smirked.

"I did," I said, keeping my voice neutral. "It seems your son was attempting to put the moves on Timberlynn last night, so I came to her rescue."

That caused Brock to look slightly surprised. "Define 'put the moves on her.'"

Timberlynn chuckled. "He said he was tossing his hat into the ring along with Dirk and Tanner. Calling dibs on me."

"What?" Ty and Brock said at the same time.

This time it was my turn to laugh. "I guess he overheard me and Dirk discussing Timberlynn at the wedding."

Timberlynn turned and faced me. "You called dibs on me, Tanner. How is that...discussing me?"

I simply shrugged and gave her a wink. Some expression moved over her face, but it was gone before I could read it.

Ty and Brock looked speechless as they stood there and stared at us.

Finally, Brock cleared his throat. "I see. My son thought he would jump in on this."

"Stella and I both explained to him how...*wrong*... that was." She tossed a look of displeasure my way as she stressed the word wrong.

Brock seemed relieved. "That boy is going to give me ulcers."

"If he hasn't already," Ty said with a slap against Brock's back. "This should make for an interesting Christmas, though."

"Why's that?" Timberlynn asked as she slipped her foot into the stirrup and lifted herself easily over Rosie.

If I had any doubts about her riding skills, she had long since put them to rest. I walked over to adjust the stirrups for her. The smell of her soap or perfume, whatever the neck it was on her, floated in the air, and I had to fight the urge to take in a deep breath. It was subtle, but damn did it make my insides warm. I'd never be able to smell coconut again without thinking of this woman.

"Dirk informed me last night that his folks are out of town for the holidays. It appears he'll be spending Christmas with us," Brock said. I could hear the humor in his voice and didn't dare look at him. Dirk was not only Brock's best friend, but a bull rider and current PBR World Champion.

I groaned internally so Timberlynn couldn't hear my displeasure with that bit of news. Dirk had stepped aside at the wedding, saying Timberlynn was too young for him, but a part of me knew the moment he got to know her, the more he'd try to get into her pants. It was Dirk, after all. If you looked up manwhore in the dictionary, Dirk Littlewood's picture would be there.

"And this will make for an interesting Christmas because?" Timberlynn asked as both of my brothers turned their attention on me. I adjusted the second stirrup and shot them the finger from down below so Timberlynn couldn't see it.

"Three guys, all working for your attention," Brock stated, his gaze focused on me as I walked around to my horse. "This is going to be like one of those bachelorette reality shows or something."

Timberlynn watched me as I pulled myself up on Pogo. "Is that what this is, Tanner?" she asked, with a playful tone to her voice.

My God, she was certainly direct. Instead of answering her, I looked at Ty and Brock. "We won't be gone long. I was going to take Timberlynn up the west trail a bit, then head on back. I've got my phone on me if you need anything."

Brock nodded. Ty stood behind Timberlynn and made a money sign with his fingers, clearly implying that he was winning the bet with Brock.

Assholes.

"You two have fun!" Ty called out as I nudged Pogo into a walk.

Rosie and Timberlynn walked up next to us, and Timberlynn called back over her shoulder, "Oh, we will, don't worry!"

With a groan, I added, "Christ, don't egg them on."

She giggled and looked at me. "Isn't that what brothers are supposed to do? Pick on each other?"

"Yeah, I suppose so. But those two have had years to perfect their craft."

I could feel her eyes on me, and I turned to look at her. She grinned, and I swore I instantly went hard. "You don't like to be teased, Tanner?"

"I don't mind it. I just don't want them making you feel uncomfortable or make you think I'm..."

"Working to get my attention?" she cut in.

"I'll be upfront and honest with you on that. I am most definitely working to get your attention, Ms. Holden."

She smiled sweetly as she looked ahead on the trail. "What exactly are you hoping will happen between us, Tanner?"

"What will happen? Let's see. I was hoping we could make it up to this small overlook, so you could get a look at some of the ranch. Give you a chance to see a bit more of the Montana countryside, especially since I now know we have to compete with Park City."

Her eyes danced with excitement, and I instantly felt a connection spark between us. I liked it. A lot.

"Then, I thought maybe we would swing by this old cabin that my grandfather used to use as a hunter's cabin."

"A cabin? Really?"

I heard the hesitation in her voice. Or maybe it was a bit of anger. "Yep. Figured we could have a quick..."

She cut me off once again. "Tanner—"

I didn't let her finish this time. "A quick breakfast and then head on back, so I can help my father with a fence that needs mending."

When she didn't say anything, I turned to look at her. Both of our horses walked side by side, making it easy for us to talk to one another. "Breakfast?" she asked. Her eyes narrowed as if she didn't believe me.

"Yeah. What did you think I was going to say?" I knew exactly what she thought, but I wanted to see if she'd say it out loud.

Her mouth opened and closed a few times before she looked back onto the trail in front of us. "Nothing. Um, breakfast sounds good, especially since I didn't have any this morning." Then she glanced back to me and searched all around the saddle. "Where is this breakfast?"

"Don't you worry that pretty little head of yours, I've got it all taken care of."

She tried to hide the grin, but the corners of her mouth lifted slightly, her eyes lighting up. "Is that right?"

"Yes, ma'am. People don't know this about me, but I'm a bit of a..."

"Romantic?"

I laughed. "Hell no. I've never been accused of that before, and don't you go startin' rumors with nonsense like that. I have a reputation to uphold."

She lifted a hand in defense. "I wouldn't dream of it."

"I was going to say a bit of a food lover. I knew I'd be starving and wouldn't be able to eat until well after lunch, so I planned on having one of the ranch hands bring us something to eat."

She shook her head. "I guess I called that one all wrong."

"Yes, you did. A romantic, pffttt. Good thing my brothers weren't around to hear that."

From the corner of my eye I saw her watching me. "Good thing," she said softly as she urged Rosie into a trot.

Chapter Eight

TIMBERLYNN

To say that Tanner Shaw was not what I expected would be the understatement of the year. The few rumors I heard about him could still be true. A guy this good-looking surely bounced in and out of beds like he bounced from rodeo to rodeo. Yet, there was something about him that made me want to know more. And that worried me. I would not allow myself to ever get hurt by a man again. Never. And Tanner Shaw scared me. Not in a physical way, but more emotionally. With the way I already felt about him, the dreams, the moments I caught myself daydreaming about him, I couldn't allow myself to be hurt again.

I stole a quick glance at Tanner. He sat up straight and confident on his horse. The way his strong, muscular legs fit against the horse made my stomach flip. I let my gaze move up and sighed inwardly. Something about this man in that cowboy hat made my insides melt.

He was funny. Kind. A gentleman to the core. And he genuinely showed interest in everything I said. He asked questions about me, but not too many. He was even respectful when it appeared I didn't want to elaborate on something.

"Okay, right over this ridge is what I want you to see," he said as we came up to an open stretch of land. "Close your eyes."

With a confused laugh, I asked, "You want me to close my eyes as I walk the horse toward a ridge?"

"Trust me, Rosie knows where we're headed." His voice was so soft that goosebumps emerged across my entire body.

Trust me.

Lord, those were two words I had serious issues with.

Something about Tanner felt so different, though. I wanted to trust him. I had no doubt in my mind he would keep me physically safe. But when it came to my heart... well, that was another matter altogether.

With my eyes closed, I felt the horse come to a stop, then a moment later, Tanner's hand gently touched the back of my leg. Heat zipped through my body, and I quickly forced it away.

"Don't open your eyes yet. Swing your other leg around, and I'll help you down."

I did as he asked, and when I slid off the horse, he effortlessly held onto me and ever so slowly set me down. My body pressed against his made me inhale sharply as I opened my eyes.

The most beautiful blue eyes I'd ever seen were staring straight back at me. Tanner looked as confused as I felt. He leaned his head down, and I found myself slightly lifting up onto my toes, the vow I had made about him last night a long-forgotten memory. Scared or not, the feelings I had for this man were unlike anything I had ever experienced before.

His gaze moved to my mouth, and I couldn't help but let my tongue sweep out and lick my lips before I pressed them together. He stared for the longest time before he smiled and met my gaze once more.

In a voice so soft and quiet, he whispered, "Close your eyes, Timber."

I smiled as I heard Candace's nickname for me slip off his lips. I liked hearing Tanner say it. I liked it a lot more than I should.

I did as he asked. One of his hands went around to the small of my back while the other took my elbow. He guided me up a slight slope, and then said, "Stop right here."

I inhaled the clean, crisp air and nearly sighed with happiness. Or maybe it was excitement. Whatever it was, I hadn't felt this way in years. "I'm ready," I heard myself say.

Warm breath hit my neck, and I leaned my head to feel more of it. Tanner's soft lips moved gently over my ear as he whispered, "Open your eyes, darlin'."

The endearment alone made my knees weak, but when I opened my eyes and saw the view in front of me, I leaned into his body, forcing him to wrap his arm around me tighter.

For the first time in my life, I found myself utterly speechless. Directly below the ridge was pastureland that looked endless. There must have been a dozen horses turned out, all meandering through the partially snow-covered fields dotted with trees. Some of the horses wore blankets, some running and jumping as they played in the warm sunlight. Beyond that was more land that seemed to stretch on for eternity. My eyes swept over the snow-capped mountains in the distance. I slowly shook my head. "Is this all your family's ranch?"

"Yes," Tanner answered.

I continued to take it all in and stopped when my eyes landed on a lake in the distance. The reflection of the mountains on the lake made it all look like a painting. The sky was the most brilliant shade of blue I'd ever seen. Surely nothing this beautiful could be real.

I closed my eyes and opened them again. I had seen that blue before. A chill raced up my body and Tanner held me closer, probably thinking I was cold.

With a smile, I realized I'd seen that blue only moments ago. The man currently standing next to me had eyes the color of the Montana sky.

"It's...the most beautiful thing I've ever seen," I whispered softly.

"I think this is one of my favorite places on the ranch. There are higher spots, places that are probably more beautiful, but there's something about this one. That's Crystal Lake tucked in between the earth and the mountains, like she's the bridge that links the two together. The reason this place thrives like it does." He laughed slightly. "Stupid sounding, I guess."

"No, not at all," I replied, my eyes locked on the distant lake before I turned and looked at him. He was staring out over the land, a smile on his face that made me smile too. "It's stunning."

"It doesn't matter what time of year it is, this is my favorite spot, hands down. No matter what season it is, the view is beautiful and so different from winter to summer and fall and spring."

I swallowed hard. No man had ever spoken like that around me, and it filled my chilled body with warmth. If I let my guard down, I was positive this man would sneak in and climb over all the walls I had in place. Walls that protected me from ever being hurt or used again.

Turning away from him, I focused on the lake in the distance. My heart raced in my chest as I realized I *wanted* to let Tanner in. And that scared me. "The lake looks beautiful."

"Yeah, next to where we're standing, the lake is actually my favorite spot on the ranch. There's a log cabin there that I like to spend time at. It's a great fishing spot."

I smiled. "I bet it is. And I bet it's cold."

He laughed. "Most of the year it's pretty cold, yes."

"Thank you for showing me this," I said, turning to face him once more. He was still looking out over the ranch with an expression of utter peace on his face. What must it feel like to have that sort of contentment? I had grown up in a beautiful home, had the best of everything money could buy, yet I doubt I ever had that expression that Tanner wore on his face right then. The happiness he felt from looking at this ranch was so evident. I could practically feel the love for this place ebbing off of him. I suddenly had the urge to know more about Tanner Shaw.

"Do you miss it when you're gone?"

He didn't look at me as he answered. "Yes, but I was happy doing what I did. Not until recently did I realize how much this place means to me. I loved being on the road, roping, winning money." He glanced down at me and gave me a sexy smirk.

I rolled my eyes but laughed. "Why are you talking in the past tense? Are you giving it up?"

He looked away, but before he did, I saw the conflict in his eyes. "The last few months I've been missing this place so much. I feel an emptiness inside of me, and I don't know what it is."

I knew that feeling.

"Do you think it's because your brothers are both working the ranch with your daddy? That you maybe feel like you're missing out?"

He lifted a brow. "Are you trying to crawl into my head and figure shit out?"

I lifted my shoulder in a half shrug. "Maybe. You're a mystery to me, Tanner Shaw. The things I heard about you aren't making much sense now."

Both brows rose in a questioning look. "Tell me what you heard."

I looked up, pretending to be in deep thought. "Let's see. You love being on the rodeo circuit and have no desire to settle down. You love women even more, and you've never had a serious girlfriend and most likely *never* will. And you like to sleep around. A lot."

His head jerked back slightly. "Wow. It appears you had some rather spotty intelligence. Who was it, Nelly at the local five and dime?"

With a grin, I answered him. "No, I believe her name was Lindsey."

Tanner's smile dropped instantly. "You talked to Lindsey about me? When?"

The coldness in his voice wasn't hard to miss. "Um, it was the day after the wedding. I was at a little coffee shop on Main Street, and she approached Kaylee to offer her congratulations. When Kaylee introduced me, she seemed very keen on joining us."

Something that looked like anger moved across his face, but he quickly let it fade away. "Is that so? Did she bring me up, or did you?"

I gave him a quizzical look. "Um, I believe Lindsey brought you up after Kaylee mentioned how we danced a few times. She was teasing me about it."

He rolled his eyes and cursed under his breath.

My stomach felt slightly ill as I asked a question I wasn't sure I really wanted to know. "Is something going on between the two of you?"

Tanner let out a sarcastic laugh. "No. Not at all. Lindsey Johnson is...how do I put this so I don't sound like an asshole?"

"How about the simple truth," I said as I followed Tanner over to a large rock. He sat on it, and I did the same. Our bodies weren't touching, but the feel of heat between us was noticeable, at least it was for me.

"Okay, the truth it is, then. Lindsey was a fuck buddy of mine."

My eyes went wide at his blunt words. I knew something was going on with how Lindsey acted when Kaylee briefly mentioned Tanner, but I honestly thought it was just a crush or something.

"She's the girl I used to call when I needed a date to an industry function and didn't want to have to deal with someone thinking I liked them more than I did."

He cleared his throat, looking down. "She's the person I called when I wanted to hook up with someone."

"And you don't think that made her see herself as something more to you in her eyes?"

He shook his head and gave me a bemused look. "Why would she? You heard how she described me. She knew there was nothing and would never be anything between us. I was always up front with her on that. I liked her, but we were never anything more than friends with benefits. She's shallow and trust me when I say she enjoyed bragging to everyone about our hook-ups."

"You said she *was* a hook-up. When did it stop?"

"A while ago."

Tanner looked out over the countryside, and before long his brows drew in and he almost looked annoyed. "Shit." He scrubbed his hand over his face and cursed under his breath. "Maybe she did think there was something more. Last year my folks had an anniversary dinner. I asked Lindsey to go with me because, well, I needed a date."

I nodded.

"After the party she wanted me to come to her place for a drink. I declined."

"Why?"

Tanner turned and looked directly into my eyes. "I wasn't in the mood for a mindless fuck that night. So I said no. She got pissed off and said something about getting tired of being used by me and that she wanted more. I had no idea what she meant, but all I had to hear was that she thought I was using her. I stopped calling her after that. I thought we had an understanding. I would have never intentionally led her on."

"Ahh, so now you're putting two and two together and realizing that Ms. Johnson wanted *more,* as in a relationship more."

His eyes were still locked with mine. "Yeah, I guess so."

"Well, she didn't say anything bad about you, so I'm sure she's not going around spreading nasty rumors."

When he didn't answer me, I smiled and asked, "Are you upset she was talking about you at all?"

That seemed to break the weird spell he was under. "No, it was true at the time. Well, most of it."

I raised a brow. "It's no longer true?"

"I'm not sure," Tanner said as he turned and stared off in the distance once more.

A part of me wanted to ask him what he wasn't sure of and what hadn't been true, but before I could, he stood and reached down to help me up. "We need to head on down and to the cabin. We should reach it about the same time as the guys."

I let him help me up and tried to ignore the dip in my stomach that seemed to happen every time he touched me. His slight change in breathing told me he felt it as well, and that made me dizzy. This was happening too fast and I was starting to lose a bit of control over my emotions when it came to Tanner. One look into those baby blues, and I no longer seemed to care about keeping him at a distance. I liked the way we bantered back and forth. The way he looked at me like I took his breath away. No man had ever looked at me like that. Tanner made me feel different, in the most amazing way. But how could I be sure it wasn't all an act? The few guys I had dated had been sweet, but it didn't take them long to show their true colors. Most simply wanted sex. Plain and simple. How could I be sure of anything when it came to Tanner?

I was losing my focus and forgetting all the reasons that I was here. I pushed away all thoughts of my past and drew in a deep breath.

But a tiny voice inside me was saying that maybe, for once in my life, I needed to let go of my fears. The question was, could I actually do it?

Chapter Nine

TANNER

It didn't take Timberlynn long to strike up a conversation as we rode back down to the valley. "Your older brothers all did bull riding?" she asked as we rode side by side.

"Not all of them. My brother Beck wasn't interested in anything that had to do with the rodeo."

I could feel her eyes on me. "I haven't met Beck yet," she said.

With a deep breath in, I let it out slowly. "Damn, I'm sorry. I thought you knew. My brother Beck died in the Marines a few years ago. My mother didn't really like to talk about him until recently. For a long time, she sorta pretended he was off on a mission and would be back home."

Timberlynn stared at me with a blank expression.

"Again, I'm sorry. I figured Kaylee told you about him. It's okay, I don't mind talking about it. In fact, it makes me feel closer to Beck when I do. For years, Ty and Brock followed my mother's silence. It wasn't until recently that we really started to speak about him a lot more. I think it had to do with Lincoln and Kaylee coming into the family. They showed us it was okay to talk about it. To begin to heal from the loss."

When Timberlynn didn't say anything, I glanced her way. She looked white as a ghost.

I slowed down my horse, which caused Rosie to slow down as well. The horses came to a stop and I leaned over and touched Timberlynn's leg. "Hey, it's okay, you didn't know."

She swallowed hard and then quickly looked away.

"You don't have to feel bad for asking about him, Timberlynn, honestly."

"It's not...I...I know how your mother feels, that's all." When she finally looked back at me, she attempted to smile but failed. I saw the sadness in her eyes and waited for her to decide if she wanted to tell me what caused it.

She looked down and spoke so low, I had to strain to hear her. "I lost my mother when I was six. It was a car accident. My father told me to keep my eyes closed, not to look."

Her voice shook slightly, and I wanted to pull her into my arms and hold her.

"He handed me to another person and ran over to my mother. I tried not to look, but I did. And I still sometimes have nightmares about what I saw. My father holding my mother. She was...already gone, I think. He's never told me. He won't talk about my mom. Ever."

She quickly wiped a tear away and stared straight ahead. "I really wish I hadn't looked."

My lungs felt as if someone had reached in and ripped them out of my chest. I had a hard time finding air to breathe for a few moments as I let her words settle into my head. "Timberlynn, I didn't know. I'm so sorry."

She finally lifted her gaze back to mine, and a single tear slipped down her cheek. The urge to jump off my horse and pull her into my arms was so strong, I had to will myself not to move. I hated to see women cry, but that single tear making a path down this particular woman's cheek did something strange to me. I would have done anything to take her pain away.

With a quick sweep of her hand, the tear was gone, and she was sitting up straight once again. Her voice was clear and strong, as if she hadn't just told me her mother had been taken from her at the age of six. "I never talk about that day. I'm not even sure I've ever told anyone outside of a therapist all of that before," she said with a nervous chuckle. "Besides Kaylee, that is."

"I can't even imagine what that had to be like for you and your father."

Her head snapped up, and she looked at me. "It was hard on us both."

I nodded. "I'm sure it was."

"About your mom..." Timberlynn took a deep breath. "I guess I understand her thought process, not wanting to talk about the profound loss, so I can see why she shuts down about your brother. Sometimes when I try to talk about my mom, the pain hurts so bad that it's better if I don't talk at all. I think it's because my father would never talk about her. I'm almost positive he still hasn't gotten over her death." She paused for a few moments. "But if it helps you to heal from your brother's death, I think it's a good thing you and your brothers talk about him."

I nodded. "If you ever want to talk about your mom, I'm here to listen."

Her eyes filled with tears, and she quickly looked away. She shook her head as if to shed a thought, a feeling, a memory, maybe? Before I could get another word out, she lightly kicked Rosie's side and took off into a trot. She called back over her shoulder, "We should get going!"

I followed her and made a mental note not to push her when it came to her mother. She needed to learn to trust me first, and I could be patient.

A few minutes later, we were on another path and heading to the cabin. Timberlynn had been silent for about five minutes or so, and then started asking me questions about the area. Where the closest large animal vet was. How many large horse breeders there were in Hamilton. I answered them to the best of my knowledge, but I had no idea how many breeders were now in the Hamilton area since I was usually gone more than I was home.

"My mother would be the best person to ask," I finally said. "She's always had a love of horses. Bogo here is a rescue horse himself."

"Is he? How wonderful!" Timberlynn exclaimed, her eyes finally coming back to life.

"Do all these questions mean you're looking to change from nursing to becoming a vet or something?"

She laughed. "No."

"What made you pick nursing, then?" I asked as we walked the horses side by side up to the cabin. The path was flanked by tall trees dusted in snow.

"My mother was a nurse, as was her mom. It was something my mother and father both wanted me to do. So, I did it."

"Did you not want to be a nurse?" I asked as I slid off of Pogo and helped her down once more.

"Yes, I wanted to be a nurse."

I gave her a look that said I knew she was lying through her teeth.

With a laugh, she looked up at me, her head tilted and an adorable smirk on her face. "Was it that obvious of a lie?"

Motioning for her to head up the small set of steps to the cabin porch, I replied, "Yes. Although it wasn't how you answered, it was in your eyes."

"In my eyes?" she asked.

Before I opened the door, we faced each other. Her eyes moved quickly as she studied every inch of my face while I stared at her. One thing was for sure, there were gold specks in those eyes that seemed to light up only when she was happy. I liked that about her. Her eyes told their own story. "Yes, in your eyes. You can read a lot about a person when you learn to read their eyes."

"Is this something you learned on the rodeo circuit to pick up women?" she asked with laughter in her voice.

"No, my granddaddy used to take us fishing up in the mountains at a lake called Hidden Pines. It's a magical place, just ask Ty and Kaylee. They exchanged wedding vows up there. Their first exchange of vows, that is."

Her brows rose in surprise.

"My brothers and I loved the time we got to spend with him. He would always give us some worldly advice, and once he told us you can tell a person's truths by watching their eyes. When I asked you about nursing, you spoke in a cool, easy tone. Almost like it was rehearsed.

But your eyes said something different. They disagreed with you, told a different story."

Timberlynn gazed up at me with an expression I wasn't able to read. I wanted desperately to cup her face with my hands and tell her that no matter what she wanted to say or not say, I didn't care. I simply wanted to be near her, and she could hide whatever she wanted to.

A laugh tumbled out of her lips, and she rolled her eyes. "Okay, never had a guy try to use that approach on me before. Good try, cowboy." She patted me on the chest, then reached for the door to open it. When she walked past me, I had to fight the urge to grab her and kiss her senseless. I wanted to know every single thing about Timberlynn Holden, but it was clear I would have to work a lot harder for it than I thought.

"Right on time, kids!"

I stopped when I saw my mother standing at the table in the small cabin. I should have known when she said she'd help me with the food that she'd stick her nose in my plan.

"What are you doing here, Mama? I thought Greg or Jimmy was bringing up the food for us."

"They both needed to run into town to pick up some fencing supplies for your daddy, so I offered to bring it up."

Timberlynn walked up to the spread of food and moaned. "Oh my gosh, this looks so good! I'm starving!"

My mother stood a little taller and smiled proudly.

So that's where Blayze gets that from.

"I made my famous chicken salad and put it on homemade rye bread. I noticed neither of you ate breakfast this morning, so I was sure you'd both be hungry and wouldn't mind an early lunch. I've got a fruit salad here with some dip."

Timberlynn took a strawberry, dunked it into the white creamy dip, and then closed her eyes and let out another moan. "That is so good."

"It's our mama's secret weapon," I said as I took off my cowboy hat and set it down on the table by the door.

"Cream cheese mixed with marshmallow fluff," my mother said with a wicked grin.

Timberlynn's eyes widened in pure delight. "I could eat the whole bowl."

I laughed. "You wouldn't be the first."

With a grin, Mom started to pack up a few things. "About six years ago we were hosting a huge Christmas Eve party for the ranch hands and some friends of ours. I made two batches of that dip. Two very large batches. When it came time to set out the food, it was nowhere to be found. I asked all the boys if they knew what happened to it, and all four of them claimed to have no idea. Two weeks later, I was in the barn when I stumbled upon the two bowls I had used for the dip. Licked completely clean."

Timberlynn smiled wide and looked at me.

"Beck, Brock, and I snuck out to the barn and ate all the dip, even after Ty warned us not to."

"Tell her about the black eye," Mama said.

Timberlynn cocked her head at me.

I couldn't help but chuckle as the memory came back. Plus, it was nice to hear my mother talking about Beck so casually. "Brock was, of course, older, so he got one bowl, while Beck and I had to share the other one. He wanted to lick it clean, and so did I. Brock told us we'd have to fight over it."

"No!" Timberlynn gasped as she covered her mouth to keep from laughing. One look at my mother showed me she wasn't the least bit sad that I was talking about Beck. She smiled in delight at the memory, and that warmed my heart. How crazy it was that Timberlynn and I had been talking about him.

"Yes. Needless to say, we fought, and I won. Beck walked around with a black eye our whole Christmas break, and when we got back to school, he told everyone he'd been kicked by a horse he was trying to break."

My mother laughed softly. "God forbid he told anyone his younger brother had bested him."

"Y'all had to have been sick as dogs!" Timberlynn stated.

"Let's just say I didn't eat that stuff for at least two years."

"The joys of having boys," Mama said as she walked up and kissed me on the side of the cheek. "You enjoy the early lunch and be sure to bring me back the dishes, please."

"Thank you, Mama."

She tossed a smile back over to Timberlynn. "Enjoy your lunch!"

"We will, thank you so much."

When the door shut, I turned back to see that Timberlynn was smiling too.

"Sorry about that," I said as I made my way over to the table and grabbed a plate.

"Don't be. I adore your mom."

"And she clearly adores you. Kaylee must have told her you were thinking of moving here and she's trying to tempt you to vote for Montana. She doesn't make her homemade chicken salad for just anyone."

Her cheeks turned a slight pink. "I'm honored she thinks so highly of me."

We settled onto the sofa, each of us with a plate piled high with food.

Timberlynn took a bite of her sandwich and then smiled as she chewed. "Okay, if your mom made me this chicken salad every day, I'd totally move here."

"I'll make sure she stocks up."

I watched Timberlynn take another bite. Fucking hell, this felt so damn right. I could do this every day for the rest of my life and feel content. Was that what falling in love was like? Could I really be falling for this woman after a few days? I frowned as I stared down at my food.

"So, Tanner Shaw, I want to know more about you, other than what your jilted ex-lover has to say."

I shot her a smirk. "I'm an open book, Ms. Holden. Ask away."

"Okay, why don't you bull ride?"

"Because I'm not stupid."

She lost it laughing and caused me to laugh as well. "Good answer. But give me the honest one."

"Okay, I tried it once, and when I got thrown, I decided I liked my body and my face too much to risk a bull hurting it...*and*, did I mention that I'm not stupid?"

I loved the way she was looking at me. Her smile was so natural and carefree. This was a side of Timberlynn I thoroughly enjoyed.

"Why roping?"

"I don't know any little boy who grows up on a ranch who doesn't want to rope a cow. Rope fence posts, rope a pretty girl." I winked, and Timberlynn shook her head at me.

"That last one doesn't surprise me."

"You'll be happy to know I have yet to rope a girl."

"Why not?"

I shrugged. "Haven't met one yet I wanted to."

Her brows raised slightly. "Not interested in settling down then."

"If you had asked me six months ago, I'd have told you there was no way in hell I wanted to settle down, at least not anytime soon."

She tossed a strawberry into her mouth, and I watched as she chewed it. "And now?"

My eyes bounced back up to meet her inquisitive gaze. Was she flirting with me? "When I figure it out, I'll let you know, but it doesn't seem like something I'd be afraid of doing now."

"Fair enough," she replied with a soft smile.

"What about you? Are you ready to settle down, get married, have a couple kids?"

Her smile faded slightly before she pulled out her phone and looked at it. "Crap, I told Kaylee I'd call her about going shopping with her and Lincoln. She mentioned wanting to show me something today."

I didn't say anything as I motioned for her to make the call. She clearly didn't want to talk about marriage and kids, but I was patient.

She frowned as she stared at her phone. "I don't have a signal."

"You might have to stand by the window."

Timberlynn got up and walked over to the window and then gasped. "Tanner! I thought you said it was going to be warm today."

I stood and made my way to where she was standing.

"It's snowing!" she exclaimed. "Oh my gosh, look at how beautiful it is. Wow."

I turned to look at her and felt my chest squeeze. She was practically shaking she was so giddy. My feelings for Timberlynn hit me all at once so freaking hard that I nearly jumped back from her. I wanted her, that much I knew, but not in the usual way. I wanted to wrap my arms around her, have her lean back against me and simply watch the snow fall together.

Hell, this was confusing and exciting all at once.

Not taking my eyes off of her, I said, "Very beautiful, indeed."

Chapter Ten

TIMBERLYNN

A day had passed since the morning ride I took with Tanner. We had walked the horses back since it was snowing and neither of us wanted to risk them slipping. Tanner went to help his father on the ranch, and I met Lincoln and Kaylee in town for some last-minute Christmas shopping. Whatever Kaylee wanted to show me had been pushed off for reasons she didn't share. Interesting...

The stores in Hamilton were darling, and I quickly fell in love with the town all over again. I could easily find myself living here, and knew I had already made my decision. If I was honest, I'd most likely made it weeks ago.

When I came for Kaylee's wedding a few months back, I hadn't been able to stay long. With just having graduated school and being new at work, I wasn't given many days off, so the trip was short. I wasn't able to look around like I had in Park City. But what I had seen today had pretty much sealed Hamilton as my new home.

"Penny for your thoughts," Kaylee said as she bumped my arm.

We were sitting on the living room floor of Stella and Ty Senior's house, where Lincoln was knee-deep in present wrapping. Kaylee and I were helping her wrap Blayze and Morgan's Christmas gifts. "Sorry, I was thinking about how cute Hamilton is."

"Isn't it?" Kaylee said with a wide smile. "Tomorrow we're going to see the little surprise I have for you. Sorry we had to bump it out a few days."

"You like to torture me because you know I hate surprises."

"Lincoln, can you come too?"

Lincoln glanced up at the mention of her name. "I wish I could, but I need to go into the office tomorrow. I've got a client who wants to redo her living room, dining, and kitchen, and I'm presenting the drawings to her. If she likes them, I'll be able to get a number of things ordered before the holidays and get a jump start."

Lincoln was an interior designer who had once owned her own business in Atlanta. From what Kaylee told me, it sounded like Lincoln had a controlling father who was hell-bent on making her successful, even if that meant paying for—and sometimes threatening—people to use her for their design needs. Once Lincoln found out how much her father had been stepping into her business, she sold her company and moved across the country to start over on her own.

"What time are you meeting them?" Kaylee asked.

"One."

"That's perfect! I've got an appointment at nine tomorrow morning. You'll have plenty of time to get back home and head into work."

Lincoln nibbled on her lower lip as she thought about it. "I can't ask Stella to watch Blayze and Morgan all day. I really do want to come, but I think I have to pass."

Kaylee tossed a crinkled-up piece of wrapping paper at Lincoln. "Boo. You're no fun."

She smiled, then stopped suddenly. "Oh no."

Lincoln suddenly stood and ran out of the room. I'd never seen anyone move so fast in my life.

"Morning sickness?" I asked as Kaylee got up and made her way after her.

"Yep, but it's not nearly as bad as it was with Morgan."

I laughed and reached for another present.

"Keep wrapping, I'm gonna check on her," Kaylee called out.

"No rush!" I replied as I searched for which wrapping paper to use next.

The air in the room suddenly felt charged with a delicious electricity, and I didn't even have to look up to know he was there. "Don't tell me my sisters-in-law left you with all the wrapping?"

With a smile, I cut a piece of red-and-white-striped paper and answered him. "I wouldn't step foot in this room unless you're ready to commit to helping."

When I looked up at him, my breath caught. His large frame leaned against the wall, and the smile he wore made my insides tingle. The cowboy hat was gone, and his brown hair looked slightly messy, as if he might have run his hand through it a number of times. Those blue eyes seemed to light up the entire room. It should be against the law for a man to be that good looking. Tanner simply grinned and walked closer to me, where he surveyed the pile of toys. "All of this is for two kids?"

I laughed as I let my gaze take it all in. "Yes, but to be fair, it isn't just presents from Santa. Some of these are from your parents, as well as from Ty and Kaylee."

Tanner frowned.

"What's wrong?"

"Well, I think I'm going to have to go shopping. I only got Blayze and Morgan one gift each. It was what my mom told me to buy them."

Laughing, I went back to wrapping a toy that was clearly meant for Morgan. "I'm sure it's okay. I don't think Ty and Kaylee got them very many. Maybe two...three presents total?"

"Shit. That's two more than I got them." He reached for my hand and pulled me up.

"What in the world are you doing?" I asked as I attempted not to fall over the pile of toys and clothes.

"I'm forcing you to come help me shop. I have no clue what to get them."

I stared at him in disbelief. "And what in the world makes you think I do?"

"You're a woman. Isn't that like...bred in you, straight from the womb?"

My hands went to my hips. From the look on his face and the way he took a step back, he clearly realized he had said the wrong thing.

"No, wait, that came out all wrong."

"Did it now?" I asked.

"Yes. What I meant to say was, I could really use the advice of a pretty lady who clearly is good at gift giving."

It was my turn to frown. "That didn't make it any better, Tanner."

"Fine." He gave me a pleading look. "I want to spend some time with you, Timber, so will you please go shopping with me? I really do need to pick up a few more things."

Despite my annoyance, I couldn't help but smile. "You want me to go shopping with you?"

"Yes, I really do. I'll even take you to lunch."

"Well, when you throw food into the equation, how can I refuse?"

He winked and I suddenly got dizzy, positive the room had shifted slightly.

Kaylee walked back into the living room and smiled when she saw Tanner.

"What's going on?" she asked, glancing between the two of us.

I pointed to him. "Tanner here has asked me to go shopping with him. Apparently, he needs my womanly advice on a few things."

Kaylee glared at Tanner as he held up his hands and laughed. "Honestly, I need to buy my folks something, and maybe another gift or two for the kids. But I more or less just want her company."

That seemed to spark something in Kaylee's eyes, and she nearly pushed me into his arms, offering me up as some sort of sacrifice. "Then, yes, y'all should totally go shopping. Don't worry about this. We've got it covered. Stella should be back any minute now to help."

I glanced down at all the presents. "Are you sure? How is Lincoln feeling?"

"She's already back to her normal self and mixing a bowl of chocolate ice cream and pickles."

Tanner gagged, then asked, "Are you serious? That's really a thing? Pickles and ice cream?"

Kaylee shrugged. "I guess so. She's currently making herself a giant bowl, and not even moments ago she was hurling in the toilet."

"That's disgusting," Tanner and I said in unison.

He smiled. "Great minds think alike," he said as he reached for my hand. "Let's go put that to good use."

I took his hand and let him lead me through the pile of wrapping paper, bows, and presents.

"You two kids have fun, but not too much fun! And sex in the back of a truck is not all you think it is, Timberlynn!"

I glanced back at her, positive I had a shocked expression on my face. Tanner wrapped his arm around my waist and said loud enough for her to hear, "Don't listen to her, sweetheart. Besides, I'd take you in the bed of my truck, not the back seat."

I couldn't help but laugh at Kaylee's expression, not sure if he was teasing or not—and not wanting to admit that I hoped he wasn't.

"Tanner Shaw!" Kaylee cried out, but she was cut off as we rounded the corner.

"I don't know what I should be more disturbed by," I said. "The fact that my cousin had sex in the backseat of Ty's truck and I have to sit back there, or the fact that you've used the bed of your truck as an actual...bed."

He chuckled and wrapped his fingers around mine, guiding me through the house while holding my hand. I knew I should pull it away so I didn't give him the wrong impression, but my goodness, it felt good to have a man treat me like this. The skin-to-skin contact did things to my body that I rather enjoyed. "Do you need to get anything out of your room?" Tanner asked.

I swallowed hard, suddenly feeling like I desperately needed water for my dry mouth and throat. "No, my purse is by the front door with my coat."

His blue eyes danced with excitement, or maybe it was mischief. I couldn't tell. But he smiled ever so slightly, and I tried not to look at the small dimple in his right cheek. I failed. My heart hammered in my chest, and I had the sudden urge to turn and run from him. Or maybe it was an urge to ask him to touch me. Anywhere. Everywhere. I needed to feel his hands on me, and I had never longed for that before. Not that I didn't enjoy a man's touch—I had, but only when I was in full control over it all. With Tanner, I had no control, and that was slowly starting to not bother me. Lord, what was he doing to me?

"Don't knock it until you try it," he said, dropping my hand as we reached the door. "I lost my virginity in the bed of a truck."

"Are you serious?" I reached for my coat that was hung up at the front door. My scarf and gloves were sitting on top of my purse. Tanner reached for the scarf, wrapping it around my neck and pulling me to him. Our faces were so close that his breath mixed with mine, and I found myself searching for air.

"Yep. With a woman three years older than me."

I stared at him. "What?"

He laughed, then leaned in even closer. "I was fifteen and she was eighteen."

I was positive my jaw was on the ground.

"That's...you were a child!" I said with horror in my voice. Had she forced him? Seduced him and made him do something he hadn't wanted to do? The thought made me both angry and sick to my stomach.

A sexy smile spread over his face. "She thought I was older. I told her I was seventeen because I *really* wanted to have sex with her."

"Tanner Shaw. You lied to have sex?"

"At first. I told her the truth before things went too far, and then in her eyes I became a little project. She taught me how to satisfy a woman that night."

I swallowed hard as his body pressed up against mine. He hadn't let go of the scarf yet, and I certainly didn't want him to. My mind raced for something to say. "Did she...I mean, did you learn a lot from her?"

I regretted the words almost instantly.

He leaned in and pressed his mouth to my ear. My entire body shuttered, and I was positive he felt it because a soft chuckle slipped from between his lips before he spoke. His warm breath made my body feel as if I had melted into him. "Yes, want me to show you some of it?"

I needed to take back control. I laughed as I placed my hand on his chest and gently pushed him away. "You are a rake and a shameless flirt, Tanner Shaw."

He tied the scarf around my neck before he tapped the tip of my nose with his finger. "I don't know about a rake, but a flirt, most certainly."

I rolled my eyes and smirked as I watched him step away and open the front door. "Where's your coat?" I asked as I followed him out the door.

He gave me a mock wounded look. "A coat? Please, I grew up here. I don't need a coat."

I shivered when a blast of air hit me, cold enough to steal my breath. "It's freezing! How can you not wear a coat?" I yelled while I ran past him to the passenger side of one of the trucks in the driveway.

"That's not mine, sweetheart. This one is."

When I turned and saw a Jeep, I frowned.

"Disappointed there's no truck bed?" he asked as he opened the passenger door for me.

"What? No, I mean, I guess I assumed you drove a truck."

"I do, but the Jeep is easier to get around in the snow, and my truck needs a much-needed break from all the driving I do."

"That makes sense," I said as I slipped into the seat.

Tanner turned the Jeep on as soon as he got in. Heat instantly blew out of the vents, and I sighed in relief.

"If you don't like cold weather, why in the world are you looking to move somewhere cold?"

I took off the gloves, removed my scarf, and pushed them both into my purse. "I love the cold."

"Really? Could have fooled me with the way you raced over to my dad's truck."

"Well, to be honest, I like the cold enough to live where it's cold. I don't mind it, but there are some days it feels like it chills me to the bones. If it had been this cold the other morning, I would never have gone riding with you."

He chuckled. "You'd never make it as a rancher."

"If I decide to move here, I'll have to get used to the winters. The perfect winter day for me is sitting on a large, oversized window bench, a cup of tea in my hands, a book nearby, and snow falling outside."

"That does sound like the perfect day."

"Really? I would assume you couldn't stand to be still."

Tanner let out a scoff. "Why would you say that?"

"I don't know. From what I've seen so far of your family, none of y'all just chill. You're always going and doing something."

"I guess we're just a busy family. There are moments we relax, but this time of year I don't know anyone who relaxes."

"Touché."

We drove in pleasant silence for a while, and it felt nice to take in my surroundings. When I was with Kaylee, we talked and talked. I was never really able to experience the Montana landscape while we were out and about together.

It felt good to be with someone who didn't fill every single moment with words. Not that I didn't love spending time with Kaylee. I adored her, but sometimes I needed a few moments to just *be*. Silence was something I valued. My ex never understood that and always thought it was a sign I was mad or frustrated.

I turned to look at Tanner. He was focused on the road and didn't seem the least bit concerned that we had spent the past ten minutes not uttering a word. "I feel like you have a window or something into my mind," I said, breaking the silence between us.

Tanner laughed. "Why would you say that?"

"I don't know. How did you know to give me a few minutes of silence without feeling like I was ignoring you or asking me if anything was wrong?"

He glanced at me with a perplexed look before he turned back to the road.

"It felt comfortable, the silence. I didn't get the vibe from you that anything was wrong. Just the opposite. You seemed to be enjoying the view, so I let you."

I stared at him, trying to figure out what it was that drew me to him like a moth to a flame. It was like we had this connection I had never felt with anyone before. How in the world could he read me so well? It didn't mean anything was wrong; I simply wanted to be alone in my thoughts. Tanner recognized that almost instantly. I frowned slightly as I let that sink in. Then looked back at him. "Thank you for giving me those few moments. I love Kaylee to death, but man can she talk and talk. Sometimes I like to enjoy the quiet and let what's around me speak. If that makes sense."

He smiled, but didn't look my way. "Makes perfect sense to me."

I found myself smiling as well. "It doesn't make sense to everyone."

"I guess not. But I think everyone needs to enjoy a little bit of silence once in a while."

I cleared my throat and asked, "What do you do for fun when you're not roping?"

He let out a quick breath and said, "Hmm. What do I do for fun?"

"Yeah. You know, fun. Things you do for amusement. Entertainment, pleasure."

The moment the words were out of my mouth, I knew he was going to come back with something sexual.

"I'm not sure you're ready to hear what my ideas of pleasure are."

"Dear God," I said with a chuckle. "Can you be serious for once?"

"I am!" he said, turning onto another road. I remembered from the few times I'd gone into Hamilton that this would lead us right to Main Street.

"You asked me what I liked to do for pleasure."

"I said fun! Like playing video games, or golf, or something like that."

Tanner looked at me, his lip curled up on one side. My body instantly felt hot. Goodness, every expression he had was so hot. How was it possible his snarl would make my lady bits go insane?

"Golf? Video games? Do you honestly see me doing either of those things?"

I giggled and shook my head. "Honestly, no. But you know what I mean."

"Yes, I know what you mean. Let's see, I like horses, so any free time I get I'll usually ride or work with them."

"Work with them?" I asked.

"Yeah, sometimes we'll have some ready to be trained, and I really enjoy doing that."

"Really?" I asked as my pulse sped up. To hear that Tanner was interested in something I was had me feeling excited for some reason.

He laughed. "Don't sound so surprised. The first time I climbed up on Trigger, she damn near threw me over two fences. It was thrilling to break her, though. She's a damn good horse, and there's something special about it being the two of us."

"The two of you?"

"Yeah, I'm the only person who's ever ridden her. She throws off anyone but me."

"Really?"

"Yep."

"So even though your job has you on a horse all the time, you still enjoy working with them?" I asked.

"It honestly doesn't feel like roping is a job. I know I'm blessed to feel that way. I have friends who utterly hate their lives because they're miserable at work. I don't ever want that. When I start to lose the love of it, I'll step away."

I nodded and looked down at my hands. "I know how that feels."

I felt his gaze on me. "You don't like your job?"

"No, not really."

"What would you like to do, instead?" His voice sounded genuinely interested.

"Train horses and set up a stable for rescue horses."

From the corner of my eye, I saw his head snap. "What? Are you serious?"

I chuckled and looked directly into those baby blues of his. We were at a stop sign and he stared at me, in no hurry to keep driving. "What, you don't think I know enough about horses?"

"That's not it at all. I knew from the way you handled the horse the other day that you knew exactly what you were doing. How long have you been around horses?"

The smile on my face couldn't be helped.

"For as long as I can remember. After my mother died, my father didn't know what to do with me because I all but stopped talking. A therapist suggested horses. From the moment I walked into that barn, I felt a peace that I couldn't explain. Even as little as I was, I knew I was safe. Happy. Being with the horses helped me forget for a little awhile. I guess it's always been my escape, and there were plenty of moments in my life growing up that I needed an escape."

My voice trailed off and Tanner took my hand in his as he started to drive again. The way his fingers seamlessly intertwined with mine felt so right. I didn't even bother to pull it away, even though that tiny voice in my head told me to. The contact made me feel...content.

"I'm sorry you had those moments in your life, Timber. I can't even begin to imagine what it was like."

A sense of warmth rushed through my body as I stole a glance at Tanner. I knew with all my heart he meant every word he said. I looked back out the window and let my mind wander. All the times I tried to explain to my father why I spent so much time at the stables, he had never let a word of it sink in. Or at least that was how it had seemed.

I shook the thought away.

"You seem to enjoy being around horses as well," I said.

Tanner smiled. "I love it. Always have. I'm pretty sure my mom had all of us boys on a horse before we were even able to sit up on our own."

We both laughed.

"Horses really do make you happy, don't they?"

He nodded and smiled again. I could stare at him all day when he smiled like that. So carefree and beautiful. And that dimple. Lord, that dimple.

"Yeah. Her folks raised and trained horses mostly for barrel racing. My mama won her fair share of buckles herself."

My grin widened on my face. "I can totally see that."

"Yeah, she did it all through high school and college. Probably could have taken it as far as she wanted to, but she longed to be a rancher's wife."

"Did your father rope or bull ride?"

Tanner pulled into a parking spot in front of a store on Main Street. "He did both. Gave it all up, though, to run the ranch. That was his one and only dream—to be a rancher like his daddy and his granddaddy before that. He always said the other stuff was just for fun, but it somehow got passed down to his three sons."

After Tanner shut off the Jeep, we both got out and met at the front of it. "Did your father's dad pressure him to be on the ranch working?" I asked.

Tanner gazed down at me. "Nah, not at all. He was my granddad's only living son. He lost his older son in a car accident."

"I'm so sorry."

"I didn't know him, and I don't think my father really did either. Dad was an...accident. His older brother was gone and out of the house after dad came along."

I nodded. "Oh, I see."

We walked slowly down the sidewalk. It was covered with a light dusting of snow, and the streetlights dotted here and there were decorated in Christmas decorations of silver and red. Strings of holiday lights ran from one side of the road to the other. It almost felt like the set of a Hallmark Christmas movie, it was so beautiful.

"Whoever decorates does a beautiful job of it," I said as we walked.

"They do a great job with each holiday. When I was a kid, one of my favorite things ever was the July Fourth parade. Now I get to watch Blayze and Morgan experience all the things we got to when we were little."

Even though it was freezing outside, my body warmed as I listened to Tanner speak of his niece and nephew. "They both seem to adore you."

He grinned. "I love those two. It's hard to be away from them so much and see how much they've grown when I come back home."

I focused straight ahead as we walked along the sidewalks of Hamilton. It really was such a charming town. A part of me hoped that Tanner would take my hand again, especially since I had purposely not worn my gloves since I knew we would be walking in and out of stores.

Ugh. I needed to stop thinking about him like that.

"I'm sure that must be the hardest thing," I said. "You said your grandfather left it up to your dad to work the ranch, though. What about you three boys? Has your father done the same with y'all?"

He nodded. "Yeah, he's let us pursue our own dreams. Obviously, Brock and Ty are helping to run the ranch now, but I'm pretty sure if Ty hadn't gotten hurt, or Brock hadn't met Lincoln, they'd still be bull riding for a few more years."

Tanner stopped in front of a home décor store and looked up at the sign. It was clear his mind was drifting somewhere else.

"What about you, Tanner? When will you work on the ranch? What's your dream besides roping?"

He simply smiled and then motioned for me to walk into the store without answering my question.

Chapter Eleven

TANNER

Six stores later and I had a plethora of bags in my arms. It appeared that Timberlynn also had some more shopping of her own to do.

"I hate shopping," I grumbled as we walked into the seventh store.

With a light pat on my chest, Timberlynn winked at me. "It was your idea. I saw a scarf in here earlier with Lincoln and Kaylee that I think your mother would love!"

"From me or you? You've already bought her three things to my one."

She giggled, and a shock of lust raced through my body at the simple sound of it. The more time I spent getting to know Timberlynn, the more I fell for her. And the more I ached to be inside her. I had never been so attracted to a woman before. Why in the hell that didn't spook me was something I didn't understand, but also something I didn't care to worry much about.

"This present is from you," Timberlynn said. "I think your mom will love it."

"Why does she need another scarf? She probably has fifty of them."

"Not that kind of scarf, Tanner. This kind. It's silk and stunning!"

I frowned as I looked down at the dainty, light-blue scarf. "You think she'll like it?"

Timberlynn nodded. "Trust me. Timberlynn is wise. Timberlynn knows all."

She smiled, and my knees trembled. I decided to finally say what I was thinking.

"Does Timberlynn have any idea how much I want to kiss her right now?" The words flowed out of my mouth effortlessly.

Her cheeks went pink with a light flush, and I fucking loved it. "You are a shameful flirt, Tanner Shaw."

"I don't disagree with you, but I did mean it. I want to kiss you."

Timberlynn bit into her lower lip and then shook her head shyly before she turned and headed across the store to look at something else. I released the breath I was holding and looked around. As soon as I did, I groaned. Lindsey Johnson stood near the counter with two of her friends. One look at me and she seemed to come to life. She started my way, and I couldn't help but glance over at Timberlynn. When I looked back at the approaching Lindsey, I saw that she had caught my quick glance. She frowned, her brows pulling slightly, but then quickly wiped the expression from her face. When our eyes met, she smiled widely.

"Fancy meeting you here, cowboy. Wasn't thinking you would be back into town for another few days."

I took a step back from her, crossing my arms over my chest. The last thing I wanted was to give her any wrong impressions. "Well, I'm back. Chance and I decided to take a longer holiday break this year."

"That's great. I haven't seen either of you in town, though...been hiding?"

"Something like that," I replied. Even I heard how clipped my voice was.

She forced a smile. "There's a party tonight at the Blue Moose."

"What for?"

"Jeremy and Kimmy are engaged and celebrating. I know Jeremy would love to see you. If he knew you were in town, he'd have invited you for sure."

I nodded. "I guess it's no surprise they're finally getting married."

Lindsey laughed, a little too loudly. It was obvious she wanted Timberlynn to see us talking. "Dating since freshman year of high school. It's about time he popped the question. So, what do you say? You want to go?"

That was Lindsey's way of asking me if I wanted to go with her, meaning we would probably end the night back at her place for a quick fuck. At least that was her plan, not mine.

"Maybe I'll show up. I'm not sure if my folks have anything planned." I purposely looked over to Timberlynn, then back to Lindsey. Her eyes followed mine. Timberlynn stood there, a beautiful smile on her face as she spoke with a sales associate. It felt like my heart may have jumped slightly when she laughed at something that the associate said.

Lindsey frowned. "Is there something going on there, Tanner? You seemed to be into her at Ty's wedding, and now she's back in town for what?"

"Christmas with her cousin Kaylee. Plus, she's thinking of moving here."

"Moving here!" Lindsey nearly shouted. I glanced at Timberlynn to see her still talking to the sales associate, so she hadn't heard Lindsey...hopefully. Or maybe she was pretending not to hear.

"Yes. It's a free country, and people are allowed to move to Montana."

She rolled her eyes. "I don't like it. There's something off about her."

I looked once more at the only stunningly beautiful woman in the whole damn store. She turned her head and caught me staring at her. I watched as she recognized Lindsey, a slight frown forming between her brows. When she looked back at me, she smiled, but it didn't quite reach her eyes. I returned it, adding a wink that made her cheeks go slightly pink as she shook her head and turned to look at something on a shelf.

"Holy shit. You can't be serious," Lindsey hissed.

I kept my gaze on Timberlynn a moment longer before I focused back on Lindsey and sighed.

She let out a forced, uninterested laugh. "You like her, Tanner? Tell me this is just a fling."

I glared at Lindsey, though she was too busy giving Timberlynn the evil eye to notice. "We're friends, Lindsey, so I would appreciate it if you kept your thoughts to yourself."

"Friends? What kind of friends? The same kind of friends that we are?"

"There is no longer a 'we', and there never will be." I tipped my head to her. "It was good seeing you, but I've got to get back over to Timberlynn. We're shopping for my mama."

That made Lindsey's nose flare. "She's helping you shop for your mama?"

I decided to ignore her question and cut the conversation off. "Good seeing you, Lindsey."

When I turned and walked away, I swore the heat from Lindsey's angry gaze pierced right through me, but it didn't matter. The only thing that mattered was the smile on Timberlynn's face as I walked up to her.

◆ ◆ ◆

Four hours and one-and-a-half bottles of wine later, Timberlynn and I were sitting in the middle of her bedroom laughing and attempting to wrap the many presents we had bought. I honestly couldn't remember when I had enjoyed myself so much. I glanced around the room and saw wrapped presents scattered across the floor around us in a rainbow of green, red, gold, and silver. We could have used the living room, but my folks had some friends over, and they were all watching a documentary on TV. It gave me the perfect excuse to spend more alone time with Timberlynn.

"Oh, man," I said, popping a French fry into my mouth, then leaning back on the floor. My mother had brought up some hamburgers and fries for us since we were elbow deep in presents. Timberlynn had not only bought gifts for my parents, but she bought stuff for the kids, Kaylee, Lincoln, and even Brock and Ty. The Christmas shopping bug had hit her for sure.

"What's wrong, did wrapping presents wear you out?" she asked.

"Hell yes. I think you bought enough gifts for the next two years' worth of Christmases."

She chuckled. "I did not. And the third gift to your parents is for letting me stay here. It's kind of them to host me."

"My folks love having people here. The more the merrier. Especially my mother. She loves to have company, even better if they're female. All those years she was outnumbered by males and all."

Timberlynn grinned, then took a sip of her wine and stared at me before she spoke again. "You never did answer me earlier."

"About what?"

"Your dreams. If you want to work on the ranch."

I sat back up and looked into her eyes. "Yes, it's always been the long-term goal of mine. It's in my blood, in my heart. I'm not sure when that long-term goal is going to start."

Her brows rose. "Sooner rather than later?"

"If you had asked me a few months back, I'd have said later. My ropin' partner, Chance, is giving me the vibe that he's ready to quit. He met a girl last year and fell in love. He was ready to walk away from his career for her. She had other plans, though."

Timberlynn raised a brow in question.

"She ran off with some hotshot guy from New York City."

"Ouch. I'm sure that took a hit to his pride."

"Did it ever," I agreed.

"Can you not find another partner?"

I nodded. "I could, yeah. The question is, do I want to?"

She tilted her head and regarded me for a few moments. "What is your heart telling you to do?"

My eyes found hers once again, and I swore she looked like she sucked in a quick breath. "Well, my heart seems to be as confused as my head is right now."

"Oh," she whispered while her eyes drifted down to my mouth.

I wanted to pounce on her and take her right there on the damn floor like a fucking beast. But Timberlynn wasn't the type of girl I wanted to simply have a quick fuck with. Hell no. I wanted her like I had never wanted any other woman, and I wasn't going to simply romp around on the floor with her and walk out. I wanted to make love to her. Learn what it felt like to be buried deep inside of her. What made her moan, dig her nails into my back, and arch to take me in deeper.

If I didn't get my thoughts in another place soon, I'd let the animal in me take over.

"Your turn," I managed to say without sounding like I was in physical pain from not kissing or touching her.

"Right. Well, I'd really love to have a place with a good chunk of land. Equine training has been a dream of mine since I can remember, to be honest with you."

"Anything you want to specialize in? And what about a degree? Most trainers have one."

She flashed me a wide grin. "I have an associates in equine science. I might have taken a few extra classes here and there."

I laughed. "Damn, woman, you are impressive."

Her cheeks flushed, and she looked down at her hands. "I'd love to focus on equestrian sporting, but I think therapeutic training would be amazing as well. Especially if I could find some good rescue horses for that. I also love the thrill of training a horse under saddle. Something about that connection you have with a horse when you're trying to get them to trust you. I love it. And maybe when I'm more settled in, I'll do a bit of breeding as well."

My brows raised. "If my mother hears you talking like this, you may have a partner."

That made her smile. "I love working with young horses too. There's almost an adrenaline rush with it."

I swear to God, my heart skipped a few beats. Where had this woman been all my life? "Have you started many young horses under saddle?"

She grinned. "I've had my fair share, yes. Enough to make a business out of it, if people gave me a chance."

I placed my hand over my heart and slowly shook my head. "You are the girl of my dreams. I think I'm falling in love with you."

Timberlynn laughed, and I took in the sound of it. When she truly laughed, like wholeheartedly, there was something so beautiful about it. I loved the way it made me feel. She held something deep down inside of her that she didn't want anyone to see or know. I wasn't sure what it was, but all I knew was that I loved seeing her with her guard down. It was a bonus knowing it was me who helped her relax like this. And to see her talk about her future was exciting, to say the least. Hopefully her future intertwined with mine in some way.

"Don't hold out for me. I have no intentions of ever falling in love again." Her voice sounded somber, even though she tried to make it light. My heart sank at the word *again*.

Who in the hell had she loved, and what had happened? And how in the hell could I be so jealous of someone who didn't have a name or a face? I could feel it bubbling up inside of me. "And why not?" I asked, honestly curious if she would answer.

When she finished off her wine, I figured she'd brush me off. But she surprised me once more. "Because I'm obviously not the type of woman a man wants."

I stared at her, stunned. "Why in the hell would you say that?"

I almost willed her to tell me why she was so scared to let her walls down.

Standing, I walked over to her and reached down to lift her up. Timberlynn couldn't have been taller than five foot three, if that. The way she tilted her head to look up at my six-foot frame was adorable. Her eyes were so green tonight. They took my breath away. She swallowed hard, and I felt my blood course through my body, almost leaving me dizzy from the rush.

"Why would you say something like that?" I asked again, in more of a demanding voice.

"Track record," she whispered.

"Whoever he was, he was an idiot for letting you go."

She looked away. I placed my finger on her chin and moved her head until her eyes met mine again.

"*I* want you, Timber," I whispered before I brushed my lips over hers softly and quickly.

Her reply came out breathy and unsure. "You don't even know me."

"Well, based on what you've shared with me tonight, I know you like to listen to Taylor Swift, your favorite color is blue, and your favorite movie is *Steel* something."

"*Magnolias,*" she whispered, her smile ever so faint.

"That's right," I murmured. "You might not have noticed, but I've hung on every word you've spoken tonight."

Timberlynn closed her eyes, and I knew it was because she was fighting to hold back her own emotions.

"Timber, let me in, please."

She slowly shook her head and whispered, "I can't, Tanner. I can't."

When she opened her eyes and a single tear slipped free, I nearly fell to the floor. I used the pad of my thumb to wipe it away, then cupped her face in my hands. "I'm going to kiss you some more, but if you don't want me to, tell me now. Because once I start, I'm not going to want to stop."

Her mouth opened, then shut. When her tongue swept over her dry lips, I took it as an invitation.

Then she nodded, giving me the yes she couldn't verbalize.

I closed my eyes and whispered, "Finally." I opened my eyes and saw her gaze search my face intently, but she didn't say anything. When she lifted up on her toes to bridge the gap between us, I took advantage of it.

The kiss started off slow and sweet. But when she moaned and opened more for me, I lost the battle of what little control I had. Everything seemed to heat up in the room. My body, the kiss, the energy between us—it all pulsed through my veins. I reached down and grabbed her by the ass as I picked her up, not breaking the kiss. Timberlynn wrapped her arms around my neck and sucked my lower lip into her mouth while she held onto me with her legs, which had me releasing a growl. She smiled, and when I lowered her onto the bed, I looked into her eyes once more. "Tell me to stop if you don't want this."

She shook her head as she moved farther up her bed. "Don't stop."

I crawled over her and pressed my body against hers. Nearly coming undone simply from the contact, and that was while we were both fully dressed. I'd never survive skin on skin.

"Tanner," she gasped as my hand slipped under her shirt and played with her already hardened nipple through her bra. I pushed her shirt up and sucked her nipple through the lace fabric, which caused her to let out a low, soft moan. Her fingers pushed into my hair and she tugged slightly.

"I want to kiss every inch of you," I groaned as my eyes quickly swept over her body. She was perfect in every way. Her curves made my mouth water. I loved that she wasn't a damn stick. Her breasts looked like they would fit perfectly in my hands, and I itched to cup them both and play with her nipples until she begged for more.

"Yes," she whimpered as I moved to the other breast. This time I pushed her bra up and took the nipple into my mouth. My hand moved down her flat stomach. She didn't stop me when I slowly pushed my hand into the sweatpants she had changed into earlier. I paused for a moment, careful to make sure this was what she wanted. She didn't stop me, so I moved my hand into her panties. She was soaking wet.

"Fuck," I groaned, moving my mouth back to hers. I pushed her leg open to allow me to feel more of her. When she didn't argue, I had to remind myself to slow the hell down. I had never desired a woman like this before, and I wanted to remember every single moment of this for the rest of my life.

"Oh God!" she whispered when I slipped my finger inside her and used my thumb to rub her clit. Her hips jerked and rotated as I took her mouth once more.

I pushed another finger inside and heard her softly moan. She was so wet, so tight. I knew the moment she came there was a strong possibility I'd come in my own pants like a damn teenage boy.

"Tanner, oh God. Tanner," she whispered, her eyes closed tightly; her arms wrapped around me as if her life depended on it.

"Does that feel good, darlin'?" I asked, finding a spot inside her that made her back arch.

"Don't stop. Please, don't stop."

I smiled, then kissed along her neck and jawline. I loved hearing the small whimpers and moans I pulled out of her as I moved my fingers inside her.

When I lifted my head to look at her, I longed to see those eyes. "Look at me, Timber."

She shook her head.

"Please, look at me, sweetheart."

Her eyes opened and our gazes locked. Everything inside of me screamed that this woman was the missing piece of my soul. That she was the one thing I had been longing for, and that I would gladly walk away from everything and anything simply to share the same air as her. I now knew what was going through Chance's mind when he said he had considered walking away from roping.

She grabbed onto me with one hand, and then covered her mouth with the other hand as her orgasm rolled through her. I could feel her pussy pulse around my fingers, and I knew in that moment I would never want any other woman except for this one. I was done. Finished. I'd do whatever she wanted if she would let me make her come like this every single day. That emptiness I had felt over these last few months instantly filled when she whispered my name.

Finally, when her body stopped trembling, she dropped her hand away. I smiled and pressed my mouth to hers. We were soon lost in another kiss. I rubbed my hard dick against her, and we both moaned softly.

I pulled back and looked at her. She was still dazed from her orgasm as she looked up at me with nothing but desire in her eyes. "Timber, tell me if you want more."

She lifted her hips up to press against mine as she whispered, "Yes. I want so much more."

"Are you sure?" I asked, knowing we had both had a good amount of wine and that maybe she was tipsy. I knew she wasn't drunk, but I still wanted to make sure this was what she wanted.

Her eyes searched my face, then locked on my gaze once more. "I'm sure."

Our mouths once again pressed together. The kiss was so slow but so fucking amazing. I'd never experienced kissing like this before in my life. There was so much passion. So much emotion in it. God, I needed to go slow so I could remember every single moment.

I was about to push her pants down when, fuck, someone knocked on the bedroom door. Timberlynn and I stopped kissing and both froze. Like two goddamn teenagers. Jesus.

Then my mother's voice came from the other side of the door. "Tanner? Timberlynn? Are you still wrapping presents?"

Timberlynn pushed me off of her so hard, I nearly fell off the bed.

"We are, so don't you dare come in! We've only got two more to go!" Timberlynn called out.

I was stunned by how normal she sounded. As if I hadn't just had my fingers inside her. Hell, we were about to make love until my mother interrupted. My whole world was turned upside down from what we had shared, and she sounded perfectly normal. Not a quiver to her voice. Not a breath out of place.

"Okay, well, our guests are gone, so when you kids are done, come on down and watch a movie with us! Kaylee and Ty are on their way over as well."

Timberlynn stood there, staring at the door, her hand over her mouth and her other arm wrapped around her body. She dropped her hand as if she was going to say something but couldn't.

"Sounds great, Mom. We'll be right down," I said, adjusting my hard as a rock cock. Timberlynn looked over at me, and then down to the bulge in my pants. She quickly looked away and shook her head.

"I can't believe we did that and with your parents right downstairs," she whispered. "I almost let you...we almost...oh God."

With a slight grin, I made my way over to her and placed my hands on her arms. Her back was faced toward me as she stared out the window. The moment I touched her, though, she jerked away.

"Don't touch me."

My hands instantly went up. She spun around and looked at me like I was some sort of monster. My heart sank to my stomach.

"That shouldn't have happened," she stated.

"Why not?" I asked. "I wanted to do that, and I'm pretty damn sure you told me yes."

Her throat bobbed as she forced herself to swallow and find the words to speak. "I did, I mean, I wanted you... but no. It can never happen again, Tanner."

"Never?" I asked with a smirk and took a step toward her.

"Never!" she shouted. "It was a mistake, and if I hadn't been drinking, I would never have allowed you to touch me. Ever."

I took a step back in shock. "Are you saying I took advantage of you? I told you to tell me to stop if you didn't want me to touch you."

"No, I'm not saying that at all. I did want you, but it was only because I had a moment of insanity and irrational thoughts."

It felt like a dagger hit me right in the heart. Timberlynn looked as if she might burst into tears.

"A moment of insanity and irrational thoughts?" I asked in a confused voice.

She looked down, then back up. For a moment I thought she was going to come to me. She looked so lost. Then her body went rigidly straight and she lifted her chin. "I'm not Lindsey or some girl on the rodeo circuit, or your special friend you can fuck and then walk away from."

I narrowed my eyes at her. "I never said you were. I don't want a quick fuck with you. I want more, and I thought you knew that. I thought you felt the same way."

She let out a shallow laugh. "Oh, so you want *more*? Is that what this is? Mess around with me, and see if you're ready to settle down for a bit?"

I shook my head as I tried to make sense of what was happening. "What are you even talking about?"

"No, thank you, Tanner. Not interested."

My confusion was replaced by anger. "You sure as hell were interested a few moments ago, and all day when you let me flirt with you, even hold your hand."

Panic flashed across her face as she looked away. She was thinking of something to say, a response that would invalidate what we'd shared that day. I saw the moment she picked the words she would use as her weapon. Her entire body went stiff. She didn't bother to look at me when she launched them out in full attack. "You're the last man I would want to have a relationship with."

I inhaled sharply. That hurt a hell of a lot more than I thought it would. I was positive my body reacted as if someone had hurled a hammer at my chest, because the moment she said the words, she flinched.

I nodded and took a few steps back. My hand went to the back of my neck to rub away the instant ache. I had no idea what had caused the turnaround. Embarrassment that my mother had almost caught us? Maybe I wasn't the type of guy she was interested in after all. I honestly had no clue. The only thing I knew was my head was fucking spinning, and she was making it clear she wasn't interested.

With a quick nod in her direction, I made my voice void of any emotion. I sure as hell wasn't going to let her know her words had affected me. "Okay, well, thank you for making that clear to me, Timberlynn."

Without another word, I turned to leave. The anger built faster than I had ever experienced before in my life. Or maybe it was the hurt of her rejection sinking in. Her words replayed in my head. She had hurled them out at me so easily, I almost believed her. I knew she had been hurt by someone, but that didn't mean she had any reason to hurt me too.

"Tanner. I didn't..."

I got to the door and threw it open so hard it slammed against the wall. I didn't hear the rest of what she was saying because I walked away so fast, I nearly sprinted.

You're the last man I would want to have a relationship with.

As I made my way down the steps, my mother called out for me. "Tanner? Honey, where are you going?"

"I'm going out, Mama," I said as I glanced back over my shoulder.

Timberlynn stood at the top of the steps, her face a mixture of emotions.

"I'm going to the Blue Moose. Don't wait up for me, I'll be home late."

Timberlynn didn't say a word, she simply stood there. I willed her to ask me not to go, but she didn't. I turned and headed down the hall to the front door. Opening the door, I didn't bother to look back as I shut it behind me.

Chapter Twelve

TIMBERLYNN

The next morning I sat at the kitchen table as Stella and Kaylee talked about the New Year's Eve party Stella and Ty Senior were going to throw. "I hope the weather is good, and we don't have a storm blow in," Stella said as she made a list of things to buy and things to do to prepare for the party.

Staring at the empty chair that Tanner normally sat in, I tried not to think about where he had gone last night. After a quick google search on my phone, I knew the Blue Moose was a bar, and my mind raced all evening and half the night. What had he done? Did he meet up with anyone? Leave with anyone? Stay the night at a friend's house? It drove me mad last night, and I ended up getting up at four in the morning to read a book. I knew I had absolutely no right to even care, but I did. It felt like I was being torn apart inside by the things I said to him. Things I didn't even mean.

I had loved Tanner's hands on me. His fingers inside me. The orgasm he brought out in me was so different from what I had ever experienced before. Sure, I'd had orgasms before, but never one like this. I'd never wanted a man to touch me like I had wanted Tanner to last night. Lord, last night. I had been so out of my mind with passion and lust, I had forgotten where we were. In his parents' house. With them downstairs. How could I be so foolish? I had promised myself I would never let a man make me feel out of control ever again. And with Tanner, I had felt so beautifully out of control, and in the moment, I had loved it. Until that knock on the door had pulled me back to reality.

I closed my eyes tightly. I was lying to myself. I had felt in control the entire time because Tanner had given me all the control. He had asked permission before he did anything.

Oh God. Why had I reacted that way?

I opened my eyes and rubbed my hand over my chest in an attempt to ease the tightness. I knew why I reacted that way. I was letting Tanner in, and that scared the living piss out of me.

"Timberlynn?"

Kaylee's voice pulled me from my thoughts, and I snapped my eyes over to her. "I'm sorry, what did you say?"

"Daydreaming, were you?" Kaylee asked with a soft smile. Her eyes silently asked if I was okay, and I gave her a simple grin in return.

"Something like that. Trying to guess what this surprise is you're going to show me today."

Kaylee's faced beamed with excitement, then she looked at her phone. "If you're ready to go, we should probably be heading out."

"Sure, I'm ready."

Stella looked at me with an odd expression on her face, but then it was gone in an instant as she stood and flashed that sweet smile of hers. It reminded me so much of Tanner's smile, and it was hard to ignore the way my stomach dropped as I thought once more about how I had reacted last night.

"When you come back, we're baking for the holidays," Stella said.

I looked between her and Kaylee. Neither one of us was used to these sorts of activities. Kaylee's parents were always out of town, and Lord knows my father was never around for any pre-holiday activities. My nanny had tried a few times to arrange for Christmas cookie baking and decorating with a promise from my father that he would be there. He never showed up, and after three years in a row of him being a no-show, and me growing old enough to know he didn't give a damn about my feelings, I asked Rachel to stop planning them.

Kaylee winked at me, most likely knowing where my thoughts were.

"I've never baked for the holidays before," I admitted.

Stella looked stunned. "Why not?" She seemed apologetic as soon as she said it.

I shrugged. "My father was a doctor and worked a lot, so we never got to the whole before-Christmas cookie baking."

"Ever?" Stella asked.

"No, ma'am. Not once that I can remember."

"But you had presents and such?"

I turned and looked at Kaylee. "Shall we go?" I knew it was rude, but with the way I was feeling about everything with Tanner, the last thing I wanted to talk about was my lack of happy childhood Christmas memories.

"Yeah, let me text Ty that we're leaving and I'm taking his truck."

Stella walked us to the back door where Kaylee had parked Ty's truck.

"You girls have fun. Be sure to stop at Nelly's for a piece of pie, at least, Kaylee."

I wanted to groan. I'd only been here a week and I was positive I had gained ten pounds already. If I moved here, I'd have to rein in my eating some.

Kaylee chuckled. "I think I'll save the calories for baking later!"

Stella laughed. "Have fun!"

Kaylee walked out first, and I had to catch my breath at the shock from the cold wind. "Holy shit!" I shouted as I ran past Kaylee to the truck. I didn't see the small patch of ice and slipped. I was about to fall when strong arms grabbed me from behind.

"Whoa, be careful, or you'll break your neck. And you're too beautiful to die."

When I was firmly on my feet, I turned to see Dirk Littlewood standing there, all six foot two of him. His dark hair was covered by a black cowboy hat that made those meadow green eyes of his flash with excitement. To say he was handsome was an understatement. Of course, Tanner was far more handsome, in my opinion. But Dirk had a forbidden look about him. He was good looking and he knew it, yet he didn't act cocky. He truly seemed liked a gentleman. He was Brock's age, twenty-nine I believed Kaylee had said, and seemed to be the only one in this little group not ready to settle down.

"Dirk, thank you so much. I didn't even see that patch of ice." My voice was unsteady from almost falling and busting my ass.

He winked. "It's hard to see it sometimes. Just don't go running around like that in the winter, and you'll be fine."

I laughed and was surprised at how nervous it sounded. I wasn't the least bit attracted to Dirk. "How's the bull riding going?" I asked.

He grinned so wide I returned one of my own. "You're looking at the world champion."

I gasped. "That's amazing, Dirk! Congratulations."

He tipped his cowboy hat at me. "It took Brock retiring for me to get my spot, so I'll gladly take it."

"I told Ty and Brock we needed to celebrate!" Kaylee said from next to me. Dirk gave her a big hug and a kiss on the cheek before he looked her over. He lifted a brow and she winked at him. I couldn't help but notice the interaction between the two of them. Kaylee had told me Dirk was one of her closest and dearest friends. She even called him her male version of Lincoln, which said a lot considering Kaylee had known Dirk for not even two years. Looking at the way the two of them acted, you could see the friendship there. He adored her, but not in a sexual kind of way. She was a like a sister to him. But then, Dirk seemed to adore Lincoln as well, yet he had that sisterly connection with Kaylee.

"Look at you, you're beautiful," Dirk said to Kaylee.

"And still my wife, so get your paws off of her, Littlewood," Ty shouted.

Dirk tossed his head back and laughed as Ty and Brock approached us. "Christ Almighty, if it isn't the oldest Shaw brothers."

There was a round of handshakes and quick bro hugs with hard back slaps. What was it about these men and the back slapping?

"You're looking good. How have things been?" Brock asked.

"Busy. I shot a few commercials this past weekend," Dirk said. "That shit is a lot crazier with a championship under your belt."

Both Ty and Brock laughed because they knew what it was like, both being previous PBR world champions themselves.

Ty walked up to Kaylee and kissed her on the lips, then whispered something into her ear. I loved seeing her cheeks blush ever so slightly, but a small pang of jealousy ripped through me, shocking me for the briefest of moments.

I focused my attention back on Brock and Dirk who were talking about bulls or something. My mind drifted off once more as I tried to think of warm things to keep my body from freezing. Then Brock said something that caused me to jerk my head up and focus on his conversation with Dirk. "I haven't seen him at all this morning, Dad said he's not even sure he came home."

Dirk nodded. "I saw him at the Blue Moose last night. He was on his way to getting pretty wasted. One of his friends was having some sort of party or something. Lindsey Johnson was hanging all over him, but he didn't seem the least bit interested in her. I can't tell you how many times he peeled her arms off of him."

My heart fell to my stomach, but at least Tanner hadn't been interested in Lindsey. "Tanner didn't come home last night?" I heard myself asking. That caused both Dirk and Brock to look at me. Brock nodded, but Dirk smiled as if he knew something no one else did.

"We need to get going, y'all. I've got an appointment and we can't be late," Kaylee said.

Dirk reached for my hand and removed the glove, then placed a kiss on top. I rolled my eyes as he winked.

"Oh, how I will miss you, Ms. Holden. If you haven't noticed, I have a fondness for the women in your family." He waggled his brows dramatically, and I couldn't help but laugh, knowing he was only kidding.

"I had noticed, yes."

He flashed me a sinful smile. "Hopefully that doesn't scare you away."

"If she's smart, it will." *That voice.*

Dirk's smile turned into a full-blown grin, as if he had planned this whole scene to happen. I jerked my eyes away from Dirk to see Tanner standing there. My breath was nearly stolen once again, and this time the cold air had nothing to do with it. I was hot all over, and the memory of his hands on me caused my body to tremble and my cheeks to burn.

Dirk stepped closer to me, leaned down and whispered so only I could hear him. "I fear I'm too late to win your heart, ma'am."

I turned and looked at him. He was teasing, and I knew what his main objective was with the whisper... agitate Tanner at all costs. Well, two could play at that game. With a sinful smile of my own, I whispered back, "I don't know what you're talking about, sir."

Dirk let out a roar of laughter, as if I had said the funniest thing in the world. Then he took his little game a step further and kissed me on the cheek. "I'll see you around, beautiful."

When he stepped away, I looked at Tanner and my smile faltered slightly. He looked furious as he glared at Dirk. When he let his gaze move over to me, he softened his expression, but I still couldn't read it. He was totally emotionless now as he stared at me.

I turned and climbed up into the Ford F-250 truck. Kaylee hopped in and fired up the engine. "Damn it, I should have started it remotely. It's freezing," she said.

"It's okay," I said, needing the cold air to diffuse the instant rush of heat that enveloped me when I saw Tanner.

By the time we pulled out of the entrance to the ranch, the truck's heater was blasting hot air, and I could breathe normally again.

"Do you want to talk about what's happening with you and Tanner?"

"What?" I asked in a stunned voice as I looked at Kaylee.

She gave me an expression that said I wasn't fooling anyone. "Timberlynn, please. From the first time the two of you saw each other, it's been like a moth to a flame. Ty said he's never seen Tanner so taken with anyone before. He thinks Tanner really likes you."

I was positive my mouth dropped open. "Please, don't be ridiculous! That's insane."

Ugh. I spat my words out way too fast because Kaylee looked at me and slightly frowned. "Why is that insane?"

"He's a player, and from what I've heard, he likes to fuck them and leave them."

Kaylee didn't look back at me when she replied in an almost angry tone, "No, that would be Dirk who fucks them and leaves them. The rumors about Tanner are fabricated by girls who want to brag they've slept with him, or by those who wished they had."

"How do you know it's not true?" I asked bitterly.

This time she did look at me, and a quick smile flashed across her face. "Dear sweet cousin, be careful there, or I may just think I've hit a nerve."

I sighed. "You haven't hit anything."

"You don't like him, then?"

"Yes. No. I mean, I don't...I don't know what I feel toward Tanner, Kaylee."

"Okay. Would it be so bad if you did like him?"

"Yes!" I practically shouted. "I can't open myself up to someone like him. I just can't. And I don't want to."

Silence filled the air between us when she didn't respond. Outside, the fields flew past, covered in snow. Kaylee cleared her throat before she finally spoke. "Are you only interested in a quick fling with him, because I'm not so sure he's on the same page, Timberlynn. I don't want to see either one of you hurt."

Frustration bubbled up inside of me and I turned to look at her. She had her eyes on the road in front of us, both hands on the steering wheel. "How exactly do you know what page he's on, Kaylee? Has he told you he has feelings for me?"

"No."

"Has he told his brothers?"

She shook her head and softly replied, "Not that I know of."

"Then can we stop this conversation?"

"No."

My eyes widened in shock. "What do you mean, no?"

"I mean, no, Timberlynn. Listen, I get the hurt and anger you have for your father and what that can do to you. Believe me, if anyone gets that, I do. But I've watched you put up a wall for fear of getting hurt again. Tanner isn't going to hurt you."

My body nearly shook with anger. "And you know this because you have a crystal ball that you can see the future with?"

She gave me a halfhearted chuckle. "No, I don't, smartass. I'm simply saying that both Ty and Brock have noticed how he looks at you. How when you walk into the room he lights up. And did you not notice how insanely jealous he was just now when Dirk flirted with you?"

I rolled my eyes.

"Did something happen between the two of you last night? Stella swears she might have interrupted something between y'all."

My cheeks heated, and I wanted to crawl under a rock. "Oh, perfect! Just freaking perfect. Oh my God. She thinks we were..."

"No!" Kaylee said, laughing again. "No, she simply sees the attraction as well and said Tanner came barreling downstairs from your room and declared he was going out. He didn't come home last night, so she put two and two together. She figured y'all might have had an argument about something."

I shrugged nonchalantly. "We were wrapping presents, that's all. He mentioned something about his partner maybe not wanting to rope anymore, and I think that turned his mood sour."

Ugh, I hated lying to Kaylee of all people. My stomach rolled as I fought the urge to be sick.

Kaylee gave me a quick look. "What? Chance doesn't want to rope anymore?"

"Maybe not, I don't think he's sure. Tanner seems to be a bit unsure of his future as well. His mood...it, um...it changed suddenly."

"Oh man, no wonder they came home early. I wonder if he's talked to his brothers about it yet."

"Let Tanner bring it up if he hasn't already."

"Of course, yeah, I won't say anything."

"Good, then can we move on from this nonsense of Tanner liking me? I'm simply a distraction that he needs right now."

Kaylee huffed, but it was so low I barely heard it. I knew I was being a bitch, and I knew I needed to talk to Tanner about last night. It was wrong what I did to him. The things I said to him. The hurt that crossed his face gutted me. Especially after the moment we shared together.

I turned and looked out at the countryside and decided I'd deal with it all later. There wasn't anything I could do about it now, so I focused on the snow-covered pastures and mountains that instantly made me smile. "It's so beautiful here."

"Just you wait, I've got something that's going to blow your mind."

I figured she was taking me somewhere special, in hopes I would fall in love and decide to make Hamilton my home. It wasn't hard to fall in love with the area. The open land, the beautiful, sweeping blue skies that seemed to go on forever. All of it screamed this was the place I needed to be.

"We're going toward the mountains," I said.

"Yep, and this is the road I needed."

She turned off a side road that had been cleared by a plow, so it must be a heavily used road.

"It's four miles down this side road."

"Can you finally tell me what exactly is down the road?"

She giggled. "You'll see! And the best part is that it isn't very far from the Shaw Ranch."

I couldn't help but giggle as well, a sudden sense of excitement building up inside of me and threatening to burst free. I had no idea what or why I was excited, but something told me everything in my life was about to change.

Chapter Thirteen

Tanner

"Tanner, you might want to slow down there before you wear yourself out."

I dug the hooks into the bale of hay and tossed it onto the back of the trailer as I ignored Brock.

"Or don't," he mumbled.

"I'm fine," I snapped.

Brock walked over and stood between me and the trailer. "I didn't ask if you were fine. You're acting like those bales of hay are someone you want to throttle."

I sighed, wiped the sweat from my brow, and then shot my brother a dirty look.

"You want to talk about it?" he asked as he took a seat on the back of the trailer.

"No," I bit back.

With a raised brow, he pulled his work gloves off and set them down. "The cattle can wait a few extra minutes for lunch. Talk to me, Tanner. Something has been on your mind since you got home from the road, and earlier you looked like you wanted to knock Dirk into the next county when he was talking to Timberlynn."

I let out a frustrated sigh. "I don't really know what's going on...with anything."

"Okay, let's start small. Why did you and Chance really come home early after y'all nearly broke the world record in Colorado? I know you guys, and you both would have run off to the next rodeo itching to try for that record again. Instead, you're here."

I dropped the hay hooks and sat on a bale. "I'm pretty sure Chance wants to give up roping."

He nodded and gave me a thoughtful look. "Okay, well, I'm sure that sucks since you've been together for so long, but you can pick up a new partner...you've done it before."

My eyes met his, and I didn't say anything.

"Oh, I see. You're not sure you want to go back on the road yourself."

I pointed to him. "Bingo. I love ropin', I do, but something seems missing from my life, Brock. I feel... empty." I shook my head and laughed. "I fucking blame you and Ty for this bullshit. Getting married, popping out kids."

"You're still young, Tanner. You've got plenty of time to settle down and have kids."

"I know that. And if you had asked me a year ago, I would have told you I'd be roping cattle until I couldn't ride anymore. Something has made that change, and I have no fucking clue what it is."

"What or who?"

I looked away. "I love being on the ranch, and now with you here, it's the three of us. I like being home. I like seeing Mom and Dad happy. I liked those months I was here when my ankle was broken. I felt content."

"There's nothing wrong with wanting to be home, Tanner. Why do you think I retired from bull riding?"

"You met Lincoln."

He smiled and nodded. "I did meet Lincoln, and she changed the way I looked at everything. Then when we found out she was pregnant I didn't need to search for the answers anymore. I knew what I had to do, and I was okay with it."

"Lincoln wanted you, though."

Recognition hit his face. "Now we're getting to the someone part. Timberlynn?"

I blew out a breath. "I don't know what it is about her, Brock. From the moment I met her at Ty and Kaylee's wedding, she's been on my mind constantly. I've been thinking about her for months. Hell, she's in my dreams. I've never been attracted to a woman like this, and I'm not the least bit scared. Well, that's not true, I'm scared she doesn't feel the same way."

He laughed and shook his head. "Tanner, you don't see the way she lights up when you walk into a room. You light up just as much, by the way. We've all noticed it. What makes you think she doesn't feel the same way?"

I looked directly into his eyes. "She told me so."

That caused him to sit up straighter and raise his brows. "What did she say?"

I rubbed my hands over my thighs; the idea of repeating what Timberlynn said to me made me queasy. Especially after the moment we had shared on her bed. Her whispered moans, the way she arched and held me so tight when she came. The way she said yes to me making love to her...her eyes even said it too.

What in the hell had changed? I'd thought about it nearly all damn night. "Oh, let's see, she said I was the last man she'd ever want to have a relationship with."

Brock looked stunned. He opened his mouth only to close it, then open it again. When words failed him, I decided to tell him what had happened between us last night.

"We had a...moment in her room last night. A pretty intimate moment."

Brock narrowed his eyes at me.

"We didn't sleep together, but if Mom hadn't knocked on the door, I don't know where it would have gone."

"Talk about a cock block," Brock said with a chuckle.

I laughed. "Yeah. I think the idea of almost being caught by Mom did something to Timberlynn. She instantly changed. Acted like she was repulsed by my touch and told me she only allowed me to do it because she'd had a few drinks. She said it was a *moment of insanity and irrational thought.*"

Brock grimaced. "Ouch."

"Yeah. She accused me of only wanting to screw her and that was it. She made it pretty clear she wasn't interested in any sort of relationship with me."

"Okay, then why did she let you...do whatever it is you did?"

"Maybe it was a moment of weakness, I don't know. Maybe it was the wine we drank. She's flirted back with me since I met her, even let me hold her hand yesterday. I thought she wanted me as much as I wanted her. I'm honestly trying to figure it all out myself. What caused the sudden change?"

Brock nodded.

"She keeps herself pretty guarded. Her mother died when she was little, and she mentioned something about never falling in love again. Maybe that has something to do with it." I sighed and took off my hat, running my fingers through my hair. "She's fucking confusing me, Brock. What am I doing wrong? I'm being as open as I know how to be."

"Have you thought about talking to Kaylee?"

I rubbed the back of my neck and shook my head. "I don't want to do that. I'd feel like I was betraying Timberlynn."

The corner of his mouth twitched with a smile he held back.

"What?" I asked.

"Nothing. It's a little strange seeing you...have feelings for someone. Regardless of what you think the feelings are, you care about her, Tanner. If I can offer you one bit of advice, bro..."

I nodded. "Please do."

"Don't give up on her. Be patient, don't push, let her know you're there for her and that you think she's worth the wait."

"She told me..."

Brock cut me off. "She lied."

I looked down at the ground and kicked at some loose hay.

"Tanner, she likes you. Trust me. Now, as far as the roping goes, meet me in the main barn at two today."

"Why?"

He grinned mischievously. "We're gonna have us a bit of fun."

I couldn't help but smile back. "I like the sound of that."

Brock stood, and I followed his lead. He hit me on the side of the arm and said, "It really is good having you back home, little brother."

"It's good to be home."

"Let's get this finished up, shall we?"

I nodded and got back to work. The silence between me and Brock gave me time to think about what had, or hadn't, happened between me and Timberlynn last night—and I wasn't sure that was a good thing.

◆ ◆ ◆

Ty and I walked into the barn a few minutes after two. My father and Brock were leading four saddled-up horses out of the barn.

"Do you have any idea how damn stubborn your horse is, Tanner? She only wants to be turned out; it's like she knows she's on vacation," my father said as he handed me the reins to Trigger.

"Hey there, sweetheart. Are you enjoying the countryside?" I asked as I ran my hand down her neck.

Trigger bobbed her head and nickered.

"I swear she knows what you're saying to her, too," Dad stated. "And I forgot she doesn't like anyone else on her."

Unable to help myself, I laughed. "Of course, she knows what I'm saying. She isn't stupid."

"You callin' my horse stupid?" Brock asked as he led his horse out and jumped up on him.

"You said it, not me."

Brock rolled his eyes.

"Who's your heeler?" Dad asked me.

I looked between both Ty and Brock.

"I pick Dad."

Both of them looked surprised as they turned to look at our father, who sat atop his horse with a wide grin. He nudged his horse toward the corral and said, "At least I raised one of ya right."

The rest of the afternoon was spent with Ty and Brock taking turns with our father as we roped some steer. It felt good, but it didn't make me miss competing. Not one bit. One look at Brock before I nodded for Ty to let the steer go, and I knew exactly what this afternoon had been about. I could still have the best of both worlds if I wanted. Sure, there wasn't a crowd yelling out, or money to be won, but I didn't need any of that. Seeing how happy my father was helped me realize that money and crowds would never fulfill me like this afternoon had. Family. That's what this was all about. I smiled at Brock and he returned it with an even bigger shit-eating grin of his own.

"You can have it all if that's what you want, little brother," Brock said as he rode up to me after we had roped a steer in four seconds.

"I think I know what I need to do."

Brock smiled. "I think you've known it for a while now. In your heart."

"Can I give it a try?"

Timberlynn's voice took me by surprise, and apparently it did Brock as well. We both turned to see our mom, Kaylee, and Lincoln, all standing at the fence with Timberlynn seated up on Rosie.

"Which one do you want to do? Header or heeler?" I called out.

The way she smiled made me want to groan. Why was she sending me such mixed signals? It was driving me mad. I wanted to be pissed—but I couldn't be, not when she smiled at me like that. There had to be a reason she was pushing me away, and why she had acted like that last night. Simply seeing her, though, and I didn't give a shit about what had happened. She was so goddamn beautiful, she stole my breath. I'd take Brock's advice and be patient.

"Heeler, of course."

Brock laughed. "By all means, Timberlynn, have at it."

Brock and Timberlynn traded places, and I couldn't wipe the smile off my face even if I had wanted to. "You think Rosie is up for this?" I asked.

Timberlynn reached down and gave the mare a light rub along her neck, then leaned down and said something to her. I shook my head and started to tell her how it worked.

"I'll nod, Ty will let the steer go. Once I rope his head, you try for the feet. Have you ever...roped anything?"

All she did was wink at me. "Let's stop talking and do some roping."

I fell in love with her in that moment.

"This is gonna be interesting," Ty said with a hearty laugh. My father also smiled, but when I met his gaze, he simply gave me a knowing nod.

"Ready?" I asked Timberlynn.

"Ready!" she called back. The excitement in her voice made me chuckle. Ty was right...it was going to be interesting, indeed.

I nodded, the steer took off, and I had his head roped in seconds. I watched as Timberlynn roped his back legs, turned Rosie, and faced me and Trigger. She had a huge damn smile on her face at her own success.

"Four-point-five seconds. Shit, son, she did better than Ty!" my father called out.

"You better marry that girl, Tanner!" one of the ranch hands yelled as Timberlynn looked at me, beaming.

"Give it slack, Timberlynn!" Ty called, and when she did, I did the same, letting the steer get free.

I rode over to her and shook my head. "Someone has been keeping secrets."

With a casual shrug, she replied, "Don't we all have hidden secrets and talents, Mr. Shaw?"

That made my body react. "You didn't tell me you knew how to rope, Timber. I think I just fell in love with you, and apparently we now need to wed."

She laughed, then stared at me for a moment. I watched her bite into her lip as she looked up at me through those beautiful eyelashes of hers. "I do believe you've said that once already, about falling in love, at least."

I nodded. "I believe I did."

With a quick glance around, she focused back on me. "I've never done that before in my life. But I did practice at the stables I learned to ride in. They had a mechanical bull that they would let loose, and we would all take turns trying to rope its horns. I got pretty good at it."

"I'm possibly looking for a new roping partner. Are you interested in the gig?"

"How much does it pay?" she teased.

My heart felt as if it slammed against my chest. "I'm sure we could negotiate something that would be mutually beneficial to us both."

She blushed and looked around the corral as if only now remembering we were not alone. She chewed nervously on her lip and moved Rosie up next to Trigger. Both mares stared at each other in contempt, but neither moved. In a lower voice, Timberlynn said, "Tanner, I want you to know that I didn't mean what I said last night. About what happened between us being a mistake."

"Good, because I didn't think it was a mistake. It was amazing, if you ask me."

She pulled in her bottom lip but didn't say anything.

"What about that other thing you said?"

She looked confused.

"About never wanting any sort of relationship with me."

Before she could answer, my father rode up.

"Timberlynn, I'm always in need of some good ranch hands. When can you start?"

She laughed once again and shook her head. "As lovely as that sounds, Mr. Shaw, I'm going to have to pass."

"No formal names, young lady, it's Ty Senior."

Timberlynn nodded. "Well, as lovely as that sounds, Ty Senior, I'm afraid I have some plans of my own I need to tend to."

My father raised his brows. "A woman who knows how to ride, knows how to rope, *and* has a mind of her own. You will certainly make some lucky cowboy a very happy man someday."

Timberlynn blushed again and stole a quick peek in my direction.

"Don't you think, Tanner?" my father asked.

Without taking my eyes off of Timberlynn, I gave her a smile that I hoped like hell screamed how much I wanted her. "I do believe you're right, Dad. A lucky man, indeed."

Blayze came running out and up to Timberlynn. "Miss Timberlynn, I was wondering if I might be able to sit next to you at dinner tonight."

I stared down at my nephew in utter disbelief. "Dude, you're putting the moves on my girl?"

Timberlynn's gaze shot back over to me, and I ignored the surprised look on her face.

Blayze nodded and looked thoughtful for a moment. "Uncle Tanner, I called dibs on dinner, you got a date with her the other day. Miss Timberlynn, dinner tonight?"

Timberlynn was clearly trying not to laugh and doing a pretty good job of holding it in.

"Damn, son, what are you doing?" Brock said as he walked over and picked up Blayze, making him laugh as he tossed him over his shoulder. "You just got home from school, and you're already putting the moves on someone? And what did we talk about with the whole calling of dibs?"

"Dad!" Blayze protested.

"She's too old for you."

"Aw, Dad, you're embarrassin' me in front of Miss Timberlynn!"

Timberlynn covered her mouth with her hand to hold back her laughter—at least until Brock took Blayze far enough away that he wouldn't hear it.

"What is it with you Shaw men?" she asked, watching my brother and nephew walk away.

I shrugged. "I guess once we know when we want something—or someone—we fight for it."

Timberlynn dropped her hand to her side and gave me a serious look. It was her eyes, though, that threw me. They were filled with sadness. "What if that something or someone isn't...worth it?"

She nearly had me pulling her onto my horse, taking her away from everyone, and demanding why in the hell she felt like she wasn't worth it.

"You are worth it, Timber."

With a noncommittal shrug, she forced a smile. Before I could say anything else, my mother called out. "Enough playtime! It's time to bake. Let's go!"

"This year my sugar cookies will be better than yours, Tanner!" Ty called out as he helped a few of the ranch hands herd up the steers to put back out in the pasture.

Timberlynn's mouth dropped open in surprise. "Wait, y'all are going to be baking with us girls?"

I feigned a look of shock as I moved my horse back toward the barn. "Are you trying to say baking isn't something men can do? Did I have that reaction to you when you said you wanted to rope? Not only women can be in the kitchen, ya know."

Another beautiful laugh slipped free from her soft pink lips. Lips that I longed to kiss again. "I would never say that."

"Come on, help me with the horses, and then we'll go show Ty and Kaylee how to decorate the shit out of some sugar cookies."

She rode Rosie next to me, and as we slipped off the horses and started to take the saddles off, Timberlynn ducked her head under Trigger's neck and looked at me with a worried expression.

"What's wrong?"

"I should probably disclose to you that I've never made sugar cookies, let alone decorated them."

"What?"

She nodded. "You might want to pick a different partner."

I slipped under Trigger and stood in front of her. I placed my finger on her chin and tilted that beautiful face up so I could look directly into her eyes.

"You are the only partner I want."

"What if I'm not good enough at the decorating part?"

I slowly shook my head as I leaned down and kissed her gently on the lips. "Trust me, I know a good thing when I see it, darlin'."

Her breath caught for a moment as our eyes locked.

I was going to listen to Brock's advice. I'd be patient, because it was obvious there was something behind the sadness in her eyes. A reason for those walls. But I wasn't going to give up. I was going to fight for this woman, because I knew deep in my heart, I was truly starting to fall in love with her.

Chapter Fourteen

TIMBERLYNN

After Tanner and I took care of our horses, blanketed them, and turned them out, we headed toward the house. I wasn't surprised when he took my hand in his, and I fought the urge to pull it away, while at the same time holding on as tightly as I could.

I was confused. Lord, I was so confused. I wasn't sure I could open my heart, even though I desperately wanted to. I needed things to go slow, and the way things were going between the two of us, slow didn't seem to be in the cards.

It had taken everything out of me not to burst out with the news about the property Kaylee had showed me earlier. It had been perfect, and the moment I laid eyes on the darling, completely restored farmhouse, I knew it was the place I belonged. It was two-hundred acres of land tucked up against the Bitterroot Mountains, and the barn was perfect for all my needs. There was a large indoor arena, as well as one outside. Even in the winter months I could keep training horses.

Before we walked into the house, I pulled Tanner to a stop. "Tanner, I need to tell you something."

He faced me, his expression serious. "Okay. Out here or would you rather go inside?"

I shook my head, still not exactly sure what I was going to say. I glanced down as my hands twisted together nervously. Was it about the property? My decision to move to Montana? The truth about my trust issues with men? How utterly terrified I was of letting anyone in?

I'd only given my heart fully to two people. And they had ended up leaving me in some form or fashion. For years I struggled with why my mother had been taken from me when I was little. With my father's refusal to ever talk about her, it was like I lost her over and over again. Then my father's lack of interest in me seemed to be the ultimate betrayal. I always came back to the same conclusion: I wasn't good enough to have a mother in my life. I hadn't been good enough to help my father heal from my mother's death.

When I looked back up at Tanner, his brows were pulled down slightly, and those pale blue eyes stared directly into mine. "We can go into my father's office—it's too cold to stand out here and talk."

"That sounds good," I agreed as I followed him through the back door and into the large mud room. After I took off my coat and gloves, Tanner took them from me and hung them up. He truly was such a gentleman. I'd never had a man treat me like I was the only thing they thought about in the moment. I liked how that made me feel, and I felt myself smile.

"Follow me," he said with a grin that made my heartbeat race faster.

As we walked into the kitchen, I noticed everyone was already here. Lincoln glanced over and noticed us first. She had Morgan in her arms and gave me a wink when I met her gaze. How in the world was she going to bake while holding a baby? Tanner walked over to his dad. "Can we use your office for a second, Dad?"

Ty Senior looked up from the dough he was already mixing. "Of course."

Tanner gave him a quick nod of thanks, and then started walking out of the kitchen. I envied the relationship this family had with one another. How many times had I longed for a family like this? Too many to even count anymore.

Hardly anyone even noticed we had left. You could feel the excitement in the room, but even that couldn't lift my suddenly darkened mood. After being so happy with the find earlier, I was quickly falling into a depression, and I had no idea why.

Damn it all to hell! Why did I have to be so afraid to open up my heart?

We walked through the living room and to an area of the house I hadn't been in yet. Tanner opened a door at the very end of the long hallway and stepped inside. I scanned the room when I walked in. It screamed Ty Senior.

Pictures and paintings of cattle, horses, and what looked like places on the ranch were placed on every single wall. On one was a collection of paintings and drawings that looked to be from all the boys, Blayze included. I walked up to them and grinned as I read the names.

Brock Shaw, age nine. Beck S, age six. TJ, age eleven. Then I came to a painting of a horse. It was done amazingly well, even though you could tell small hands painted it. My heart tumbled as I read the name. Tanner Michael Shaw. Twelve.

I slowly shook my head. "You painted this at twelve years of age?"

The painting was of a buckskin running in an open green pasture. It was dotted with what looked like flowers. I recognized the view. It was looking down from the ridge he had taken me up to on my second day here. The sky in the back was a beautiful mixture of pinks, oranges, and yellows as the sun sank low on the horizon.

Tanner walked up and stood next to me. "I did. I was bored out of my mind one spring day, and my mother challenged me to go paint something on the ranch. It was when I discovered the ridge. I mean, I'd been up there before plenty of times, but that was the day I saw its true beauty. I started to paint it, and then waited for the sun to start setting so I could see what the sky looked like. I quickly painted what I saw, and then got my butt home. I don't even want to tell you the trouble I got into with my mama for getting back to the barn near dark."

I chuckled as I glanced from the picture to him. He was staring at it with a smile on his face.

With a spin around the office, I took the rest of it in. A large leather sofa sat at one end of the room. A giant picture window was behind it, and I gasped as I saw the view. A rolling pasture made way to a mountain range that was fairly close to the house. The way the sun reflected off the snow made it sparkle like a million diamonds. It was truly stunning. On the other side of the room was a large fireplace with two oversize leather chairs on either side. I imagined the boys playing in this room when they were younger.

"My goodness. Every single room in this house I swear has a different view."

Tanner chuckled. "You should see the view from my bedroom."

I turned and slightly raised a brow. "I'm sure it's equally impressive."

He laughed. "I like to think so."

I shook my head, and the sinking feeling of sadness suddenly came back in a whoosh. I needed to be honest with him before I let things grow between us, because I knew I was sending him mixed signals. This was the moment I needed to decide what to do about my attraction to Tanner. Give in to it or tell him we had to only be friends. I knew what I wanted, and I prayed he would be patient with me.

My phone buzzed in my pocket with an incoming text, and my heartbeat picked up slightly. I had called Cory to tell him I had decided on a piece of property to buy. Even though I had come into my trust fund, I was still relying on Cory as my financial advisor. After all, I was only twenty-four, and I now had a rather impressive bank account. So, I thought maybe it was him reaching back out to me.

I pulled the phone out and saw it was from Mary, an old high school friend and the woman who had cheated with a boyfriend of mine I had been going out with at the time. I had felt so betrayed by her, especially since she had been my best friend and the one person whom I had always counted on being there. And Jase, the guy I had finally allowed myself to open up to, had turned out to be a major dick. I knew I should have let it go. That nothing she could possibly say was anything that I wanted to hear. I hadn't talked to her since we graduated high school. Then, I caught a glimpse of the text. "I hope you've been able to forgive..."

Curious, I opened her text to see there was an attachment to it. I read her full text.

Mary J: "I hope you've been able to forgive me and that you will be able to join us."

When I opened the attachment, my stomach jerked and a wave of nausea hit me as I read the save the date announcement.

Mr. and Mrs. Jerkins have the honor of announcing the engagement of their daughter, Mary Kathleen Jerkins, to Mr. Jase Logan. Save the date of June 24th, everyone! We are having a wedding!

I stared at the beautiful scripted announcement in teal and white.

Mary and Jase were getting married. Why in the world was I acting like I had been hurt by the two of them all over again? I honestly could not have cared less about Jase Logan or Mary. So why was this wedding announcement throwing me into an emotional tailspin?

"Timber? What's wrong?"

"N-nothing," I said, my voice unsteady. I deleted the message and tossed my phone to the side. I needed to get myself back in check, but that damn voice nagging in my head reminded me that I hadn't been good enough for

Jase. That he had slept with my best friend. That Mary had betrayed our friendship.

"Hey, what's going on? What was that text about?" Tanner dropped down in front of me and lifted my face until our eyes met. "Talk to me, Timber."

I slowly shook my head as tears filled my eyes. "I don't think I can do this. I thought I could, and I don't mean to keep leading you on. It's just..."

"Lead me on?" he asked.

I attempted to keep my hands still in my lap instead of rubbing them together or against my jeans. It was something I did when I was nervous or upset. It started shortly after my mother died, and I had tried like hell to break the habit. "I'm not going to lie and say I'm not attracted to you, because I am. Very much so, Tanner."

My words made a brilliant smile appear on his face and my insides melted.

"Why do I feel like there's a very big but coming?" he asked.

"Because there is. I'm not sure I'm ready for this. I want to be, I thought I was. But I'm not sure I can trust you."

His smile faded. "And why can't you trust me?"

I laughed. "One, I don't want a boyfriend who would be gone all the time, and I wouldn't be the type of girlfriend who'd be able to join you out on the road. Not that I wouldn't like it, I'm sure it would be fun...at first... but I have my own set of dreams that I'm finally able to follow. I can't risk anyone taking that away from me."

Tanner frowned. "You think I wouldn't allow you to follow your own dreams?"

I gave him a half shrug, even though I knew he would.

His eyes flashed with anger. "I would never do that, Timberlynn."

I hated that he didn't use the nickname he had been calling me.

"I would never deny you your dreams. No one ever denied me any of mine."

With a hard swallow, I looked away from him for a moment before I gained the strength to let at least one wall down. I had to give him something. "After my mother died, my father slowly became distant with me. So much so that he hired a nanny, Rachel, who pretty much became the mother and father figures in my life. She worked for my father up until I entered my senior year of high school."

Tanner's expression softened some.

"I remember so many times I begged my father to come to a school play or a dressage competition I was in. He would promise to be there but never showed up."

Tanner took my hands in his. "I'm so sorry. Did he ever tell you why?"

My eyes stung with the threat of tears. "No. I haven't spoken to him in a while. He doesn't even know I'm here in Montana. For all he knows, I'm still in Atlanta working the nursing job he guilted me into taking." I let out an unfeeling laugh. "He didn't even wish me a happy birthday, Tanner."

I lifted my eyes to meet his. "Please don't look at me like that," I said. "I can't stand pity. I'm fine, for the most part. He always provided me with everything I could ever want or need. He spoiled me. I saw a horse I liked, he would buy it. I wanted a Jeep for my sixteenth birthday, he bought it for me. He was there for me when it came to money, just not when it came to emotions."

Tanner's face tightened and his body was tense as he watched me closely. "That had to be hard for you. I know how important my parents were in my life growing up, and you missed out on both."

I stared at him in disbelief. No one had ever acknowledged the missing pieces of my life. Kaylee had, of course, but never someone from the outside looking in.

I looked down and drew in a deep breath, slowly letting it out. "One of my good friends from high school, her name was Mary, she had always been there for me from the time we met in eighth grade and was more like a sister than a friend. I caught her and my boyfriend Jase one night. They were having sex in her bedroom while her folks were out of town. They both thought I was at a horse show that day."

I let out a gruff laugh. "They got the dates mixed up. Let's say I found them in bed together, having rather... eventful sex."

"I'm sorry, Timber," Tanner said as he ran his hand through his hair. He looked both angry and upset.

I shrugged and pulled in another deep breath. "When I walked into the room, I froze. I didn't know what to do. They didn't see me at first, but then Jase did. He pushed Mary off of him and started to beg me to let him explain."

"Tell me you didn't."

"Oh, I couldn't move." I scoffed. "He took that as me wanting to hear why he was in bed fucking my friend. I don't even know what he said, to be honest with you. I was completely zoned out. When I finally had the wits about me to leave, I turned and walked out. Mary and Jase called for a few days, but I ignored their calls. Ignored them both in school. Eventually they both stopped trying, and I was once again left alone."

"I'm so sorry that happened to you. You didn't deserve to be betrayed by the two of them like that."

I sighed. "I'm not looking for you to feel sorry for me, Tanner. It didn't take me long to realize they weren't worth it, but it still rocked me to the core. I've had a hard time trusting anyone since."

"And the text just now?" he asked as he glanced down to my phone on the sofa. "You looked like you were gonna be sick."

"I was caught off guard, that's all. It brought back those feelings of inadequacies I fought to push away."

"What did it say?" he asked.

I sat up straighter. "It was from Mary. She said she hoped I had forgiven her and Jase. She sent a save the date for their wedding and said she hoped I would make it."

Tanner seemed shocked. "She hasn't talked to you since high school, and she invited you to her wedding?"

I shrugged. "Guess she wants another present."

Silence filled the room, and I glanced at him. He looked confused.

"Are you upset he's marrying her?"

"No!" I clenched my hands together. "God, Tanner, not at all. I don't have feelings for him anymore. I was surprised. And it reminded me of all the stupid issues I have."

He sat back, watching me carefully. "So, you got a notice that your ex, who treated you like shit, is getting married, and that made you decide you can't trust me? You're basically putting me in the same category as that douchebag."

I closed my eyes and shook my head. "That's not it."

A flash of anger crossed his face. "That is it, Timberlynn. You just told me you can't trust me. Have I given you any reason why?"

I stood and let out a long, frustrated breath. "Tanner, as of thirty minutes ago, I was ready to give this a try. You and me. But I'm not sure I can take my heart being hurt again by someone else."

"I wouldn't hurt you, so why won't you even give me a chance?"

My chin wobbled, and I turned away from him. I knew with all my heart that Tanner wouldn't hurt me. It was me who would end up hurting him. There was something that made me unworthy of love, and Tanner would end up seeing it sooner or later. "You deserve someone better than me. Someone not...broken."

"For fuck's sake, you're not broken, Timberlynn."

Tears threatened to spill free as I turned to face him. My voice was barely a whisper. "I'm not sure if I gave you my body that I'd be able to survive walking away from you after that. I don't want to ruin our friendship for a fuck."

He jumped like I had slapped him. "Back to this again? A fuck? Is that what it would be, Timberlynn? Just a quick fuck, and then you think I'd walk away from you? Do you honestly think that's all I want from you?"

"I heard from someone today in town you danced with nearly every girl in the Blue Moose last night before you left. You didn't come home, so who did you sleep with last night when you couldn't sleep with me?"

His mouth opened, and he looked taken aback. "What?"

I instantly regretted the words. But something inside me was angry. Maybe it had to do with Mary and Jase, and I was taking it out on Tanner. I couldn't stop the words coming from my mouth. "You denying what happened last night will only make me think it's the truth."

He gave me a sarcastic smile and then rubbed the back of his neck in frustration. "You think because you pushed me away last night I went and found some random girl to hook-up with?"

"I don't know what you did last night," I stated.

He shot daggers at me as he answered. "I went to the Blue Moose. Danced with some old friends from high school, and a cousin of mine I hadn't seen in a while. Yes, I drank some, and yes, I saw Lindsey there. But nothing happened between us. Nothing. I left with Chance and stayed at his place last night. We stayed up half the night in the loft of his barn, drinking beer and talking about our future as roping partners. He's done with it and wants to stop roping."

My eyes widened in surprise, and even though I was angry, my heart ached for him. "I'm sorry to hear that about you and Chance."

He sighed in frustration. "Yeah, me too. But I wasn't looking to fuck anything or anyone to get you out of my head. I like you. A lot. We're only just starting to get to know each other, so why are you jumping to all of these conclusions? Why can't you believe I'm not simply trying to get into your pants? You're really starting to give me whiplash here."

I sucked in a breath at his words. I knew what he said was true, but a part of me hated that he had thrown it in my face. "Isn't that what most men like you do, Tanner? Simply try to get into a woman's pants?"

Tanner stood before me with a disbelieving expression on his face. I had basically said he was a player. A guy who simply slept with women for sex. That he was only out to sleep with me, and I knew by the way he looked at me that it wasn't true. I had let my anger at Jase and Mary take hold of me once more. And the worst part was, I had taken it all out on Tanner. I had said hurtful things to him, and I immediately wanted to take them back.

"Wow. Okay, so if that's your opinion of me, I guess I'm wasting my time trying to tell you otherwise."

I shook my head. "I..."

He cut me off and kept talking. "I do want to be with you, and yes, if my mother hadn't knocked on your door, we might have made love. But I guess all you can see is that I simply wanted to fuck you."

I swallowed hard at his words. Then he let out a laugh, but it was devoid of any humor. "Fine, is what you want to hear from me that I want to fuck you? Is this what you think I want? Hell, strip down and I'll take you right here in my father's office. That's what *guys like me* do, right? No consideration for anything or anyone. Is that what you want to hear? Because if you honestly think I'd fuck you in my father's office for the sake of having sex with you, then you really haven't gotten to know me at all."

My body trembled as I fought to keep a neutral expression on my face.

The look of defeat on his face nearly brought me to my knees.

"Tanner...I..."

My words drifted off as I saw his eyes glaze over, and I fought to keep from walking forward and wrapping my arms around him. I desperately wanted him to hold me while I took back every single word. So I did just that. I stared to walk toward him, but he put his hand up to stop me.

He shook his head and let out a long, slow breath. "We might not have known each other for very long, but I thought you knew me, Timber. Yes, I do want you. But I want more than a casual fuck. I wanted to get to know you. Spend time with you. Learn everything I could about you. What made you happy, what made you laugh, because I fucking love to hear you laugh. I wanted to make love to you as much as possible. Kiss you all over your face and body until you fell asleep next to me, then wake up and make love to you all over again. I wanted to give you something I've never given to anyone before...my heart."

I nearly cried at how sad and defeated his voice sounded. My hand came up to my mouth to keep from letting out a sob when I realized he was talking in the past tense. Oh God, what had I done?

The tears slipped free before I could stop them, and when Tanner noticed them, he looked as if he might drop to his knees. He took a few steps toward me and then stopped. "Do you really think I only thought of you that way?" he whispered.

I swallowed hard and shook my head. "I don't think so."

"You don't think so?" he asked, an edge of anger in his voice.

"No, I don't know, Tanner. Everyone has always thought of me as dispensable—it's the only thing I've ever known."

He slowly shook his head and backed toward the door. "Well, in case you haven't noticed, I'm not everyone. I don't think of you that way, and I never will. I'm going to walk away, Timberlynn, because I'm not sure what in the hell is going on, but if I don't leave, I may regret something I say."

And then he turned and walked to the door. Before he opened it, he looked back at me. "There is one thing I will say to you, though."

I held my breath as he stared at me. "I don't think my own heart can take this...game...we're playing."

A sob slipped free. "I'm not playing a game. This was never a game to me."

"Okay, then, when you figure out what you want, let me know. I'll be waiting."

"Tanner, I..."

The words died on my lips. I had no idea how to explain how I was feeling. What a selfish bitch I'd been. Earlier I was flirting with him in front of his entire family, then I lashed out and accused him of not being trustworthy.

"I didn't mean what I said. I'm just...I'm so confused, and you make me want things and feel things I've never felt before and I'm scared."

"You don't think I'm scared? Do you think giving your heart to a person is easy? I've never felt like this before in my life, Timberlynn. I'm willing to trust you with my heart...can you say the same about me?"

Before I had a chance to answer him, Dirk opened the office door. "Shit, sorry, I didn't know anyone was in here."

Tanner cleared his throat as I quickly wiped my tears away.

"Is everything okay?" Dirk asked, his eyes bouncing from Tanner to me.

Tanner didn't say a word, he simply walked past Dirk and out the door. And in that moment, I knew what a breaking heart truly felt like.

"If that little prick said anything to hurt you, I'll kill him."

A laugh mingled with a sob as I shook my head. "No, he didn't. But I'm pretty sure I just did one hell of a job pushing him away. Or, at the very least, confusing the hell out of him."

"Is that what you wanted to do?" Dirk asked as he leaned against the doorjamb.

With a shake of my head, I closed my eyes and whispered, "No."

"It's not hard to notice the connection between the two of you," Dirk stated.

I opened my eyes, wiped my damp cheeks, and took in a deep breath. No more crying for me. I was done and I needed to figure out how in the world I was going to fix this mess I had gotten myself into.

"Timberlynn." Dirk's voice was so kind and soft. "You don't have to hide your scars, you know. Open up to him, and I promise he'll help you heal them."

My jaw muscles ached as I fought to keep myself from crying once again. Everyone in my life who mattered only had kind words to say about Tanner. So why had I let the gossiping fools get into my head. "What if I've totally messed up..."

Dirk raised a brow, causing me to instantly stop speaking. He smiled. "Doll, let me tell you something about the Shaw men. When they fall, they fall hard and they fall fast. And trust me when I say that the one who just walked out of here has fallen so freaking hard for you, that I think he might have gotten the breath knocked out of him. You didn't mess anything up. He'll come back around."

"You don't know that, Dirk. You don't even know what happened."

He walked over to me, gave me a once-over, and then grinned. "What I do know is that your past is keeping you from living your future."

I lifted my chin and straightened my shoulders. "It is not. I'm moving on and I'm...I'm...."

"A future without someone to love is no future at all, Timberlynn. You and I both know that. Whatever happened can be fixed, at least I think it can. Tell me what happened."

My cheeks puffed up as I exhaled. "The short of it?"

"Yep."

"My father neglected me, my boyfriend cheated on me, my best friend at the time betrayed me, my father missed my birthday, I have some serious effed-up trust issues. I keep leading Tanner on, only to get spooked and then push him away. I told him I couldn't trust him, but that's not true. I found out tonight that my ex and the bestie are getting married. I got angry, and I took it out on

Tanner. Then I said some things that were hurtful, and I didn't mean it, and I'm pretty sure he's already sick of the whiplash I've put him through. Oh, and did I mention I had daddy issues?"

Dirk nodded. "Twice."

"Okay, then, there ya go." I tilted my head to look at him. "Did any of that make sense?"

"Weirdly enough, I think I'm up to speed. I'm going to ask you something and I want you to answer me honestly."

"Okay," I replied with a nod.

"Do you want to have a relationship with Tanner?"

"Yes, but I'm also scared."

"Fair enough. Do you want to fix this mess you've made?"

I nodded.

"Okay. Seems like you Holden women like to make big messes."

With a smile, I gave him a half shrug.

"Next big question. Do you trust me to help you?"

I chewed on my lower lip for a moment. "You're not going to try and make him jealous by acting like we're flirting or anything, are you?"

He pulled his head back and then motioned to his face. "Do I look like I want to have this face beaten to a pulp?"

There was no way I could stop the laugh that tumbled from my mouth. "No, you do not."

Dirk held out his arm and motioned for us to leave the office. "Let's go."

After another moment or two of getting my nerves settled, I nodded and took his arm. We left Ty Senior's office and headed down the hall.

"Do we have a plan?" I asked.

Dirk laughed. "*We* don't have a plan. *I* have a plan."

I closed my eyes and sighed. "Shit."

Chapter Fifteen

TANNER

"Where's Timberlynn?" my mother asked as she looked past me and into the living room.

"I'm not sure if she's in the mood to bake and decorate cookies," I stated.

"She should be! She seemed over the moon after I showed her a small little ranch out toward the mountains," Kaylee said as she focused on cutting out stockings with a cookie cutter.

"What?" I asked, my voice sounding angrier than I meant for it to. That caused Kaylee to glance up at me with a confused expression. She had probably figured that was why Timberlynn wanted to talk. To tell me this little bit of news.

"Is everything okay, Tanner?" Brock asked. He could clearly see I was still upset from my encounter with Timberlynn. I knew I had overreacted, but damnit all to hell if she hadn't frustrated the fuck out of me.

I pushed that thought away. Timberlynn wasn't just anyone. I needed to make things right. A part of me wanted to head back to my father's office, but then I realized how long I had been gone, and neither Timberlynn nor Dirk had come into the kitchen.

Brock's voice interrupted my thoughts. "Hey, Tanner, are you okay?"

I nodded. "Yeah, everything's fine."

Even I could hear the lie in my voice. I glanced back over to Kaylee. "You showed Timberlynn a piece of property?"

"Is that the old Covey property? I heard it was for sale," my father said.

Kaylee nodded, a confused expression on her face as she finally shifted her gaze from me and looked at my father. "Yes, that's who the real estate agent said owned it. It's two-hundred acres with the most adorable little ranch house. They've totally remodeled it. And the barn is amazing as well. Timberlynn can rescue a good number of horses if she wants."

"Such an amazing thing she wants to do," my mother said. "I was thrilled when she spoke to me about it this morning and asked if I would be willing to help her."

I nodded in agreement, but I was having a hard time keeping my own emotions in check. Had Timberlynn decided on staying here? Shit. This was so freaking messed up. She had trust issues, I got that. But I hadn't given her a single reason not to trust me.

"Look who I picked up along the way to all the cookie decorating fun."

Dirk's voice caused everyone to turn and look at him and Timberlynn, both standing at the entrance to the kitchen. I felt an instant rush of anger as I looked down to see Timberlynn's arm locked around Dirk's.

Fuck. I had acted like a total asshole, and Dirk walked right in after I left and saved her.

No. Timberlynn didn't need saving. She had even said so herself. She glanced my way, and I couldn't read her expression. Then she looked away, and my chest dropped.

When Dirk's gaze met mine, he raised a brow. I was positive I was shooting daggers at him. He dropped Timberlynn's arm, made his way over to me, and placed his hand on my shoulder, then motioned for me to step into the mud room. From where we were standing, I could see Timberlynn talking to my mother. "Don't let her know I'm telling you this, but she broke down in tears after you left. Like legit sobs. Dude, I don't do good when a woman is crying."

I rubbed the back of my neck and cursed.

"She was saying something about how she ruined everything. Something about a text, her being angry, and, dude..."

Dirk leaned back and looked into the kitchen to make sure no one was listening. He turned back to me and lifted his brows in concern. "I don't really know how to tell you this, but she almost said the L-word."

"The L-word?" I asked, confused.

"Yeah. The L-word."

I shook my head in confusion. "What's the fucking L-word, asshole?"

Dirk stared at me with a disbelieving expression etched on his face. "Are you fucking serious right now, Shaw? The L-word. Love. Love, dude! She almost said she was falling in love with you."

I should have been scared shitless. Instead, I smiled.

Dirk snarled his lip, then rolled his eyes. "Christ, don't get all Ty and Brock on me. You need to be careful with this one."

"Why?"

He looked back into the kitchen, and then leaned in and whispered, "She said something about being scared and having some pretty fucked-up trust issues."

"She told you that?" I found myself whispering back to him.

He nodded.

"Yeah. It was crazy. One second she was a crying mess, then the next second she wiped all the tears away, stood up tall and straight, and said she needed to win you back. It was weird, dude. She started mumbling as she wrote on a piece a paper. All I heard were a few words here and there. Something about rope and matches."

His words caught me totally off guard. "What...what does that mean?"

Dirk smiled. "She's either plannin' on tying you up, or setting something on fire. Who knows with women. Maybe she's planning make-up sex."

He simply shrugged. I was positive my mouth was gaped open. I shook my head to get all of Dirk's bullshit out. "That makes no sense at all. What are the matches for?"

Dirk tossed a piece of cookie dough into his mouth and laughed. "Beats the hell out of me, but I can't wait to find out. Keep me posted, man."

He turned and headed back into the kitchen. He must have made his way over to Kaylee because I heard Ty yell at him. "Get your paws off my wife, dickhead."

"Jealousy doesn't become you, Ty," Dirk mused.

I walked back into the room and looked once more at Timberlynn, but she was lost in a conversation with my mother. She had a smile on her face and seemed to be fine.

"That will not do!" I heard my mother say as she walked Timberlynn over to my father.

"Ty, our sweet Timberlynn has never made sugar cookies or decorated them. I'm officially making her your partner."

My father gave Timberlynn a wide smile. "Finally, a girl partner and not Tanner."

"Hey!" I said as everyone laughed, including Timberlynn. She looked at me and smiled. It was a smile that said a million different things. She was okay. She was happy. She was sorry. Or maybe I hoped it said all of that.

"Granddaddy, may I bake with you and Timberlynn?" Blayze asked with as innocent of a smile as he could muster.

"Oh Lord, son, why?" Brock said as Lincoln giggled and handed Morgan to him.

"Blayze, I was really hoping we could be partners," Lincoln called out.

Blayze's eyes lit up. "You don't want to be partners with Dad?"

Lincoln scrunched her face up and shook her head. She pretended to whisper, "He rushes the decorating."

Brock rolled his eyes, but then gave Lincoln a loving smile.

"We're going to win, Mama!" Blayze said as he rushed over, climbed up on the stepstool, and got to work helping Lincoln.

"Traitor," Brock mumbled.

My mother took my arm and pulled me to the other side of the kitchen. "I'll take Tanner and Dirk."

"Why does that make me feel cheapened?" Dirk said, tossing another piece of cookie dough into his mouth as he made his way over to Mom's area of the kitchen.

Mom simply laughed and put both of us to work rolling out the dough and cutting out shapes. She declared she'd be decorating. She lost that battle, though, when Dirk and I started to compete with one another on who could decorate the best cookie.

I won. At least, in my eyes I had. Every so often I'd sneak a glance over at Timberlynn. She truly was enjoying herself with my father, and that made me both happy and sad. I felt bad for the way her father had treated her, but happy as a fucking clam at how my father was doting on her. I looked at my mother and asked in a low voice, "You put her with Dad on purpose, didn't you?"

She nodded. "Kaylee told me a little bit about Timberlynn's past with her mother dying and how she and her father aren't very close. I thought maybe she might like the experience with more of a male parental figure."

"When did you become so smart, Mama?"

"When did I become so smart? Son, I've always been smart. I'll have you know, Tanner Shaw, I don't miss a thing. Like how you left to go to the office with Timberlynn, yet came back alone and she came back looking very confused and on the arm of Dirk. Or how Dirk ushered you into the mud room for a little chat. Don't think I haven't noticed how you and Timberlynn keep looking at one another when the other one isn't paying attention. I see all, child. I see all."

"You saw all that, huh?" I asked.

She nodded and kept speaking in a hushed voice. "Timberlynn seemed a bit off when she came back. Did you two argue?"

"You could say that. I got a bit...upset."

"Why?" she asked as she wiped her hand on her apron.

"We'll talk later, not here."

With a gentle nod of her head and a warm smile, she replied, "Of course, sweetheart."

Hours later, we had hundreds of sugar cookies all ready to be packed up into boxes and delivered to various locations. Some went to friends and family, some to the retirement home in town, some to neighbors. My mother had a list every year of where the cookies went. We had voted long ago that we would only stick to baking sugar cookies. The year we tried to do five types of cookies turned out to be a failed attempt. My mother saw how competitive we were with the sugar cookie decorating and used it to her advantage. Long ago we accused her of using child labor to pump out her cookies, and she had admitted to doing just that.

It only made me realize even more that I had done the right thing by coming home early. December twenty-second, the official cookie baking day, would always be one of my favorite days. My only regret was the fight Timberlynn and I had gotten into earlier.

One more glance over at Timberlynn, and I caught her looking at me. Our eyes met, and before I could do anything, Dirk walked up and threw his arm over her shoulders. "Come on, little one. We're going to play charades, and you and I are going to kick everyone's ass."

Timberlynn laughed and allowed Dirk to lead her out of the kitchen. Brock stopped next to me and said, "He's not interested in her, you know that."

I nodded. "Yeah, I know."

He smiled. "Good. I don't think Mom and Dad want to see you and Dirk break out into a fist fight so close to Christmas. Plus, Mom needs you to help her pack up these cookies."

"Why me?" I protested.

Brock looked around the kitchen. "'Cause everyone else left, and it's you and me. I'm older, so I delegate it to you."

Before I had a chance to argue, our mother walked back into the kitchen. "Oh, Brock, Tanner. You both stayed back to help me! You're so sweet."

I smiled and looked at Brock.

"Mom, I was just..." he started.

She handed him a tin. "About to fill this up with cookies. Let's get to work, boys, we have a lot of cookies to pack up!"

For the next couple of days, I did my best to give Timberlynn the space I figured she needed. I got up early, ate a quick breakfast while everyone else was still sleeping, and then headed out to work on the ranch. Jimmy, Greg, and I had been busting our asses to make sure everything was winterized, and ensuring that nothing had been missed a few months back when they had first prepped for winter. We worked almost until sundown each day. It made sense for me to grab dinner with them rather than try and make it up to the house for dinner. That meant I hadn't seen Timberlynn in a while...besides a quick moment or two when I'd see her at the barn, or with my mother when they went riding.

It had nearly killed me, not being able to talk to her. See that smile. Hear her sweet voice. Just a couple of days of not being close to her was starting to get to me. Especially since we had left things on not-so-great terms.

Tonight, I would get to see her, though, and I had been counting down the hours all day. It was Christmas Eve, and the family always went to church together.

As I walked out of my bedroom, I heard Blayze and my father playing a videogame on the TV. Judging by Blayze's belly laughs, it was clear he was enjoying himself immensely. I smiled. He was growing up so fast and so was Morgan. I was glad Lincoln was expecting another baby. The housed needed to be filled with kids again, especially with how happy it made my parents. I knew Mom and Dad missed having Blayze here at the house so much when Brock was still bull riding. He still came over often, but not as much as I knew my folks wanted.

As I went to walk down the steps, I paused and looked down the hall where Timberlynn's bedroom was. With a deep breath, I walked to her door and knocked. It opened, and my breath caught in my throat at the sight before me. She looked beautiful, dressed in a red dress that was off her shoulders ever so slightly and hugged the top half of her body. The front of her dress fell to her knees with the back longer, almost to the floor. For a moment I found it hard to even speak. "Wow. You look beautiful, Timberlynn."

Her cheeks flushed. "Well, Stella told me to dress up since we were going to dinner afterwards at the country club. Apparently, Brock's treat," she said in a teasing voice.

I smiled and then noticed her eyes giving me a once-over. I was in dress slacks, a button-up shirt, tie, and, of course, I carried a black cowboy hat in my hand. "You sure do shine up nice, cowboy. I don't think I've ever seen you in anything other than jeans and boots, except for the tux at Kaylee and Ty's wedding."

This time I laughed. "Well, it makes my mom happy, and she doesn't ask us to do it too often."

Her eyes met mine. I could see the confusion in them. The uncertainty of something. Me? What had happened between us? Her feelings toward me? I had so many questions, and the urge to haul her into my arms and kiss her was almost overwhelming. And what in the hell did she need rope and matches for?

I cleared my throat. "I wanted to apologize for the way things were left the other day. I didn't mean to make you upset, and I hope you know I didn't mean the things I said. I would never disrespect you, Timberlynn. I need you to know that. I was angry because you were pushing me away."

She nodded. "I know you didn't mean it."

I looked down at the floor, trying to figure out what to say to make her understand that she could trust me. I decided to simply be honest. After all, that was the advice Mom and Dad had both given me when I talked to them this morning about what had happened in Dad's office between me and Timberlynn. They suggested I talk to Timberlynn and be honest with my feelings, so that was what I was going to do. And be patient. There was that word again. After everything she had told me about her father, I could now see why she had such trust issues. But it still bugged the shit out of me that she thought I was simply a player. My father had said it right when he cautioned that I was going to have to work to earn Timberlynn's trust.

"I don't want to lose your friendship, Timberlynn."

Her mouth turned up at the corners slightly. "I don't want to lose that either."

"Good. I also want you to know that I want to be more than friends with you, and if that's not something you're able to do, or not wanting to do, then I guess it's best if you just tell me now. But I did want you to know that I care about you, deeply. I have feelings for you that are stronger than...friendship."

Her cheeks turned pink.

"But if this isn't something you're ready for now, but could possibly be in the future, then I'll wait."

"You'll...wait?" she softly whispered.

I shrugged. "If that's what you need me to do."

Her eyes widened and she stared at me for a few moments. She went to speak, but then closed her mouth.

"We're going to be late, Tanner!" my father called out.

"You're driving with Ty and Kaylee?" I asked.

"Um, yes. Kaylee texted they're on their way."

I gave her another once-over, then winked. "I'll let you finish getting ready to meet them."

Her eyes searched my face before she finally smiled and said, "I'll see you there, then."

The corner of my mouth twitched before I gave her a nod. I turned and walked away, only to stop when she called out my name.

"Tanner?"

Turning around, I watched as she took a few steps closer to me. "Do you think we can talk later? Alone."

With a smile, I nodded again. "Sure. Tell me when and where, and I'll be there."

"After dinner, the barn loft? Maybe give me time to change clothes and I'll meet you there?"

My chest felt heavy, and she must have seen the worry on my face, remembering how we'd attempted to talk a couple of days ago and it had turned out disastrously.

"I promise not to get any texts that will alter my mood. And if anyone interrupts us, I won't flake out on you."

"Is that your Christmas promise?" I asked, a teasing tone in my voice.

Timberlynn giggled. "Yes! That is my Christmas promise to you."

"Then, it's a date."

Her face lit up as she smiled. "Great."

"See you at the church, Timber."

"See you there."

Nearly an hour later, we were all sitting in church waiting for the Christmas Eve service to start. My mother glanced around nervously.

"You know how Ty is, Mama. He'll be here," I said as I squeezed her arm.

"He'll be here alright, and walking in after the service starts." She crossed her arms over her chest and turned to look forward. My father was busying himself talking to Brock and holding a sleeping Morgan in his arms.

Leaning closer to me, my mother hissed, "You know how Pastor Steve is about things like this! Not to mention, the women's prayer group I'm in. I can hear them now, 'Stella Shaw's son walked into Christmas Even mass late!' Oh, won't Gidget love this. She's been itching to talk smack about me."

I attempted not to laugh. "Talk...smack...about you? Mama, where in the world did you even learn that word?"

She turned to glare at me. "I have Facebook, Tanner. I keep up with the trends on there."

It took everything I had not to bust out laughing. My phone buzzed and I pulled it out of my pocket. I grinned even more when I read the text from Ty.

Ty: Tell our mother to stop pouting. We're walking into the church right now.

"He's walking in right now."

My mother's entire body relaxed, and she dropped her arms to her side. Not thirty seconds later, Ty, Kaylee, and Timberlynn slipped into the pews in front of us.

"Go stand next to Timberlynn, Tanner. Lori Williams, the town gossip, is here. So is her son, and he's making eyes at Timberlynn. He'll come and sit next to her, and then we'll have to hear him shouting during worship songs."

I tipped my pretend hat at her and made my way around to the pews in front of us. I leaned past Timberlynn and Kaylee and met Ty's gaze. "You were two minutes from being cut out of the will and becoming the subject of the lady's prayer group gossip."

He grinned, then turned and gave our mother a kiss. I laughed and looked down at Timberlynn.

"What's going on?" she asked.

I leaned down to talk softer now that nearly all the seats around us were taken. It wasn't lost on me that Lori Williams' son, Pete, did indeed sit directly in front of Timberlynn. "Nothing, my mother nearly got her panties in a twist because Ty was almost late for service."

The music started and Timberlynn took a quick glance around. "Looks like we got here right on time."

"Ty has it down to the second. He does it purely to agitate our mother. Every year."

Timberlynn giggled. "That's terrible."

I shrugged. "That's Ty."

As the service began, Timberlynn relaxed next to me. Once or twice, Pete turned and flashed her a smile if she glanced his way. By the time he turned around for the fourth time, Timberlynn had reached down and took my hand in hers as we stood and sang one of the worship songs. Pete glanced around, then looked at our joined hands. He turned back around and didn't look our way the rest of the service. Timberlynn also didn't let go of my hand. And that left me feeling like a fucking giddy school boy.

Chapter Sixteen

TANNER

CHRISTMAS EVE

After the service was over, my folks introduced Timberlynn to a few people. I watched as she smiled politely and spoke to folks.

As Kaylee and Lincoln introduced Timberlynn to a couple of their friends, I stood off near the entrance of the church and waited patiently. Lincoln and Brock were showing off Blayze and Morgan and answering the same questions over and over again. No, they didn't know if it was a boy or girl yet; no, they were not finding out ahead of time; and yes, they would be happy with either a boy or a girl.

My mind drifted to Timberlynn's father. What was he doing tonight on Christmas Eve? Had he not even thought about his own daughter at all? How could a father not want to be involved in his only daughter's life?

Finally, everyone started to make their way over to me. Timberlynn stood by my side as we all waited for my father to finish his conversation with the pastor. I looked around at the church, which was quickly emptying out. I nearly groaned when I saw Lindsey walking my way.

I pulled my hands out of my pockets and laced my arm around Timberlynn's waist. She didn't so much as flinch.

"Why, Mr. Shaw, are you using me to distract a certain ex?"

"She is not an ex, and yes, I am totally using you right now. Is that okay?"

When she leaned into me more, I smiled and tried not to let her know both my heartrate and breathing had sped up. "Is that your answer?"

"Yes, plus, I've missed being near you."

As Lindsey made her way through the small crowd, her eyes locked on my arm wrapped around Timberlynn. She frowned and then turned to speak to my mother. "Why, Stella, it's so very nice to see you."

My mother flashed Lindsey a polite smile. "You, as well, Lindsey."

She glanced my way and then back to my mother and gave her a fake pout before she spoke. "I'm hoping you can talk Tanner into attending one of our closest friend's weddings. I've asked him, and he's turned me down."

Mom looked at me with my arm around Timberlynn, then focused back on Lindsey. "Honey, I'm guessing he said no because he has a good reason to say no. You have a lovely holiday season. Tell your mama I said hi."

And like that, my mother dismissed Lindsey who huffed, spun on her heels, and walked away.

Without missing a beat, my mother gave my father a knowing head bob.

"Okay, Shaw crew, let's head on out!" my father announced as we all piled out of the church and made our way to the parking lot.

"Did you want to ride with Ty and Kaylee, or with me and my folks?" I asked Timberlynn, not letting go of her.

Her eyes lit up. "As much as I love my cousin, seeing her and Ty kiss the back of each other's hands every two minutes does get a little old."

I laughed. "Have you ridden with my parents anywhere yet?"

She rolled her eyes and let out a fake moan.

Blayze ran up to us and faced Timberlynn. "Miss Timberlynn! Will you sit next to me at the restaurant?"

Timberlynn dropped down some and smiled at Blayze. "Why, I would be honored to sit next to you."

My nephew beamed with happiness before he shot me a triumphant grin. Cocky little bastard. He was going to be upset when he found out I was sitting on the other side of her. My folks walked and stopped next to Blayze. When my mother looked my way and winked, I knew she was up to something.

"Timberlynn, sweetheart. Would you mind terribly riding over to the restaurant with Tanner in his daddy's truck? Morgan is acting up a bit, and Lincoln has some serious morning sickness. I told her Ty Senior and I would ride in the back with the kids."

My father's head snapped over to look at my mother, and I almost laughed at his confused expression. "We are?" he asked, only to have my mother wave him off.

"Would you mind riding with Tanner?" Mom asked again.

Timberlynn smiled politely. "I don't mind at all."

"Great! We'll see the two of you there."

I held my arm out for Timberlynn, and she took it without a second thought.

"Save me a seat, Miss Timberlynn!" Blayze called out as he walked away, his hand in my mother's.

She glanced back over her shoulder and replied, "I will, I promise."

As we headed over to my father's truck, I chuckled. "Seems Blayze has high hopes that his hat is still in the ring."

Timberlynn giggled and shook her head. "He is such a sweet little boy. Did you see him singing that hymn? He was practically shouting to the heavens."

I smiled. "Yeah, he's a special little man."

"He's a lucky little man to have such a loving family. Parents and grandparents who love him, and of course, you and Ty."

"Yeah, he's blessed. We're all blessed to have parents like my mom and dad. When they love, they love fiercely. It's a Shaw trait, really."

Her eyes met mine as we came to a stop at the passenger side of the truck. "I can see that. I mean, it's obvious how much your family means to each other. And I didn't believe for one minute that Brock and Lincoln needed your folks' help in the truck."

I rubbed the back of my neck and sighed. "She isn't subtle, is she?"

Timberlynn laughed. "No, she isn't."

"She cares, that's all. I hope you don't mind her butting in."

"Not at all," Timberlynn said as she allowed me to help her up into the truck. I shut the door and jogged around to the other side, climbed in, and started up the engine.

"It's pretty obvious how much your family loves and takes care of one another," she said. "That's not something I'm used to at all."

"Yeah, it's nice when they're not all trying to meddle and butt into your life."

"I guess that's fair enough."

"There isn't anything we wouldn't do for each other, though. Family or not. That's the funny thing about love. It looks past all the faults, forgives easily, and has a way of changing people."

Timberlynn stared at me for a moment or two before she sighed and looked out the window. "Well, some of us haven't experienced that type of love, so..."

I took her hand in mine and kissed the back of it, breaking the intensity of the moment and causing us both to laugh.

"Okay, that must be bred into you guys!"

I winked. "Must be."

Timberlynn Holden didn't know it yet, but she was about to experience that type of love...and a hell of a lot of it.

Chapter Seventeen

TIMBERLYNN

CHRISTMAS EVE DINNER

Laughter.

It was something that was in abundance with the Shaw family. Even at a fancy country club filled with uptight, rich people, this family seemed to be at ease. Not one of them seemed to have a care in the world.

"Does the whole family belong to this country club?" I leaned over and asked Tanner.

He laughed. "Yes. Hard to believe, right? A bunch of ranchers belonging to a country club."

I shook my head. "No, it just doesn't seem like your dad or Ty—hell, even Brock—would fit in here."

Tanner leaned in closer and the smell of his cologne filled the air around me, causing me to take in a long, deep breath. I'd missed that smell more than I had wanted to admit. "You'll find this hard to believe, but my granddaddy formed this country club."

"What?" I asked, surprise in my voice.

"Yeah, he and one of his good friends. Of course, back when they started the club it was mainly just a place for the guys to go and play some golf and some poker, and God knows what else they did. Granddaddy's best friend was the one with the money to back it all, pretty much. Granddaddy did put in a good chunk, though, and my father is still part owner to this day."

"No!" I said again, peeking over at Ty Senior. He looked ready to crawl out of his skin. He kept tugging on his tie and asking Stella if he could take it off, to which she simply glared at him and said no.

"They had the golf course designed and built before they even had the main building started. Then it became a place for Howard to entertain his business partners, and less of a place for them to escape and sit and smoke cigars and hit a few rounds of golf."

"So was your mother joking when she said Brock was treating for dinner?" I asked.

Tanner laughed. "Yes. We don't get charged for anything here at the country club, and honestly, we don't ever really come here. My dad will maybe play a few rounds of golf, but my brothers and I never picked up the game."

"Too busy riding bulls and roping calves?"

"Something like that," he said with a wide grin.

My eyes immediately went to the dimple in his cheek. His smile made it even more pronounced. My entire body tingled with how close he was to me.

Tanner picked up his glass of beer and took a drink. Something made the hairs on the back of my neck prickle up. I took a look around the country club and nearly choked on my own tongue. Sitting a table down from us was Lindsey. Our eyes met, and she flashed me a fake smile. I forced my own smile back. I looked away and attempted to focus on what Tanner and Ty had been talking about, but every single time I glanced back her way, she was staring at Tanner.

Her gaze slipped to mine and I glared at her. I wanted to hold up a sign and tell her to back off, he was mine. The sound of Blayze's voice made me look away before I did something I'd regret.

"Miss Timberlynn, is it true you're buying a house here?" Blazye asked.

I could feel Tanner's gaze on me, and I realized I had yet to tell him. I was positive someone in his family had already told him by now, but I had hoped to tell him myself tonight.

"It is. I won't be living very far from y'all's ranch, as a matter of fact."

Blayze's little blue eyes lit up. "How far will you be?"

"Maybe twenty minutes or so from your front gate," I answered with a shrug.

"The Covey ranch, is that right?" Tanner asked.

"Yes. I, um, I went and saw it a few days ago with Kaylee. It was perfect for what I need. It'll be a wonderful fit for me."

Tanner flashed me a smile as he said, "I'm really happy for you, Timber. I think you're going to love it here."

My heartbeat picked up when he used the nickname once again. He genuinely looked happy for me. It wasn't like I didn't think he would be happy; I just didn't want him to be upset that I hadn't mentioned it yet. "I think so as well. What about you?"

"What about me?" he asked as he finished off his beer and motioned to the waiter for another one.

"You mentioned Chance not wanting to go back out on the road with you. What are you going to do?"

"I'll be your new partner, Uncle Tanner! I can do it, you know!" Blayze announced.

Tanner leaned forward and looked around me at his nephew. "I do believe you could do it, buddy. You have to stay home and finish school, though."

Blayze leaned back in his seat and folded his arms across his chest. "Stupid school."

Tanner chuckled, and so did I.

"I loved school," I said, causing Blayze to look up at me.

"You did?"

"Yep. I was involved in a few extra things at school that made me love it even more."

"Extra things?" Blayze asked. "Like what kind of extra things?"

"Well," I said as I set my napkin down on my empty plate. "I loved horses, and we had a 4-H club."

"What's a 4-H club?" Blayze asked.

"It's sort of like a club for people who love animals and raising animals and showing them," I replied.

"Showing them?" Blayze asked.

"Abort. Abort! Abort this now!" Tanner said in a whispered voice as he hit me on the leg.

I glanced back at him with a confused look.

"Trust me, Lincoln will have your head on a plate if you don't stop now."

"Daddy, what does it mean to show an animal in 4-H?"

Tanner closed his eyes. "Shit. It's too late. The seed has been planted and is taking root."

I turned back and looked across the table at Brock who had his fork frozen in his mouth. Lincoln stared at me with a not-so-happy look on her face.

Without even thinking, I reached down next to me and grabbed Tanner's hand. "Oh no. Oh. No. The pregnant one is giving me the death stare," I softly said as he squeezed my hand.

"Don't worry, I have lots of places on the ranch we can hide you for a few days."

I snapped my head to look at him. "Are you serious?" I asked with a laugh that was more filled with fright than humor.

He nodded with a somber look on his face. "Do you not see the way Lincoln is boring her crazy mom eyes into you right now?"

Slowly, I turned back to see her doing just that. Clearing my throat, I tried to fix my mistake. "Well, it's when older students, much older students, like high school age, um, they get an animal and then raise it. Which is a very difficult thing to do. They have to get up early in the mornings, and by early, I mean way before the sun gets up. Then they have to brush them and feed them and then walk them."

"Walk them? Like a dog!" he said, getting excited.

"You are losing it, Timber!" Tanner whispered as Lincoln cleared her throat.

"No! No, not a dog. Dogs are not allowed in the 4-H. So, anyway, it takes a lot of work, and they have to give up a lot of time with their friends and it's super hard. It takes away from a lot of play time. Then they take them to the rodeo, and people bid on them."

"What happens, then? What is bidding?" Blayze asked me. His blue eyes reminded me so much of Tanner, and I couldn't help but wonder what type of little boy he had been. Did he get into trouble a lot? Was he a good student? Did he flirt with girls at the age of six like his nephew did?

"Well, people say how much they'll pay for the animals, and the person with the highest amount wins the animal. Then they take them home," I said.

Blayze looked down at his plate, his facial expression tight as he thought about it. "Why would you want to do all that work, miss play time with your friends, and then sell the animal?"

I looked around the table to see if anyone would jump in and help. Not one person said a word. No one besides Lincoln was even making eye contact. Even Kaylee seemed to be enjoying the hole I had dug myself into.

"You're on your own with this one, Timber," Tanner said. I even looked over at Dirk, who had joined the family after church and slipped into a spot at the table without so much as a raised brow. Surely, he would help. If only to annoy Tanner.

"Don't look at me, doll," came his answer.

I sighed. "That is a good question. I wouldn't recommend doing it. At all. It really isn't any fun for boys."

Blayze nodded his head, then looked at Brock and Lincoln. "Put me down for no 4-H, Mommy and Daddy."

Lincoln grinned. "Done."

I leaned back in my chair and sighed. Tanner leaned over and whispered against my ear, "It may be wrong, but that totally turned me on."

With a quick motion, I grabbed my glass of wine and hid both my smile and the blush I knew was splashed across my cheeks.

◆ ◆ ◆

The craziness that was Christmas Eve started the moment we walked into Stella and Ty Senior's house after dinner. Stella made a mad dash to her room to change for movie night. Everyone was meeting at the house for a movie marathon. Everyone except for me and Tanner.

Stella wasn't the only person to quickly run to her room and change. I slipped into a pair of yoga pants, a sweatshirt and threw my hair up into a messy bun on top of my head.

As I made my way through the kitchen and toward the mud room, I was stopped in my tracks by my cousin's voice. "Where are you sneaking off to?" Kaylee asked.

I turned and looked at her, then pointed at myself. "Me?"

She nodded. "I don't see anyone else in here, Timberlynn."

I smiled. "I'm going to the barn."

"Why?"

With a nonchalant shrug of my shoulder, I replied, "To check on the horses and just give myself some alone time."

Her brow quirked up. "Alone time?"

"Yep!" I said.

She leaned against the counter, folded her arms, and eyed me with suspicion. "So, the fact that Tanner literally just left for the barn is what...a coincidence?"

"Did he?" I said, my voice sounding a little too high-pitched.

"He did. I might add he was carrying something in his arms. Not sure what it was, since his brothers seemed to be helping him with this little mission."

"Really?" I did my best to seem interested, but not too interested. "That is a coincidence."

She harrumphed. "You have always been a terrible liar. What are you up to, little cousin?"

With a smile, I started to walk backward toward the mud room where my coat, hat, and gloves were hanging. "I'm learning to trust again."

Her eyes lit up, and a huge smile played across her face. "Good. He's a great guy, Timberlynn."

"I know he is," I said softly.

"Have fun, but not too much fun. Trust me, sex on hay is not as great as it sounds."

My mouth dropped open. "My God, how many places have you and Ty had sex outside of a bed?"

She winked. "I'd go down the complete list, but I'm sure Tanner is waiting."

I laughed, and then turned to grab my stuff and headed toward the barn.

By the time I got there, my nerves had kicked up a few notches. I forced myself to calm down. This was what I wanted. I was scared, but letting someone into your heart would be a scary thing no matter what.

"Timber, over here."

I looked to see Tanner coming out of a stall. "I wanted to check on this mare. She's been acting off for a few days."

"Is she okay?" I asked.

"Yeah, vet came earlier today and said she has a cold."

I looked at the mare, who was now staring out at us. "Poor baby."

Tanner took my hand and led me over to the stairs that led up the loft. "She'll be fine. Lots of rest and spoiled by everyone with carrots and she'll be back to normal in no time."

I glanced back over my shoulder to see the mare bopping her head, almost as if she was agreeing with Tanner.

When we got to the top of the loft, I took a quick glance around. It was your typical loft, nothing very fancy about it. What caught my eye were the doors that swung open to the balcony. I could see the massive Montana sky spread out, just as impressive at night as it was during the day. "Wow. Look at the stars," I said.

As we got closer, I noticed a quilt was laid out; a basket sat on it, along with a portable gas heater. Tanner motioned for me to sit down, so I did. He sat across from me and smiled. The soft light that cascaded down from the bulb above us lit up Tanner's face just the right amount. He was so handsome I almost had the urge to pinch myself. Was this even real?

"What is all of this?" I asked.

"Well, I figured this was our second date, if you don't count the shopping trip. I wanted to make it special. I'm competing with an awfully cute six-year-old who's putting up a pretty big fight for your heart."

I laughed and pushed a piece of hair that had fallen from my bun behind my ear. "He is cute, I won't argue with you on that one."

Tanner rolled his eyes and then held up his finger. "But...he doesn't have this."

I watched as Tanner pulled out a Tupperware container along with some fruit. He opened the container, and I looked at the contents. "Is that what I think it is?"

"Yes, ma'am, that is the famous cream cheese mixed with marshmallow fluff."

Tanner handed me a strawberry, and I dipped it into the dip, then took a bite. "I totally see why y'all snuck up here and ate all of this. It's so good!"

He laughed. "I told you! Lincoln made some for me."

"I owe her my thanks."

Tanner grinned and popped a strawberry into his mouth, then looked up at the night sky. Most likely waiting for me to start talking since I was the one who asked him up here.

"I wanted to apologize for the things I said to you the other day," I said. "It wasn't the conversation I had planned on having with you."

He chuckled softly. "I figured."

I took a deep breath and slowly blew it out. "I'm not the least bit hung up on my ex, I want you to know that. It was more about what was happening in my head."

"Okay, do you want to talk about that?"

I looked out into the massive night sky that seemed to go on for miles and miles. I was starting a new life, and I knew with every ounce of my being that I very much wanted this man in it. "Yes."

Tanner waited patiently for me to begin as he stared at me. I could almost feel the intensity of his eyes.

"I don't know why, but I've always felt like a part of me was missing." I reached down and played with the blanket. "Well, maybe I do know why. With my mother gone, something was so very different. I barely remember what life was like when she was alive. My mother and father were over the moon happy and in love. I might have been young, but I remember the way they looked at one another."

I glanced up and met his intense gaze. "Your parents remind me a lot of them. When my mother died and my father pushed me away, I always wondered if it had something to do with me. I didn't feel like I was good enough for him to love me. And by good enough, I don't mean I was bad. More that I lacked something. I still feel like I do, where he's concerned. I guess I wasn't my mother, and maybe being around me reminds him too much of what he lost. Then, with Jase..." I sighed once more. "I trusted him with my heart, and he didn't value it. It was another blow. All those years I spent with my feelings bottled up about losing my mother—and my father, in a sense—and then experiencing the ultimate betrayal from my boyfriend. I lost it. Once I finally got my shit together, I knew I couldn't put myself in that situation again. I told myself I wouldn't ever find true happiness because it didn't exist for me."

Tanner shook his head and placed his finger on my lips to silence me. "You, Timberlynn Holden, are good enough. Too good, if you ask me. I look at you sometimes and think that there's no way someone like me deserves to be with a woman like you."

I went to talk, but he pushed against my lips harder. "I don't know about you, but I'm tired of worrying about things. I want that peace and happiness my heart has been searching for, and when you walked into my life, I got a taste of it." He dropped his finger from my mouth.

"I feel the same way, Tanner. When I'm with you I feel...happy. Content. Sometimes you look at me and I feel so..." I released a nervous chuckle.

"Tell me," he pressed.

"I feel sexy. I feel desired. I feel wanted. But wanted in more than just a sexual way. I think I was so stuck in my head that I didn't know if I was dreaming that feeling up, or if it was really happening."

Tanner almost looked relieved. "I do want you, but not just in my bed. I want to be by your side for whatever life throws at us, Timber. And trust me when I say you're not the only one who's scared. I've never felt this way in my life. Hell, I've had dreams of us walking hand in hand with kids running around us. I'm not entirely positive, but I'm pretty sure that's not normal for a couple who've only been on two dates. And the first one was unofficial."

My breath caught in my throat. "You've had...dreams like that? About us?"

He nodded. "Hell, Timber, I've been dreaming about you since I first met you in September."

My teeth dug into my bottom lip, and I let out a small chuckle. "So have I."

Tanner took my hands in his, and my stomach fluttered as he rubbed his thumbs over the back of my hands. "I want you to know that I'll go as slow as you want. As long as I get to see your smile every day, hear your laughter on the breeze, and see those beautiful eyes of yours, I'll wait as long as you need me to, for whatever happens next. But I need you to know that I'm in this for the long haul, and I will fight for us. And I swear on my life, I will never hurt you, Timber."

The tears I tried to hold back slipped free and trailed down my face. Tanner watched them fall and then met my gaze again. "I don't want to say those words too soon, so I'll just do this instead."

He placed my hand on his chest. My breath stilled as his heart raced under my touch. His hand landed over mine. With my gaze locked on our joined hands, I finally let the last wall down.

Slowly, I lifted my eyes to his and smiled as I took his other hand and placed it on my chest too. I put my hand over his. "I feel it too," I whispered.

Tanner smiled and leaned over to kiss me. The moment our lips touched, I heard voices climbing up the steps to the loft and smiled.

With a growl of frustration, Tanner dropped his forehead to mine.

"I heard there was cream cheese fluff up here!" Ty called out.

Chapter Eighteen

TIMBERLYNN

CHRISTMAS MORNING

A soft knock at my bedroom door had me opening my eyes and stretching. I sat up and asked, "Who is it?"

"Tanner."

I jumped out of the bed and reached for my robe. A quick glance at the clock on the bedside table said it was only six in the morning.

"One second," I said as I slid on my slippers and went to the door. I smiled the instant I saw him in his PJs and rumpled hair. Lord, how did he look so handsome straight out of bed?

"Merry Christmas, Timber."

His voice sounded breathy, and butterflies fluttered in my stomach. "Merry Christmas, Tanner."

He held out a package, and I let the door fall all the way open. "For me?" I asked, taking the small gift.

Tanner nodded.

"Why are you giving it to me now, Tanner? At six in the morning?" I asked with a slight giggle.

He shrugged. "I didn't want anyone else to see me give it to you."

I raised a brow. "Oh? Should I be worried?"

With a shake of his head and a smile, he replied, "No."

I motioned for him to come into my room, but he shook his head. "I don't think that's such a good idea."

My cheeks heated, and I focused on the gift in my hand. I pulled the ribbon and carefully took off the wrapping paper.

"You're one of those types of people, are you?"

"What do you mean?" I asked, stopping my process of carefully not ripping the wrapping paper.

He gifted me with a brilliant smile and my insides pulsed with desire. I nearly moaned in pleasure. "The type of person who tries not to rip the paper and then folds it up and keeps it."

I simply shrugged and replied, "Maybe..."

"Go on, keep going. At this rate you'll have it open by breakfast time."

I rolled my eyes, then got back to my task. Once the red paper was off, I held my breath and opened the box. "Oh, Tanner!" I gasped as I handed him the ribbon, bow, and paper. I reached in and took out a beautiful key chain with a horse on it.

"This is so stunning." I looked up at him. "It's so heavy!" I giggled.

"It's white gold. I overheard you telling Kaylee you weren't a fan of yellow gold."

My mouth fell open in shock as I stared at him. He suddenly looked nervous and took a few steps away from me.

"Do you like it? I thought you could put the house key on it when, you know, you finally purchase the Covey place." He laughed nervously. "I mean, if you don't like it..."

"I love it," I said softly as I looked back down at it. "It's the most thoughtful gift I've ever gotten."

My hand came up to my mouth as I stared at the keychain. No one had ever done anything so thoughtful for me before. I was shocked by the feeling of utter joy as it wrapped around my body like a warm blanket. This man was unbelievable. "I'll cherish this gift forever," I said as I clutched it to my chest.

A wide smile broke out over Tanner's face. He let his gaze take in all of me before he locked eyes with me once more.

It was then I realized how I must look. "Geesh, do I look awful?" I said, running my hand through my hair.

Tanner shook his head and replied, "No way. You're beautiful, even first thing in the morning."

"I swear, if I had brushed my teeth, I'd pull you into this room and kiss you!"

With a smug smile, Tanner replied, "If I told you I hadn't brushed my teeth yet, would that change the situation any?"

Laughing, I shook my head.

"Damn. Just to be clear, though, I have brushed my teeth."

I was so light on my feet and over-the-moon happy that I let out a giggle. It sounded like a small child was in my room. "How about you let me brush my teeth, get dressed, and then you and I can get a head start on breakfast."

Tanner winked. "I like this plan. I'll meet you downstairs, sweetheart."

"I won't be long!" I called out before I shut the door, rushed back into the room, and carefully placed the keychain on my bedside table.

No words could describe my excitement at finally being able to share in a Christmas that was normal. One filled with love and laughter and happiness. The little girl in me who hadn't been able to experience that in so long was itching to come out and enjoy the day.

I heard laughter from the kitchen and paused at the door as I took in the scene before me. Apparently, Tanner wasn't the only early riser in the family. He and his mom were placing what looked like cinnamon rolls onto a cookie sheet. She hit him on the back of the head and told him to stop eating the frosting, and I had to cover my mouth to keep from laughing. Before I had the chance to step into the kitchen, someone tapped me on my shoulder, and I turned to see Ty Senior standing there. He motioned with his head for me to follow him.

"Is everything okay, Ty?" I asked, unsure of why he would want to speak with me alone.

"Yes, of course. Let me get right to it, sweetheart. I overheard you speaking to Lincoln last night at dinner about finding a place to rent until you close on the Covey ranch and can move in."

I nodded. "Yes, it looks like it could be a few weeks still, even with how fast everything is moving. They mentioned something about a possible hiccup."

He smiled, and I was hit by how much his younger son looked like him. The same smile. The same dimple. The same stunning, pale blue eyes.

"Well, I want you to know that you're welcome to stay here. You're family now, Timberlynn, and this is your home. Plus, I'd hate to think how Tanner would react if he knew you were leaving the house. With how smitten he is with you and all."

With a chuckle, I replied, "Smitten?"

He nodded. "Well, I'm sure he's more than simply smitten, but I'll just leave it at that. Because he is a Shaw after all, I need you to know that he'll most likely...to put it bluntly...fuck up something at some point without meaning to do it."

I brought my hand up to my mouth to keep from laughing.

"It's true. He's going to say or do something he thinks is the right thing, and it won't be, and you'll most likely want to walk away or kick him where it counts."

I couldn't help but laugh now. If he only knew that we had already both done exactly that.

"I'm simply saying to give the boy a chance. That's all I ask, if you have the same feelings. And by the way you light up when my son walks into the room, I'm going to go with my hunch on this one and say you do."

I dropped my hand and stared at the floor for a moment before I lifted my gaze back to his. "Thank you for letting me stay with y'all. This is all really new to me. This environment with a loving family," I said, motioning around the room. "I had loving parents until my mother died and my father...well, he sort of slipped away. Spending time with your family has truly been a blessing."

Ty Senior leaned down and kissed me on the cheek. "It's been a blessing for us to have you here, Timberlynn."

"First Dirk, then Blayze, and now you, Dad?"

The sound of Tanner's voice made my entire body come to attention and buzz with excitement.

Tanner's father winked at me, and then looked at Tanner. "Nothing to worry about here, son. I am very much in love with the woman in the other room. Now, if you'll excuse me, I best go help her with breakfast before all the gang gets here.

I laughed, as did Tanner before he said, "Mom said Brock called—they'll be over shortly. Ty and Kaylee said they'd be here soon as well."

As Ty Senior walked into the kitchen, Tanner reached for me and pulled me into his arms.

My teeth dug into my bottom lip. My stomach flipped when Tanner reached up and gently set it free. "I've been dying to kiss you again," Tanner said.

I lifted up onto my toes and grinned. "Then, kiss me."

His hands went to both sides of my face while I grabbed onto his T-shirt to keep my balance as he kissed me. We both moaned softly, and something jerked in my chest when he deepened the kiss.

This was how I wanted to start every day of my life. Kissing this man.

I pulled back when I figured we both needed a breath. Tanner's chest rose and fell nearly as fast as mine. "Wow, that was..."

"Amazing," Tanner finished.

Chuckling, I added, "So amazing."

"I want to do that a lot more."

The feeling of heat in my cheeks made me smile up at him. "I want you to do that a lot more as well."

He leaned down, and once more bridged the distance between us with another heart-pounding kiss.

"Well, I see someone got his Christmas wish," Brock called out with a bark of laughter.

I couldn't help but smile against Tanner's mouth as we drew apart slowly.

"When do you close on your house?" he asked in a hushed voice, ignoring Brock.

"Soon. A few weeks, maybe."

He closed his eyes and groaned. "A few weeks, that's too long!"

Brock walked by Tanner and slapped him on the shoulder, causing him to lose his balance some. I tried not to laugh, but I couldn't help it.

"Trust me, it's going to feel like forever," he said, glaring at Brock.

I tried to give him my best sexy smirk as I whispered, "We could find lots of ways of being alone, ya know."

His eyes went dark, and then he called out. "Chop! Chop! Time to open presents!"

"Okay!" Blayze said with a huge smile. I hit Tanner on the chest and shook my head.

"Sorry, buddy, we need to wait for Uncle Ty and Aunt Kaylee," Lincoln stated.

Blayze pouted. "Aw, man."

Tanner grabbed Blayze and started to play as I headed into the kitchen to see if Stella needed any help.

When I walked in, Ty Senior and Stella were dancing to "White Christmas," sung by Elvis Presley. It was such a sweet moment that I tried to back out of the kitchen, but Stella caught sight of me.

"Timberlynn, come take my spot so I can stir the hash browns."

"Me?" I asked, pointing to myself. Stella nodded as Ty Senior motioned for me to come to him.

I walked over and he took me in his arms and danced me flawlessly around the kitchen.

"Find a man who will dance you across the kitchen floor, Timberlynn. Those are the keepers. That type of man will be devoted and love you forever."

I giggled when Ty Senior dipped me.

"Just try not to compare their dancing to mine," he said. "I wouldn't want you to be disappointed when you can't find an equal."

This time I found myself laughing so hard I was nearly in tears. This was turning out to be the best Christmas of my entire life.

Ty Senior spun me and let go as he gracefully went to the oven and took out the cinnamon rolls.

"So, this is Christmas," I said softly as I watched a husband and wife work flawlessly next to one another as they laughed and stole a kiss every so often.

It truly was the best Christmas ever.

Chapter Nineteen

TIMBERLYNN

CHRISTMAS DAY

As I helped Stella get all the food out into the dining room, I asked her what a typical Christmas looked like for their family.

"I guess like any other family. I've always liked having the main meal on Christmas Day be breakfast. The kids hated it, still do, but that was how it was when I grew up. My grandmother and mother would be in the kitchen at the crack of dawn making all the breakfast goodies."

She smiled at the memory. "It was always my favorite part of the day, eating amazing food around the giant table and hearing all the grownups talk about whatever it was they talked about. Then, after we ate, my mother used to say the dishes could wait, and off it was to open gifts. No one took turns, we all ripped into presents like it was the first time we'd ever seen them. Ty and I decided early on that's what we would do. It's a madhouse, I'll tell you right now. It should be a little less crazy this year since it's just the kids and no one from my family or Ty's will be here. Most of the older folk have passed on and most, like us, simply want to be with the immediate family."

"It sounds like fun."

She winked. "It is. And I'm so glad you're a part of it, sweetheart. So very glad."

"I am too. My only concern is who's going to tell Blayze that I'm officially off the market and spoken for by his uncle?"

Stella's face went bright with happiness. "Both uncles stealing women out from under him. How will he survive?"

We both laughed.

Stella let out a sigh and then said with a straight face. "Well, good luck telling him."

"Wait, what?"

She looked back over at me. "I'm not going to be the one to tell Blayze. And I'm pretty sure it won't be Tanner. So, that leaves you."

"Oh no. There is no way I am breaking that little boy's heart. Stella! You're his grandmother, isn't this like your area of specialty?"

She laughed. Hard. "My area of specialty is spoiling my grandkids. Butting into my kids' business, keeping up with the gossip in town, not letting anyone know I'm keeping up with the gossip in town, and being able to mend any piece of clothing in any sort of emergency. Oh, and I can gut a deer faster than any of the Shaw men."

The last one made me curl my lip. "Eeeww!"

She shrugged.

"But I don't see why..."

Stella held up her hand, and I instantly stopped talking. "It's your heart he wants, so it's got to be you who breaks it into a million little pieces." And with that she walked away.

"Okay, what just happened?" I asked as I looked around the empty room.

Before I had a chance to walk out of the room, Blayze walked in.

Oh. No.

"Hey, Miss Timberlynn! Merry Christmas."

"Merry Christmas, Blayze. So how did Santa treat you?"

Blayze looked around and then motioned for me to come closer so he could whisper. "Can you keep a secret?"

Good Lord, what was this little boy going to tell me? Would it be something I'd need to tell his parents and then he'd never trust me again? What if it was something bad? Oh my gosh, what if he didn't believe in Santa anymore and didn't have the heart to tell anyone else?!

"What kind of secret?" I asked wearily.

He giggled. "The only kind there is, silly!"

I laughed and hit my forehead with my hand. Okay, this would be easy to handle, no problem. "Of course, silly me! Okay, I promise I can keep a secret. Hit me with it."

Blayze frowned. "I can't hit you with it. It might hurt it."

It was my turn to be confused, but then I realized it was my choice of words. "No, I mean go ahead and tell me the secret."

Then what Blayze said finally registered.

"Wait, what do you mean it might hurt it?"

"The baby rabbit I snuck into the barn yesterday."

My eyes widened in shock, and I nearly fell back on my ass. "The baby rabbit?"

He nodded. "She's really pretty. And Renee, my friend from Sunday school, told me I could have the puppy too."

This time I let myself sit. "The...the puppy?"

"Yeah, they were moving and stopped by so that Daddy could give Renee's daddy a name of some guy he knows in Colorado where Renee is moving. She showed me the bunny and puppy that were in the backseat of her daddy's truck. She said they were giving them away. So, I took them." He said it with a little shrug, so matter of fact that I almost laughed.

"What did you do with them?" I asked.

"I put them in the barn, back in a stall that Daddy or Mommy aren't using."

"You're hiding a puppy and bunny in your folks' barn?" I asked, making sure I got the secret right.

"Yep! I'll take you to see them later."

Oh, heck no. I would definitely be spilling this secret, but to whom? Lincoln or Brock? I figured Brock was the safer pick.

I forced a smile. "Blayze, I think this is really big news. Such big news that you really should tell your daddy about it."

"But Renee said I had to keep it a secret, or she'd get in trouble."

I rubbed my temples. This was not territory I was used to dealing with. "Um, well, I think if you keep this a secret much longer, you're going to be the one getting in trouble, Blayze. You need to come clean and tell your folks about the rabbit and puppy."

His face went white as a sheet.

Tanner and Brock walked into the dining room and saw me on the floor. They both frowned.

"Why are you sitting on the floor?" Tanner asked.

I jumped up and went to make an excuse, when Blayze suddenly decided that coming clean in that moment was the right thing to do. "So, Daddy, I have a rabbit and a puppy, and Miss Timberlynn said I needed to...what was it? Come clean?"

Brock drew his brows in tight and then looked at me. I held up my hands. "Nothing to do with this at all. Nothing. At. All." With my hands in the air, Tanner came to my side.

Brock looked back down at Blayze. "What do you mean, you have a rabbit and puppy?"

"Renee...she gave me her rabbit and puppy."

Brock closed his eyes. "Lincoln is going to...I don't even want to think about it, to be honest with you."

Tanner tugged me closer to him, clearly trying not to smile.

Brock's phone rang, and he pulled it out. "It's Paul," he said with a confused expression. "Hey, Paul, what's going on?"

Brock kept his face neutral, but at one point I swear the corner of his mouth twitched with a hidden smile. "No problem, Paul, the gate's open. Completely understand."

He hung up and looked down at Blayze. "Your life has been spared, son. Renee confessed to giving you the rabbit and puppy. Paul had already promised them to another family in town."

I was positive we all let out a collective sigh of relief. Blayze took it a step further. "Good thing Renee came clean too, huh, Dad?"

Brock laughed. "Yeah, buddy. It's always best not to keep secrets."

Blayze nodded. "Hear that, Miss Timberlynn? You shouldn't keep secrets."

And with that, he turned and headed out of the room as Brock and Tanner both looked at me.

"I only promised to keep the secret when I thought it was going to be something cute!"

Brock nodded. "Best you learn this now, Timberlynn. If that boy asks you to keep a secret…"

"Run," Tanner and Brock both said in unison.

Chapter Twenty

TIMBERLYNN

CHRISTMAS DAY

Lincoln walked over, wrapped her arm around my waist, and pulled me off to the side. "Okay, you cannot leave me in the dark until we get alone time with Kaylee. She'll understand if you tell me first."

I gave her a confused look. "Tell you what first."

She rolled her eyes. "Don't play innocent. You and Tanner! I've never seen him look so utterly happy."

I knew if I could look at myself right now, I'd most likely be blushing. Good grief, if I kept getting embarrassed like this, I wouldn't ever have to wear makeup again.

"By the way you're blushing, I'm going to guess y'all are growing closer?"

A wide smile spread across my face. Before I had a chance to say anything, though, Stella called out, "Ty and Kaylee are here! It's breakfast time!"

Kaylee came rushing over as if her radar had been activated. "Oh, hell no. I know you are not trying to get information before me!" she stated as she shot Lincoln a friendly, but still disapproving, look. Lincoln simply shrugged.

"Like you wouldn't have done the same thing," she countered.

Kaylee smirked, then turned her attention to me. She gave me a quick once-over, and her smirk turned into a full-blown smile. "Tell us everything, but make it quick. I'm pretty sure the family is about to go insane since I clearly won the gift giving this morning."

"Why?" Lincoln and I asked at once.

She waved her hands in the air and said, "Tell us! Quickly, before they figure out the shirt!"

"What are you talking about?" Lincoln asked.

Kaylee grabbed onto my upper arms and gave me a light shake. "Are you dating him or not, man?!"

I laughed. "Yes! We are officially dating! Now will you stop manhandling me, woman?!"

My cousin pulled me into her arms and hugged me tightly, then whispered, "Oh, sweetie, I'm so glad you let your guard down. You won't regret it. Tanner is such a great guy."

I giggled, overcome with excitement. "I know he is."

Before I knew it, Lincoln had us both wrapped up in her arms. "This is amazing! Three Georgia girls snagging the Shaw brothers!"

Kaylee and I both laughed. Then we heard Stella scream.

The three of us quickly looked toward the kitchen.

"Stella figured it out," Kaylee said. She grabbed both our hands and pulled us behind her as she made her way toward the kitchen.

When we walked into the room, Stella had her face buried in her hands, crying.

"I am so confused right now," Tanner said as Brock stared at his mother.

"Sweetheart, what's wrong?" Ty Senior asked, drawing his wife into his arms.

"This...is...the best...Christmas...ever!" Stella stammered out. I looked at Ty, who was beaming. Then my eyes went down and I read his t-shirt.

Certified DILF

Est. 2020

My hand came up to my mouth, and I looked over to Kaylee. She smiled and nodded.

"What does your shirt mean, Uncle Ty?" Blayze said.

"OH. MY. GAWD!" Lincoln cried out, then started to jump. Kaylee laughed and they hugged.

"We're doing this together! At the same time!" Lincoln said.

"What does DILF mean?" Tanner asked.

I peeked over at Brock who looked just as confused.

"It means Dad I'd like to F. U. C. K!" Stella cried out as she made her way over to Kaylee and hugged her.

Ty Senior stared at the shirt. "Should I be worried my wife knows what that means?" he asked more to himself than anyone else.

"I'm more worried I didn't know," Brock stated.

"Oh, holy shit, dude!" Tanner grabbed Ty by the back of the neck and pulled him in for a quick hug. "I should have caught on. I'm slipping," Tanner said as he stepped out of the way, giving Brock room to congratulate his brother.

"Another baby! Oh, my goodness. Another baby!" Stella cried out.

As I stood back and watched the family all exchange congratulations with Kaylee and Ty, I couldn't help but feel a strange ache in my chest. Was this...jealousy I was feeling?

My eyes caught Tanner's, and he smiled. I made my way over to him, and he slipped his arm around my waist. The ache that had been in my chest was exchanged for a fluttery feeling. I leaned my head onto Tanner's shoulder and watched everyone. A sense of peace and happiness washed over me as I observed my cousin. She looked so happy, and I had the same sense of joy.

Ty Senior looked over at us and winked before he flashed that famous Shaw smile that each of the boys had inherited from their daddy.

"Wow, Ty's going to be a dad," Tanner mused.

"I think he'll make a wonderful father," I said.

He nodded. "I agree. We had a good example to follow."

My eyes stung with the threat of tears. I was truly so happy for my cousin and Ty. Kaylee was having a baby. I covered my mouth and tried not to cry.

Tanner held onto me tighter.

Once the crowds backed away, I made my way over to Kaylee. We held hands, and I slowly shook my head. "I knew it."

She rolled her eyes. "You didn't say anything."

I shrugged. "I figured you'd tell everyone when you were ready, and I didn't want to ruin your plans by mentioning it. I'm so happy for you, Kaylee. So very happy!" We hugged once more.

"You'll know this same happiness someday, Timber," she whispered in my ear as we embraced.

I hugged her tighter. "This is about you right now, not me."

When we pulled apart, I turned to Ty. "I'm so happy for you, Ty!"

He drew me into a hug, then whispered in my ear, "Did I see my baby brother's arm around you?"

I chuckled. "You did," I whispered back.

"Are you finally together?" he asked as we stepped apart.

"We are."

He pumped his fist in the air, then shoved Brock on the back. "Pay up. I won. Little brother has himself a girlfriend." Brock groaned and pulled out his wallet.

"You did not bet on Tanner and Timberlynn!" Lincoln admonished the two of them.

"Sure as heck did!" Ty stated as he waved his money in the air, only to have Kaylee grab it from his hands.

"Thanks! I can get an early start on baby shopping." We all watched as Ty's face went from *excited as hell* to *oh shit*.

Everyone laughed again as Ty's brothers started to take a few teasing jabs at him.

"Okay, into the dining room before breakfast gets cold!" Stella said, motioning for everyone to go and sit.

I noticed Blayze standing off to the side, a stricken look on his face.

"Um, Stella, do you mind if I have a word with Blayze really quickly?"

Stella stole a glance in her grandson's direction and smiled softly. "Oh no. His little heart is broken yet again."

She reached for my hand and squeezed it. "Take your time, sweetheart."

I walked over to Blayze and stretched my hand out. He took it and we made our way out of the kitchen and into the living room.

The moment he sat down on the sofa, he let out a long, loud sigh. "Well, looks like I lost the girl again."

It took everything in me not to smile. This little boy was so much like his father and uncles. And if I had to guess, like his granddad too.

"Blayze, you had to know it wasn't going to work. I'm simply too old for you."

He nodded. "Do you like Uncle Tanner? I mean, do you really like him?"

"Yes, very much so. I've liked him since I first met him at your Uncle Ty's wedding."

He looked at me with a thoughtful expression. "There's this girl in my class and, um, she said there's a thing called *love at first sight*. Do you think that's true?"

I thought back to the very first time Tanner walked up to me. That cowboy hat, the jeans and button-down shirt that showcased his amazing body. The smile that instantly lit something up inside of me. The countless hours I thought about him, dreamt of him. With a smile, I answered Blayze honestly. "Up until I met your Uncle Tanner, I wouldn't have believed in it."

"But ya do now?"

I nodded. "I believe I do."

He sighed once more and looked down at his little cowboy boots.

"What's the little girl's name?" I asked.

"Lilly."

Trying to be careful with where this conversation was going, I asked, "Did Lilly mention why she believed in love at first sight?"

He nodded. "Yeah. She said she fell in love with me when she first saw me."

"Oh dear," I said softly, frantically looking over my shoulder for Lincoln or Stella. Hell, even Kaylee would be better than me at this.

"I wasn't thinkin' I liked her, 'cause you know, you came to town and all."

Suddenly this six-year-old felt like a little adult.

"I see. But how do you feel about her now?"

He shrugged. "My friend Tommy says we ain't supposed to like girls. At least not now."

I nodded, glancing over my shoulder again and whispering, "Help!"

"But I don't think he's right. Daddy says girls don't have cooties like Tommy says. Do you think only girls in my class have them?"

What is the right answer here?! Oh gosh.

"Um...well...no...girls don't have cooties at any age."

Blayze lit up like the Fourth of July. Shoot, maybe that wasn't the right answer. "It's okay to like her? I mean, I'm pretty sure Lilly will be easy to win."

I closed my eyes and groaned internally. With a quick prayer to give me the right words to say, I took Blayze's hands and gave him a sweet smile. "Blayze, the first mistake a young man, I mean, *a man* can make is thinking he can easily win the heart of girl. She needs to know you like her for her. For who she is."

"What does that mean, Miss Timber?"

My heart melted at how he shortened my name. "It means you like her for things like her smile or for how smart she is. Girls should always be treated with respect, and one should never assume she's a prize to be won. Giving your heart to someone is a big thing, and asking for it in return is just as big."

His little brows drew in closer and I cringed inwardly. Was that too much for a six-year-old to process? Hell, according to Tanner, Blayze had finally stopped using the W sound for his Ls not that long ago, and here I was giving him love advice.

Finally, after what felt like an eternity, Blayze stood. "Tommy was right. Girls can make a man go crazy."

My mouth fell open, and I stared at him. He shook his head, gave a half shrug, and then walked back toward the kitchen.

After a moment or two, I found myself laughing.

"That was some good advice you gave him."

I stood and faced Lincoln, who had come into the room at some point. "Wow. I don't know how you do it."

She smiled. "Some days neither do I. You're really good with him, Timberlynn. Thank you for thinking of him and talking to him. It means a lot to me and Brock."

"I just hope I didn't confuse him more. Maybe I should have kept it simple and told him that girls do, in fact, have cooties."

She rolled her eyes. "He has Shaw blood running through him, so that would never work."

We both laughed and headed back into the dining room. About that time, Dirk showed up for breakfast, and the moment he caught sight of Ty's shirt, I saw something I thought I would never see.

He looked at Kaylee, smiled, and let a single tear slip free.

Maybe there was hope for that man yet.

Chapter Twenty-One

TANNER

The day after Christmas, I walked into the kitchen and poured myself a cup of coffee, smiling as I watched my mother stir blueberry muffin mix. My father sat reading the paper like he did every morning. Last night, after all the excitement had died down, I announced that I was retiring from roping. Everyone in the family was supportive of my decision, as I knew they would be, but I could especially see it in my folks' eyes. They were happy to have all of their sons back home, that was clear to see.

"It's a beautiful morning," I said before I took a sip of my coffee.

My mother beamed at me. "The best morning ever!"

"I'll agree with your mother," Dad said. "I think this has been one hell of a good Christmas."

He glanced over the paper and gave me a smile. I returned it, then pushed off the counter. "I'm off to do some chores."

As I walked out of the kitchen, I heard my father sigh in delight. "Yes, indeed, one hell of a good Christmas."

After shooting the shit with Jimmy and finishing my coffee, I walked into the barn and came to a stop at the sight in front of me. Dirk was standing there in a yoga pose.

"Okay, what the fuck has happened to you, dude?" I asked, making him jump. "First you cried yesterday, and now you're doing yoga? Who the hell are you lately?"

"You dickhead, you scared the piss out of me. And for the one-millionth time, I didn't cry. Something was in my eye at that particular moment!"

"You cried. We all saw it."

He sighed, then rolled his eyes. "Fine. It was a tear of happiness for Kaylee. You know how she's like a sister to me. It was for her. And I quickly wiped *it* away."

"There was more than one...*it*...and you didn't wipe it quickly enough," I mumbled.

"What are you even doing here this early?" Dirk asked as he balanced once again in a one-legged stance.

"Um, ranching. It's like downward dog, but it's called feed the horses," I replied. As I walked by him, I barely touched his shoulder with the tip of my finger, causing him to go off balance again.

He put his other foot down and quickly recovered.

"What are you doing yoga in the barn for? Why didn't you do it up in your room? You know if Brock and Tanner see you doing this, you'll never live it down."

He huffed. "Please, Brock is the one who told me how good it would be for my balance on the bull."

I stopped walking and turned to faced him. "*Brock* does yoga?"

"Did. Past tense. I doubt he does it now."

With a smile, I secretly contemplated how this little tidbit of info would benefit me. I also tried to figure out how I could gather any evidence of my older brother doing yoga.

"It'd be good for you as well."

"I don't ride bulls, Dirk, remember?"

He chuckled, and then switched his pose. "You still need good balance for roping. I can show you a few moves if you want."

I reached for the feed bucket and answered him over my shoulder. "Hard pass, but thanks for the offer."

"Your loss. It could improve your time."

Once I got a few buckets filled with feed, I made my way back out into the stall area. We only had a few horses who were stalled, a mare who was pregnant, a stallion who was healing from a crazy jump over a fence, and foal who had lost her mother during childbirth and was now with a surrogate. "That's not something I need to worry about anymore," I stated as I opened the first stall door and poured the grain into the feeding dish.

"Come again?" Dirk said. His voice sounded closer, and I could tell he had made his way over to me.

I faced him. "I'm done. Retiring from roping."

Dirk's mouth nearly fell to the floor. "Tanner, you can find another roping partner. Just because Chance doesn't have his heart in it anymore doesn't mean you have to give it up."

I smiled and walked out of the stall, locking it behind me. "I appreciate you giving me advice, Dirk, but my heart hasn't been in it a hundred percent for a while now. I think I was actually ready to leave before Chance decided he was."

"What?" Dirk asked, his voice laced with surprise. "But you love it."

With a nod, I agreed. "I do...I did. But the last few months I've discovered I love this more. The ranch. My family. Being home."

He grinned. "Does a little blonde, green-eyed beauty have anything to do with this decision?"

I returned his grin with one of my own. "She has something to do with it, yes."

Dirk almost looked relieved. "I'm glad you both realized your attraction to each other like the rest of us did."

"We're taking it slow."

He placed his hand on my shoulder and gave it a squeeze. "I really am happy for you, Tanner." Dirk walked back over to his mat and got into another weird ass position.

"What about you, Dirk? You ever going to take the leap and settle down with one woman?"

He laughed. "Hell no. I've got a plethora of women at my disposal. Why would I want to give that up?"

"So no plans to slow down?" I asked.

He looked up at me from where he was sitting on the floor. "Slow down? I just won the world championship. I'm going to give it my all to win it again next year. Hell-to-the-no am I going to slow down. Not for anyone, especially *one woman*."

I chuckled. "Yeah, a year ago I thought the same damn thing."

"No offense, Tanner, but you and I are nothing alike. I like my endless flow of women who are eager to share my bed. I like the no commitment. The thrill of chasing a woman. I like my life exactly how it is. You may have acted like you played the field, but we both know the truth. You've most likely been itching to settle down for a while and just didn't realize it."

It wasn't long ago that I thought along the same lines. Not as extreme as Dirk, who gave new meaning to the word manwhore. But a part of what he said was true. I had known something was missing for a while now. Just took me coming back home after a long-ass time on the road to finally figure it out.

I shrugged and gave him a smile. "You don't see yourself wanting to settle down? Have a family?"

He scoffed. "A family! Bite your damn tongue, son!" He stood, his entire body shivering before he dropped back down on the mat. "Jesus, you're giving me the heebie-jeebies, dude!"

"Heebie-jeebies?" I repeated as I tossed my head back in laughter. I glanced down at him as I walked by and said, "What are you, in middle school?"

Dirk laughed and then bent his back so much that I nearly gagged at how he was contorting his body.

"Right, I'm going to let you get back to your...yoga. Have fun."

Dirk drew in a deep breath, then let it out. "You don't know what you're missing out on, Tanner."

Grabbing another feed bucket on my way out of the barn, I called out, "I'll take your word for it, Dirk."

As I continued walking away from him, I mumbled under my breath, *"What the fuck happened to you, dude?"*

◆ ◆ ◆

We all spent the rest of the day getting everything ready for a major storm that was approaching later in the evening. Needless to say, everyone was running around like the damn world was ending. It was the first major winter storm of the season, and it looked to be a big one.

"Did you get the water trough heaters in?" my father asked as he walked into the small office in the main barn.

Brock sat at the desk as Ty looked over Brock's shoulder as they read the weather report. I sat in the corner, attempting to rest my body for a few minutes. I'd been going nonstop since daylight.

"Yes, they're all in," Ty answered, not looking over at my father.

"What are they looking at?" Dad asked, sitting down next to me.

"The latest weather report. Sounds like it's going to be worse than they thought. I'm thinking we bring the horses in from the pastures."

Dad nodded. "There's plenty of room in the barns; let's do it."

I stood. "I'll take Rosie—she doesn't mind the wind and she's already in the barn."

Brock turned and looked at me. "Rosie isn't in the barn."

"What do you mean? I put her in the stall a few hours ago next to the new mare we got in. I figured if anyone could calm that mare, it would be Rosie."

Ty and Brock exchanged a concerned look. "Tanner, I just checked the water in all the stalls in the main barn, Rosie's stall was empty. I wasn't sure if you turned her out again or what. I meant to ask you and got sidetracked."

A feeling of dread came over me for some reason. Had she gotten out somehow?

A light knock came on the office door, and our mom poked her head in.

She looked directly at me and asked, "Do you know when Timberlynn will be back? She said she was only going on a short ride, since bad weather was coming in later."

"A ride?" I asked. The dread I had felt only moments ago quickly turned to full-on fear.

"Yes, she said she was going to ask you boys if she could take Rosie out for a ride. About an hour-and-a-half ago. She said she'd be gone an hour, maybe less. I thought maybe I missed her coming back in, but I went up to her room and she wasn't back yet. I just heard the storm is moving in a lot faster than they predicted. I'm worried she might have gotten turned around and can't get a cell signal."

I quickly pushed past my mother and nearly sprinted to the saddle shed.

"Tanner! Tanner, wait!" Ty called out.

"She's out there, Ty. You and I both know it. She's also not used to these fast-moving snowstorms."

He grabbed my arm and pulled me to a stop. "No, we don't know she's out there."

Jimmy walked into the barn. His face was etched with concern as he looked at me. "I've been trying to call you."

"Who?" we all said at once, including my father.

Jimmy looked at Ty, then Brock, then me. "The three of you."

Kaylee walked into the barn, her entire body wrapped up in a winter coat, a scarf and gloves. "My gosh, looks like the storm is moving in early." She looked around at each of us. "Ty, I've been trying to call you, but I don't have a cell signal. The wind is so bad, I'm wondering if it knocked down a tower or something. I finally just drove over here."

We all pulled out our phones. "I don't have a signal either," I said.

"Me neither," Ty stated. He looked at Brock who simply shook his head.

"Jimmy, where's Rosie?" I asked, already knowing the answer by the look on his face.

"That's why I was calling. Ms. Holden asked me to saddle up Rosie about an hour-and-a-half ago. Said she was only taking her on a short ride since she wasn't familiar with the ranch. I advised her there was a storm moving in later this afternoon, and she said she wouldn't be gone long. She asked me to let you know, Tanner. I called and left a message on your cell that she took Rosie out."

"If I'd gotten the call, I'd have told you to not let her leave," I stated.

He rubbed the back of his neck. "When I couldn't get a hold of any of you, I figured we needed to get Ms. Holden back on in. I went looking for her. I figured she might have gone on the trail you all took the first time you went riding. Then I remembered that she mentioned the lake."

"The lake! Did you tell her how far off it was?" I nearly shouted.

He nodded. "I did, yes. She said okay, so I figured she wasn't heading up that way. I'm thinking she might have after all."

"I need help getting Pogo saddled up...and fast," I said.

"Jimmy, we need two more horses saddled up," I heard Ty say.

"Three," my father added.

"Dad, no. It's best if you stay here with Mom and the girls," Brock said.

Dad nodded, then looked back at the tack room. "You boys each take one of the walkie-talkies. I want you to check in every fifteen minutes. This storm could speed up even more. We've all seen it happen in the past; it can turn on a dime."

Brock quickly walked into the tack room and came out with the walkie-talkies and handed them out. "They're all charged."

"It's going to be okay," Kaylee said, but it felt like she was saying it more to herself than to anyone else. "She's an experienced rider. I'm sure she realized that the weather was turning bad too fast. She probably got twisted around and tried to find shelter for her and Rosie."

Ty walked over and kissed Kaylee on the forehead. "You're right, baby. Don't worry, okay? I'm sure she's fine."

She bit her bottom lip. "I won't. She'll be okay."

My mother and Kaylee stood off to the side as we got three horses saddled up with Jimmy's help.

Dad walked up and handed each of us a blanket. "Here, just in case."

The sound of something running toward us caught everyone's attention. Rosie was back. When she ran by us, though, my stomach dropped to the ground. No one was on her.

"Timberlynn!" Kaylee called out in fear.

"She's not on her," I said as I ran up and grabbed the reins, trying to calm down the mare.

"No! No! Where is she? Oh my God! Where is she!" Kaylee cried out.

Ty wrapped Kaylee up in his arms. "Hey, calm down, Kaylee, calm down. It's okay.

Rosie looked at me, fear in her eyes. I ran my hand down her neck to calm her down. "Where is she, girl?"

The horse bobbed her head and snorted a few times.

Kaylee turned and looked at me, tears already streaming down her face. "Tanner, you have to find her," she said between sobs.

I stood there, stunned, as I watched Rosie panting. She was out of breath. Something spooked her enough that she had run back to the barn. How far had she run, though? This horse knew the ranch just as well as I did. She would have easily been able to find her way back to the barn with Timberlynn on her back.

Staring into her eyes, I willed her to tell me where Timberlynn was.

"Tanner!" Kaylee shouted. I jumped, then looked at her. "Find her!"

"She came down the trail that goes to Crystal Lake," I said as I thought about getting on Rosie, thinking she might lead me back to Timberlynn. But she was clearly exhausted from running. I leapt up onto Pogo, reached for the walkie-talkie my father held out and took a deep breath.

"Channel three?" I asked my father.

"Yes." I walked Pogo over to Ty. "Someone needs to get the pasture horses in. You and Jimmy take care of that. Brock, you head toward the ridge I took Timberlynn to—she might have gone that way and Jimmy missed her. I'll head toward the lake."

He nodded. "Okay, be careful."

"Every fifteen minutes!" my father called out. "And if you don't find her in an hour, I'm calling the sheriff."

Chapter Twenty-Two

TIMBERLYNN

The storm had literally come out of nowhere with wind so strong it nearly knocked me off Rosie. I had stayed on the trail that Jimmy told me led to Crystal Lake. He was right. It was too far. Now I was beginning to see why he didn't want me heading this way. A large gust of wind rushed by, and I heard a cracking sound above me. Rosie reared up when the tree limb fell in front of us, and I fell off her. I couldn't believe my eyes when I saw her turn and run back down the trail we had just come up on.

"Seriously, Rosie? You're just gonna leave me?" I shouted.

She kept running, so I nodded and sighed. "Okay! Go get help," I called out like a crazy person.

I went to stand and instantly felt a pain in my ankle. I dropped back down and hissed as the pain shot through my entire foot. "Shit. Shit. Shit."

Ugh. Why had I thought this was a good idea? The lake hadn't really seemed that far away, but I had known better than to try when I knew a storm was coming. I was the only one to blame here. "I should have listened to Jimmy."

With a quick look around, I took in the area. This part of the ranch was covered in more trees. One area I saw offered a bit of shelter from the wind. It was only a few feet from the trail.

I closed my eyes and prayed my cell phone hadn't gotten damaged in the fall. I pulled it out of my back pocket and sighed with relief when I saw it wasn't broken. But when I slid my finger to open the phone, I nearly cried out in frustration. "No signal. Crap!"

I opened up the text messages and sent a text to Tanner, just in case the service was spotty.

Me: I'm on the trail that leads to the lake. Tree fell. Rosie got spooked. I'm okay, but I hurt my ankle. Staying put until someone can find me.

I hit send, but it didn't say it was delivered.

Rosie would most likely head back to the barn and alert everyone I was gone. They'd search for me, so it was best I stayed put and close to the trail.

"Okay, so rule number one in Montana. When a storm is coming in, don't go for a ride like an idiot," I said as a gust of wind whipped a light dusting of snow around me. I wrapped my scarf tighter around my face and pulled my hat down more. The only thing showing was my eyes. So far, I was okay, just a little chilled. My ankle throbbed, but I didn't think it was broken. Or maybe that was wishful thinking on my part.

"Stupid storm! You weren't supposed to come in until tonight!" I cried out as I looked up at the mountains looming above over the trees. I could see the storm moving in, and it didn't look good. I dropped down and leaned back against a tree. The sound of the wind blowing through the trees was actually calming, so I concentrated on listening to it and trying not to panic.

It had been thirty minutes since Rosie had taken off back toward the barn, and I was beginning to feel colder. I pushed back into the bushes that surrounded the group of trees I was sitting near the best I could, but I still wanted to be able to see the trail. I wasn't worried...well, at least until I looked to the north and saw the clouds moving in closer.

"Wow. I'm going to guess that's snow," I mumbled as I pulled the scarf tighter around my face.

I dropped my head down and rested my forehead on my knees. My ankle still throbbed, but not as bad. I was positive it was because I was beginning to feel the effects of being in the cold. The temperature was dropping, and I didn't have a signal to find out how cold it had gotten. It was probably for the better that I didn't know the exact temperature—it would only make me panic.

A wave of exhaustion hit me, and I closed my eyes. Was this what hypothermia felt like? No. No, I wasn't going to think in the negative. "It's going to be okay," I mumbled. "Tanner will find me."

The colder I got, the more I could feel myself drifting off to sleep, and I fought to stay awake. But it was so damn hard to keep my eyes open. I needed to be able to hear or see if someone was coming down the trail.

Slowly I drifted off into a dream. Tanner stood before me, his blue eyes looking down at me. His hands cupped my face, and he gently whispered my name. "Timberlynn?"

"Yes?" I whispered back.

"Are you okay?" his soft, sexy voice asked.

"Hmm...I am now."

A soft chuckle came from his parted lips.

"Tanner, make love to me."

He smiled, but his voice sounded surprised. "Um... you're colder than I thought."

"I want you. Touch me."

"Timber, sweetheart, I need you to open your eyes."

"Your hands feel so warm."

Then his mouth pressed against mine, and my entire body melted into a puddle on the ground.

"Darlin', open your eyes for me. We need to get you out of here."

I smiled. I loved when Tanner called me darlin'.

Another soft kiss. "Wake up, baby."

I opened my eyes and saw a beautiful sea of pale blue so striking I was lost in it for a moment. I smiled and Tanner returned it with one of his own. It was mind-blowing to me how handsome he was. And that smile of his. The way it made the corners of his eyes crinkle ever so slightly. The blue seemed to light up the longer I looked into them. And words couldn't describe the way it made me feel inside. All I knew was I felt safe and cared for like never before.

"Hi," I said softly.

"You were dreaming?" he asked, his eyes drifting to my mouth, then back up.

"I was. About you."

"I'll admit, I'm pretty damn happy you said my name, or I was gonna have to kick the ass of whoever you were asking to make love to."

My cheeks heated, and a rush of embarrassment hit me. Tanner noticed and kissed me softly. "Let's get you out of the cold, shall we?"

"I think we should. I can't feel my body anymore."

He gave me a once-over. "Are you hurt?"

My chest fluttered with a feeling that I was becoming all too familiar with when it came to Tanner Shaw. Was this what falling in love felt like? Because I hadn't felt this ever before. The way he made me feel like I was his everything. Was it just a silly notion, because for the first time in my life, someone looked at me like I *was* their everything?

With a slow, deep breath in, I stared at him, suddenly unable to find words. Snow started to softly fall all around us, and for one crazy moment I couldn't help but think how romantic this was. The wind howling through the trees, the snow falling, and the way Tanner looked at me with such a caring expression. From the moment Tanner had entered my world, it felt like something deep inside me had awakened. I was seeing everything in color instead of dull grays. I hadn't even known the difference until I experienced it.

"My ankle, I don't think it's broken, but to be honest, I haven't tried walking on it."

Tanner moved back and looked down at my feet. "Which one?"

"The left one."

He nodded, then stood. "Here, let's stand up slowly."

I reached for his hands and allowed him to help me up. As I put pressure on my ankle, I let out a small yelp. "Ouch! Okay, it hurts."

Tanner cursed, pulled out a walkie-talkie from his jacket, and talked into it. "I've got her. We're closer to the cabin on the lake than we are the house. Looks like she might have sprained her ankle and has a bit of hypothermia. I need to get her warmed up."

"Shit," came Ty's voice from the other end.

Ty Senior chimed in, "Take her to the log cabin, Tanner. I had Jimmy stock it with some food last week. The Millers were planning on staying at the cabin for the holiday. They canceled when they saw the storm coming in."

"That's luck!" Brock added.

"Sounds good." Tanner pulled my body tighter against him as we stood there. "We're heading there now. I'll check in once I get Timberlynn warm and settled."

"Got it," his father said.

"Hold this," Tanner said as he handed me the walkie-talkie, then he bent down and lifted me up. He carried me over to Pogo and put me up on the horse. Then he jumped on and sat behind me. He took the walkie-talkie from me and winked. I was stunned when I heard a girlish giggle slip from my lips.

Tanner pressed the button and spoke. "Dad, I've only got one problem. Pogo. Is there hay or anything in the barn for him? What about the water trough?"

"There's hay; I always keep it stocked just in case," Ty answered instead of their father. "As far as the water goes, you're gonna have to keep checkin' on it. Hopefully it won't freeze too bad since that barn is pretty well built and will keep all the wind out."

"Sounds good," Tanner said, then handed the walkie-talkie to me again and said, "Hang on."

He gave Pogo a kick and got him going into a trot. The cold wind felt like knives hitting me, and my body trembled.

"You okay?" he called out over the wind. I put up a thumb to indicate I was, even though I was far from okay. I was freezing, and the faster we got inside, the better.

Tanner was right—we were close to the lake and log cabin. I gasped at the sight before me as we approached. "Goodness, it's beautiful!" I took in the frozen lake and mountains that surrounded us. Sitting across from the lake was a log house that was most certainly not the little cabin I had envisioned in my mind. It was a one-story log home with a large front porch and windows that made me itch to see what the view was from the inside looking out. A small little wooden bridge was built over a creek that fed into the lake.

"I've never in my life seen anything so beautiful! Why don't your parents live here?" I asked as Tanner laughed. To the side of the house was a large wooden barn.

"The barn!" I gasped.

"That barn is my pride and damn joy. Brock, Beck, and I built that barn with our father. Ty was already out on the circuit and helped when he came back into town, but it was mostly me, Beck, and Dad who built it."

"Tanner, it's...it's beautiful," I said as he drew closer to it.

The lake was a lot bigger than I thought it would be, but then I shouldn't have been surprised considering I could see it from the main barn on the ranch. I couldn't help but smile. I knew this wasn't the most ideal situation to be in, but it occurred to me that Tanner and I would finally be alone. In this beautiful log home, on the lake, during a snowstorm. Fate had a funny way of showing up at times. My entire body trembled with anticipation, or from being cold as hell.

"We're almost to the house. We'll get you warmed up soon, babe," Tanner told me.

I shook my head and looked back at him. "It's not that. I just realized you and I are going to be completely alone."

A sexy grin appeared on his face. "That's definitely one way to warm you up." Tanner brought Pogo up to the house and jumped off. He motioned for me to lean forward so he could help me down.

"I think I can walk," I stated, but Tanner wouldn't let me. He carried me up the porch steps and to the front door. He punched in a code and then walked into the log house.

With a quick intake of air, I glanced around and instantly fell in love, almost forgetting how chilled to the bone I was. "This place is beautiful!" I said as Tanner set me down on the sofa and grabbed a small blanket and wrapped it around me.

"Wait right here. Let me go get Pogo settled, and then I'll be back in. Are you okay until I get back?"

I nodded. "You don't need help?"

He laughed. "No, you get warm."

Not wanting to admit to Tanner how heavenly the heated house felt, I simply nodded.

After Tanner left and my body warmed up, I slowly stood and put weight on my ankle. It hurt, but I was pretty positive it wasn't broken. I took off my hat, scarf, gloves, and jacket, and then took the log house in. I was still shivering, but it was starting to settle down a bit more as I got warmer.

Before me was a giant, freestanding stone fireplace. Above the massive stone mantel was a family portrait of the Shaws. I smiled at the sight of the four brothers, much younger in the photo. Maybe high-school age. All handsome and all of them with blue eyes except for Beck. His green eyes nearly jumped out at you, they were so green. Stella and Ty Senior stood in the back, and I felt my smile grow across my face. Those boys for sure got their looks from their daddy. And Stella, my goodness was she beautiful.

I turned and stared out the large wall of windows that overlooked the frozen lake. I slowly shook my head and sat down on the sofa. "Wow." It was the only word that seemed to come to mind as I stared at the view. The storm was moving in, and it was getting darker out, but I still had a clear view of everything. Including the snow that was now falling on the other side of the lake. It was coming our way.

I turned and focused on getting the boot off of my sore ankle. When I finally got it and my sock off, I grimaced. It was very swollen and now bruised. I let out a frustrated sigh. I was so angry with myself for taking Rosie out. I had been itching to ride, but I should have heeded Jimmy's warning.

Dropping back against the sofa, I stared at the ceiling and started to go over the plans I had for my own little ranch. A smile spread across my face as I thought about all the things I couldn't wait to do. It would never be as amazing as this house was with its view, at least from the little I'd seen of it, but it would be all mine.

When I heard the front door open, I lifted my head and saw Tanner. He shook off some snow. "It's snowing on this side of the lake now?" I asked.

"Yeah, it's coming down pretty good. I'm so glad I found you when I did."

I chewed nervously on my lip. "I'm so sorry, Tanner. It was stupid of me to go for a ride, but I honestly didn't think the storm would move in until later this afternoon."

Tanner hung up his coat and scarf, and dropped his gloves onto a table by the front door. He walked over and grabbed all my stuff to hang it up as well. "Don't beat yourself up about it. I'm kind of glad you got yourself lost in the woods."

With a grin, I asked, "Why?"

With his hands motioning around him, he replied, "Look where we are. Alone."

My cheeks grew hot.

"Let me take a look at that ankle," he said. He walked over and crouched down in front of me, gently touching around my foot. "It's swollen, but I think you're right. If you had broken it, it would look and feel a lot worse. Trust me, I know."

I let out a soft laugh. Tanner gently massaged my foot, which caused me to let out a soft moan of pleasure. Even with the tenderness in my ankle, it felt so good to have his warm hands on me. The feeling left me a bit breathless. A warmth rushed through my veins, instantly making my body heat and the pain in my ankle fade to a dull throb. A new throb between my legs was taking precedent.

He took off my other boot and sock and massaged that foot as well, only this time more aggressively since it wasn't injured. "You've had an adventure, haven't you? What happened with Rosie?" Tanner asked.

My eyes had closed, but at the mention of the horse, I opened them again. "She didn't make it back to the barn?"

"Oh, she did. She was in a fit; that's when we really panicked because you weren't with her."

A crackling sound came from behind Tanner. His father's voice said, "Tanner?"

Tanner reached behind and grabbed a walkie-talkie from his back pocket. "We're in the house, Dad. I got Pogo in the barn with some hay. He's got a blanket on and I was able to fill up the water for the trough. It's pretty toasty in the barn, so I don't think the water will freeze, but I'll keep an eye on it. Timberlynn and I are in the house. I'm looking at her ankle, then I'll get us settled. Looks like we'll be staying here through the storm."

"Sounds good. Check in with us, though, okay? Don't forget, the landline still works up there."

"We'll be fine, Dad. Don't worry. Let Kaylee know I'll keep Timberlynn safe." Tanner shot me a smirk and then winked.

"Will do. Stay warm and pray we don't lose power."

"Talk soon, Dad."

Tanner set the walkie-talkie down on the table and stared at me, the corner of his mouth tilted up ever so slightly. His eyes sparkled like stars in the night sky.

My chest bubbled with excitement at the look in his eyes, and it nearly had me reaching for him and begging him to kiss me. Anticipation raced through my body as he stared at me. I'd never wanted anyone to touch me, to hold me, to make love to me like I wanted Tanner to in this very moment. "What is this feeling?" I whispered.

He smiled and pushed a piece of hair behind my eyes. "I'm not sure, darlin'."

I closed my eyes and leaned into the hand he placed on the side of my face. "When I'm with you, I feel like I'm floating away from everything. I'm in a bubble of pure happiness. I have to keep asking myself if this is all real."

"It's real, Timber." Tanner leaned in and gently kissed me. The kiss was tender, almost shy at first. His tongue ran along my lips, causing me to open to him. The moment his tongue touched mine, a zap of energy raced between us. Tanner let out a soft moan, and I nearly melted. Then, the sweet heat was gone as fast as it came. Before the kiss could get out of control, Tanner pulled back.

He leaned his forehead against mine and attempted to control his breathing. Then, he smiled and said, "It's like a freefall."

I smiled as I let out a soft chuckle. "It does feel like that."

"Let me get a fire going and look at our food. If I don't, I'm going to peel your clothes off right here on the sofa, and we'll never have the energy for the things I plan on doing to you."

"Oh," I said, thinking that sounded like a rather good idea.

Tanner got up and walked over to the fireplace. He placed a few logs on it and then opened up a fire starter and slid it under the wood before he lit it. Soon the soft glow from the roaring fire sent shadows cascading across the logs. It gave off a romantic feel as I glanced around and really took everything in. I was on a simple tan leather sofa with two matching chairs that sat on each side. In the middle was a large wooden coffee table. Across the room was a dining room with a farmhouse table that sat four. One large picture window took up a good portion of the entire exterior wall.

I stood and turned around the best I could on one foot. The interior walls were all logs, with windows sprinkled throughout to take advantage of the lake and what I imagined were stunning mountain views. I looked up and saw wood plank ceilings with wooden beams going across. An antler chandelier hung from the ceiling and I smiled. That was certainly the touch of Ty Senior. Gently, I put a bit of weight on my foot as I walked.

"Hey, what are you doing?" Tanner said, coming to take hold of me.

"I wanted to see the rest of the house."

He bent to pick me up, and I stopped him. "No, let me walk on it some."

"It might be more than a sprain, Timber."

"I'll let you know if it becomes too painful."

Tanner drew in a deep breath, then sighed. "You are stubborn, aren't you?"

I flashed him my sweetest smile. He shook his head and let me put my weight on him as we walked into the kitchen.

"Wow! This kitchen is beautiful!" Dark walnut cabinets with a light gray tumbled tile backsplash gave the kitchen a simple yet elegant look. The stone counters, light in color as well, made the room feel bigger and airy. A vintage stove in cream and black served as the centerpiece for the entire kitchen. Another large window sat over the sink. "This is my dream kitchen!"

Tanner laughed. "Really? My father and I actually made all the cabinets in here."

"Shut up! Seriously?" I asked as I looked back at him.

"Yep. I'll be sure to tell him how impressed you were with them."

I chuckled and walked through the kitchen. "I may have to hire you both for my place."

"No hiring necessary, babe, I'll gladly do anything you need me to."

Wanting to continue the tour, I asked, "How many bedrooms are in the house?"

"Three bedrooms and two baths. My uncle Rob first built the log cabin, but it started out much smaller, and after he died, Granddad and my father added onto it and made it bigger. Family and friends can stay here when they visit if they don't want to stay at the main house. Most of the time, though, it sits empty. I've always had it in the back of my mind that I would live here someday."

"I'm surprised Brock and Ty haven't claimed it," I said.

Tanner chuckled. "I think they know it means more to me. Beck and I worked on the house a lot with my father, and then after Beck died, it was a project Dad and I finished up."

I could hear the pride, as well as the emotion, in his voice. "It would be a beautiful place to live."

He nodded. "I think so. But who knows what will happen?"

Tanner showed me a mudroom, a guest bedroom, another room that was set up as an office, and then the master bedroom. It was simple in size, but the massive logs and large windows made it all so beautiful. There was a screened-in porch off of the master bedroom, and I imagined it would be perfect during the summer. Large windows covered the entire wall of the master bedroom. The bathroom was also simple in size, but so beautifully done. The stand-up shower had a window in it damn near from the floor to the ceiling.

"It's like we stepped outside with all these windows," I softly said as I hobbled up to the large window to watch the snow falling outside. "Does it always snow like this in the winter?"

Tanner walked up beside me. "Sometimes, but not often. We'll get the normal snowstorms that pass through, but this one is going to dump a lot of snow. We're probably going to have to have Ty or Brock plow the road to the cabin and bring Pogo back in the trailer."

My chest pinched with the sudden rush of anxiety. Living in Atlanta, I had never really experienced being snowed in before. "You're kidding...it's going to snow that much?"

He nodded as he stared out the window.

I swallowed hard and asked, "How long will we have to be here, do you think?"

He shrugged. "Most likely just for a night, maybe two depending on how fast it moves out."

My eyes closed, and I inwardly cursed myself. "I'm so sorry, Tanner." I looked down at the floor. "It's because of me we're stuck and you're not with your family right now."

He placed his finger under my chin and lifted my head so that our gazes locked. "Trust me when I say this, I would much rather be trapped in this cabin with you for a few days. I'm sure we can find all kinds of interesting things to pass the time while we're here."

"That does sound rather nice. It will give us a chance to get to know one another even more."

He raised his brows, and I couldn't help but shake my head and laugh at him. "Stop it."

Tanner cleared his throat and glanced over toward the bathroom. "Listen, why don't you take a warm shower? You'll feel better. I've got some spare clothes in the master bedroom. I'll turn up the heat in here so it gets warmer. Then, let me go see what they stocked the kitchen with, and we can eat an early dinner."

He looked at his watch. "It's almost four, so by the time you shower, and I get something made, it'll be perfect timing."

"Sounds good," I said as I limped my way back into the master bathroom. It had the same dark cabinets as the kitchen. There was also a large soaking tub tucked into a little corner that had picture windows on all three sides. Nothing fancy, but enough room for two people to soak in it. I quickly pushed away the visual of Tanner and me in that tub together.

I placed my hands on my instantly hot cheeks and smiled.

Two sinks sat next to each other on the stone counter. It was the cutest bathroom I'd ever seen, and I couldn't help but wish for the briefest moment that this house was for sale.

I quickly stripped out of my clothes, turned on the hot shower and stepped in. It took a few moments for me to relax as I stared at the window and wondered if anyone might be able to see me. With a laugh, I brushed away my fear. Apparently, I was the only fool who went out riding with a storm on the horizon. Instead, I let the hot water run down my body and tried not to fantasize about Tanner being in this shower with me.

Chapter Twenty-Three

TANNER

After I heard the shower turn on, I made my way back to the kitchen and looked through the cabinets and refrigerator. There was plenty of food to last three to four days. I figured we'd be here for at least two.

I walked over to the landline and dialed my folks' number. My mother's voice came on the line. "Tanner, how is Timberlynn doing?"

With a smile, I replied, "She's fine. The power is on here. How about there?"

"It's on here too. How's her ankle?"

"Not broken, but she twisted it pretty good."

Mom sighed. "There should be some aspirin or Tylenol in the master bathroom in the cabinet."

"Okay, I'll be sure to check if she hasn't already. She's taking a shower."

"Thank goodness your father had Jimmy bring in that food. The storm looks to have stalled. You might be there until at least tomorrow afternoon."

"Don't worry, Mama, it's not going to be a hardship."

She laughed. "No, I imagine it won't. I'm sure Timberlynn wouldn't have gone out if she had known how fast this storm was moving in."

I rubbed the back of my neck and looked toward the hall where Timberlynn was in the master suite. I could hear the water running, so I knew she was still in the shower. "Yeah, she feels bad about it."

"Well, I might as well tell you because I'm sure Timberlynn is going to find out soon enough."

My heart dropped to my stomach. "Tell me what?"

"Your daddy ran into Richard Covey earlier. He mentioned something about Timberlynn buying the family property and Richard seemed surprised by it."

The sound of my heart beating in my ears made it almost hard to hear my mother's words. "He didn't know the family was selling?"

"He knew, but he told your daddy plans had changed. When your father asked him for more details, he simply said they had a better offer."

I closed my eyes and cursed inwardly. "She was really looking forward to that place, Mama."

"I know she was, son."

"Should I say something?"

"I wouldn't—just let it be for now. There isn't anything she can do being stuck out there, and I'm sure she's already feeling a bit stressed. The poor girl doesn't need another knockdown right now."

I remained silent on the phone as an idea hit me. A crazy, insane, brilliant idea.

"Sweetheart, is everything okay?" my mother asked.

"Yeah, yeah, everything is fine. I just had an idea pop into my head."

"What kind of idea?"

I looked around the cabin. "One that might be moving a bit too fast for Timberlynn."

It was her turn to be silent. "Lord, don't even tell me. Let's just make it through this storm first, okay?"

I nodded, even though she couldn't see me. "Are you and Dad okay? Did Ty or Brock make sure you had enough firewood? You're okay with food?"

A light chuckle filtered through the phone. "Who's the parent here, Tanner?"

"Sorry, I can't help but worry. It seems like a pretty bad storm."

"If you happen to remember, your father and I have lived through plenty of them over the decades. We're fine. Your father can always go out and get more wood. We're planning on camping out here in the living room in case the power goes out, so we'll have the fire."

I grinned. There wasn't a doubt in my mind that my father would take full advantage of that. He was, after all, a Shaw.

"You take care of our girl, okay?" Mom said.

My gaze drifted back toward the master bedroom. "Our girl?" I asked in a teasing tone.

"Yes. *Our* girl. She might not have been in our world for very long, but I adore her. And I'm pretty positive that you do too."

I rubbed my chest to ease the ache there. It was becoming a familiar feeling every time I thought about or saw Timberlynn. "I adore her, Mama."

The line was silent for a moment. "I know you do, Tanner. Check in before you go to sleep and in the morning."

"Will do. Goodnight, Mama, I love you."

"Oh, sweetheart, I love you too."

The line went dead, and I hung up. The shower had stopped, and I walked back over and took out bacon, lettuce, and tomatoes. I grabbed the bread and pulled out four slices and put them in the toaster. I searched for the right type of frying pan, and soon had some bacon cooking. I turned the heat down to low and set off for the master bedroom.

I sat down on the bed next to her. "I'm cooking up some bacon for BLTs. Does that sound okay?"

"Sounds good."

Timberlynn sat on the edge of the bed and stared down at the floor. The look on her face was one of utter devastation.

"Hey, are you okay?"

She nodded, then looked up at me and slowly shook her head to indicate she was indeed not okay. It looked like she was about to cry at any moment.

My heart raced in my chest and I tried like hell to keep my breathing controlled. She held her phone in her hand, and I glanced down to see she had an email pulled up.

"Do you have service?" I asked.

She slowly shook her head. "No. The realtor emailed me earlier, and I downloaded the message but wanted to wait until I got back to read it."

Her voice sounded defeated and I hated that. "Do you want to tell me what's wrong?"

"I lost the Covey property."

I dropped my head and stared at my hands. I wanted to tell her that I already knew, but I kept quiet.

"The realtor said they had a higher bid on the property, and they went with that person."

"I'm so sorry, Timberlynn. You'll find something else."

She wiped a tear away that had slipped free and shook her head. "Tanner, that property was perfect. And it doesn't even matter. Even if I do find something, he won't let me buy anything. He'll just keep outbidding me."

"Who?" I asked, instantly feeling a sense of anger that someone was fucking around with her.

Timberlynn blinked back tears and looked at me. "My father."

Now I was confused. "What does your father have to do with the Covey property?"

"He bought the Covey property. He outbid me on it and told me in an email he would keep outbidding me if I didn't give up this...as he put it, 'silly little dream of mine', and come back to Atlanta."

Anger moved through my body so fast it caused me to stand. "Your father was the one who outbid you? How in the hell did he even find out you were buying the place?"

She sighed. "Cory, my financial advisor, told him."

"Is he allowed to tell him that information?"

"It wasn't anything like that. He ran into him at a benefit dinner. Cory mentioned something about me being so in love with Montana and how happy he was I found a place to purchase. My father played it off at first, went along with him. He got information out of Cory by playing along, pretending that he knew I was here. Cory didn't know my father wasn't privy to that information."

"So, your father is pissed you're in Montana. He does realize he doesn't get a say in where you live or what you do with your life, right?"

Timberlynn stared down at her phone and then turned to face me. "This is what he's always done, Tanner. He attempts to control my life the only way he's ever known how. Money. Now that I have my own, this is the only way he thinks he can control what I do. He's upset with me that I left Georgia and didn't tell him. He's even more upset that I walked away from my nursing job. In some weird way, I think he thinks he's helping me."

"Helping you? By keeping you from your own damn dreams?"

She nodded.

"That doesn't make any sense."

Timberlynn exhaled and dropped back onto the bed, staring up at the ceiling. "I know it doesn't. I don't know what to do, short of changing my name and moving somewhere he can't find me. And I don't want to do that. I really do love my father, and I was hoping once I got settled, I could talk him into coming out here. Seeing how happy I am. Part of this is my fault for leaving and not telling him. I know he's more upset about that than anything. And to be honest, I've never told my father about wanting to own my own business."

She covered her mouth to keep from crying. I grabbed her hand and pulled her up. "Hey, no crying allowed, or you're going to make me want to hunt your father down and punch him for making my girl cry."

The corner of her mouth rose into a slight smile. "Your girl?"

I nodded. "Yes. You're my girl, and I'm going to make this right. I think I might have an even better solution. Will you give me a week or so to figure something out?"

She tilted her head and smiled at me. "Tanner, it is so sweet of you to want to come to my rescue. But I don't need a knight in shining armor. I just need you to support me. And I'm afraid the Covey place is gone."

"I'm not talking about the Covey place. Will you trust me with something?"

A skeptical look moved over her face.

"Timberlynn, I'm not asking you to let me rush in and be your savior, I'm asking you to let me come up with another solution for *you* to decide on. I think I might know of a property you'll love even more than the Covey ranch, and I sort of have my own selfish reasons behind it. I'll admit, it's kind of crazy, and I might very well spook you, but I really need you to trust me."

I took her hands in mine. She looked so sad, yet so intrigued. "Please, will you trust me?"

She smiled. "Yes, I'll trust you."

"Good. Now let me kiss you really quick and then go flip the bacon, because I think it's burning."

With a laugh, she leaned closer to me and I met her halfway. A quick kiss and I stood to leave. "Mom said there's aspirin in the bathroom cabinets. You might want to take some."

"I will," she said with a sweet smile.

At least she was smiling now and not on the verge of tears any longer. I'd take that as a win.

◆ ◆ ◆

Timberlynn snuggled against me on the sofa as we silently watched the fire flicker in the fireplace.

"That was the best BLT I think I've ever had," she mused.

With a laugh, I kissed her on the head. "Flattery will get you everywhere, Ms. Holden."

Her laugh vibrated against me. I looked down and saw the oversized T-shirt she had on. It was an old one of mine that I had left here at some point in the past when I stayed in the cabin. It wasn't unusual for me, Brock, and Ty to spend a few days here, especially during the spring and summer. Crystal Lake held a lot of memories for all three of us.

"How's your ankle?" I asked.

"Better. I think the hot shower and the aspirin really helped."

"Good, I'm glad it's feeling better."

She looked up at me and smiled and it felt like I forgot how to breathe for a moment. God, she truly was the most beautiful woman I had ever laid my eyes on.

I had to work at swallowing before I could make myself say anything. "You are...so beautiful."

Her cheeks turned bright pink. "I look like a mess."

I shook my head. "No, you're perfect."

She shyly looked back at the fire.

"I saw some ice cream in the refrigerator if you want dessert."

Slowly, she moved away from where she was sitting next to me and stood. She reached for me and I joined her.

We faced each other and Timberlynn gave me the sexiest smile I'd ever seen. "I'd like dessert, but not the kind you eat."

My damn knees nearly buckled under me. "Timber, are you sure?"

The way her eyes sparkled, turning dark with desire, told me everything she couldn't seem to say. I cupped her face in my hands and stared into those beautiful eyes of hers. They looked so green, reminding me of the pastures here on the ranch in spring. The gold specks could be flowers sprinkled around the land.

"I'd be content to simply hold you in my arms tonight if that was all you wanted from me," I said.

Her tongue came out and swept quickly across her dry lips. "I want you, Tanner. I almost feel like I could cry if I don't feel you touch me soon. We're finally alone," she said with a shy chuckle. "I...I need to feel you touch me."

I closed my eyes and let out a low, guttural growl. *Slow. You need to go slow.* Feelings of excitement and regret for wanting her so badly mixed together and left me feeling confused.

"Tanner?"

Her voice made me snap my eyes open.

She stepped closer and took the bottom of my shirt in her hands. She lifted it slowly as I reached behind my back and assisted her in getting it over my head. Her eyes drank in my upper body, and I loved seeing the lust written clearly on her face. I knew I had a nice body, hell, I worked hard for my muscular frame, and the fact that she enjoyed seeing it like this only made me want her to see more of my body. Timberlynn wasn't one for hiding her emotions, at least not when it came to me. She seemed to wear them so visibly on her face. In her eyes. The way she chewed on her lip or let her gaze roam freely over my body. I loved how she looked at me.

"You're incredible," she whispered as she placed her palm on my chest over my heart. Her eyes lifted to mine. "Your heart, it's beating so fast."

All I could do was nod. She smiled and the room felt like it moved under my feet. I had to concentrate on not stumbling, and I reached out for her to hold me up. I'd never experienced this feeling before when I was with a woman. I knew I never would again. "I feel like this is my first time," I said honestly.

She shyly looked down. "You know I'm not a virgin, but I don't have a lot of experience. It wasn't because of lack of interest on my end." A small, nervous laugh slipped from her lips. "I'm honestly terrified of you being bored."

I placed my finger on her chin and bent down to look into her eyes. "I can promise you right now, I'm not going to be bored. And if something doesn't feel right, or you're not comfortable, you'll tell me, right?"

She nodded. "I promise I'll tell you."

I lifted the T-shirt and gently pulled it over her head. She wasn't wearing a bra, so her breasts were the first thing I saw. I suddenly forgot how to speak. "I...um... can't...think," I stammered.

Timberlynn placed her finger on my chin and closed my mouth as she let out a giggle. "They're only breasts, Tanner."

I slowly shook my head. "No, Timber, they're so much more. You are so much more. You're perfect in every way,

Even my dreams weren't this good, and I haven't even touched you yet."

Her eyes searched my face, and I saw something that looked like a trace of worry between her brows. But then she smiled. "I don't want to let you down."

It was my turn to laugh. "Please, woman, that is not going to happen."

I let my gaze linger on her mouth as she dug her teeth into her lip once more. With a whisper so low I nearly didn't hear, she said, "Make love to me, Tanner."

I swept her off her feet so quickly that she let out a small yelp, then laughed. "Tanner!" she cried out as I nearly hurdled the sofa and made my way to the master bedroom.

When I got into the room, I gently laid her on the bed. "Do you want me to tell you one of the many fantasies I've had about you over the last few months, Timber?"

With a nod, she replied, "Yes. Tell me."

"I lie you down on my bed and kiss you slowly, everywhere. I learn what parts of your body make you tremble with desire. I learn where and how to make you come so hard you scream my name."

Her mouth dropped open, and she sucked in a breath of air. I liked that my words had that effect on her. I could see her breathing get faster.

"Then I slowly make love to you until we both lose ourselves in each other."

Timberlynn's eyes closed, and I climbed onto the bed and kissed her face softly. "Are you okay?" I asked, my lips still pressed to her cheek.

"More than okay."

"Why the tears, darlin'?"

Her eyes met mine. "You have a way of making me feel so...desired. They're not sad tears, I promise."

"Good," I said as I kissed her lips softly. "Now, you tell me one of your fantasies, and I'll see what I can do to make it come true."

I stood and unbuttoned my jeans. I'd already kicked off my boots after dinner when we were sitting on the sofa together. Timberlynn kept her eyes locked on my hands, not speaking, and when I pushed my jeans down, I tried not to laugh at how she stared at me. Then she looked up at me and grinned. "Boxers? I wouldn't have pegged you for that type of guy."

"Really? Some days I go commando," I said as I shed the boxers and dropped them next to my jeans.

That caused her eyes to darken with lust as she knelt on the bed and slowly pushed her panties down. It was my turn to stare. I had to clench my fists together to keep from pulling her to me and going all caveman on her.

With her finger, she motioned for me to come closer to her. Both of us now completely naked. This moment felt crazy right. Like every other path we had taken in our lives had brought us to this very point in time.

Timberlynn placed her hand on my chest as her mouth curved into a soft smile. She slowly moved her hand downward, letting only two of her fingertips touch me as she went. My entire body shook with anticipation and she saw it. "I've dreamed of you looking into my eyes as you made love to me. I wondered so many times what it would feel like to have you inside me. Claiming me... making me yours."

I hissed when she ran her thumb over the head of my cock. Then she shocked the shit out of me and put her thumb into her mouth and tasted my pre-cum. Her eyes closed and she moaned ever so slightly.

"Fucking hell, Timber. Are you trying to kill me?"

She flashed me such an innocent expression that I nearly begged her to do it all over again.

"I've never had anyone kiss me on my—" Her voice trailed off as a blush moved over her cheeks.

"Never?"

She shook her head.

"Is that something you want me to do?"

Shyly, she nodded. "I've never given a guy a blowjob, so if you want me to…"

I shook my head and quickly cut her off. Lord, what an inexperienced idiot her ex must have been.

"I'm not going to ask you to do that to me tonight, baby. I want this to be about your fantasies, not mine."

"That is one of my fantasies, Tanner. To do that to you. To make you feel good by using my mouth."

When she wrapped her hand around my cock, I jumped and gasped. "Shit. You can't say those things and touch me like that at the same time. I won't last long enough to even kiss you without clothes on, darlin'."

It was taking all my control not to lose myself in her hand as she gently stroked me. "I want you, Tanner."

My cock was so damn hard, it ached to be inside her.

I cupped her face with my hands and brought my mouth to hers. "Are you sure about this?" I asked, searching her face for any signs that she wasn't a hundred percent on board with what we were doing. "I want to make this perfect for you, baby."

She smiled against my lips. "It's already perfect, simply because it's you."

Chapter Twenty-Four

TIMBERLYNN

Tanner stared into my eyes as butterflies swarm in circles in my stomach. "Stop touching me, Timber, and get your sweet ass on that bed."

His words caused my stomach to drop, the pressure between my legs growing deeper. The anticipation of what was to come was almost unbearable. The urge to pull him on top of me and beg him was a breath away on my lips.

Tanner was about to make love to me. We were about to finish what we'd almost started the night he made me orgasm. All the nights I'd dreamed of this—I could hardly believe we were here. I almost wanted to cry I was so ready for him to make love to me.

I tried my best to smile as sexy as I could, but it only made me giggle, which Tanner seemed to like more. I moved myself farther up the bed while he crawled onto it. I jumped when his hands touched my hips. An intense rush of energy or desire—hell, I didn't know what it was at this point—moved across my body. I had never experienced this with another man before. That made it all the more special, knowing that it was Tanner who made me feel this way. Made me feel so wanted, so wet that I fought to keep from touching myself. My heart pounded loudly in my chest, and I silently wondered if Tanner could hear it. I swore I could almost feel my orgasm building in the pit of my stomach, and we hadn't even really started anything yet.

Tanner's eyes darted up to mine and I nodded. "It's okay, your touch...it feels like when you touch me my entire body is surged with..." I pulled in a much-needed breath of air. "With something I've never experienced before. It's almost making me dizzy."

A crooked smile played over his face, and he winked as he moved his hands slowly up my thighs. I should have felt embarrassed to be lying there on full display, but I didn't. I felt empowered. Sexy. In control. That was something I was not used to at all.

Tanner let his eyes move slowly over my entire body as he moved back up the bed and gently pressed his mouth to mine. The kiss was sweet, yet full of passion. His hand went to one of my breasts and he cupped it gently before he moved onto my nipple. A gentle squeeze between his fingers had me moaning as I arched my back off the bed. It felt exquisite. I wanted more. *Needed* more. The need to come grew stronger, and I longed to touch myself to ease it.

"Are you wet for me, Timber?" he whispered against my lips.

I closed my eyes and felt myself holding my breath as he moved his hand down between my legs. *Yes! Yes!*

Please touch me there. The moment he touched my clit, I nearly came undone.

"Oh, shit!" I cried out. My body trembled, and I knew it wouldn't take much for me to come. I dragged in a quick breath and called out his name. "Tanner."

His mouth was back on mine as he slipped one finger inside me, then two. We both moaned, and my hips lifted as I silently begged him for more. I was positive the bedroom was cold, but all I felt was a heat building so intensely I thought I might combust from it.

He pressed his palm against my clit, and I rubbed myself against him. I didn't care that it made me seem desperate. I was. So very desperate for all the dreams I've had of this man to come true. Him kissing me. Touching me. Making love to me. God help me, I had even dreamed of him doing naughty things that I had heard Candace and Kaylee talk about. The last few weeks of being near him had nearly driven me insane. When I was with Tanner, everything else in the world faded away. It was only the two of us. The pulse of passion, desire, need, and maybe even love, rushed through my body as he moved his fingers in and out of me, bringing me to the edge of pleasure.

"Please. More," I gasped.

"Does it feel good, having me touch you?" Tanner softly asked as he placed soft kisses along my neck and down my chest.

I nodded, my hands fisting the sheets. "Y-yes. So...so good."

He took one of my nipples into his mouth and gently sucked on it.

"Oh God. That feels so good!" I panted as I arched my back to push my body closer to his mouth. He liked teasing me. Driving me nearly mad. I wasn't sure how much more I could take before I finished myself off.

Then he removed his fingers and I whimpered in protest. Before I could say anything, his entire body shifted, and his head was between my legs. He kissed the side of my thigh, and I melted into the bed. My body trembled with excitement, excitement for the unknown of what he was about to do to me, and my cheeks flushed with embarrassment. God, how I wanted his mouth between my legs. More than I had realized. Tanner was about to fulfill one of my fantasies, and my entire body trembled with anticipation.

My chest rose and fell as I lifted my head and watched him make his way between my thighs.

"May I?" he asked with a devilish grin on his handsome face.

I said the only thing I could manage to get out. "God, please."

Tanner chuckled, then leaned forward and licked me like I was his favorite ice cream cone, not once taking his eyes from mine. When the tip of his tongue flicked my clit, I gasped and dropped my head back onto the bed. It wasn't going to take me long to come, hell, if I hadn't known better, I would think it was already starting. My toes tingled, my lower stomach pulsed, and my clit throbbed.

My fingers pushed into his thick brown hair as he took my clit into his mouth and sucked gently. It felt heavenly. His fingers entered me once again, and everything exploded all at once. My orgasm hit me so fast, I cried out his name and surrendered to the most amazing pleasure I had ever experienced before in my entire life. I shamelessly pushed myself against his face and held him there as I tumbled into a euphoria of utter bliss. I cried out his name over and over until I heard myself begging him to stop. The orgasm was so intense...it felt like it would start to fade, only to explode once again.

He didn't stop though. Tanner sucked, nibbled, and licked while I fell apart into another mind-blowing orgasm. I was positive I would never experience anything like that ever again for as long as I lived. If I was even still alive after this was over.

"Oh, God! Tanner, stop! No...don't stop! Please. Oh my God!" I cried out as wave after wave of pleasure tore through my body. "Stop! I can't breathe!"

My fingers pushed into his soft brown hair, and all I could feel was myself rubbing against his face. When I couldn't take it any longer, I said the one thing I knew would make him stop.

"Tanner! Please! I need to feel you inside me."

He moved, and when I finally managed to open my eyes, I had to blink rapidly to see clearly. I heard something crinkle, and I watched as Tanner slid on a condom. The way his muscles flexed at the movement only turned me on more...if that were possible.

When he saw me staring at him, he said, "We're damn lucky I knew Ty had some stashed here in one of the bedrooms." He came back over to me.

"Spread your legs wider for me, baby," Tanner said, his voice sounded strained. As if he was having a hard time speaking.

I did as he asked, and when I felt his cock at my entrance, I tensed for a moment. A reflex because it had been a really, really long time.

Tanner's eyes met mine, and I instantly relaxed from the way he looked at me. Without saying the words, he was once again asking if I was okay with this. I smiled and nodded, granting him permission for what had been a long time coming. He laced his hand with mine and pushed it over my head as he used his other arm to keep himself from crushing me.

He opened his mouth to say something, but no words came out. I lifted my hips, pushing the tip of him inside me slightly, answering every question he might have had with that one movement. He closed his eyes and moaned in pleasure.

"Tanner, please," I begged.

When his eyes opened and met mine, he pushed slowly inside of me. His jaw muscles twitched as he moaned softly. "Jesus," he whispered.

"Yes, finally," I said as I squeezed his hand.

"God," he rasped. "You're so fucking tight."

I let my legs fall open more as I lifted my hips to him. He filled my body in the most delicious way. With Tanner, I knew I was giving a piece of myself to him, and I knew he would cherish it. I saw it in his eyes.

Once he was fully inside me, he paused, breathing heavily as he dropped his head down and buried his face in my neck.

I lifted my free hand and gently ran my fingers over his back. "Are you okay?" I asked in an unsure voice.

He looked up and met my gaze. Even though the room was dark, I could see those blue eyes of his. There was something so different about them. They seemed to be even more blue, if that was at all possible. God, he was so handsome. And he was mine. This incredibly amazing man was mine.

"Am I okay?" he asked with a slight chuckle. "I'm more than okay. I'm afraid if I move, I'm going to go entirely too fast. Need to focus for a moment is all."

I laughed and moved my hand to the side of his face. Tanner let my other hand go, resting on his elbows and cupping my face in his hands. "I'm falling in love with you, Timberlynn."

I gasped and felt my stomach flutter as my chest tightened in the most delicious way. I was filled with a rush of happiness that I'd never felt before, and it seemed to expand out into the rest of the room as well. I felt light. Unburdened by something that I hadn't even realized I had been carrying with me.

His eyes searched mine, and I knew I needed to be honest with him. "I believe I fell in love with you the first moment I saw you, Tanner."

A wide smile appeared on his face and he pressed his mouth to mine as he gently withdrew from me, then slowly pushed back in. The movement felt so amazing, I dug my fingers into his back.

If asked to describe what it felt like to have Tanner make love to me, I would fail. Words could never describe the sensation of him moving inside me. I was taken to another place. A beautiful meadow. Spring flowers in bloom. Riding free on the back of a horse with Tanner's arms wrapped tightly around me. This moment would be burned into my memory forever. He kissed me again, this time deeper. Then his pace picked up and I wrapped my arms and legs around him and found my own rhythm.

"Tanner...I need more."

He groaned and leaned his forehead to mine as he moved in and out of me a bit faster.

"Yes! Oh, God, yes!" I cried out. I'd never really been vocal during sex. Never telling my partner what I wanted. Embarrassed, maybe? But when Tanner asked me how it felt, I knew it was because he was solely focused on bringing me pleasure—so I told him exactly what I needed. Him. More of him.

"Timber, talk to me."

I lifted my hips to meet him thrust for thrust. "Harder. God, I need it harder and faster."

He gave me exactly what I asked for.

"I'm not going to last much longer," he said. Then he moved, and I dug my nails into his back as a tingle started deep in my stomach and rushed up my entire body.

"Yes! Tanner, I'm going to come again!"

Never before had I come when a guy was inside me. Never. Friends of mine talked about how amazing it was to come that way, but I had yet to experience it. But with the way Tanner was moving, and how he was hitting something so deep inside of me, my toes curled and the room started spinning. "Tanner!" I cried out as an orgasm hit me once again. I could feel myself clench around him.

Tanner's body tensed, and he trembled as he buried his face into my neck. He lifted his head and our eyes met. "I'm going to come, Timberlynn," he panted out before he groaned again.

"Oh God," I said as another wave of passion rolled through me. Again?

Tanner's mouth claimed mine, and we fell apart together. For a brief moment I wished he hadn't been wearing a condom. The need to have him fill me popped into my head, but I pushed it away quickly. That was reckless thinking on my part.

Soon his body stopped moving and he hovered, keeping his weight slightly off me but not completely. The feeling of his body pressed against mine while he was still inside me was my new favorite thing. Both of us panted for air. I saw that the pulse on the side of Tanner's neck matched my own.

I placed my hand against the side of his face, and our eyes met once again.

He smiled. "That was...it was..."

With a nod, I simply replied, "I feel the same way."

He smiled, and if hearts really could skip a beat, mine did when I looked at that smile of his.

"I want to stay inside you forever. I don't want this moment to ever end," he whispered before he placed a soft kiss on my lips.

My heart hammered in my chest. "I would totally be okay with that."

After another few moments, Tanner kissed me quickly on the lips, then said, "Let me get us cleaned up."

He slowly pulled out of me, and I instantly felt the loss of him. I grabbed onto him and shook my head. "Don't leave, not yet."

Tanner smiled, but I saw the concern in his eyes. "I'm not going anywhere, Timber. I swear to you."

I nodded as I pushed the sudden wariness away.

"Let me take this off and bring back a washcloth for you."

My mouth opened to say something, but I quickly shut it. Was he really offering to take care of me after we just made love? The gesture was so sweet, I nearly swooned while lying down.

"Do you want to lie out by the fire or in here?"

"I want to stay in here."

He grinned, then kissed me. "Okay, be right back."

My body was completely relaxed, and my eyes drifted slowly shut. I opened them when I felt a warm washcloth between my legs. I smiled and let Tanner take care of me. I'd never been taken care of like this before. It warmed my entire body, and I couldn't help but let out a soft moan of pleasure as he moved the cloth over me. My body and my mind were hyperaware of his every touch.

Tanner removed the washcloth, walked into the bathroom and then made his way back to me. I watched in awe as he walked across the room completely naked, with no care in the world. Would I ever be that confident to just stroll naked in front of him?

Once he got into the bed, he pulled me to his side, covered us with the blankets, and we both sighed with contentment. "Is it wrong that I want you again so soon?" Tanner asked.

I grinned while I played with the hairs on his chest. "Not wrong at all, cowboy, the feeling's mutual."

Tanner reached for me and pulled me onto his body as I straddled him. I could feel his length already hard underneath me. I moved slowly and caused him to hiss. He grabbed my hips and raised a brow.

"I'm impressed, Mr. Shaw."

He laughed. "You should be."

Tanner reached for a condom, then flipped me over. He quickly rolled the condom on, then settled between my legs. "I plan on keeping you up all night, Ms. Holden."

My arms wrapped around his neck, and I pulled his mouth inches from mine. "If you meant that as a threat, it didn't work."

"No threat, simply a promise."

Tanner pushed inside me again, making good on his promise.

Chapter Twenty-Five

Tanner

I stared out the window as the snow slowly fell. Timberlynn and I had barely gotten out of the bed except to grab something to eat, take a shower, then climb back under the covers. The strangest sensation of warmth had filled my chest when I first made love to her last night. Or yesterday afternoon. Hell, I had lost track of time.

Timberlynn stirred in my arms, and I glanced down at the sleeping beauty and smiled, then turned my attention back to the snow. I had been up for over an hour trying to think of a way to pitch my idea to both my parents and to Timberlynn. She'd think I was insane—after all, we'd only known each other for a brief time. I had promised her we'd go slow, and this idea was definitely not slow and most definitely crazy. I had a feeling my folks would go for it. Even Brock and Ty would be on board. The one I worried about the most was Timberlynn and getting her to see why this plan would work.

Fingers gently moved across my lower stomach, and my body instantly became aware of her touch.

"Are you awake?" she softly whispered.

"Yes."

Moving her head, she propped her chin on her hand and looked at me. The sweet smile that she wore had my heart beating like a hummingbird's. I was definitely falling hard for this woman, and there was no doubt in my mind I wanted her in my future. "How's your ankle?" I asked.

"I feel a dull ache, but it's much better."

"Did you sleep okay?" I moved my hand lazily up and down her back.

Her cheeks turned slightly pink. "Considering you wore me out with the best sex of my life, and I had no choice but to pass out from exhaustion, yes, I slept the best I have in years."

My brow raised. "Best sex of your life, huh?"

She giggled. "Yes. It was. I don't even have words to describe what I feel like when I'm in your arms. It's... peaceful. It's just perfect."

I pulled her body a little closer, if that were even possible. I would crawl inside her if I thought I could. She was heaven on Earth. The one thing I had been longing for. My missing piece. "I feel the same way, darlin'."

She smiled. "I really hope this isn't a dream."

I pulled her on top of me and she sat up. Her blonde hair tumbled down and hid her breasts slightly. The feel of her sitting on me had my cock rock hard in an instant.

Timberlynn smiled and gently rocked against me. "But then I feel this, and I know it's definitely not a dream.

You bring something out in me, Tanner," she said shyly. "You make me feel so..."

"So what?" I asked as I lifted my hips and caused her to moan.

"Sexy. Powerful. Naughty."

I lifted up my pelvis once more as I waggled my brows. "I think you need to elaborate on the naughty thing."

She giggled. "Do you have another condom?"

That had me pause for a moment. "No, I don't."

Her eyes moved greedily over my body, and for a quick second I wanted to slip inside her free of a condom, but I knew that wasn't the smart thing to do.

Timberlynn looked as if she might have been thinking the same thing.

"I know of other ways to be naughty, and we don't need a condom," I said softly.

She smiled. "Is that so?"

I grabbed her ass and pushed up against her.

"Tanner," she gasped. "You're teasing me."

"Roll back over, baby. Let me make you come with my mouth again."

Her breath picked up in speed, and she rolled off of me and spread her legs. I held the laughter that threatened to escape. She definitely didn't hesitate.

I settled between her legs and licked slowly up to her clit. Timberlynn moaned in pleasure, then whispered, "Yes. Oh, that feels so good."

My fingers slipped inside her as I continued to suck on her clit. I could feel her pulse and squeeze against my fingers, and I damn near came.

I was in the middle of bliss when my cell phone rang.

"Is that...a phone?" Timberlynn asked in a pleasure-induced haze.

Fuck. I quickly moved and grabbed my cell phone from the side table. I saw my brother's name on the screen.

"It's Ty."

Timberlynn moaned, then grabbed a pillow and pushed it on her face as she laughed. "We always get interrupted by a Shaw."

"What the fuck do you want, Ty?"

I could hear Timberlynn's muffled giggle from under the pillow.

"Good morning to you too, baby brother."

"I'm busy, what do you want?"

He laughed. "Busy, huh? My guess is you probably don't want to hear that I was going to make my way to you with the plow."

"Don't you dare."

A roar of laughter came from the other side of the line. "I take it you two enjoyed your evening together."

"Again, what do you want, Ty?"

"You little ungrateful ass. I was calling to check up on you. Thought I might even risk my life to hitch up the plow and come save your ass."

"We don't need saving. We're absolutely fine, dipshit."

"I guess it's a good thing, then, since the snow is coming down again pretty hard."

"Good, leave us alone. And thanks for checking on us. Don't call for another twelve hours or so, at least."

I hit End as I heard the asshole laughing and tossed my phone onto the table. I made my way back over to where I was before.

Timberlynn smiled, and just as I was about to have my fill of her, the phone rang...again.

"Don't answer it!" Timberlynn said.

"It's not my phone. It's yours."

Timberlynn sighed and then sat up. "Where's my phone?"

"Sounds like it's in the kitchen."

"Then, leave it!"

It stopped ringing and we both smiled.

Timberlynn dropped back onto the pillow and I buried my face between her legs before anyone else could interrupt us again.

Then, Timberlynn's phone started to ring once more.

"Okay, I can't do this. What if it's important?" Timberlynn said. "Ugh!"

I moved and let her crawl off the bed. She grabbed a quilt that was on the back of a chair in the bedroom and made her way out of the room.

With a frustrated groan, I dropped onto my back. It was my turn to bury my face with the pillow. I heard Timberlynn answer the phone. "Hello?"

It sounded like she was walking back to the bedroom. "I don't need you checking up on me, I'm twenty-four years old."

Tossing the pillow off of me, I sat up.

"You stole it right out from under me!"

One quick look, and I found my jeans. Without a second thought, I got out of bed, pulled on my jeans and made my way out of the room. I could hear Timberlynn talking in the living room.

"Dad, you can't swoop in after years of having nothing to do with my life and then claim you're protecting me. I want to be in Montana. I'm staying here whether you like it or not."

I couldn't help but smile.

Timberlynn's head dropped, and I watched as her whole body seemed to slump. "Nursing was Mom's passion. Not mine. I wasn't happy. I'm not sure what she would say, Dad. She died when I was six. I barely remember her, and you never talked about her with me."

I made my way into the kitchen and opened up the cabinets. Surely Jimmy would have stocked the place with coffee. After another minute of looking, I finally found it. In the refrigerator. Okay, wasn't expecting it there.

Timberlynn sighed. "I'm not coming back to Georgia, Dad. I've met someone and..."

She looked over her shoulder to see me standing in the kitchen, holding a bag of coffee. A bright smile moved across her face. "And we're dating. I really like him. His name is Tanner. He's Kaylee's brother-in-law."

I winked and her cheeks turned pink. Then, her smile dropped, and she turned away from me.

A part of me wanted to pull the phone from her ear and listen to what her asshole father was saying. She wasn't speaking, so he must have been doing all the talking. I poured the ground-up coffee into the pot, filled it up with water, and hit the brew button. Then I made my way over to Timberlynn.

She sat down on the sofa and leaned back on it with her eyes closed. "I'm sorry you feel that way, but I'm not a child and I'm able to make my own decisions. I'm not asking you for any money, Dad. I have my own, remember? Yes, I'm sure you didn't mean to forget my birthday or Christmas. After all, I am your only child."

When I sat down next to her, she opened her eyes. I hated that she looked so sad. That defeated look she sometimes had in her eyes came creeping back in. "You do what you have to do, Dad. I need to go, there's a storm here and I need to take care of some things."

I could barely hear a man's voice coming through the phone. He didn't sound angry.

"Dad, my signal is bad. I can only hear every other word. Dad? Dad?"

She pulled the phone away and hit End.

"Do you want to call him back?"

She shook her head. "No, he said he was being paged." Timberlynn was holding the phone so tightly, her fingers were turning white. I reached over and gently took it from her hand, placing it on the sofa.

"Are you okay?" I asked.

She slowly shook her head and stared across the room. "He wants me to come back to Georgia. I just need a good talking to, he said. Like I'm a child."

I didn't say anything. Not because I didn't want to console her, but I honestly didn't know what to say. I got that her father was upset. She had left without telling him. Regardless of how often or not they talked, she was his only daughter.

"He's going to make this as difficult as he can, Tanner. He's already taken one piece of property from me. What's to stop him from doing it again and again?"

"We'll figure out a way, I promise."

Tears pooled in her eyes. "How can you promise that?"

I smiled and pulled her onto me. She straddled my legs and I pushed the quilt away from her shoulders, exposing her breasts. "I swear to you, Timber, I'll make it work. All of it."

My tongue flicked her nipple and she moaned as she dropped her head back. "Tanner. Make me forget it all."

Her words sounded needy. She pushed the quilt completely off of her and wrapped her arms around my neck.

I took in her body, and a rush of desire swept over me like wind in a storm. If she needed me to help her forget, I'd damn well help her forget.

"Christ, you're so damn beautiful," I whispered as I cupped her breasts in my hands and pulled her other nipple closer to my mouth. I sucked, pulled, and lightly bit on it as Timberlynn squirmed in my lap. When I felt her hands working to get my jeans unbuttoned, I lifted up and helped her pull them down, kicking them off like my life depended on it. We were both naked on the sofa, and a part of me knew we should stop; she was emotional after her phone call with her father. But she asked me to make her forget, and hell if I wasn't going to do everything in my power to do just that.

Timberlynn slid her warm pussy down onto my cock, and we both moaned as she rubbed against it. My mind went fuzzy with the feel of her against me.

"I want to stay like this forever. I don't want to think about what's waiting for us on the other side of the door," she said as she pushed her fingers into my hair and drew my mouth to hers. We kissed, and soon we were both lost to everything other than the feel of our tongues dancing together. Her breasts pressed against my chest nearly had me losing my mind. Things got hot and heavy real fast. My hands went to her ass, and I squeezed as she lifted up.

"Tanner, yes. Please," she begged as she rubbed against me.

Whatever she was doing to me, it was like I was floating above us on a high I'd never felt before. "Fucking hell, Timberlynn. God, don't stop."

She moved faster and the feeling started to take over. Oh hell, I was about to come.

I snapped my eyes open to see Timberlynn riding me. Her head dropped back. Her hands were on my chest and her mouth was shaped into a perfect O as she rode me. Her breasts bounced and I grabbed onto her hips, meeting her as I thrust up.

"Tanner, I'm going to come. Come with me. Please."

"Jesus," I hissed as I pounded into her harder—the sound of our bodies hitting together pushed me even more. "That's it, baby. God, I'm going to come."

And then everything exploded, and I came so hard I was pretty sure I saw God.

Timberlynn cried out my name, and suddenly I realized why it felt so damn good.

Oh, fuck. Fuck. Fuck. Fuck.

I was inside her. With no condom on.

My hands dug into her hips and stared at where we were still joined together. Timberlynn's head was down and she was breathing heavily.

"Timber, I'm so sorry. God, I've...I've never done that before. I've never..."

She lifted her head and looked at me, then down at the same place I'd looked only moments before.

I lifted her gently off of me and she reached for the quilt. "It's okay. We both got caught up in it all. It was my fault for..."

I pressed my finger to her mouth and shook my head. "No." I stood and pulled her to me. "It takes two, remember? I was caught up just as much as you. Hell, I think for a moment I must have blacked out when you sat down on my cock."

She giggled as I ran my hand up and down her back. I secretly wished the quilt wasn't between us.

"I'm so sorry I didn't realize before I came. We haven't even talked about birth control or anything. You know, that talk?"

"The talk?" she asked, a dazed expression on her face.

"Yeah, the one where we talk about past partners. I tell you I've never had sex without a condom because I'm a responsible guy and all, but after what just happened, you might question that."

Her eyes were gray today, and I wondered if it had anything to do with all the snow falling.

"Have you never, really?"

"Have I never really what?" I asked, my mind forgetting what we were even talking about as I got lost in those eyes.

"Had sex with anyone without a condom?"

I cleared my throat. "Oh, I've always worn a condom. I've never even come close to not wearing one, so I don't know what sort of bewitching spell you just put on me, but that was the first time."

Timberlynn's cheeks went pink. "Me too."

I smiled, not wanting to tell her I'd had my fair share of sexual partners, but nothing crazy like Chance or Dirk. Hell, not even as crazy as my two older brothers. I decided to let it go unless she asked.

"Are you on the pill?" I asked.

She shook her head and said, "No. But I can get on them, if you want. I really liked the way you felt inside me without a condom on."

My heart felt like it slammed against the wall of my chest. "Yeah, that was fucking phenomenal. I've also been regularly tested for STDs. That was drilled into me at an early age. Besides, I haven't been with another woman in months."

She nodded and looked down at the floor. I placed my finger on her chin and lifted until her eyes met mine. "We both know I haven't exactly been a Boy Scout when it comes to women, but I'm also not a manwhore. When I say I haven't been with anyone in months, I mean it. There hasn't been anyone since I met you last September."

Her eyes widened. "Why not?"

I shrugged. "They weren't you."

"Tanner," she whispered as she came up on her toes and kissed me. She slowly drew back, and I placed my forehead against hers.

"Babe, how soon can you get on the pill? I can drive you there myself through the snow if need be."

Timberlynn laughed. "I'll ask Kaylee who her doctor is and make an appointment."

"Sounds like a plan."

She looked down at my naked body and flashed me a sexy grin. "I know something else we can do to make me forget my father's call."

"More oral sex?" I replied as I waggled my brows.

"No," she said, laughing. "You could make me breakfast. Naked."

"As long as you don't request bacon, I'm totally down for that."

Chapter Twenty-Six

TIMBERLYNN

Tanner truly made me forget all about my father's phone call. First with the crazy hot sex on the sofa, then with cooking for me naked. It was the hottest thing I'd ever seen. He was so comfortable in his own skin, which made him even sexier. Of course, midway through cooking he did get dressed, as did I.

I leaned back in the chair and sighed. "Wow! You must have really paid attention in the kitchen growing up. Though I have to say, I've never had spaghetti for breakfast before!"

Tanner laughed and pushed his plate to the side. "It wasn't hard. It was spaghetti. And that was my mom's homemade sauce in the freezer."

"I want to learn to do that."

He lifted a brow. "Make sauce?"

I nodded. "Yes. I never was able to learn things like that, since my mother passed away."

"Your father never met anyone else?"

With a scoff, I looked down at my empty plate. Memories of women coming in and out of my life were like a blur. My father was good-looking for a man in his early fifties. Women still flocked to him like he was a twenty-something guy. Of course, the fact that he had money and was a doctor played a big role in that.

"He's dated. A lot. But no, he's never remarried, and I'm pretty sure he won't. The girlfriends last until they find out Daddy has no plans of putting a ring on their finger. Then, they move on, or he gets tired of them and breaks it off. There was one I really liked. I think my father liked her too, but when she started to want to spend more time with me, he ended things with her. I hated him for months after that."

"Why?" Tanner asked as he stood and took both of our plates.

"I guess it was because she was the first female in my life since my mother and my nanny. I was certainly craving that maternal figure. I guess he didn't want me to have it. So, he broke up with her. From that point on, he kept the women he dated rather distant from me."

"I'm so sorry, Timber."

I shrugged. "It is what it is. When I have a child someday, I'm going to make sure they know what it feels like to be loved."

Tanner smiled and placed his hand on the side of my cheek. "You're going to make an amazing mother."

I stared into his blue eyes and took a deep breath, letting it out slowly. "Tanner, I know this is probably not something a couple talks about when they've literally just started a relationship, but how do you feel about kids? I mean, I see you with your niece and nephew, and you're amazing with them. Do you want kids of your own someday?"

"Hell yes, I do."

Relief flooded through me. I hadn't really thought much about kids before, but being with the Shaw family, I quickly realized I wanted a family of my own. One where love and laughter filled each room. "Since I've been spending time here with your family, seeing Morgan and Blayze, and then hearing Kaylee was pregnant, I realized that I want a family more than I thought I did."

"Good," Tanner said, throwing in a wink on top of his sexy smile.

The phone on the wall rang, and Tanner got up to answer it. "Hello? Nah, we're good. We ate spaghetti for breakfast."

I laughed and stood. Since Tanner cooked, I would clean.

Tanner was obviously speaking to his father. Something about a tractor, hooking up a plow, and the storm moving out. A part of me wanted to be stuck here forever. The cabin, as Tanner kept calling it, was beautiful, and now with the snow no longer falling, I was able to see Crystal Lake through the living room window. It was breathtaking. The mountain range beyond was just as stunning, if not more so. The snow sparkled when the sun peeked out from the clouds every so often. Kaylee had once described it as someone throwing out diamonds onto the mountains, and when the sun hit just right, they cast off beams of sparkly light. It was so beautiful I had a hard time believing it was real. *Picture perfect* didn't even begin to describe the view I was looking at.

"It's beautiful, isn't it?" Tanner asked as he stood next to me. He grabbed a dishtowel and picked up a pot and started drying it off.

"There honestly isn't a place on this ranch that isn't beautiful."

"All of Montana is like this."

With the last dish washed, I placed it in the dish drainer and turned to Tanner. "By the way, I've been thinking. I'm going to need a truck for sure. And a horse trailer."

"Okay," he said with a chuckle. "What kind of truck?"

"The lady who owned the horse ranch back in Georgia where I first started to take lessons...she had a Dodge."

Tanner screwed up his face and shook his head. "A Dodge! No. No girlfriend of mine is driving a...a Dodge."

I swooned hearing Tanner call me his girlfriend. Had we really come this far in only a few short weeks? I had been so hell bent on keeping this man far away from me, and here I was talking about kids with him. My future. A future I wasn't really sure about since my father was bound and determined to undermine my life in Montana.

"What's wrong with a Dodge?" I asked.

"If my father saw you drive up in a Dodge, he'd ban you from the ranch. You need a Ford."

"Why a Ford? What's wrong with Dodge, or even the Toyota trucks?"

He closed his eyes. "I'm not even going to give that a response."

I laughed. "Why, Tanner Shaw, are you a truck snob?"

He scoffed. "I'm not a truck snob; I simply know a

good truck when I see one and a Ford is a good truck. Everyone on the ranch has Ford trucks."

"Well, I'm not going to be living on the ranch."

A strange emotion moved quickly across his face. If I hadn't been looking so intently at him, I might have missed it. "What was that look for?" I asked.

"I didn't give a look."

I raised a brow and thought about questioning him, but for some reason decided to let it go.

"Dad said Brock is hitching up the plow to his truck and should be heading this way soon," Tanner said.

With a quick look around, I said, "We should clean up."

He winked. "My thoughts exactly. I thought maybe we could be stranded another day, but it looks like the next round of storms won't be here until late tonight or tomorrow morning."

"Should I take the kitchen or bedroom?" I asked.

"I'll do the kitchen; you take the bedroom. Just toss the sheets and towels we used into the washer. There's a quick wash setting."

"Got it!" I said and went to turn to head to the bedroom. Before I could take a step though, Tanner pulled me into his arms and kissed me.

My legs felt weak and I held onto his arms, a soft moan mixing with one of his own. When he pulled back, my entire body swayed. "Your kisses, Mr. Shaw..."

"Good or bad?" he asked, a wicked gleam in his eyes.

"Very good. They leave me weak."

A wide smile erupted across his face. "You better leave before I decide to have my way with you again."

I laughed. "No more condoms."

He frowned. "Oh, we've already covered that there are plenty of ways to make you come without using my cock."

My mouth dropped open and I knew I should be shocked, but instead I was turned on. I took a few steps back and flashed him a grin. "You wicked, wicked man."

◆ ◆ ◆

With the house cleaned and straightened up, Tanner headed out to the barn once again to check on Pogo. He had gone earlier in the morning to check on him, but was now going to clear a path for me so I could help him. I insisted on going, especially after he had found some crutches that he'd left behind when he'd stayed here for a few days with a broken ankle. It seemed to me that Tanner really enjoyed being in the log home. I could see why he always thought he'd end up living here. A part of me could see myself living here too, but I wasn't ready to go that way with my thinking. Not yet, at least.

The front door opened as I wrapped my scarf around my face. "You sure you want to attempt this?" Tanner asked.

"Yep. You can be there in case I slip."

He rolled his eyes as he held his arm out for me. "And sprain your other ankle. If you fall and hurt yourself more, my mother is going to kill us both."

I laughed. "Let's go before your brother gets here."

Ever so carefully, Tanner and I made our way from the house to the barn. It wasn't far from the house, so the walk over wasn't bad. Tanner had shoveled a path for us, but snow was starting to fall once again, making me feel a bit nervous about slipping.

The moment I stepped into the barn, I let out a sigh of relief. Tanner did as well.

"How did he do through the night?" I asked as I hobbled over to Pogo in the stall.

"He's fine, aren't you, boy?" Tanner asked while Pogo bobbed his head like he knew exactly what Tanner had asked.

"I swear they understand you," I stated as I ran my hand down the side of Pogo's neck. "You're sure it'll be safe to ride him back?"

"Yeah, as long as the snow doesn't come down too much between the time Brock gets here and we get back. I'll take it slow."

The sound of a truck honking caused us both to look toward the entrance of the barn. Brock drove by slowly, plowing a path. He then backed up and made another pass until he had the whole area cleared out between the house and the barn.

Then, I saw another truck with a horse trailer. "They brought a horse trailer!" I exclaimed as I turned back to Pogo. "Look at that, boy, you don't have to worry now."

Tanner smiled and offered his arm as we slowly made our way out of the barn. I was surprised to see this barn was almost as big as the main barn on the ranch.

"Greetings!" Ty shouted as he got out of his truck. He made his way over and shook Tanner's hand quickly, then leaned down and kissed me on the cheek. "Did you know Kaylee and I were once stuck together during a snowstorm?"

I shook my head. "I didn't. Is that when the sparks flew between y'all?"

Tanner and Brock both laughed.

"Please, the fireworks went off the first time the two of them met. They were both just too damn stubborn to admit it," Tanner said.

I smiled and focused back on Ty.

"Nothing happened between us that night," he said, "but by the glow on your face and the way my baby brother is grinning from ear to ear, I'm going to guess your night wasn't so boring."

"That's none of your business, Ty," Tanner quickly said as he wrapped his arm around my waist and tugged me closer to him.

"Jesus, Mama is going to be over the moon when she gets a look at you two. She has a weird way of knowing these things. Just watch out, she'll be planning weddings and grandbabies if you don't set her straight right off the bat," Ty stated.

"She will not," Tanner said, kissing me on the top of my head. I knew he was worried I'd be spooked by what Ty was saying, but it was the opposite. This whole thing was a far cry from what I thought I wanted only a few months ago.

"Let me help Ty get Pogo loaded up," Tanner said.

I nodded and turned my attention to Brock. "We need to get you guys back to the house and get Pogo settled while there's a break," he said. "Another system is moving down, and you saw yesterday that it can come in faster than expected."

I grimaced. "I'm so sorry. Y'all wouldn't have to do this if I hadn't been so stupid to take Rosie for a ride."

"Nah, don't think twice about it. You didn't know, but better to learn early on."

I nodded in agreement.

Tanner and Ty got Pogo safely loaded up in the horse trailer as Brock helped me up into his truck. Tanner rode with me and Brock while Ty followed behind. Brock kept plowing the new snow as it came down. It was light, but from the looks of the dark sky in the north, another heavy round was about to move in.

It didn't take long to get back to the main barn. Brock kept the plow on his truck, said his goodbyes, and headed back to Lincoln and the kids. Tanner helped Ty get the trailer off his truck, and before he took off back home to Kaylee, Stella gave him a casserole.

We watched as Ty drove off, then Stella turned and looked at me. "Your ankle?"

"Is doing much better. Tanner found crutches for me to use, but I really don't think I'll need them. I think I just twisted it good when I was thrown from Rosie."

"Well, let's get you both into the house, and I'll start making some lunch."

"We ate a pretty big breakfast, Mama," Tanner stated as we followed his mother back down the path toward their house.

"That's fine, I'll make some sandwiches and soup. Maybe later we can even make an apple pie, Timberlynn."

"Oh, I've never baked a pie before."

Stella turned and gave me a look of pure disbelief. "First the cookies, now pie! Lord, we've got some catching up to do with baking!"

"I can almost read her mind now," Tanner whispered. "She's thinking if you intend on being with me, you need to be able to cook so her precious baby boy doesn't starve!"

I giggled and hit him on the chest. I'd never in my life felt so happy. Coming to Montana was the best decision I'd ever made, and one I knew I wouldn't regret.

Now the only hurdle was figuring out how to buy a piece of property without my father attempting to block it.

Chapter Twenty-Seven

TANNER

NEW YEAR'S EVE

The last week had been pure bliss. Even if I had to sneak around my folks' house like a high school boy attempting to get laid for the first time. Each night I found myself in Timberlynn's bed. We woke up each morning, kissed and fooled around like kids, then I'd leave to head back to my room before things got too hot and heavy. We had even snuck away to the barn a few times with some blankets, a lantern we used for camping, and some wine. Somehow sex in my folks' barn loft had become my new favorite thing. At least when I could push away the memory of Ty telling me he'd lost his virginity in the same spot.

"Thank goodness the snow has let up enough for folks to make it to the party tonight!" my mother said as she looked up from the little smokie sausage rolls she was wrapping up in crescent rolls. Kaylee and Timberlynn were working alongside my mother, each super focused on the task of rolling them up. My mother had taught Timberlynn how to make an apple pie from scratch, right down to the crust, as well as at least ten different types of casseroles and the homemade ragu her Italian best friend had taught her how to make after my mother married my father. They also made countless amounts of cookies, brownies, fudge, and three cakes. With homemade buttercream frosting and all. I was positive I'd gained at least ten pounds since Christmas.

"How many people are coming?" Kaylee asked.

My mother handed me a bowl, marshmallow fluff, and cream cheese. "You know what to do with this. And do not eat it, Tanner!" my mother demanded.

I gave her a salute and winked at Timberlynn, who blushed. I was quickly falling madly, head over heels in love with Timberlynn, and a part of me wanted to shout it from the rooftops.

"Timberlynn, Kaylee can finish up the wraps. Can you start on cutting up the fruit for the tray?"

"Certainly." Like a dutiful young apprentice, Timberlynn took the containers of fruit and started to cut and arrange them onto a tray.

"Let's see, pretty much everyone we invited will be here. This year we kept the list on the smaller side."

Dirk walked into the kitchen and everyone looked over at him.

"Hey, Dirk. We haven't seen you in a few days," Kaylee said as she tilted her head for him to kiss her on the cheek. Timberlynn turned and smiled.

"Hi, Dirk."

He winked at Timberlynn, and I sent him a dirty look, which he pretended not to notice.

"Good afternoon, Timberlynn. Kaylee, Stella." He finally looked my way and nodded. "Tanner."

"Dirk. Where have you been?" Kaylee asked.

He grinned as he reached for a grape and popped it into his mouth. "Been stuck at home and just enjoying the silence. I forgot how nice it was to just be alone for a few days." He looked around. "Where is everyone?"

Mom answered. "Brock, Ty, and their daddy are out driving the fence. With all the high winds, they wanted to make sure no trees fell down."

Dirk caught my eye again. "Why didn't you go?"

"I met up with Chance earlier to go over the press release announcing that we're both stepping down from roping."

His brow raised. "No shit?"

I smiled. "No shit."

The feel of Timberlynn's gaze made me look over to her. She looked unsure, so I smiled and gave her my own wink. Her cheeks flushed slightly, and something deep in my chest grew warm.

"I bet you're happy as a clam, Stella," Dirk stated.

"To have all my boys home? You better believe it. Now we just need you to come on back home, and everything will be perfect."

Dirk nearly choked on the piece of kiwi he had tossed into his mouth. "You're going to be waiting a long time on me, Stella."

She grinned, but I knew what that grin meant. It was the one that said she knew something no one else did. Dirk's brows pulled in slightly. He had seen it as well. "What's on the smaller side?" Dirk asked as he focused on my mother.

"What?" she asked, confused.

"When I walked in, you said something was on the smaller side."

She shook her head and laughed slightly. "Oh, the guest list for the New Year's Eve party tonight. Now, I want to make sure you've made plans to stay here this evening, Dirk. No drinking and then heading back home."

He saluted and gave my mother the smile that I was positive had landed him in a woman's bed a dozen times or more. "I've already made arrangements to stay the night at Brock and Lincoln's place. No need to worry about me, Mama Shaw."

She rolled her eyes.

"Who all is going to be here tonight?" Kaylee asked.

My mother started naming names, most of them were friends she and my father had known for years. A few relatives and some folks who lived on ranches around us. "The Edens will be here as well."

Dirk froze as he was reaching across Timberlynn to grab another piece of fruit. He looked stunned. "The Edens?"

I watched with curiosity, and so did Kaylee. The only person who hadn't caught Dirk's pause was Timberlynn. She was still cutting up the fruit and arranging them on the platter.

"Yes, their farm is right next to your folks' ranch, isn't it?" my mother casually asked. She knew damn well it was.

"What's the difference between a farm and a ranch?" Kaylee asked, totally not seeing what was going on. "I never really thought about it before when y'all mention a farm versus a ranch."

My mother shrugged. "Well, on a farm they focus more on the soil for growing crops. A ranch, like ours, is land where livestock is raised. On the Eden's farm, they grow crops such a strawberries, corn, wheat. They also have dairy cows, but not many. They also grow pumpkins and let folks in town come in and pick their own right from the fields. I get all my eggs from them when I shop at Pete's Grocery in town."

"They have blueberries too. Their strawberry and blueberry crops are you-pick-it, and they have folks come to the farm and pick the berries. That allows them to sell other stuff while they're there. Like tomatoes and other veggies," I added.

My mother smiled. "Yes, as a matter of fact, those strawberries came from their greenhouse. They grow them all year long."

"Do they still grow Christmas trees?" I asked.

Dirk leaned against the counter, silently taking in the entire conversation. The look on his face, though, had me curious as hell. Apparently, Kaylee was on the same page as I was. We glanced at each other and the corner of her mouth rose slightly, as did her brows. If my memory served me right, Dirk had a fling with Merit Eden his senior year of high school...but that was a long time ago, so I wasn't sure what was going on.

"You know, I'm not sure," my mother stated. "Dirk, do they still grow trees?"

"What?" Dirk asked as he glanced up from the strawberry he had been staring at.

"The Eden family, do they still sell Christmas trees?"

"I'm not sure. Last I heard, their son Michael was running that part of the farm."

There was a moment of silence in the kitchen and I turned to look at my mother. She wore a smile on her face that said she was about to go in for the kill.

Oh, holy hell.

"I know when I talked to Lori Eden—" She looked at Kaylee and Timberlynn. "She's the mother."

They both nodded to show they were keeping up.

"When I talked to Lori, she mentioned that Merit was back in Hamilton for good. She's working on the farm, but I totally forgot to ask about Michael."

I couldn't hide my smile. My mama was good. Damn good. Dirk stared at her with a befuddled expression. I made a mental note to ask Brock about Dirk and Merit, and then let it slip to Kaylee. She'd bug the hell out of Dirk about it.

"Merit's back in town? For good?" Dirk finally managed to ask, his voice sounding a little off.

Kaylee turned and looked at him, as did Timberlynn.

"Did y'all date?" Kaylee asked, clearly noticing his reaction.

Dirk dropped his eyes down and laughed. "Why would you ask me that?"

"Your tone changed."

His brows crinkled. "What do you mean, my tone changed? Nothing changed."

"It did change, I noticed it too," Timberlynn said with a grin. I couldn't hold it in. I laughed out loud, and Dirk shot me a look that said I needed to stop, or he was going to throttle me. I held up my hands in defense and looked at my mother.

She wore a huge smile on her face as she started mixing together some kind of dough.

Clearing his voice, Dirk stated, "Nothing changed, you're both insane."

"Normally when you talk about girls you went to school with, your tone is normal. But when you talked about...what was her name again, Stella?" Kaylee asked.

"Merit," my mother and I said at the same time, neither of us missing a beat. Dirk shot me another dirty look.

"When you talked about Merit, your voice went slightly higher," Kaylee said.

Dirk laughed. Hard. "Your pregnancy brain is playing tricks on you, sweetheart."

Then my mother really went in for the kill. "I do believe you were her first kiss, at least that is what her mama always says. Dirk Littlewood was the first boy to ever kiss my little Merit back behind the chicken coop! Imagine that, a pro bull rider kissing my little Merit!"

Everyone in the room laughed...everyone except for Dirk. "We were ten, for fuck's sake! How does that count or even matter?"

My mother chuckled. "She always did think you two would end up together. You always were like peas and carrots. I imagine she'd probably talk about the whole barn incident, if given the chance."

Dirk's face went pale. "Wh-what? How do you even know about that?"

With a wink, my mother answered, "Roger told Ty Senior. Said he was about ready to rip your head off the night he caught the two up there in the hay loft."

Dirk gave her a smug grin. "I'd imagined he was a bit pissed, considering we had been...doing more than kissing."

My mother huffed. "Lori might be happy to brag about that early on kiss, but Roger isn't very keen on his daughter losing her virginity to a bull rider who was supposed to be like a brother to his daughter."

"Oh. My. Gawd!" Kaylee gasped.

"What!" Timberlynn shrieked as she turned and looked at Dirk. "You were ten when you lost your virginity?"

Kaylee reached over and smacked Timberlynn on the back of the head.

"Ouch! What in the heck, Kaylee?!" Timberlynn said as my mother and I both laughed.

"He was ten when they first kissed, fool, not when he popped her cherry!" Kaylee corrected as only she could.

Timberlynn's mouth made the cutest little O as it all settled into place for her. Damn if she wasn't the sweetest thing. Her gaze met mine and she half shrugged as I laughed.

"You lost your virginity to the...to the girl next door! How romantic is that!" Kaylee busted out, then fell into a fit of laughter.

"Ha ha. She was hot, and just to be clear, Timberlynn, we were both in high school when we had sex, and she was the one who lost her virginity to me, thank you very much. And what in the heck, Stella Shaw! Why are you talking about this?"

About that time, Brock walked in, and without so much as missing a beat, he said, "Hey, Dirk, you hear that Merit Eden's back in town?"

Everyone, and I mean everyone, started laughing... everyone but Dirk.

◆ ◆ ◆

I knocked on Timberlynn's bedroom door and waited for her to answer.

"Come in!"

With a smile, I opened the door and walked in. Timberlynn stepped out of the bathroom that was attached to her room, and I nearly dropped to my knees.

She smiled and I was positive I tripped.

"Do you like it? When I found out your folks were having a party, I ordered it from a college friend who designs gowns. She's making it pretty big in New York City with her designs and all. She had one in my size and sent it overnight, which isn't really overnight to get here, but more like three days!"

I went to open my mouth to speak, but nothing came out.

Timberlynn chewed on her lip, and I could see her cheeks turn the slightest shade of pink.

"You look...I mean...you look beautiful. Sexy beautiful. Like I want to slowly take that dress off of you beautiful."

A big smile appeared on her face.

The dress was black and hugged her body in the most amazing ways. It fell below her knees, but on one side was a slit that came up her thigh. One shoulder had a ruffley-type sleeve on it, and the other shoulder was bare...and her breasts. My God, her breasts were on full display. I wanted to throw a blanket around her torso, but at the same time parade her around so every man in the room could envy the hell out of me.

"Do you like it?"

"Like it? My cock is so hard right now I may have to sit the party out."

Timberlynn laughed.

"How does your ankle feel in those shoes?"

"It's a bit sore, but nothing bad." She reached down for a necklace that was laying on the side table by her bed.

"Would you put this on for me?"

Her long blonde hair was down and fell in soft waves around her face. Her makeup was light, but her red lips screamed that she was classy as hell.

I took the necklace and noticed that my hands shook as I moved toward her. Timberlynn turned around and lifted her hair, exposing her back to me. I leaned down and kissed her bare skin. Instantly, a rush of heat flowed through my body.

Her entire body trembled, and I couldn't help but smile as I moved my lips up her neck. "Tanner," she whispered as I blew softly on her ear.

"I want you, Timber."

She dropped her head back as my hand came up and moved to her breasts. "No, we can't."

"We can."

My other hand moved slowly under her dress. When I felt a bare ass cheek, I lost all control. "Are you wearing panties?"

She turned and smiled. "I didn't want a panty line to show."

I took a few steps away from her. "You're not wearing panties?"

"I said I had a thong on."

In my crazed mind I hadn't even heard her say that. My eyes went over her body again, and it only took me two seconds to make my decision.

Two steps and my mouth pressed against hers. She wrapped her arms around my neck, and I walked her back until she hit the wall.

I dropped down and carefully pushed her dress up. The black thong was nothing but a piece of thin lace. I licked my lips and pushed the fabric to the side as I lifted her leg.

"Tanner!" she gasped, then covered her mouth with her hand when I licked her, flicking her clit with my tongue. "Oh God."

It didn't take long for her to come. The moment I slipped my fingers inside her and sucked on her clit, she was bucking her hips into my mouth and covering her moans with both hands.

Jesus, she was wet now. So I stood, unzipped my dress pants and pulled my cock out. I dipped my fingers back inside her and then stroked myself a few times.

Timberlynn looked at me with a pleasure-induced smile. "There are condoms in the side table drawer."

Since we were waiting on Timberlynn to get into the doctor—and silently hoping her period came—we were still wearing condoms. I reached into the side table of her nightstand and grabbed one. After ripping it open and sheathing myself, I moved and positioned myself at her entrance, rubbing my cock against her clit.

Timberlynn's eyes were hooded and cloudy, as if she was still in the aftermaths of her first orgasm. She placed her hands on my shoulders and whimpered, "Don't tease, Tanner."

She moved her hips toward me, and I slid myself into her warm, tight body.

"Fuck," I moaned as I started to move. I wanted to go slow. To enjoy simply being inside her. But slow wasn't on either of our minds.

"Faster, Tanner. Oh, God, yes!" she whispered before she dropped her head into my chest.

I pumped fast and hard as I pressed her against the wall. My body must have been hitting hers in all the right ways, because she buried her face into my jacket and moaned as her orgasm rocketed through her. I could feel her tighten on me. Feel how wet her body got as my cock slid in and out more easily after she came. Then I felt my own build up.

"Timberlynn, I can't hold back, baby."

"Yes. Tanner, yes."

The moment I came, I let out a low growl. The fucking room felt like it was spinning out of control. I pumped inside her a few more times, and then her fingers dug deep into my shoulders.

"Tanner."

Reality floated back in, and I hated that I had lost control like that. I'd just fucked her against the wall while my folks had a freaking party going on downstairs. That wasn't the type of man I promised her I would be.

She dropped her head against my chest again and we both fought to regain our breathing. I stayed inside her, afraid to move. Afraid to acknowledge my own selfish behavior. "I'm sorry," I mumbled as I pulled out of her slowly.

Timberlynn looked at me and she frowned. "Sorry for what?"

"I...lost control and acted like a damn animal just now."

She smiled. "If my memory is right, I didn't stop you."

"I promised you I'd always respect you, and I just fucked you like a mad man."

Timberlynn cupped my face within her hands. "Tanner, you made me feel desired. Sexy. I love that I make you lose control like that. Don't say you're sorry for making me feel like a woman who's desired."

With a forced smile, I nodded. "I won't lose control like that again."

Timberlynn fixed her gown and took a step back, then straightened my jacket. "Bite your tongue, Tanner Shaw. I think my new favorite thing is to be fucked against a wall."

My mouth dropped open, and she winked. "Come on, let's get to the party before we're late."

Chapter Twenty-Eight

TIMBERLYNN

Conversations flowed easily around the room as people talked, laughed, and exchanged stories. My mind was not on the conversation going on around me as Lincoln, Kaylee, and a woman a few years older than me, Libby was her name, I think, were engaged in a conversation about food cravings during pregnancy.

I took a sip of my wine and glanced around the room as I searched for Tanner. My body, I swore, was still humming from earlier. Tanner had apologized several more times since we'd gotten to the party, but I assured him he had nothing to apologize for.

Across the room I saw Ty Senior, Stella, and Brock talking to a couple. They all smiled and waved over a woman who had just walked into the room. She looked to be Lincoln and Kaylee's age, around twenty-nine. She was beautiful. Her dark brown hair was swept up into an elegant bun with a few strands of curls that framed her face and neck. Her dress was equally elegant. An ombre, long-sleeved, curve-hugging dress that fell just above her knees. I glanced down and smiled at the Jimmy Choo black crisscross heels she had on. At least I wasn't the only one in the room wearing seven-hundred-dollar heels. I peeked down at Kaylee's heels and then over to Lincoln's. I covered my smile with my wine glass. Okay, correction, there were four of us in the room with excellent taste in black shoes.

When I looked back over, I found Tanner. He leaned in and gave the woman a kiss on the cheek. An instant rush of jealousy rolled over me, and I had to force myself not to squeeze the wine tumbler any harder.

Well, goodness, Timberlynn, where on Earth had that come from?

"There's nothing to worry about there, Timberlynn," Libby's voice said. I turned and looked at the three women, all now staring in the same direction I had been.

"Who is that?" Lincoln asked.

"That is Merit Eden."

"*That's* Merit Eden?" Kaylee practically shouted as I quickly placed my hand over her mouth.

"Jesus, Kaylee, shout it out to the whole room, why don't you!" Lincoln snapped.

Libby laughed. "Before I let my inner gossip girl come out, tell me what you know."

Kaylee pointed her bottle of water to Libby. "I knew we were going to be friends the moment you walked into this room," she mused.

With another chuckle, Libby winked at Kaylee. "I'm mostly a listen-to-the-gossip kind of person, but every now and then a girl has to fill in her new friends."

"Yeah, I like you. I think we'll keep you," Lincoln stated.

I leaned in closer to Libby and said, "Stella seemed to be picking at Dirk about Merit. Something about being caught in the hay loft by Merit's daddy."

Libby nodded, looked around, cleared her throat, then motioned for the three of us to come closer.

"Okay, so I feel sort of bad for talking about Merit, we were close in high school, but I don't want you to hear the wrong version."

We all nodded. "Go on," Lincoln stated.

"Everyone in school knew Dirk and Merit were close. Like best friends' kind of close. They grew up next door to each other, and Dirk protected her like a big brother would. Then, one day out of the blue, Merit told us she wanted Dirk to take her virginity."

"Did she say why?" Kaylee asked.

Libby took another quick look in Merit's direction. "She said she trusted him, and he had sorta been hinting at wanting her. That was all she told us, but we all knew she had a crush on Dirk. She wouldn't admit it, because so did her best friend, Kaci."

Lincoln and Kaylee gasped.

I knew Kaci was Brock's first wife, but was unaware of why they gasped.

Libby went on. "The next week in school, everyone was talking about how Mr. Eden found Dirk and Merit up in her daddy's hay loft. It was apparent something had happened between the two of them."

"Had he caught them in the act?" I gasped.

Libby shook her head. "No, but it was clear they had done something. When we asked Merit about it, though, she almost cried. She said it was all a joke and that she hated Dirk and never wanted to talk about him or what had happened ever again."

We all frowned. "What did she mean, it was all a joke?" Kaylee asked.

With a half shrug, Libby replied, "No one really knows. Merit *never* talked about it again, and from what I know, Dirk has never mentioned it either. Everyone knew Dirk had a thing for Kaci, but I also used to see the way he looked at Merit. Dirk didn't look at her like a guy who thought of her as a sister, if you know what I mean. And truth be told, he never looked at Kaci that way either. I always sort of thought Dirk had a thing for Merit, but was maybe too afraid of losing their friendship."

"Kaci, Brock's first wife?" I asked.

"Ugh, long story, but yes, Dirk liked her," Kaylee said as Lincoln nodded.

Libby went on. "Anyway, they both pretty much swept it under the rug. Then after graduation, Merit went off to college at NYU. She got her degree and stayed in New York City. She always comes home to visit her folks—apparently always when Dirk is on the circuit. She never really tried to connect much with any of us from high school. She had kept in touch with me for a little while, then we kind of lost touch. Last month, though, she moved back home. For good, according to her mother. I haven't had a chance to catch up with her, so I have no idea why she's here. Of course, the rumor mill of Hamilton says she was dumped by her longtime boyfriend, fired from her job, and had no choice but to move back home. I know Merit, though, and she's not that type of woman. If she has a problem, she isn't slinking back into town with her head hanging down. She's home for a reason. A big one."

We all turned and looked over to where Merit had been standing. The Eden family was no longer talking to Stella and Ty Senior.

"I wonder why she's back home?" Lincoln asked, the gossip clearly intriguing her.

Libby drew in a deep breath and slowly let it out. "My best guess is it has something to do with the family farm. I think they're in a bit of a financial mess, and Merit came home with the intention of fixing it. That farm means everything to her and her brother."

Kaylee took a sip of her water. "Well, by the look on Dirk's face when he found out she was back in town, and the way he was staring at her earlier, I'm going to guess there was more to that lose-her-virginity-night than we know, and I intend on finding out what happened."

"How are you going to find out, Kaylee?" Lincoln asked.

With a slow shake of her head, Kaylee replied, "I don't know. But I'll come up with something."

"Dear God, those are words I do not want to hear come out of my wife's mouth," Ty said as he kissed a surprised Kaylee on the lips.

"Ty, did you happen to see where Tanner went?" I asked.

"Yeah, I think he offered to show Merit something my father's working on. I'm guessing maybe he's with her in Dad's office."

"Oh," I said as I looked toward the hallway that led to Ty Senior's office.

Libby touched my arm, and I glanced her way. "Don't worry."

I forced a smile. "Oh, I'm not the least bit worried."

It was a lie. Those old insecurities had a way of creeping back in so fast they nearly left me dizzy. I excused myself and mingled with the people in the room as I made my way toward the hall.

Moments later, I found myself standing outside of Ty Senior's office. The door was shut, and a sick feeling hit my stomach. Then another emotion pushed that ill feeling away.

Trust.

A calmness washed over my body, and I knew in that moment that Tanner wasn't going to hurt me. He wasn't going to sneak off into another room with another woman and cheat on me. For the first time in a very long time, I realized that I trusted someone completely.

I saw the way Tanner looked at me from across a room. The way his eyes met mine when we made love. The way he felt only hours ago inside me, how our passion had been unlike anything I'd ever experienced before in my life. I knew he was upset about what had happened earlier because he cared about me. He always wanted to make me feel cherished, and I loved him for that.

I loved him.

With a smile on my face, I turned and walked back down the hall to the large living room where most everyone was gathered. When I stepped into the room, I saw Tanner. He threw his head back and laughed at something an older woman said. Butterflies danced in my stomach as I watched him flirt with a woman who could be his grandmother. She had a huge smile on her face and was eating up the attention the younger man was giving her.

"Oh, Tanner," I softly whispered. "I am so in love with you."

I was about to walk over to him when I felt a hand on my arm. Turning, I smiled when I saw Dirk...and Merit.

"Timberlynn."

"Dirk, how are you?"

He smiled. "Everything is, um, fine. I was just showing Merit something in Ty senior's office. Before you run off to find Tanner, I'd like for you to meet Merit Eden. Merit, this is Timberlynn, Tanner's girlfriend and Kaylee's cousin. Kaylee is Ty's wife."

Merit flashed me a bright smile. She was even more beautiful up close. Her eyes looked almost violet.

"Wow, your eyes!" I shook my head and covered my now-heated cheeks. "That was so rude. I mean, it's a pleasure to meet you, Merit. Forgive me, I've just never seen anyone who had eyes that looked...purple!"

She laughed. "No worries. A lot of people are thrown off by the violet color."

"They're stunning."

Her smile widened, and there was something about her that I immediately liked. "Thank you for your sweet words. They're definitely a good conversation starter!"

I laughed. "I'm sure they are!"

A hand moved around my waist, and I didn't even have to look to see who it was. I knew it was Tanner. I could smell his cologne, and with only his touch, my entire body came alive.

My cheeks felt warm and I looked up, only to find him smiling down at me. "Hey, I've been looking for you," he said.

There went that feeling in my chest again, and my stomach flipped and flopped like I was on a carnival ride. "You found me. Dirk was just introducing me to Merit."

Tanner stared at me for another half second with that breathtaking smile of his before he turned to look at Merit. "Dad said you might be able to help out with a situation I presented him with."

Merit's eyes darted over to mine, then back to Tanner. "Yes. It's simple to do. No different from when they pieced off the two parcels of land for Brock. From the quick look at the survey Dirk just showed me, I'd say the one road used now would work perfectly with your parents still maintaining ownership of it. Just like with Brock's house now. The piece of land that Ty and Kaylee have is completely separate from the ranch, since it was on the outer edge of the property, but with the land purchased up to the easement and with the next ranch over, you could purchase a parcel of land from them and put in your own road. Although, I don't see the need for it, and I doubt your parents would either."

Tanner nodded and pulled me closer to his side. I wasn't sure if he'd even noticed he'd done it. I couldn't help but look up at him. His brow was pulled in slightly. Was he planning on building a house on his parents' ranch?

"That's what I wanted to hear," he said.

Merit smiled. "Let me know if you need any help with permits and such. I'm more than happy to help."

"I will. Thanks, Merit."

Dirk gave me a wink and then said, "Merit here is a civil engineer."

"Oh, wow! Libby didn't say that."

My mouth instantly shut tight at my slipup. Merit raised a brow, then glanced across the room, most likely searching for Libby.

"I'm so sorry, Merit, she wasn't gossiping about you at all. She simply saw you talking to Stella and Ty Senior and mentioned you had left Hamilton after graduation and went to NYU for a business degree. That's all."

"It's fine. Originally I was going for business, but changed my major. I'll have to get used to the small-town gossip mill again," she said with a wink. I felt my body relax, but I still kicked myself internally.

"Well, it was nice meeting you, Timberlynn. Tanner, good seeing you again."

Her body stiffened when she turned to Dirk. "Thank you for showing me that, Dirk."

He nodded and gave her a smile. "My pleasure. I'll, um, see you around."

Merit's smile was genuine. "Well, with you bull riding, I doubt we'll see each other much."

"We do live next door to each other."

Merit gave a half-hearted laugh. "Well, lots of land separating us, so I doubt it."

"I may want some...strawberries."

It was like I was watching a tennis match. Tanner and I both looked at Merit for a follow-up response to Dirk's ridiculous reasoning.

"You like them now?" she asked, her smile now forced. "I seem to recall you picking them on the farm only to get Kaci's attention."

Dirk physically flinched.

I looked at Merit, who turned to Tanner and me. "I'm going to go track down my parents and say hello to some of the other guests. Happy New Year's, Tanner and Timberlynn."

"Happy New Year's," we replied in unison.

I glanced back to Dirk and watched his face as Merit walked away and blended into the large group of people who were now gathered in the living room. The tension in the air was palpable.

"She's beautiful," I said as I glanced in the direction Merit had just walked.

"Yeah, she is." Dirk nodded toward Tanner's possessive grip around my waist. "Hold on to her tight. the good ones can slip away easily if you don't," he said before turning and walking away.

I stared at him, then turned to Tanner. "What in the world was that?"

He shrugged. "About earlier," Tanner started to say.

I grabbed his hand and pulled him down the hall to his father's office.

With a quick look behind me, I opened the door, motioned for him to go in, then shut it. Before Tanner had a chance to talk, I pushed him against the door, then pulled his mouth to mine.

We both moaned and I wrapped my arms around his neck, falling easily into the kiss.

"Tanner," I whispered as he softly placed kisses down my neck. With a deep breath, I dropped down and started to unbutton his dress pants.

"Timberlynn, what are you doing?"

I unzipped them and pulled his boxers down until his semi-hard cock sprang free.

"Timber, I—"

His voice was cut off when I took him into my mouth.

"Christ," he cried out and grabbed onto the coat rack that stood next to him.

I worked him with my mouth and hand, and when he touched the side of my face, I couldn't help but smile. I could hear the way he was panting. I looked up and saw his eyes closed and a look of utter pleasure on his face.

He opened his eyes and looked directly at me. "Baby, stop, or I'm going to come."

I took him deeper and moaned. Tanner jerked a few times, and I felt the warmth of his cum hit the back of my throat. I swallowed it as fast as I could while still working him. This was my first time doing this, and I definitely wasn't a fan of swallowing, but I wanted to show him that losing control earlier was exactly what I had wanted.

When he stopped, I slowly took him out of my mouth.

"Holy shit." He gasped. "I need to sit down."

I smiled and wiped the corners of my mouth as Tanner stumbled over to the sofa and fell into it.

"I can't breathe. That felt so damn amazing. Why did you do that?"

"Because I want you to know that in this relationship, we're both in control, Tanner. I don't want you to feel like you have to worry about treating me like I'm going to break."

He frowned.

"You thought by taking me upstairs you did something wrong. I know if I had said no, you would have stopped. I wanted you just as much, and knowing that you had that reaction turned me on."

He smiled. "It did?"

"Yes, very much so."

He took my hand in his. "I'm just glad I had the wits about me to wear the condom this time."

I looked down at my hands and then at him.

"What's wrong? Why do you look like you want to say something?"

"I almost told you not to put one on."

A soft chuckle came from his lips. "I almost asked not to."

We both laughed. "I will be getting on birth control ASAP."

"Good!" he said. Then he stood and cupped my face with his hands. "But it's not just about the crazy hot sex we have, or the fact that you just gave me a blowjob in my father's office."

I laughed and dropped my head onto his chest.

"I want to spend the rest of my life with you, Timber."

My breath caught in my throat and tears pooled in my eyes as I looked up at him. "What did you just say?"

Tanner took my hand and placed it on his chest.

"Do you feel that?"

I nodded.

"It beats only for you. I knew it the first time I saw you, and I know it even more now. Some people don't believe in love at first sight, and I think at one point in my life I was one of those people. But I'm a believer now."

"Me too," I softly whispered.

"I'm about to ask you something, and I'm not sure what you're going to say."

I laughed. "What is it?"

"Move in with me, Timberlynn."

I was positive my eyes nearly popped out of my head. "You want me to move into your bedroom with you? In your folks' house?"

Tanner laughed, hard. "God, no, Timber. I mean, let's move into a house together."

This time I smiled. "You want to move in together?"

"Yes."

I sighed, my happy bubble deflating as real life poked its ugly head back in. "My father, he's..."

"Wait...before you say anything, I have an idea that I want to run by you. I've already spoken to my parents about it. It's actually what Merit was talking about."

"Okay."

"I've asked my folks if we can purchase the cabin on the lake."

His words rattled around in my head for a few moments. "The cabin? You mean the house on the lake? Because it's not a cabin, Tanner."

"Yes," he chuckled. "The house on the lake."

I shook my head. "Wait, you said we. As in, me and you?"

"Yes. I know it's a huge leap on your part, and a big risk. But I don't really see us breaking up, so..."

I put my hand to my forehead to ward off the instant headache. "Tanner, wait. This is moving way too fast."

He stared at me like I just said the craziest thing. "I just told you I wanted to spend my future with you, what difference does it make if we start early? If we purchase this land from my parents, your father won't even know about it because it'll all be done in-house. He can't interfere or outbid anyone."

I swallowed hard and looked out one of the windows toward the lake in the distance. His thinking made sense. But a million what-ifs ran through my mind. I pulled in a deep breath and faced him.

"Buying a house together is a huge leap in any relationship. But buying a house that sits on *your* family's land is altogether insane. Tanner, as much as I want a future with you, what if things don't work out? Then what would I do? I'd have all of my money invested into a house and land that was sitting on your family's property. I can't do that. It's not that I don't trust you or trust us, but we're still so new in this relationship. I just now got control over my future, Tanner. I don't want to risk losing it again."

After a few moments of thinking, he nodded his head. "I can understand your worry. There's about two-hundred acres that separate the cabin..."

I raised a brow.

"Fine, the *lake house* from the next ranch. The Peterson's own it."

"Okay, but what does that have to do with anything?"

"When Brock and his first wife got married, my folks gifted him the house my granddaddy had built. It sat on the edge of the ranch's perimeter, so it was easy for them to simply cut off a small portion of the ranch and give it to Brock and Kaci. Well, Kaylee and Ty now own it. There's a couple hundred acres of land with it. Then Brock had a house he built on the ranch. Again, my folks carved out a piece of the ranch and gave it to him. What if I talked to the Peterson family and asked them if they'd be interested in selling you some of the land that butts up to the land that I'm going to buy from my folks?"

My heart started to beat a little faster in my chest. "Do you think they'd be willing to sell some land? And do it privately?"

"We could ask them. Or the other option is, you hang onto your money and start your business now on the land I buy. Plus, you'll have full use of the entire ranch. If things work out, then we make it all legal with your name on it."

I chewed on my lip and thought about what he was saying. "Will you give me some time to think about it?"

Tanner smiled. "Of course, but I'm still buying the cabin, er, lake house. So even if you didn't want to buy it with me—and I totally understand why you would have reservations about it—you could still move in with me. You said so yourself. You could see yourself living there."

I laughed. "It is a beautiful spot."

He nodded. "I wanted it before you came into my life. And us making love in that house for the first time only sealed the deal for me. Brock and Ty are fully on board and happy to see someone's actually going to move into the place."

"So, no matter what, you're buying it?"

He nodded. "And you can move in with me."

I rolled my eyes and laughed.

"If you think for one minute I don't intend on falling asleep next to you every night and waking up every morning with you in my arms, then you are crazy," he said.

"That's moving supersonic fast."

He smiled and his dimples were on full display. "Sweetheart, have you never seen me rope a calf before? Supersonic is the only speed I know."

Chapter Twenty-Nine

TANNER

The most beautiful smile appeared on Timberlynn's face before she laughed. "You're serious. You're really going to buy the house on the lake? And you want me to move in with you?"

I cupped her face in my hands. "I wasn't just talking out of my ass when I said I was falling in love with you, Timber. I want to be a part of your life in every single way. And I want you to be a part of mine."

"So, what you're saying is, I'm your new partner?"

With a chuckle, I nodded, then pulled her face to mine and kissed her. Her fingers laced into my hair, and she let out a moan so sexy it shot a bolt of electricity straight to my cock.

I walked her back slowly until she was pressed against the door.

"Tanner," she whispered against my mouth as she pulled on my hair gently. "We already desecrated your daddy's office once."

With a quick look around, I laughed. "Good point. So you'll think about everything I said?"

She nodded. "I will. I promise."

"We better get back out there, or someone will come looking for us."

"Okay."

As we headed out the door, Timberlynn reached for my hand and pulled me to a stop. "I want you to know something."

"What's that?"

"I trust you with all my heart, and I don't think we're going to fail."

With a soft kiss on her forehead, I nodded. "I know. My folks tried to tell me to wait a bit before I talked to you about my plan, but I really wanted you to know how I felt and what I wanted for our future. I won't hold you back from your dreams, Timber. I swear to you. If you want to purchase your own place, I'll support you a hundred percent."

She placed her hand on the side of my face. "You really are so amazing, do you know that?"

"Midnight is in fifteen minutes!" someone shouted.

"Come on, let's go grab some champagne and get ready to start the New Year together. You and me."

With a smile, she repeated, "You and me."

As Timberlynn and I made our way back to the crowd, I realized that people had started to make their way outside. "Let's grab our coats and join them."

Timberlynn stopped walking. "Outside? It's freezing out there!"

I gave her a wink and said, "Trust me, it'll be worth it."

Ty was headed our way, both our coats in his hands. Kaylee followed behind him.

"Thought you might want these," Ty said as he handed us our jackets.

"Why are we going outside?" Timberlynn asked. I helped slip her coat on.

"You'll see!" Kaylee said. "Here, at least one of us can drink the new year in!"

Timberlynn took the two glasses of champagne from Kaylee and handed one to me. "Now I'm curious!" she said with a slight giggle.

As we stepped outside, I noticed the fire my dad had started in the pit. Brock stood next to our parents with his arms around Lincoln. Blayze sat on top of my father's shoulders, and my mother seemed to have a glow about her that I could see thanks to the fire's light. I knew she was happy to have us all home and together.

I did a quick sweep of the outstretched ranch before us. The moon hit the snow and lit it up like a nighttime candle. Damn, I loved this place, and I knew I had made the right decision in staying. Every day that passed, working alongside my father and brothers, I knew in my heart that this was where I needed to be. And the woman standing next to me was the person I wanted to spend the rest of my life with. I didn't have a doubt in the world about that.

Timberlynn leaned into me, so I wrapped my arm around her waist. Ty and Kaylee had joined us and stood between Timberlynn and my folks. My mother turned to see us all there and smiled so big I couldn't help but smile back. "I'm so happy to have all my kids home. I love you all so much! I'm sure Beck is looking down smiling on us this evening. Happy to see all of his brothers are home safe and sound."

Ty leaned down and kissed our mother on the cheek, followed by Brock, then me.

Timberlynn smiled up at me.

"What?" I asked.

"I just love your family is all."

"You're a part of it now, darlin'."

Her cheeks turned slightly pink, and she jumped when Dad shouted, "It's almost time! Grab the person you want to ring in the New Year with!"

"Where's Dirk?" I asked Brock. We both searched the crowd. He always rang in the New Year with us when he was home.

"He probably can't find anyone to kiss at midnight!" Brock said with a laugh.

"What about Merit?" Timberlynn asked.

Brock laughed again. "That was a long time ago and only a one-time thing." He frowned, though, and looked around once more. "Last I saw him, he had taken Merit to look at the ranch survey."

Lincoln, Kaylee, and Timberlynn all exchanged a look. "That's funny. Dirk is missing. Merit is missing. Interesting," Kaylee mused.

"Don't go starting anything with that, Kaylee," Ty warned. "That happened a long time ago, and I doubt Merit wants anything to do with Dirk's whorish ways."

Kaylee shrugged. "Stranger things have happened." I laughed as she pointed to each of the Shaw brothers.

"A toast, before the New Year rolls in!" my mother shouted. "To love, happiness, family, and health!"

"Well said!" Brock called out as everyone took a drink of champagne. Well, everyone but Lincoln and Kaylee. They both held up glasses of water.

"One minute!" Dad yelled out.

Timberlynn pulled out her phone from the small purse she had tucked under her arm. She stared at it, and I instantly saw the tears forming in her eyes.

"Hey," I asked, tipping her chin up so our eyes met. "Is everything okay?"

"Twenty seconds!" Ty cried out.

She nodded. "My dad sent me a text. He said Happy New Year and that he loved me."

I smiled. "That's a good thing, right?"

Timberlynn chewed on her lip. "Yes."

"Ten!"

"Come here," I said as I drew her closer to me.

"Seven!"

I used my thumb to wipe away the tear that had started to fall down her beautiful face.

"Four!"

"I'll fix it all, Timber. I swear to you."

"Two! One!"

Happy New Year was shouted as I leaned down and kissed her lips gently, fireworks exploding above us.

The whole world faded away as Timberlynn wrapped her arms around my neck, and I laughed as she kissed me.

I loved this woman; I felt it in the depths of my heart and soul. And I knew exactly how to make good on the promise I had just made her.

◆ ◆ ◆

My father and two brothers stared at me like I had lost my mind.

"Tanner, you can't be serious," Brock said, his arms folded across his chest and a serious expression on his face.

"I've seen that look before," Ty stated. "He's dead serious."

"What do you expect to gain from flying to Georgia and talking to Timberlynn's father?" Dad asked.

"Well, for one thing, I'm going to tell him I'm in love with his daughter and to ask him to come to Montana."

"You're going to do what?!" Ty said, his eyes wide. "Do you think it's wise to tell her father you're in love with her when you've only been dating for a month or so?"

It had been exactly a month and some change since Timberlynn and I had officially started dating. After the New Year, my folks and I quickly worked on me buying the lake house, and I had moved in a few days ago. My folks sold me the house fully furnished, but there were still a few things I wanted to do to update things and make it my own. Timberlynn decided she would move in with me, but she was still keeping an eye out for her own place to buy. And she had made arrangements to speak with the Peterson's about buying some of their land that backed up to the parcel of the ranch that I now owned.

I followed my father's advice and hadn't pressed the issue of Timberlynn starting her business on the ranch. She had also insisted on paying me rent, which had caused our first fight. It didn't last long, and we both agreed she would pay the utilities. Then we had make-up sex on the kitchen island.

My father sighed, took off his hat, and ran his fingers through his hair before he carefully placed it on top of his head again. "Tanner, a lot has happened in your world in the last month. You've retired from ropin', you bought a house, and you entered into your first real relationship."

"I dated in high school, Dad. I'm not a relationship virgin."

"Son, high school doesn't count. You are living with Timberlynn. This is a relationship, not sex in the back of your truck and a trip to Sonic afterwards for dinner and a chocolate shake."

Ty and Brock both laughed, and I shot them each a dirty look.

"You yourself said that this is the first time Timberlynn has been free to do what she wants. Now you're asking her to set up shop in a place that isn't hers."

I rubbed the back of my neck and sighed. I knew he was right. Hell, Timberlynn and I were moving faster than fast, but it felt right.

"Fast is something we do in this family, Dad," Brock said. "Look at how fast Lincoln and I went."

"Lincoln was also pregnant and…"

Three sets of blue eyes looked at me. Ty and Brock suddenly seemed amused, and my father had a stern expression on his face. "Good Lord, tell me you haven't gone and gotten the girl pregnant."

I laughed. Only because now I could laugh. For a few weeks I did my fair share of silently freaking the fuck out until Timberlynn went to the doctor and got the all clear she wasn't pregnant. She was now on birth control, though the doctor advised her to continue the condoms for at least a month. I even had the damn day marked in my phone when I could make love to her bareback again.

"Timberlynn is not pregnant."

"Thank goodness," my father said.

"Would that be a bad thing, Dad?" I asked.

"Yes, in a way. I want the girl to pursue her dreams, Tanner, and so should you."

"I do want that. I'm not ready to have kids, but if it happened, I wouldn't be upset either."

"Christ Almighty, is there something in the water you boys are drinking? You all have lost your damn minds."

All heads swung around to see Dirk walking up. Brock pushed off the wall and made his way over to him. "What are you doing here? I thought you were riding this weekend."

"I am. I flew back in to help my folks with some repairs they needed done on the well."

"I could have helped them," I said.

Dirk gave me a smile and nodded his head. "I know, but it sounded like they were itching for me to come home for a few days. What's this about kids?"

"Nothing," I stated as I looked back at my father quickly. "I was trying to tell my dad and brothers that I think I need to go to Atlanta to talk to Lincoln's father. I can't stand to see the sadness in her eyes every time she mentions him. He sends her exactly one text a week now, and he ends it by asking her when she's coming home."

My father shook his head. "So strange."

"I think there's more to it," Ty said.

"Like PTSD from the mother dying?" Dirk added.

I looked between the two of them. "What?"

Ty took in a deep breath and then exhaled. "From what Kaylee has told me, Timberlynn's parents were the classic love story. Met in college, got married right after. She said she can remember her parents making comments about how the two were inseparable. The fact that the man has never remarried also says something."

"From what Timberlynn says, he's played the field. Maybe he likes the freedom of all the women," I said.

"Or, he doesn't want anyone in the same way that he wanted his wife. Didn't you mention that Timberlynn said that if anyone her father dated got to close to her, he would break up with them?" my father asked.

I thought about it for a moment. "Yes. She did mention that. So, the dad doesn't get married again because he was madly in love with his wife. I get that. But that doesn't explain why he's kept Timberlynn at arm's length all these years. Why treat her like she isn't even there?"

This time Brock spoke. "To guard his own heart. Maybe he was so heartbroken about his wife's death, he figured he'd be safe if he kept Timberlynn at a distance. Out of fear of losing her too."

I nodded. "That makes sense. But shouldn't that be all the more reason for me to go and talk to him? He needs to know how much his daughter has needed him. I love her, and I don't want to see her hurting like this. Plus, if he comes to Montana and sees how happy she is, he'll back off the bullshit of blocking her from purchasing anything here."

The four of them exchanged looks, and my father finally nodded. "Do you want me to fly out with you?" he asked.

"No, I don't want him to think we're double-teaming him," I replied.

"True," Brock stated.

Dirk cleared his throat and smirked. "My question is, are you going to tell Timberlynn you're going to Atlanta to talk to her dad?"

My father, Ty, and Brock all looked my way, waiting for my answer.

Chapter Thirty

TIMBERLYNN

I sat on the kitchen counter of the lake house and stared at Tanner. "You want to go to Atlanta? What on Earth for?"

Tanner tossed the kitchen towel over his shoulder and turned to face me. I licked my lips and tried not to ogle his body but failed. There was something incredibly sexy about this man cooking. He wore his signature jeans, a black T-shirt that showcased his broad chest and shoulders, and his hair was rumpled from his fingers raking through it all day. He had gotten into the habit of taking his cowboy hat off at the door, like at his folks' house, and I loved it. Don't get me wrong, I loved seeing a hat on him too. But that brown hair, rumpled and sexy looking—Lord, it was one of my favorite things.

"I want to meet your father."

I jerked my head back up and laughed. "Wait, I could have swore you just said you wanted to meet my father."

"I did say that."

"Have you lost your mind?"

"Well, for starters, we're dating, and although it's still early on, I think it's important he meets me and knows my intentions for our relationship. Plus, I think he needs to know you have another reason for wanting to live in Montana."

Anger pulsed through my body. "I don't need to give him any reasons, Tanner. He doesn't control my life anymore, and besides, I've already told him about you."

He sighed. "That's where you're wrong, Timber. He does control it still. Have you forgotten about the house you tried to buy? He sends you a text at least once a week asking when you're moving back to Atlanta. He's not coming to terms with you moving to Montana."

"He doesn't get a say in it."

Tanner raised a brow. "Do you really want to cut your father out of your life? You don't want me to meet him? Have him be a part of our lives?"

I let out a defeated breath. "Tanner, he's never wanted to be a part of my life before. Why should I worry about it now?"

Tanner walked up to me and stood between my legs. His expression was so serious. "What if the reason your dad kept you at a distance wasn't because he didn't love you or want you in his life. What if it was because he was scared?"

"Scared?" I asked, confused. "Scared of what?"

"Losing you like he did your mother. Have you ever thought about it like that, or had a therapist mentioned that to you?"

I looked down for a moment and thought about what he just said. Slowly, I shook my head. "No one has ever said that before, and honestly, I've never even thought of it."

Tanner pulled me closer to him, and I draped my arms over his shoulders. "Think about it," he said. "You told me that anytime someone he dated got close to you, your father broke up with them. Maybe it was because he didn't want you to think it was a replacement for your mother?"

I let his words simmer in my brain.

"And his distance from you? Maybe in some weird sort of post-traumatic stress way he kept you at arm's length thinking it would somehow keep you both safe?"

My eyes met his. "I...I hadn't ever thought of it that way."

"Timber, do you doubt your father loves you?"

I swallowed hard and pressed my lips together tightly. If I spoke right then, I knew I was going to cry. So I shrugged.

"He's scared right now. The whole move with blocking you from buying the Covey place, maybe it was his way of showing you that he isn't okay with losing you."

"He hasn't lost me," I whispered.

Tanner raised a brow. "Maybe you both need to hear each other say that."

My eyes stung as I tried to hold back my emotions. "I don't honestly think I could take being hurt again by him, Tanner. All the moments in my life when my father promised to be there for me, and he never...he never really was."

Tanner cupped my face in his hands and bent to look me straight in the eye. "Trust me on this? Please. Let me take you back to Atlanta to meet your dad. If you don't want to go back, we could invite him here."

"Here?"

"Yeah, he can stay with us."

I smiled. "Is this a way to get me to fully move in with you and stop looking for my own property?"

"No, but if you think it would work, I'm down for it."

Laughing, I pulled him closer to me and quickly kissed him before resting my forehead against his. "I don't want to go back to Atlanta, and I don't want you going either."

"Okay."

"Okay?" I asked as I drew back to look at him. "You wouldn't go if I asked you not to?"

The corner of his mouth rose into a sexy half smile. "No, baby, I would not go if you asked me not to. This relationship is based on trust and honesty. If you asked me not to go, I'd honor that. But I do think we should invite him here."

I pulled in a deep breath and held it for a moment before I slowly let it out. With each second of breath leaving my body, I allowed everything that Tanner was saying to absorb into me. "I'll call him tonight and invite him to visit."

A wide smile erupted across his face.

I held up my hand. "Don't get your hopes up, Tanner. He's a busy man, and I don't think I've ever known him to just drop everything and leave town, unless it was work related."

He winked and then pulled me into him so that I was forced to wrap my legs around his body. "I have a feeling you're wrong on this one."

"Oh, really?" I said as I pressed my mouth to his. Tanner lifted me off the counter and started walking down the hall to our bedroom.

With a laugh, I drew back from his mouth and asked, "Where are you going?"

"To our room, to make love to you."

My body ached instantly for him. "What about dinner?"

"Don't you worry that pretty little head of yours. I can be fast when I need to be."

◆ ◆ ◆

I sat on the front porch and stared out at the lake. It was cold outside, but I was bundled up and warmed still from Tanner making love to me earlier.

My eyes closed, and I drifted back to his mouth moving slowly over me. His hands had explored my body like it was the first time he'd ever seen me naked. The words he'd whispered in my ear made my entire body shiver, and it wasn't from the cold air.

"Hungry?" Tanner asked as he stood next to me on the porch.

I stood and smiled as I made my way over to him and back into the house. "Starving!"

Tanner had made lasagna, and boy howdy, did my man know how to cook.

"I'll grab the salad," I said.

"I made a lemon vinaigrette that's in the fridge."

Pausing, I looked in the refrigerator and shook my head. "What, you just whipped up a vinaigrette while I was on the porch?"

He laughed. "It wasn't hard...remember, I had a good teacher when it comes to cooking."

That I had no doubt believing.

"After dinner, I have a little surprise for you."

I set the salad and dressing on the table and smiled up at him. "Really? Do I get any hints?"

"No, you have to wait and see."

I pushed my lip out into a pout, and Tanner laughed. He placed the lasagna down on the table, and then started to cut us each a piece while I held out the plates. "Not even one hint?"

"No, not even one hint, and stop pouting. All it does is turn me on and make me want to push everything off the table and take you right here."

My lip drew in, and I gently bit down on it as I tried to ignore the way my lower stomach pulled with desire at the mental picture Tanner had painted. "That would be a shame since you spent so much time making this delicious meal."

He winked. "It's a sacrifice I'd be willing to make. We can always have frozen pizza."

I laughed and shook my head as I used the tongs to put salad on each of our plates.

I took one bite of the lasagna and let out a long, soft moan. Tanner grinned. "I take it you like it?"

"Like it? Tanner, this is amazing!"

"It's the homemade ragu. It's a recipe my mother got from her friend Tina. She's Italian and makes some of the best Italian food I've ever eaten in my life."

"I love authentic Italian food, and I can honestly say I haven't had a sauce this good ever before!" I replied before I shoved another forkful in my mouth.

"Word of warning, don't ever tell Tina you're eating jar from a sauce. She'll drag you into the kitchen to cook up a pot of ragu on the spot, then send you home hours later with jars of it. Each time she converts a jar sauce lover to fresh ragu, she says she's doing the Lord's work."

I closed my eyes and moaned again as I let each spice from the homemade ragu settle in my mouth.

Tanner and I spent the rest of our meal in a comfortable silence. I knew he was leaving me to my thoughts about my father. A part of me knew that what Tanner said made sense. Maybe all those years of distance was my father's own mechanism for keeping himself from being hurt again. It still didn't make it right. I would never be able to get back all the moments I wished my father had been there for me.

I must have sighed, because Tanner reached across the table and squeezed my hand. "Let's leave the dishes for now, and before you call your father, let me take you to the barn. I have that surprise for you."

"The barn?" I asked, instantly perking up. I knew Tanner had set up a stall for his horse Trigger and one for Rosie. He knew I had taken a liking to her. But I also knew they were both turned out in the smaller pasture that was set off to the side from the lake. Tanner and Ty had fenced it in after Tanner bought the lake house and two-hundred acres from his folks.

I had gone over it in my mind a thousand times. I could buy that land from the Peterson's and that would put my own investment in, but I knew deep within in my heart that I would have a long future with Tanner. I couldn't explain how I knew it or why it felt so different, but I knew this relationship with Tanner was it. He was my future. Yet, I still wanted to have something that was mine. As much as I loved Tanner, I didn't need him to rush in on a white horse to save me. Tanner himself told me that he'd always wanted the lake house—and Kaylee and Lincoln had talked to Ty and Brock and confirmed it. Yet, I couldn't bring myself to jump on board with his plan. Maybe someday, when we were engaged, it would feel different. Right now, it simply felt like Tanner was handing me my dream. I loved him for that, but I needed to work it out for myself.

After we wrapped ourselves up in jackets, gloves, and hats, we made our way to the barn. A light snow was falling, dusting the ground just enough to take my breath away once more. Something about a fresh snowfall on the rolling hills and mountainsides made me feel so at peace.

When we walked into the barn, I stopped at the sight of a horse in a stall. He was a chestnut thoroughbred and he looked very malnourished. "What happened?" I asked as I rushed over to him.

"Someone my mother knows from the Hamilton SPCA called her yesterday and said they had a rescue horse they needed to find a permanent home for," Tanner said with a nonchalant shrug. "The owner had been given the horse in hopes of training him to race. He hit some hard times and thought maybe he could hold onto the horse, but realized he needed to give him up. They asked if she was interested in taking him on. She told them she knew of someone who would be starting a new training business, but who was also interested in rescue horses."

I placed my hand out for the beautiful chestnut to smell before I gently rubbed down the side of his face. He let out a sad nicker. I softly rubbed his neck. He looked like he had been left to starve, and that broke my heart.

"I know you're not ready to start training yet or take on rescues, but my mother thought it would be good for both of you to help each other out," Tanner said.

With a smile, I unlatched the stall door and slipped inside. The gelding looked down at me, and when his eyes met mine, I felt the instant connection. "Hey there, beautiful. You're safe now. We're going to take care of you."

Tanner watched as I cooed to the horse. "I was thinking this spring we could make a corral off the side of the barn to do some rope work with him. I don't think he's trained at all."

I nodded and ran my hand over his back. "I'd like to talk to your mom about what she thinks is the best approach feed-wise."

"She'd love that," Tanner said as he joined me in the stall. "He seems to like you. He's a sweet boy, and didn't give Chance any issues when he picked him up from the Hamilton SPCA. As a matter of fact, Chance said the horse almost knew he was there to take him out of that place."

"Chance brought him here?"

"Yeah. I gave him a call and asked if he'd be interested in picking him up for me. He was more than happy to do it."

I smiled and focused back on the horse. This was my first recuse horse, and how fitting that he was here in Tanner's barn and that we were doing it together.

My heart skipped a beat as I turned and looked at Tanner. He slowly ran his hand down the gelding's leg, and then lifted it to examine his shoe.

In a sudden rush of realization, I took a few steps back and watched Tanner interact with the horse. Everything I had been through had brought me to this very moment. The only thing I needed in my life was this man. This wonderful, caring, amazing man who was starting his own journey in life, and bought a freaking house and land so that I could start a dream I'd had for so long. The one person I knew I was destined to spend the rest of my life with. There was a reason he had pushed his way into my heart, and I wasn't afraid to take the leap with him. Not anymore. Faith and trust were the two things that stood out when it came to Tanner Shaw.

"We could do this together," I softly whispered.

"What was that?" Tanner asked as he looked up at me and let the horse's leg down.

"Nothing, I was just thinking out loud."

He smiled, and I couldn't help but smile back. "Do you think you'll have time to maybe work him with me?"

Tanner's smile morphed into a wide grin. "I was hoping you'd ask. I'd love to work with him. He looks like he could be a great horse. If you wanted to get back into dressage competition, he'd be perfect for that. I can see it in his eyes."

I looked at the pathetic-looking horse. He looked tired, and only someone who truly loved horses could look past what was on the outside to see what potential this horse had. I sensed it the moment I stepped into the stall with him, and clearly Tanner had as well. "If you don't mind, I think I'm going to call my father."

Tanner looked surprised. "Right now?"

I nodded. "Yes. Right now."

Chapter Thirty-One

TIMBERLYNN

My heart pounded so loudly, I was positive everyone in the Missoula airport heard it.

"Don't be nervous," Tanner whispered as he pulled me closer to him.

"I can't believe he agreed to come."

"And why wouldn't he?"

Slowly, I shook my head. "Because he's never come to anything. Ever. Tanner, he wasn't even at my high school graduation."

Tanner frowned. "He wasn't?"

"No! Or my college graduation."

Without saying a word, Tanner kissed me on the forehead. "Well, he's here now."

I blew out a breath and mumbled, "He's about eighteen years too late."

My breath caught in my throat as I saw my father heading down the escalator. He scanned the area, and when he saw me, he smiled. I smiled back, almost without meaning to. Things had been tense between us the last few years, but that one smile gave me the slightest bit of hope. I wasn't going to go crazy, though. My father had let me down so many times in my past, and I knew this feeling was only temporary.

"There he is," I softly said as Tanner dropped his arm from around my waist.

In a minute he was there. Standing in front of me, the smile still on his face. He truly looked happy to see me.

"Dad," I said as I walked up and kissed him on the cheek. I was stunned when he pulled me into a hug and held onto me.

"Timberlynn, I've missed you so much, sweetheart."

Then he let me go and looked at Tanner.

Tanner stuck out his hand to give him a firm shake. "Mr. Holden, I'm Tanner Shaw, it's a real pleasure to meet you."

My father gave Tanner a good once-over. His smile was still there, yet it had faded ever so slightly. "Tanner, it's good to meet you. It's also good to put a face to the name."

I smiled nervously.

"Your luggage will be coming off of this belt," Tanner stated.

"I carried mine on, learned my lesson a time or two."

Tanner laughed an honest laugh, while I let out a nervous-sounding chuckle. My father turned to look at me, and I forced myself to smile wide. "Did you have a good flight?"

He nodded.

Tanner reached for his suitcase. "Let me take that for you, sir. I hope you don't mind, but my parents have planned a small lunch with my two older brothers and their wives to welcome you to Montana."

My father kept the pleasant smile on his face. "That sounds nice."

As we walked out of the airport, my father stopped. I turned and looked at him.

"Dad? What's wrong?"

He stared straight ahead, and I heard Tanner chuckle. "They're beautiful, aren't they?" Tanner said.

With a slow nod of his head, my father replied, "They don't look real. It looks like a picture."

I turned to see where he was looking. The mountains. They were covered in a fresh snowfall, and it looked like a winter wonderland.

Smiling, I stared out at the same view. They were part of the reason I was drawn to Montana. But the man standing there, telling my father what mountain range he was looking at—he was the reason I had come here. I hadn't known it at the time, or maybe I had. But Tanner Shaw was one of the reasons I fell for Montana.

My father turned and looked at me. "Well, I certainly see the appeal."

"Just wait until you see Hamilton. Kaylee is so excited to see you."

His brows narrowed ever so slightly. "I don't even know when the last time I saw Kaylee was. I think you were in high school, and she might have been in college."

I laughed. "Most likely."

We made our way to Tanner's truck as my father kept talking. "I haven't heard or seen her parents in a while either."

"Kaylee said they were in Austria. Or maybe it was Australia. I don't remember."

He let out a halfhearted laugh. "They always did like to travel."

"Yes, they did," I replied.

When a silence settled over us, Tanner started to talk. "So, Timberlynn tells me you're a doctor."

My father smiled politely. "Yes, I am. Right now, though, I do mostly consulting work for hospitals."

When we got to Tanner's truck, Tanner opened the front door for me, held his hand out to help me in, then assisted my father with his suitcase.

"How long will you be able to stay?" I asked my father.

"I'm not sure. I told my secretary to put everything on hold for at least a week."

I felt Tanner turn and look at me. I was too nervous to meet his gaze.

A week. My father had planned on staying in Hamilton for a least a week. Was he going to try and talk me out of living here? That had to be why he planned on staying so long.

"Well, we've got you set up to stay with us, but my folks have also offered the use of their house as well. It's whatever makes you feel more comfortable."

"I appreciate that, Tanner. Now, how long have you and my daughter been living together?"

Oh. Shit.

This time I did look at Tanner, who simply took a quick look my way and winked.

"Not that long, sir. I've only just recently purchased a cabin that was on my folks' ranch."

I let out a nervous laugh. "It's not a cabin, it's a log house that sits on a crystal-clear lake. Dad, you should see it. If you thought the mountains outside the airport looked too pretty to be real, wait until you see the Shaw ranch."

"I'm excited to see it," my father said.

As we drove, my father asked Tanner questions about what type of ranch his family owned. Did they have cattle? Did they grow things? How long had it been in their family? Then he moved on to Tanner's recent career.

"You roped cows?"

"Yes, sir, I did. We mostly used Corriente cattle."

"And you made a decent living at it?"

"I did, yes. I was a four-time WNFR qualifier and won the world championship once."

"Are you able to make it with that sort of a living?"

My jaw dropped open, and I quickly turned to look at my father. "Dad!"

Tanner laughed. "It's okay, Timber. And yes, you can make money at it. My career earnings were around one-point-two million, give or take. I also still get asked to do endorsements. I'm set to fly to Colorado for a Wrangler commercial in March."

This time I looked at Tanner, my jaw even wider open at what he just said. "What?"

I hadn't even thought of asking Tanner what kind of money he made while roping. It honestly wasn't even something I thought about. I knew he had money, especially since he paid his folks cash for the lake house. He had never asked about my trust fund, and I had never asked him about his money. It never mattered to me, and I knew it didn't matter to him.

Tanner didn't look at me as he said, "Sorry, Timber, I just found out about that this morning. I was going to talk to you about the upcoming trip this evening."

I laughed. "I'm not surprised about your commercial... or maybe I am."

He shrugged as if it wasn't a big deal.

"Have you invested your winnings, Tanner?" my father asked.

"I have, yes, sir. I've learned a lot from my older brothers and have taken advice from them and my folks. I bought my house from my parents in cash, and it'll all be legally divided so that the house and acreage is in my name."

"Hmm."

It was the only response from my father before he cleared his throat. "And what about you, Timberlynn? Since you clearly haven't spoken to Tanner about his income, does he have any idea of what your net worth currently is, or what you stand to inherit once I pass away?"

My mouth felt like it turned to cotton. I tried to speak, but nothing came out. The idea of my father dying was something I didn't like to think about. At all.

I could feel Tanner's eyes on me. "We have not spoken about that, Mr. Holden," he said. "I need you to know I have no intentions of holding Timberlynn back from pursuing her dreams of horse training and rescue. I have no intentions of using any of Timberlynn's money. That is for her to use to pursue her own dreams."

"What about nursing?"

"Dad, I told you I'm not interested in nursing."

"What you're telling me, then, is that I paid for you to go to college for nothing."

I closed my eyes and slowly drew in a deep breath. "Do you think we could talk about this later, in private?"

"Why? If you've decided to move in with this... cowboy...and didn't bother to talk to him about your finances or his, why feel the need to hide anything?"

Tanner reached for my hand and gave it a squeeze before our fingers laced together.

"My daughter happens to have a small fortune of her own, Mr. Shaw. And when I pass away, she'll inherit even more. If you think for one second you're going to get your hands on—"

"With all due respect, Mr. Holden, I'm not the least bit interested in your daughter's current or future financial holdings. If we decided to marry and Timberlynn asks me to sign a prenuptial agreement, you will not hear any arguments from me. I'm a rancher by nature, sir. Money isn't something my family has strived for. It's been nice to have, but it doesn't buy my happiness. What makes me happy is seeing your daughter smile at me first thing in the morning. Hearing my niece and nephew laughing as they run around the yard. Seeing my folks dancing in the kitchen while my mama hums her favorite song. Those are the things in this life that make me happy. Not money."

I placed my hand over my stomach to calm the sudden rush of flurries. If my father hadn't been in the truck, I would have told Tanner right then and there how much I loved him.

Tanner looked at me and smiled. Those blue eyes of his sparkled, and his dimples were on full display, which caused my heart to speed up ever so slightly.

"That was a nice speech," my father said.

I closed my eyes and sighed.

"I'm sorry you thought it was a speech because it was from my heart."

The rest of the drive was made in silence. We pulled up to the gate of the Shaw ranch and Tanner clicked the gate opener.

"Did you want to freshen up first before you meet the rest of Tanner's family?" I asked.

My father didn't reply. I turned around in my seat to find him staring intently out the window. "Dad?"

He didn't respond, so I followed his gaze. Six horses were out in the pasture. It was a stunning sight to see with the Bitterroot Mountains in the background and the sky turning a soft pink as the sun dipped lower.

I focused back on my father. "Dad?"

"Your mother would have loved it here," he softly said as he smiled. It was such a genuine smile. "She loved horses, like you do, Timberlynn."

My throat worked to swallow the emotion that had suddenly built up. It was the first time he'd mentioned my mother in...I didn't even know how long. "I know she did."

He broke his gaze and looked at me. "What did you ask me?"

"Would you like to freshen up before you meet the rest of Tanner's family?"

He shook his head. "No, I'm fine, sweetheart."

I smiled softly and then turned to look straight ahead. My father had just gone from ice cold to warm. It was something he had done often when thoughts of my mother hit him.

We drove down the long driveway, winding around snow-covered pastures dotted with both horses and cattle.

"What's down there?" my father asked as we passed a road off the main drive that went to the left and had a little gate on it.

"That takes you to my brother Brock's house," Tanner said. "We'll pass a few more roads, mostly dirt roads that take you to various parts of the ranch. Then as we get closer to my folks' place, we'll pass the road that takes you to Crystal Lake and my house."

"And your other brother? He lives on the ranch too?"

"He lives with Kaylee on a piece of property that's adjacent to the ranch," I said.

Tanner nodded. "It used to be part of the ranch, but my parents subdivided it for my brother a number of years ago."

"I see, like they did for you?" my father asked.

"Yes," Tanner answered, not giving him any more details.

The house soon came into view, and I took in a deep breath. I had no idea how this night was going to go, and I couldn't shake the strange feeling of uneasiness that bubbled up in my chest.

But suddenly, my father said the one thing I hadn't expected him to. "I'm sorry for coming off as a hard ass, Tanner. It's just...she's my only daughter."

Tanner looked in the rearview mirror and nodded. "No apology needed, sir."

Chapter Thirty-Two

TANNER

The moment I parked in front of my folks' house, the front door flew open and out piled the entire Shaw clan.

"Oh no," Timberlynn whispered.

"Looks like they're excited to meet me," Frank said with a chuckle. His mood had lightened, and to say I had been shocked when he apologized would be an understatement. Timberlynn still seemed to be stunned by Frank's apology. I took the excitement in Frank's voice as a good sign. Timberlynn hadn't noticed it though, because it appeared she was attempting to keep herself from hyperventilating at the thought of her father meeting my whole family.

"Hey, it's okay," I said as I squeezed her leg.

She looked at me, and I smiled. I instantly saw her relax, and she mouthed *thank you* before looking back at her dad. She went to say something, but he was already halfway out the door. He got out and shut it and glanced back at us as if wondering why we were still sitting in the truck.

"Looks like he's ready to meet everyone."

Timberlynn looked at her father as he stood there and waited for us to get out of the truck. She turned back to me and let out a disbelieving laugh. "I guess so."

"Come on, let's do this." I jumped out of the truck and jogged around to help Timberlynn down. The three of us made our way toward the front porch.

"Uncle Frank!" Kaylee said, the first one to hold out her arms for a hug.

"It's good to see you, Kaylee. You look..." he gave her a once-over and smiled. "You look very happy."

She laughed. "It could be the pregnancy giving me a glow."

He hugged her again as he chuckled. "I knew it. It showed in your eyes."

I turned and looked at Timberlynn, wondering if she had remembered our conversation about the emotions our eyes held. She gave me a knowing smile.

"When are you due?"

"August fifth."

"Well, congratulations are definitely in order," Frank told her.

"Mr. Holden, this is my father and mother, Stella and Ty Senior. Mom, Dad, this is Dr. Frank Holden."

Frank waved his hand off. "No need to be formal. Frank will do."

My father was first to approach. He held out his hand. "It's good to have you here, Frank. We've sort of taken to that daughter of yours. She's something special."

Frank looked at Timberlynn and winked. "That she is."

I could see the confused expression on Timberlynn's face before she covered it with a soft smile.

My mother spoke next. "Frank, I'm so glad you've come to visit. Now, if you don't want to stay with the kids, we have the guest room all set up and ready for you. Timberlynn was staying there before she moved out with Tanner, but it's yours if you need it."

Timberlynn squeezed my hand, and I gave her a squeeze back.

"Thank you, Stella. I think I'll take you up on that offer of staying here."

That made both me and Timberlynn jerk our heads to Frank.

"You don't want to stay with us?" Timberlynn asked. Even I could hear the hurt in her voice.

Frank looked at her, and it was evident he heard it as well. "It's not that I don't want to stay with you, sweetheart, I just think it's better this way. Let me get used to you living with a man before you throw me full on into it."

Everyone laughed, and Timberlynn's body relaxed a bit. I knew Timberlynn had some issues with her father, but I was beginning to think they went much deeper than I had thought. I looked over at Ty and our eyes met. It was like he could read my mind because he gave me a nod. I wasn't sure why, but it reassured me some.

Brock and Lincoln were next with the introductions. Then came the kids.

"This is Morgan," Brock said, "and we've got another one baking away."

Lincoln rolled her eyes. "Not sure if it's a boy or a girl just yet."

"When are you due?" Frank asked.

"May fifteenth."

Frank looked at Kaylee. "That's nice that you're both pregnant at the same time."

Kaylee nodded.

"I'm Blayze Shaw. It's a real pleasure to meet ya, sir."

Frank knelt down and got eye level with Blayze. "My, you are a fine-looking cowboy."

Blayze stood a little taller. "I threw my hat in the ring for Timberlynn, but my Uncle Tanner won her heart. But that's okay 'cause there's this girl in my class I like. Her name is Morgan, just like my sister's. I used to like Lilly, but she kicked me, so now I like Morgan. She asked me to kiss her, but I told her she'd have to change her name because that would be gross."

Frank lifted his brows as Blayze continued on.

"See, that would be gross 'cause that's my sister's name," Blayze stuttered. "That would be like kissing my sister."

"That is a fair and good point you've got there," Frank said.

"She asked you to kiss her?" Lincoln asked as she stared down at Blayze.

"Don't worry, Mama, I told her I wasn't allowed to be kissing girls on the lips, but that I could give her a kiss on the cheek. Well, if her name wasn't Morgan."

Both Lincoln and Brock let out a groan while the rest of us tried not to laugh.

"Uncle Frank, this is my husband Ty," Kaylee said.

Ty shook Frank's hand. "Welcome to Montana, sir."

"Thank you. The beauty here is beyond words, and I'm not normally at a loss for words."

"Do you ride?" my father asked.

The question seemed to take Frank aback. "Honestly, I haven't been on a horse since I rode with my wife last, so I'm a bit rusty."

I heard the intake of air from Timberlynn. Clearly that little bit of information took her by surprise.

"It's like riding a bike. Would you be up for a ride tomorrow morning? I'd love to show you the ranch," my father said.

Frank smiled. "I would like that very much. Tanner, would you be able to join us?"

Okay, that took me by surprise. At least my father would be there to protect me. "Yes, I'd love to come along."

My mother motioned for everyone to head into the house. "Let's all get inside. The sun is going down and the temperature is dropping. Frank, I hope you like roast and vegetables."

"One of my favorite meals."

Everyone piled into the house, but before I could step through the door, I was yanked back by Timberlynn. She looked utterly panicked.

"What is happening?" she asked as her eyes darted from the front door, back to me, then the door again.

"What do you mean?"

"I mean, he wants to stay here with your folks. He's going riding with your dad and asked you to come along, and do not even get me started on him not riding a horse since my mother! What in the hell?"

I laughed and kissed her on the forehead. "Were you expecting it to be worse?"

"Yes! No! I don't know, Tanner. I'm so nervous and I don't know why!"

I pulled her into my arms and held her. "Take a deep breath, baby. It's going to be okay. Your father already seems like he's going to fit in just fine."

"He doesn't do family, Tanner."

Gently, I pushed her out some and looked into her eyes. "Maybe he's never known how to do family without your mother, Timber."

Her eyes filled with tears.

"No, baby, don't cry. Come here."

Timberlynn buried her face into my chest, and I held her. "I'm so confused by everything, Tanner. I don't know how I'm supposed to feel. A part of me thinks this is why I picked Montana to live—it was far away from my father and the constant reminder that I was never good enough for him."

"Hey, don't say that, okay? You are more than good enough. Please don't think like that. Let's just take it a day at a time."

She nodded, then rubbed her nose all on my shirt. I was pretty sure I was madly in love with the woman because it didn't bother me a single bit that her snot was now all over me.

I tipped her chin so our eyes met. I took a deep breath and said, "I love you, Timberlynn. I'm never going to let anything or anyone hurt you. I swear it."

Her chin quivered, and she smiled. "I love you too, Tanner."

Leaning down, I paused at her mouth and whispered, "Say it again."

She giggled. "I love you."

My lips brushed softly over hers in a tender kiss. "Now, take a few deep breaths, wipe away the tears, and let's head on inside. I'll be by your side the entire time."

Timberlynn nodded. "Okay. Let's go."

◆ ◆ ◆

I placed the saddle on the back of Trigger while Brock saddled up Pogo.

He cleared his throat and broke our silence. "Last night went pretty good, don't you think?"

"Yeah, I think it went a lot better than Timberlynn expected. To be honest, with the way she described him, I figured he might be a snob. But he really hit it off with Dad."

Brock laughed. "I'd say they hit it off. Mom said they were on the back porch smoking cigars half the night. She fell asleep at one, and dad was still out there with Frank."

"Really?"

"Yep. How's Timberlynn? She looked so off-balance last night."

I sighed. "Yeah, I think she's trying to figure out this side of her father she's never seen."

"Do you think it's because he's relaxed? Or around people who don't really know him?"

"Could be."

"Well, we all know why he wanted you on this ride."

I laughed. "So why do you think Dad and Frank went out a bit earlier on their own?"

Brock finished getting Pogo ready and faced me. "My thoughts are they wanted to talk about you and Timberlynn."

"Yeah, mine too. What about us?"

He shrugged. "Listen, I'm playing devil's advocate, so don't think I'm judging. Lincoln and I moved faster than any couple I've ever known, but maybe Frank has an issue with how quickly things are going with you two. It's been what, two months since you became official?"

"About that. And I know we're moving fast, but I love her, Brock."

My brother smiled. "I know you do, Tanner. I think you fell in love with her the moment you first saw her. It's not hard to see how you two feel about each other. It's written all over your faces."

A sound from outside caused Brock and me to turn and look.

"Sounds like they're back. Were your ears burning?" Brock asked while he walked Pogo out of the barn.

I shot him a go-to-hell smirk, and then gave Trigger a quick pat on the neck. "Come on, girl, let's get some exercise."

As I walked out of the barn, I watched Brock swing up on Pogo. Dad was sitting on top of his favorite quarter horse, Russ, while Frank rode on a mare named Lucy that my mother had rescued a few years back.

"How's Lucy treating you?" I asked as I swung up onto Trigger. I could feel her tremble lightly under me. I reached down and rubbed along her neck to calm her down. She was itching to get after some cows. As soon as the snow melted in the corral, I'd have to have Ty rope some with me.

Frank ran a hand over Lucy. "She's a beautiful horse. Your father told me all about how your mother saved her from the slaughterhouse."

I nodded. "She's saved a number of them, and all of them turned out to be damn good horses. I have to say, she's pretty excited Timberlynn is interested in starting a rescue."

Frank smiled and nodded his head while his gaze drifted down to Lucy. I knew my father put him up on that horse for a reason.

"Let's head out," my father stated as he turned Russ around and headed toward one of the trails. Brock rode up next to my father, so that Frank and I rode side by side. As we walked farther along, I noticed Frank slowed down the pace of his horse, while my father and Brock damn near almost trotted away.

"Your family seems to really love my daughter," Frank said.

"They're not the only ones who love her, sir."

I felt his eyes on me, so I turned to face him. "She loves you too—she told me when she called to invite me here. Sounds like it was a love-at-first-sight sorta thing."

How in the hell was I supposed to respond to that?

Before I had a chance to say anything, Frank kept going. "That was how it was with Lynn, my wife. I knew the moment I saw her I was going to marry her. I wasn't even looking for someone to be in a relationship with. There was something so wonderful about her. I see the same thing in Timberlynn, so I'm not surprised you fell like you did."

"She's pretty amazing."

He nodded and stared straight ahead before he spoke again. "She reminds me so much of her mother. Looks just like her. After her mother died, I got so lost in myself.

I tried so hard to be there for Timberlynn. I kept her close to me right after the accident. Then one day she was on a swing, and she fell and got hurt. I remember standing there, looking at the blood coming from her knee, and I was transported back to the day her mother died."

He turned and faced me, a look of sadness etched on his face that made my own chest hurt for him. "Everything changed that day, and by the time I realized I had pushed my own daughter away, it was too late. I didn't know how to reach out to her."

"I don't think it is too late. She loves you, and I know she desperately wants you in her life. I honestly don't think either one of you know how to have a relationship with each other."

He cleared his throat and looked at me. "I'm certainly not earning any bonus points lately. Did she tell you I bought the property she wanted and then sold it?"

"Yes, she was pretty angry about it."

"Don't blame her," he said with a sigh. "It was a pretty dick move on my part. I panicked when I found out she had left Atlanta. I haven't been there for her a whole lot since we lost her mother. I thought by keeping her at a safe distance, I was saving us both from any potential hurt. Then the day after she turned twenty-four, I was in a meeting with some doctors and lawyers from a pharmaceutical company, and I glanced down at the date. I'd forgotten my only daughter's birthday. Forgotten it. Then I got the notice she'd gotten her trust and found out she was buying that property the Covey family had for sale. In a span of thirty minutes I found out my daughter had quit her job and left the state. I was so pissed off that

I didn't dare call or text her. Then one day turned into a week, then two, and then I wasn't even sure what to say to her. Looking back now, of course, I know it was the wrong thing to do."

"With all due respect, I don't think it was."

Frank looked at me with a confused look. "You don't?"

"No," I said with a smile. "If you hadn't bought it out from under her, then I wouldn't have bought the lake house from my parents, and Timberlynn wouldn't be living with me. She wouldn't be working with a rescue horse right now, and I wouldn't be working alongside her."

Frank nodded. "I like you, Tanner. I like your family as well. I see why Timberlynn has fallen in love with Montana. I feel...different here. More at ease, and it's the first time that I don't feel guilty for feeling happy."

"Why on Earth would you feel guilty for being happy?"

The horses walked on as Frank and I rode in silence. I could see he was working through some emotions, so I waited for him to speak when he was ready.

"Timberlynn doesn't know this, but she was a bit of a miracle child. Lynn, my wife, was told she couldn't have kids. When we ended up getting pregnant with Timberlynn, I had never seen her so happy. She loved that little girl so much. Prayed for years for her, and cried so much when she found out she was pregnant. When she died, I couldn't understand why God would do something like that. My wife should have been there for every moment of Timberlynn's life. The guilt I felt was, at times, almost too much for me to handle."

"Is that part of the reason you stayed away from her? She told me you never came to any of her events, no school functions. Nothing."

He cleared his throat and quickly wiped a tear away. "Yes, that is part of the reason. And because of the guilt. I caused the accident."

That took me by surprise. "Sir?"

"I looked back at Timberlynn in the seat. Took my eyes off the road. If I had been paying better attention..."

His voice trailed off, and he looked away. I noticed where we were and saw that my father and Brock had kept going on the trail. I stopped Trigger, and Frank did the same with Lucy.

"I'd like to show you something, Frank. If you don't mind getting off our horses and taking a small walk up that hill."

He glanced over his shoulder and then nodded. "Okay."

"We don't have to tie the horses up; they'll stay right here."

As we walked up the small hill to the overlook, I tried to figure out what I wanted to say. In the end, I left it up to the man upstairs to get all my words straight in my head.

"This is where I brought Timberlynn on our first unofficial date."

Frank laughed, then stopped when he saw the view. For miles before us stretched open pastures, some more covered in snow than others. Cattle and horses walked freely, some even running and enjoying the warmth of the sun beaming down on them. Crystal Lake was iced over, but somehow she managed to reflect the snow-covered mountains around her.

"That house, next to the lake there, is where Timberlynn and I live."

"It's...beyond words. The sky here looks so...massive. Like it goes on forever."

I laughed. "Welcome to Montana. Big sky country. You should see it in the spring and the summer. And if you think this is beautiful, you should see it in the fall."

"I see why Timberlynn wants to live here. It's so different from Georgia."

Turning, I faced Frank. "Frank, have you ever talked to anyone about the accident? Losing your wife? Raising Timberlynn alone?"

He shook his head. "No. Timberlynn had a therapist for a little while, but I pretty much went right back to work and have buried myself in it since."

"You realize it wasn't your fault, the accident."

His body slumped. "I needed to get Timberlynn out of the car first. She begged me not to leave her, but I had to go back and get Lynn. Someone was trying to help Lynn out of the car, and when I got there, they told me she was gone. I pulled her out of the car and just remember screaming out her name. For the briefest moment I wondered if I hadn't gotten Timberlynn out first, if I had gone to Lynn, would it have made a difference. I hate that I even had that thought."

I could feel my throat aching as I attempted to hold back my emotions listening to Timberlynn's father relive that awful day.

"The doctors told me she had broken her neck, so she most likely died instantly. It still didn't make me feel any better. I replayed it over and over in my head. Why did I look away from the road?"

Frank rubbed the back of his neck and then let out a humorless laugh. "I've never talked to anyone about that day. Never."

"Must be something in the air here—your daughter told me pretty much the same thing."

He looked at me and smiled weakly. "Must be the Shaw family. I opened up to your father this morning as well."

I grinned, then looked back out over the ranch. "Sir, please forgive me if you think I'm interfering in your life with what I'm about to say."

When he didn't say anything, I went on.

"I think maybe you and Timberlynn are long overdue for a heart-to-heart. And, I think you could do with speaking with someone. My brother Ty went through a rough patch a few years ago, and he sees a therapist. It might do you some good being away from familiar grounds, talking to someone neutral. Heck, just talking to someone at all."

I looked over and saw him nod.

When he didn't say anything, I let out a slow breath, then said, "Should we catch up with my father and Brock?"

He stared straight ahead and smiled. "Yes, I think we should. And Tanner?"

We faced each other and he looked directly at me. "I didn't mean to come off as not liking you when we were coming back from the airport. You seem like a fine young man and I trust my daughter to know what she's doing. But if you ever hurt her, I'm honestly not sure I could keep myself from hurting you."

I tipped my hat at him. "Noted. And for the record, I'd lay down my life to protect her, sir. Everything I do, I do it for her."

He clapped me on the shoulder and grinned. "Thank you for taking care of our girl. Let's go catch up with your daddy and brother, shall we?"

Chapter Thirty-Three

TIMBERLYNN

I paced the kitchen and rubbed my hands together as Stella and Kaylee sat at the small table and drank coffee.

"Timberlynn, you're starting to make me tired with the walking back and forth. Will you please sit down?" Kaylee said.

"Where do you think they are? You said Ty Senior and Brock went as well?"

Stella nodded. "Ty and Frank actually went out a bit earlier for a ride together before they met up with Tanner and Brock, I believe."

I was positive my eyes nearly jumped out of my head. "What? Why did they go out earlier, just the two of them?"

Stella laughed. "They seemed to have hit it off."

"Right. The cigars and all," I said as I went back to pacing. "This isn't my father. He doesn't do sitting on back porches, bullshitting, or riding. I didn't even know my father rode horses!"

Kaylee gave me a sympathetic smile. "Why don't you grab a few blueberry muffins, slather some butter all over them, sit down, and eat your emotions."

"I can't eat, my stomach is upset. Do you think he likes Tanner?" I asked as my gaze bounced between the two of them.

"Why wouldn't he?" Kaylee asked.

"Of course, he does. What's not to like?" Stella countered.

At that, I smiled. Then I saw Kaylee pick up a stick of butter and take a bite out of it. I blinked a few times to make sure I was seeing correctly. Another bite and I gagged.

"Oh my gawd!" I cried. "You just ate butter, Kaylee!"

She glanced down, and then looked back up at me. "Can you hand me a blueberry muffin if you're not going to eat one?"

I shot a look at Stella who simply gave me a sweet smile. After getting a muffin for Kaylee, I handed it to her.

"Thanks!" she said as she took a bite of the muffin, then another bite of the butter. "Hmm, so good."

I slapped my hand over my mouth as I gagged again. Stella jumped up and started to guide me out of the kitchen.

I went to glance back, and she said, "Don't look back, it's for the best."

"But...she...the butter...she ate it!"

Stella nodded. "Yes, I know. Don't even get me started on what she ate that made poor Blayze throw up."

"What?" I cried out as Stella walked us into her sewing room and shut the door. "She made Blayze throw up?!"

"Yes, and Lincoln wasn't too far behind. But luckily Brock got her out of the kitchen while I tended to Blayze. Morgan sat in her highchair oblivious to all of it. The joys of being a baby."

I opened my mouth to ask what it was she ate, then quickly shut it.

"Smart move, sweetheart. You don't want to know."

"Ugh. Why does pregnancy make women eat such weird things?"

She shrugged and motioned for us to sit down on the small sofa. "I'm not sure, but when I was pregnant with Ty and Brock, I had the urge to eat dirt."

I couldn't help but laugh. "Dirt?"

"Yes," she replied with a slight chuckle. "Ty Senior swears I snuck off and ate some, and that's why the boys love to bull ride so much."

Stella rolled her eyes while I shook my head in disbelief. Then she took my hands in hers. "Timberlynn, stop worrying so much about your daddy. He's fine. Tanner is fine, all is going to be fine."

"Stella, I don't have a relationship with my father like you and Ty Senior do with the boys. I feel like I hardly even know him. He's never been there for me in all the years I've grown up, and honestly, I'm afraid to start counting on him now. Look what he did with the Covey place."

"Timberlynn, I never had a little girl, but you, Lincoln, and crazy-eating Kaylee out there are my daughters. I know you're not married to Tanner, but I think of you as family. And I know that what you and Kaylee grew up with is completely different than how my boys grew up. But I saw something in your daddy last night and this morning that tells me there's going to be some healing between the two of you. Just take a deep breath, and let it be."

I closed my eyes and blew out a breath. "Let it be."

"Yes. Let it be. There's something in the Montana air, just trust it."

Tears filled my eyes. "I want him in my life, Stella. I truly do. But I know the moment I let myself believe he'll be there, he'll be gone again."

She squeezed my hand. "I know how to cheer you up. Put your coat on—we're going to visit the Pocket Kings."

"Is that a horse?"

She stared at me with a dumbfounded look on her face and then laughed. "No, sweetheart. We've got some work to do. Let's go."

◆　◆　◆

Two hours later and I was laughing alongside Stella as she taught me how to play Texas Hold'em. I heard my father's voice behind me and turned to see him standing there, a smile on his face and a gleam in his eyes. I don't think I had ever seen him look so at ease.

"You two look like you're having fun," he said as he glanced down at the cards in our hands.

"I'm teaching your daughter how to play Texas Hold'em. Once every few months we all get together for a fun—and profiting—game of family poker. The women are on a winning streak the last few months, and I'd like to keep it that way. Game night is next week."

I laughed and placed my cards on the table as I looked at Stella. "Full house."

She pretended to wipe a tear away as she smiled and nodded. "Yes, indeed. You will make a fine addition to the women's team, especially with Kaylee and her pregnancy eating. She might eat a can of Crisco and be out for the entire game."

We all laughed as my father came and sat down at the small table that was in the main barn's office.

"How was your ride?" I asked as my heart sped up a bit.

"It was great. This ranch is probably one of the most beautiful places I've ever seen, Stella."

Pride showed on her face as she grinned. "I won't argue with you on that. Well, look at the time. Do you know how to play, Frank?"

"It's been a while, but yes."

Stella handed me the cards and stood. "Enjoy, then. I'm off to start a late lunch."

"Thank you, Stella, I had fun."

She winked and replied, "So did I, sweetheart. Work up a good appetite, Frank, I'm making burgers with homemade fries."

"Sounds good," my father answered.

Stella turned and quickly left the small office, shutting the door quietly behind her.

"Want to play?" I asked as I held up the cards.

"Deal away, sweetheart."

I did and we played the first few games while making small talk about the ranch, like the horse he had ridden that morning and Stella's amazing cooking skills. I also found out what Kaylee had eaten that caused Blayze to throw up.

"Liver and onions?" I repeated.

My father shuddered. "Yeah. Brock was telling us about it on the ride. She asked Stella if she could make some when Ty refused to allow her to cook it in their house."

I laughed. "That's gross."

"Women get some pretty weird cravings. Your mother ate watermelon with chocolate syrup on it."

I stared at him. "Is that why I hate watermelon so much?"

"Probably."

We both laughed. It was nice to hear my father talk about my mother. It was something he rarely did.

I went to deal again when he held out his hand. "I was wondering if we might simply talk, sweetheart."

My heart dropped, and I set the cards down carefully. "Dad, if you're going to demand that I return to Georgia, I'm not leaving Montana."

He smiled and shook his head as he looked down, then back up at me. "No, I'm not ever going to demand anything from you, Timberlynn."

"You're okay with me living here?"

He slowly drew in a deep breath, then quickly let it out and sat back in his chair. "Timberlynn, you're a grown woman with a pretty hefty bank account. You can do whatever it is you'd like. And I don't want me, or anyone, to hold you back any longer from the dreams you have."

I was positive my jaw was on the table. "I'm sorry, what did you just say?"

"Which part?"

"The part about me following my own dreams. What about mom's wish for me to be a nurse?"

He let out a grim laugh. "It's pretty obvious, Timberlynn, that it's not what you want to do. Although, it would have been nice for you to tell me, so you could have gone to school for a business degree instead of nursing."

I stood and shook my head to clear all the thoughts racing through it. "Wait. I thought you were going to be angry. You *were* angry."

He nodded and calmly folded his arms over his chest. "Yes, I was angry. I was angry you left and didn't tell me. I was hurt as well."

"Hurt?" I asked.

"Yes, but pretty angry. But not just at you, sweetheart. At myself for not knowing, or seeing, that nursing was not the career you wanted. If I had been paying better attention, that would have been clear to me."

I was stunned into silence. Then, I frowned. "Did you drink on the ride this morning? How did you sleep? Have you had the water here? I think something might be in it."

This time my father tossed his head back and let out a roar of laughter. "I'm not drunk, I slept the best I have in years, and I think the mountain air is clearing my head some. Maybe the water too," he said with a wink. "Timberlynn, honey, I've been wanting to talk to you for months now, and I just never knew how to start a conversation or what to say. Less than twenty-four hours with the Shaw family, and I'm confessing things I've never shared with anyone, and telling your boyfriend my feelings about your mother's death."

Slowly, I sat down as I kept my gaze on him. "Yeah, I think it's something in the water here. Or it's their eyes. Have you seen how blue they are?"

He laughed, then reached for my hand. "The first thing I want to say to you is I'm sorry. I'm sorry I missed your birthday. It's no excuse, but when I realized I had missed it the day after, I was so upset I couldn't bring myself to call you. I was...embarrassed."

"Dad—"

"No, let me get this out. I know I wasn't always there for you, but I've always remembered the best day of my life. When you were born."

Tears built in my eyes and I blinked rapidly to keep them back.

"I'm sorry I wasn't there for you when you were growing up. I was selfish and unsure of so many things, and in a strange way I thought I was doing the right thing for both of us."

My brows pulled in as I tried to understand his words. "The right thing? What do you mean?"

He took my hand and gently rubbed his thumb over it while he tried to think of his next words. "You don't know this, but your mother was told she'd never have a child."

I inhaled sharply. "What?"

He nodded. "We tried to get pregnant almost immediately after we got married. Months turned into a year, then two. They did every test they could, and then determined she wasn't able to get pregnant. When we ended up getting pregnant with you—" He let out a soft laugh and looked into my eyes. "We had never been so happy, and your mother, God, Timberlynn, it was like her purpose in life was being filled. She was so happy."

I smiled and let my tears fall freely.

"No, baby girl, don't cry. Please don't cry."

I sniffled and wiped my tears with my free hand, before drawing in a shaky breath. "Don't stop talking, Dad. Please don't stop telling me about her."

He closed his eyes and then opened them. I could see the sadness, and I wasn't sure if it was from talking about my mother, or simply because this was the first time in years, maybe in forever, that he'd shared anything with me about her.

"I had never seen her so happy. She prayed so hard for you, Timberlynn. Wanted you desperately." He cleared his voice when it cracked.

"When she died in the accident, I was so angry with God for taking her away from you. Why would He give her this gift, only to take it away? She should have been there to see you grow up. To see all the amazing things you've accomplished."

"Dad, is that why you never remarried?"

He rubbed the back of his neck and then let go of my hand to drag his own down his face. "Hell, Timberlynn. I don't know how to explain to you how messed up I was after losing your mom. And when I saw someone get too close to you, I'd panic. Yes, I was lonely, but none of those women would ever be able to replace your mother."

"But she'd want you to be happy."

"I'm not sure I know how to be happy that way again, sweetheart." He exhaled quickly and then slowly shook his head. "After your mother died, I sort of lost a piece of myself. She was my entire world, and when she was gone, I was confused. Angry. Hurt. Filled with guilt that I got to see you grow up, our little miracle baby, and she couldn't. Then one day you were on a swing and you fell.

Your knee got busted up, and I saw the blood. Something inside me switched, and I closed down. The thought of you being hurt or taken away from me was something I knew I couldn't mentally handle. And the more you grew up, the more I saw your mother in you."

"You didn't want to be around me because I reminded you of her?" I asked so softly even I had a hard time hearing myself.

"No, sweetheart, God, no. I wanted to be there for you, but I was afraid that I'd let myself get...I don't know... too close to you and something would happen. I couldn't stand the thought of losing you like I did your mother. I also felt responsible for the accident."

I gasped and reached for his hand. "Daddy, no. It wasn't your fault."

Tears filled his eyes and he closed them. My heart broke as I watched him deal with all of this. Had he held all of this in for so many years?

"Dad, the accident wasn't your fault. You have to know that."

He nodded. "I want you to know I was there, sometimes, at your events. Especially the dressage events. I showed up late a few times," he said with a laugh. "But I did watch you. You reminded me so much of your mother. It was hard for me to be there, and looking back on it now, I know it had to have hurt you to think I wasn't there. I'm so sorry, Timberlynn. God, I'm so sorry."

"You were there? I never saw you."

"Like I said, my way of thinking since your mother passed away probably hasn't been very healthy for either of us."

I looked down at the table and let everything he said process, then I looked up at him again. "Why now? Why are you telling me this all now?"

"When I found out you had left Atlanta and moved to Montana, I nearly fell to the floor. In that moment I realized that after all those years of keeping myself guarded, I had lost you anyway. I was so angry, but not at you. At myself. Then when I found out you were buying property here, I sort of..."

"Lost your damn mind?"

He chuckled. "Yes. Exactly. But I think it's worked out for the best. At least Tanner thinks it has."

I smiled. "What do you think about Tanner, Daddy?"

His eyes lit up like Christmas morning. "God, how I've missed hearing you call me that, Timberlynn."

"I've really missed saying it."

With a nod, he went on. "I like that boy. He's smart and madly in love with you and wants to make your dreams come true. Plus, I like his father. He reminds me of my best friend from college."

I laughed. "I think he likes you as well. Stella likes you too."

"That's good, because I came to a decision today."

My heart sped up and I had to force myself to breathe. "Wh-what decision is that?"

"I'd like to stay in Hamilton for a few extra weeks. Look around, take it all in."

"Are you serious? Do you want to move here?"

He held up his hands and laughed. "Hold on now, I'm not saying that. But if my only daughter is going to be living here, starting a new business, and possibly getting married someday, I want to be a part of it. I've missed so much, and I don't want to miss anything else."

My hand came up to my mouth, and I couldn't contain my sobs.

"Would you like it, if I stayed and checked out the area?"

I did the only thing I could. I nodded and stood up. My father stood as well, and I launched myself into his arms. "Nothing would make me happier, Daddy. Nothing."

Chapter Thirty-Four

TIMBERLYNN

APRIL

"One month to go," Lincoln said as she slowly sat down in one of her kitchen chairs.

Kaylee laughed. "Three more for me! Or is it four? Hell, I can't even remember anymore."

I smiled as I placed grass into Morgan's Easter basket. "The weather looks like it's going to be perfect for Easter on Sunday.

Kaylee smiled as she looked at the baskets I was making. "I'm so glad. This past winter was hell with those three major storms. I thought at one point I was going to punch Ty after he took the butter from me and hid it."

Lincoln moaned. "I'm so glad you're out of the butter phase."

"So am I," I added.

Kaylee shrugged. "I think this little girl is finally giving her mother a break with the morning sickness and weird cravings."

"Are you still not finding out the sex of the baby?" I asked Lincoln.

"Nope!" she said as she popped the P. "I really want to be surprised. I'm looking forward to seeing Brock's face. Deep down I'm thinking it's a boy. Your father says he's almost positive it's a boy from the way I'm carrying. And how hard the little guy kicks. Stella is still set on a girl."

A warm sensation ran through my body at the mention of my father. He had stayed those few extra weeks after New Year's to check out Montana and spend time with me. He'd helped me set up my new business, and I'd already gotten two rescue horses and three clients to train.

Dad had formed a bromance with Ty Senior, fell hard for Stella's home cooking, and learned that the hospital in town was in need of a consultant with a new wing they wanted to build. Needless to say, they didn't waste time bringing him on considering who my father was in the medical industry. Dad bought a cute little house right outside of town with a short commute to the hospital and ended up selling my childhood home back in Georgia. The fact that he had moved here to be with me still made me teary-eyed when I thought about it. He came over every Tuesday night for dinner with me and Tanner and joined us every Sunday night at Stella and Ty Senior's house for their weekly family dinner. We still had a ways to go with our healing, but with both of us going to a counselor together, and Dad seeing one of his own, things were progressing well.

"Do you think he snuck a peek at your last ultrasound?" Kaylee asked.

Lincoln laughed. "Don't even let Brock hear you say that. He'll try to talk Frank into giving him the information."

I laughed as I tied a yellow bow on Morgan's basket. "There. Finished."

Lincoln sighed happily. "Oh, Timberlynn, thank you so much. I don't have the energy to put into anything right now, so you've saved me. I don't remember being this tired with Morgan."

"That's because you didn't have two kids then. You only had Blayze, and I swear that boy could probably take care of himself if he really wanted to," Kaylee said.

We all laughed, then turned when we heard the sound of male voices growing closer.

Brock, Ty, and Tanner all walked into the kitchen. Brock saw Lincoln sitting in the chair and rushed over to her. "Are you okay? What's wrong?"

She giggled. "Yes, I'm fine. I'm just tired."

He kissed her quickly on the lips, then bent down to kiss her stomach.

Ty was currently talking to Kaylee's stomach and telling their child how much he loved him or her, while Tanner came up and kissed me like he hadn't seen me in weeks.

"I have a surprise for you," he said.

Brock laughed. "Why is it every time you tell her you have a surprise, it's a horse?"

"Or a puppy! I'm still jealous," Kaylee said.

Tanner had bought me a silver lab for Valentine's day. We named her Millie, and she was the perfect dog. Tanner was training her to bird hunt while I trained her to jump up into bed and snuggle on the sofa when I said it was movie night. Millie was meant for me, but she adored Tanner and followed him everywhere.

"Kaylee, we're about to have a baby and you want a puppy?" Ty said with a disbelieving laugh.

Kaylee rolled her eyes. "If Lincoln can handle two kids and a newborn, I'm pretty sure I can handle a puppy and a newborn."

I smiled as Ty let out a sigh, then he winked at Lincoln when Kaylee wasn't looking. I must have had a curious look on my face, because Tanner leaned in and whispered, "She's getting a black lab puppy in her Easter basket."

I gasped, then covered my mouth.

"What?" Kaylee said as she narrowed her eyes at me. "You know something."

With a shake of my head, I turned to Tanner in an attempt to change the subject. "What's this surprise you have for me?"

"A hundred bucks it's another horse," Ty called out.

Brock pushed Ty. "I already said that. That's my bet."

Ty shook his head and said, "No, you didn't call it, I did. It's my bet."

Tanner rolled his eyes and then winked at me, which still gave me butterflies in my stomach. Then he turned and faced everyone. "You'll have to wait until later. I believe right now, Ty, you challenged me to a roping contest."

"Lord, not again," Kaylee groaned. "Ty, the boy did it for a living. He won a championship doing it. Why do you insist on challenging him every month?"

"I do it so that that *boy,* as you call him, can get some roping time in because I'm a damn good brother. And I've been practicing this month, so I think I can beat him."

Everyone laughed.

"Blayze will want to be there, Ty. You know how upset he was last time y'all did it without him," Lincoln stated.

"Where is he?" Tanner asked.

Brock smiled and shook his head slowly. "He's with Mom and Dad. He spent the night there last night. Said he missed spending time with them, but I think he just wanted to be away from us since he got into trouble."

I placed my hand over my chest. "Oh, he is so sweet. I find it hard to believe he would ever get into trouble."

"Ha!" Lincoln said as she reached for Brock to help her out of the chair. "He was called to the principal's office at school last week."

"Why?" Kaylee and I asked at the same time.

Brock laughed, and Lincoln hit him as she answered. "It's not funny, Brock."

"It's kind of funny," Brock stated. "He was called in for telling his teacher he didn't think she picked very good books to read during reading hour."

"Then," Lincoln added as she gave Brock a side eye, "he proceeded to hand her the books he felt she should be reading."

"Oh. No," Ty said. "I hope he didn't find Tanner's collection of old naughty magazines."

"My collection? Dude, those were yours and Brock's! Beck and I begged y'all to share those with us," Tanner said.

Lincoln chuckled and shook her head. "No, thank goodness it wasn't that. But now I'm gonna have to make Stella search your old rooms before he does find them. He gave her books on roping and raising cattle, and the best one of all was raising a calf for beef. That one made two little girls in the classroom burst into tears, which made Blayze tell them it was okay. Then he proceeded to ask where they thought their hamburgers and steaks came from. One of the little girl's mother called us to let us know her daughter now refuses to eat anything made from a cow."

I covered my mouth to keep from laughing. Ty, Tanner, and Kaylee all laughed out loud, and Brock did his best not to.

"Y'all think it's funny," Lincoln said, then pointed at Kaylee. "Your time is coming. Just wait."

Ty reached over and rubbed Kaylee's stomach. The way he looked at her made me swoon.

Then Tanner took my hand, and I went from swooning caused by one Shaw brother to full-on heart palpitations from the Shaw brother I loved so dearly.

"Come on, let's go rope some cows," Tanner said, guiding me to the door.

"Yes!" Ty said as Lincoln asked Brock if he could just carry her. She was, of course, kidding. Although, I had a feeling if he offered to do it, she would take him up on it.

An hour later and everyone was at the corral. Even my father had showed up, which surprised me. I rushed over to give him a hug and stopped when I saw the smile on his face. He seemed lighter on his feet, a spark in his eye that made my heart feel happy.

"Dad, you have a look about you," I said.

He laughed and kissed me on the cheek. "It's the fresh mountain air here. Does a soul good."

"The mountain air, huh?" Stella countered. "That pep in your step wouldn't have anything to do with the rumor going around town that you had lunch with a lady yesterday."

I spun back around to look at my father. "Dad, is it true?! Did you go on a date?"

He held up his hands and laughed. "Don't get all excited."

"Was it a date?" Stella asked. "Betty Lou told me she saw you and Molly Walker having lunch together. I was just teasing, but do tell!"

"Yes, Uncle Frank, do tell!" Kaylee added.

"Goodness, there's no getting away with anything in this town, is there?" my father said as he smiled and then looked at me. "I was going to talk to you about it. It was just a friendly lunch, but I do like Molly. She's...nice."

"Nice?" every woman said at the same time.

"Yes. Nice."

"Frank, have I not taught you anything yet about these women?" Ty Senior asked.

"Oh hush, Ty," Stella said, then motioned for my father to keep talking. "Tell us more, Frank."

My father blushed, and I was hit right in the middle of my chest with a happiness I hadn't realized I could experience.

"Daddy," I said softly as I took his hands in mine. "You don't have to talk to me about dating anyone."

He nodded. "I know, but I wanted to let you know first. Guess I better move faster than the gossip chain next time." He shot a quick look at Stella who pretended not to hear him.

I leaned up and kissed him on the cheek. "You don't need my permission to date anyone. I've met Molly. She's very nice."

"Not to mention, hot as hell for her age. You know she teaches the spin class at the community center and she kicks ass," Kaylee said. Dad's face turned even more red with embarrassment.

"Enough about me, how are you feeling, sweetheart?" Dad asked as he walked over and kissed Kaylee.

"Great!"

Then he turned to Lincoln and gave her a sympathetic smile. "You look radiant, Lincoln."

She kissed him on the cheek and said, "Liar. But thank you."

"Frank! You made it!" Tanner called out from atop his horse.

Dad gave Tanner a thumbs up and shouted, "Wouldn't miss it for the world."

"Miss what?" I asked as I looked between them.

"Can we stop talking and do this? I feel like this is gonna be my lucky run!" Ty shouted.

Tanner laughed. "By all means, brother. Go for it."

"What do we have here, the Shaw brothers competing?" Everyone turned to see Dirk walking toward the corral.

"Dirk, what happened?" Kaylee cried out as she rushed over to him. His arm was in a sling.

"It's nothing, a torn ligament."

"Ouch," Brock and Ty said in unison.

"Bull riding?" Kaylee asked.

Dirk frowned. "Don't get me started."

"I'm so glad you're home though," Kaylee said as she kissed him on the cheek.

"My God, woman, you're huge!" Dirk leaned down to talk to the baby. "Hey, baby girl Shaw!"

"I am not huge. She's huge," Kaylee said as she pointed at Lincoln.

Dirk's eyes grew wide, and he walked over to Lincoln. "Wow. You look..."

"Like a whale." Lincoln sighed.

Dirk laughed. "I was going to say like a stunningly beautiful woman who is ready to pop."

She laughed. "I am. One month to go."

"Don't let me stop you gentlemen from your roping session," Dirk called out as he turned and kissed me on the cheek. "Hey, sweetheart, how are you?"

"I'm good. I'm sorry about your injury."

"It is what it is," Dirk said with a wink, then walked over and started shaking hands with everyone.

Once Dirk made his rounds, things got back underway.

Tanner and Ty Senior were partners, while Ty and Brock had paired up. Ty nodded for Jimmy to open the gate, then took off.

"He almost broke the line early," Tanner stated.

We all watched as Tanner roped the calf's head and Brock got his back leg.

"Five seconds," Jimmy shouted.

"Damn it all to hell, Brock!"

"Me! You took forever to rope the stupid thing."

"Last time up, Tanner and Mr. Shaw!" Jimmy cried out.

Tanner looked back at me, and I smiled and blew him a kiss. He winked, and I suddenly couldn't wait to get the man alone.

They got into position, and a calf was loaded in the shoot. "This is it, Dad. Let's show him how it's done."

Ty Senior tipped his hat toward Tanner, and Trigger stomped around, anxious to be let loose. Tanner gave the nod, and they took off. It was a blur how fast Tanner and his father went.

"Jesus! Holy shit! Oh my gosh!" Jimmy shouted as he looked at the timer in his hand.

Ty groaned, then shouted, "For the love of God, Jimmy, what was their time?"

Jimmy looked at Tanner. "Three-point-two seconds."

I let out a scream, as did Stella. Kaylee and Lincoln both cried out in celebration.

My father looked around. "What are we screaming for?"

"You broke the record! You broke the world record!" I yelled as I climbed over the fence and ran toward Tanner.

He laughed, as did Ty Senior.

"Damn, old man! Who knew you still had it in you?" Brock said as he rode up and shook his father's hand.

Tanner leaned down and kissed me.

"You did it, Tanner. You did it and no one will know," I said.

He winked. "I know I did it, that's all that matters. And I did it with my dad, which makes it all the more special."

My cheeks burned as I looked up at him and smiled. "I love you."

"I love you more, darlin'."

Ty rode over and shook Tanner's hand as I stepped out of the way. I turned to walk over to Ty Senior, who was currently off his horse and kissing Stella, bent back in a dip. I laughed and went to say something, but I came to a stop when a rope went around me.

Laughing, I turned to look at Tanner.

"What in the world are you doing?" I asked.

"Do you remember when I told you I'd never roped a woman before because I hadn't found one worth ropin'?"

"Yes!" I said with a giggle as I took the rope off of me and walked back toward him. He stopped right in front of me, then knelt down on one knee. I sucked in a breath and felt my stomach drop.

"Well, I found her, and I don't ever intend on letting you go. You have made me the happiest I've ever been, Timber, and I cannot imagine my life without you in it. I want to be by your side as every dream you've ever dreamed comes true. I want the honor of calling you mine, and I want desperately for you to be my wife. Will you marry me?"

Tears streamed down my face as I dropped down onto the dirt in front of him. I opened my mouth to speak, but no words would come out. The only thing I managed to do was nod and sob like a fool.

"I believe that's a yes, son!" my father called out.

I smiled and said, "Yes! Yes, I will marry you!

Tanner's face erupted into the most beautiful smile as he picked up my left hand and slipped on the ring. I glanced down at it and stared. Then I looked up at my father and saw him wiping away his own tears.

"Daddy," I whispered.

"She would have wanted you to have it, princess."

Tanner leaned in and whispered, "Go to him, Timber."

I turned back to Tanner, cupped his face with my hands and kissed him. "I love you so much, Tanner Shaw."

He winked. "I know. I love you too."

Tanner stood and helped me up. I hugged him tightly, then turned and ran to my father.

He held his arms open and caught me when I ran into them. "I love you, Timberlynn. So very much."

"Oh, Daddy. I love you too."

Ty walked up to Brock and slapped him on the back. "I won...pay up."

Epilogue

TIMBERLYNN

MAY

I slowly lifted the saddle pad onto the two-and-a-half-year-old gelding I was training. He stood perfectly still and turned his head ever so slightly to watch me. "That's a good boy, Romeo."

He threw his head back slightly as I rubbed the pad over him gently, then let it sit on his back.

"He looks comfortable with it on," Tanner said.

I glanced over my shoulder to see the love of my life—my fiancé—sitting on the fence. Lord, he looked so handsome with his dark cowboy hat on and that sexy smile and dimple.

"He's a trooper." I quickly lifted the saddle and placed it onto the pad and let it sit for a few minutes.

"Okay, buddy, let's cinch the girth and see how you like it." I got the saddle strap just snug enough to keep it in place, and Romeo didn't flinch.

"I'm itching to get on that horse, you know," Tanner said as he got off the fence and headed over to us.

"Patience, Tanner. You of all people know that," I said as I tightened the girth a bit more.

"He seems to be okay with it. Jasper was biting the shit out of the saddle earlier to get it off."

I laughed lightly. "Yeah, he's going to make us earn our money, that's for sure."

After Tanner and I got engaged, we sat down and talked about where we both wanted our careers to go. Tanner, of course, was still going to work on the family ranch, but we also decided to go into a partnership with the horse training and rescue. There was also the fact that Tanner had purchased the house and land we lived on from his parents. After talking with my father and Tanner, I paid Tanner fifty percent of what he'd bought the house for. Tanner then turned around and invested it into our new business, Shaw Equestrian and Rescue. Stella and Ty Senior also added the name to the main gate of the Shaw ranch. Each time I saw it driving in, my eyes teared up. It was a longtime dream of mine that was finally coming true.

Working with Tanner was another added bonus, and each time I saw him with a horse, I knew this was where he belonged. He had such a natural way with horses—I swore he knew how to communicate with them. He loved training horses under saddle and did amazingly at it.

"You've got him moving good. Look at that," Tanner said as we watched Romeo trot around the corral on his own.

"When do you want to work on the mounting block with him?" I asked.

"Later. What I really want to do is work on mounting you."

I smiled and let him pull me to him.

"Have you decided on a wedding date yet?" he asked.

"Well, I had an idea."

"Okay, hit me with it."

"I think I want to get married in the spot you took me on our first, unofficial date. The lookout over the ranch."

He smiled. "I love that idea. When?"

"My mom's birthday is May twenty-fifth. I already talked to my dad about it and he loved the idea. I know that's only a couple weeks away, but I really only want it to be just your family and my dad and Molly and of course Dirk and Candace, if they can make it."

"I bet they both could. Why don't we put Romeo up, and you let me take you into the house to make love to you. Then we'll go talk to my folks about it."

With a smile, I stretched up on my toes and kissed him. "Sounds like a plan."

Tanner got Romeo to come to him, then attached the lead to his halter. After getting the saddle off and turning him out in the pasture, I started to walk toward the house, only to have Tanner grab me and pull me back into the barn. "What are you doing?" I asked with a giggle.

"I just realized we haven't broken in this barn."

The space between my legs suddenly throbbed with need. "We should probably rectify that," I stated.

Tanner's lips moved up the side of my neck as his hand slipped under my shirt and teased my nipples. "I agree," he whispered as his other hand worked on unbuttoning my jeans. "I want you, Timber. Now."

His phone rang and we both groaned.

"Let it go," I whispered as I ran my fingers through his hair. His cowboy hat had gotten knocked off his head at some point.

"I have to get it. There was supposed to be a delivery of feed today, and they haven't shown up yet."

With a sigh, I dropped my head back against the barn wall.

"Hey, what's up?"

I mentally started to go over the list of things to do with Romeo when Tanner's voice caused me to jump.

"What! Are you kidding?"

I jerked my head up to see Tanner wearing a stunned expression. "Dude, holy shit. Okay, yeah, Timberlynn and I will meet you there. We will, you too."

He hung up and looked at me.

"What's wrong? Is everything okay?"

A brilliant smile erupted across his face. "Everything is perfect."

I couldn't help but return his smile.

"You better add another person to our wedding list."

"Who?" I asked.

Tanner's eyes filled with pure happiness as he replied, "Hunter Mason Shaw. The latest member of the Shaw family."

The End...for now.
Be on the lookout for *Strong Enough,* book four, and the final book in the Meet Me in Montana series. Coming February 9, 2021.

ABOUT THE AUTHOR

Kelly Elliott is a *New York Times* and *USA Today* bestselling contemporary romance author. Since finishing her bestselling Wanted series, Kelly has continued to spread her wings while remaining true to her roots with stories of hot men, strong women, and beautiful surroundings. Her bestselling works included *Wanted, Broken, Without You,* and *Lost Love.* Elliott has been passionate about writing since she was fifteen. After years of filling journals with stories, she finally followed her dream and published her first novel, Wanted, in November 2012.

Elliott lives in Central Texas with her husband, daughter, and two pups. When she's not writing, she enjoys reading and spending time with her family. She is down to earth and very in touch with her readers, both on social media and at signings. To learn more about Kelly and her books, you can find her through her website, www.kellyelliottauthor.com.

CONNECT WITH KELLY ELLIOTT

Kelly's Facebook Page
www.facebook.com/kellyelliottauthor

Kelly's Amazon Author Page
https://goo.gl/RGVXqv

Follow Kelly on Twitter
www.twitter.com/author_kelly

Follow Kelly on Instagram
www.instagram.com/authorkellyelliott

Follow Kelly on BookBub
www.bookbub.com/profile/kelly-elliott

Kelly's Pinterest Page
www.pinterest.com/authorkellyelliott

Kelly's Author Website
www.kellyelliottauthor.com

Made in the USA
Middletown, DE
06 October 2020